The Color of Snow

Brenda Stanley

THE COLOR OF SNOW

Brenda Stanley

ISBN: 978-1-940224-88-6
Copyright 2015

TAYLOR AND SEALE
PUBLISHING, LLC

Cover layout by White Rabbit graphix.com

This is a work of fiction. Any characters, names and incidents appearing in this work are entirely fictitious. Any resemblance to real persons, living or dead, is purely coincidental.

This book may be purchased through

Amazon.com and Amazon Kindle
Taylor and Seale Publishing.com
www.taylorandsealeeducation.com
Barnes and Noble.com
Books a Million

Taylor and Seale: Publishing, LLC
Daytona Beach, Florida 32118

Phone: 1-888-866-8248

www.taylorandseale.com

Dedication

For Beverly, my fan club president ...

and mother

Important Areas

Places: Arbon Valley, Idaho, December 2008
Malad, Idaho early spring, 1991

Main Characters

Papa: Luke Theotokis/ Miguel Sanchez
Thomas Theotokis
Vee Richardson
Gene and Molly Richardson
Pete
Sophie/Callidora
Anthony Carponelli (Carpo)
Damien
Elise
Stephanie
Uncle Lanny

Editor's Foreword

Through a juxtaposition of different time zones, *The Color of Snow,* a dramatic mystery novel, unravels layer upon layer, leaving the reader in suspense until the last chapter. Each character has strengths that reveal themselves as the reader discovers the motives behind their strong emotions and actions.

Chapter 1

Arbon Valley, Idaho, December 2008

It had snowed over five inches the day I was born, and it wasn't until the day I was saved that the snow was as deep or as blue.

I was intrigued and scared when I saw them approach the house. The cars wore the seal of the Power County Sheriff's Office on the doors. The woman looked angry and cold. She wore the same uniform as the men, but hers looked bulky and ill-fitted. She adjusted the holster around her waist and put her hand on the butt of her gun. As she did this, I looked at the pistol in my own hand and marveled at how heavy it was. I ran my thumb along the textured handle and contemplated my father's instructions. *It's up to you now*, he said. It didn't make sense, but much of what had happened the past two days didn't. My world was shattered.

The woman officer drew her gun. Another officer followed. Thin, plain and determined, he pushed against the wind toward our front door. Two other cars with two other officers were parked at odd angles in the driveway. The officers stepped onto the snow-crusted gravel, but stayed back and watched.

His voice startled me. "They're here," my father said calmly. He stood in my doorway. My gate was still locked. He shook his head, seeing I was drawn to the same window that started this terrible chain of events.

"I'm sorry, Papa," I said, looking into his eyes, hoping to see some inkling of forgiveness.

He sighed, defeated. "It's not your fault. This is my doing, but remember what I told you about us." He kept looking down the hall toward the front door. "This is what I've been warning you about all these years. None of this would be happening if I had done the right thing. It's up to you now...."

"Yes, Papa," I answered, softly, completely unaware of just how alone I was going to be.

"I love you, Sophie. Please know that. I've always loved you. It's why this is happening now."

It was the only time my father told me he loved me, and now he did it with such fervor it made my skin prickle. The words didn't comfort, they left me feeling scared and abandoned. I nodded and sat on my bed. He looked at me one last time, then put his hand to his mouth and left my doorway. I knew we were in trouble, but I didn't know what would happen next.

A loud pounding and a muffled demand came from just outside the front door. I heard my father walk toward it. I unlocked the gate and stepped from my room into the short hallway.

He saw me and stopped. "This is what I'm talking about. You don't listen. Being disobedient to your parents is like being disobedient to God." His face was pained as he lowered his head. "I didn't listen either."

I looked at the floor, the gun still dangling heavily in my hand.

Low and demanding, a man's voice called from outside. "Miguel Sanchez, open the door! We need to talk to you!"

Papa's face turned into a death mask. "Sophie, stay in your room. Pray for strength to do the right thing. Pray for me and what I didn't do."

The pounding came again. "If they ask questions, stay quiet. It must always be our secret."

"Why will they ask?"

"They'll ask because of what I did to that boy. I was trying to protect our secret. That's all I've ever done."

I turned to go back in my room and paused to ask another question, but he was already opening the door. He was thrust backward by the officers, guns drawn. His shoes scraped against the linoleum of our foyer as he struggled against them. I jumped back into my room without them seeing me.

"My daughter is in her room. She has a gun!" I heard Papa yell in the struggle.

I went to my closet and crouched in a corner. I tried to close the folding doors, but it was difficult from the inside. I dug in the carpet for my secret place and quickly disposed of the gun. My lips felt dry from breathing through my mouth, and I pulled a folded flannel blanket around my legs and over my head. My back was pressed against the wall and I heard them yelling at my father to stay still. I tried not to breathe so I could hear what was happening over my fear and panic.

I heard shuffling and then noises outside. The slam of a car door made me pull the blanket from my face, wondering if they knew I was there. Even with my father's warnings, I hoped they'd find me and wondered what to do if they didn't. I cautiously stood up and left the closet. At the window I peeked out to see a man put his hand on my father's head and direct him into the back seat of the patrol car. Papa's hands were fastened tightly behind his back and his face was a mixture of weariness and worry. I felt like I should scream or cry, but instead I worried about being abandoned.

The floor creaked in the front hallway. Someone was still in the house. I slinked back to the closet and pulled the blanket over my head. The floor moaned with each step that came closer and my heart started pounding so loudly I could feel it in my head. The front door closed and I heard a second set of footsteps.

"Do you think she's still in here?" the man asked in a loud whisper.

The woman hushed him. The creaking made its way into my room. Someone was just outside my closet door and I bowed my head, praying for help. I closed my eyes tightly and wished myself away. Then a voice called to me from behind the folding doors.

"We have guns. Open the doors and throw yours out," the man demanded.

"I don't have a gun," I said. It wasn't completely a lie, but I was terrified that God would view it as such. "Please don't shoot me."

"It's okay. We're not going to hurt you." It was the woman. Her voice was soft, but resolute.

"We're here to help," said the man, trying to sound genuine, but failing miserably.

I pulled the blanket tighter around me. I cleared my throat and tried to sound serious. "Please leave me alone. I can't talk to you."

There was a long pause. Then the woman spoke again. "You can't stay here alone. We want to get you some help. I promise we won't hurt you, but you must open the door and put your hands up so we can see them. Okay?"

"We're here to help. You don't need to hide. Please come out and talk to us."

Talk to us. The words sounded heavenly. For so long I had been lonely and wishing for more people to simply talk to, and now I was afraid to leave the closet and face these strangers.

"Where's my father?" I asked the question out of concern for him, while at the same time fearing that he'd catch me talking to people. I had witnessed what he had done to the last person I spoke to.

"He is in the car. He's going for a drive, so he can talk to some people about what he did to that boy. You must talk to us about what happened. Please come out."

I didn't want to talk about what happened because I wasn't really sure. I knew it was my fault, but the reason still puzzled me. Papa had said I couldn't have friends, and I didn't listen, and now my world was melting around me.

In the books I read, all the girls had friends. They laughed and played together. They told each other secrets and they went places...outside. My father told me so many times why I couldn't be like the girls in my books, but I still prayed every night that someday I would be.

I heard the door open further.

"It's okay," the voice said, calmly. "But please put your hands where I can see them."

"It's cold," I said. My hair fell around my face.

"It is cold," the woman agreed. "And I have a coat on. Can I get you a coat?"

I shook my head, and then peered at her. Through my hair, I saw them both staring back. The woman holstered her gun and crouched on her knees. The man stood behind her, his legs apart, his gun still drawn.

"You're going to be okay," the woman said.

5

She leaned forward and put her hands on her legs. Her fingers where long and thin and her nails were cut very short. Her round face spread out from an uneven nose, and her small, round eyes looked at me with true concern and interest. I felt safe in her gaze, and my fear subsided.

The man relaxed his stance and put his gun away. He crooked his head at me. I sat up straight, and with a small sweeping motion I lifted my long hair away from my face. I blinked up at them, and for a moment we all sat staring at each other.

The man's eyes grew large and his hands fell to his sides. The woman gasped. She sucked her breath back into her body with a long, low gasp.

Suddenly I felt naked. I retreated and dropped my face into the flannel blanket.

"No, it's okay," she pleaded.

I wondered what horrific thing they had seen. Was this why my father kept me a secret from the world? I rattled through my mind the few encounters I had with others and thought about their reactions, too. I realized Damien had gasped when we first met, but he came back. Over and over he had made his way through the fields and waited behind the hay pile in the pasture for my father to leave and for me to come outside. He no longer gasped, but he did stare. At first it made my stomach uneasy and I wanted him to stop, but I knew his reasons for it. He loved me, but that wasn't the case for the others.

The man's voice cracked oddly. "Don't be scared, little lady."

I gathered courage and looked at them again. The woman bit her lip, trying to hold her composure, but the man again let his mouth go limp and his eyes grew. I held my gaze, challenging them. I studied her face and then switched my focus to his. Wide eyes and gaping mouths.

She broke the silence. "Callidora," she said, softly. It wasn't to me or to anyone, just into the silence that surrounded us.

Her partner broke his gawking trance. "Yes—and Miguel Sanchez is Luke Theotokis."

The woman turned back to me. "Callidora, is that you?"

"No. My name is Sophie."

Chapter 2

She was whispering, but I could hear everything she said. "There were bars on the windows of her room and a cage-like door that locked...but from the inside. She wasn't locked in, but others were locked out."

The woman officer was named Ellen. She sat with three others in the room with me. "She had a suitcase packed, but there were only a few things inside...a book, a drawing pad, a Bible and an old toaster. No clothes or toiletries, especially odd for a girl. In fact, I think she had one tube of toothpaste and a comb in the bathroom, but that was it. It wasn't like she was going on a trip, but she had packed what was sentimental to her from the house. I still don't understand the toaster."

The others scribbled notes.

"Escape," a tall man with dark hair and perfect skin announced from behind her. I eventually learned that his name was Anthony Carponelli, but he was known as Carpo, and he had been an investigator with the Idaho State Police for fifteen years. It was his one big case if, in fact, I turned out to be the girl they all thought I was. "It shows she was ready to make her escape."

"I wonder why now?" Ellen asked. "What pushed her to finally do it?"

Julie Doherty was the social worker assigned to my case. Julie was quiet and simple, with hair that fell past her waist. She pulled it together in a long tight braid held with an ornate clip at the base of her neck. She had light green eyes that smiled even when she frowned, and pale freckled skin.

Ellen introduced everyone as we gathered my things from the house. "This is Officer Burns, and this is Julie Doherty. I'm Officer Richards, but you can call me Ellen. Okay?" I nodded, but said nothing. Even on the car ride over to the police station, I sat silent, wondering what was going to happen.

The ride was exhilarating. I hadn't been in a car for years and had forgotten what it felt like to travel that fast. When we pulled on to the main highway that led to the city, I saw houses everywhere. There were people who lived just a few miles from me and I never knew. I had never asked Damien how far he traveled to see me. Part of me was afraid that if he realized how long the journey was, he would stop. I couldn't bear the thought. I wondered where he was now and if he hated me for getting him shot. I bowed my head and prayed for him. My father would be furious if he knew I asked God to help Damien...but Papa was gone.

Julie gave me a pat on the head before leaving me in a hospital-like room. "Please take your clothes off and put this gown on."

I glared at her.

"It's okay, Sophie, it's just a checkup. I'll be right back," she assured me. She, too, had given me a strange stare when we first met, but then her demeanor had turned sympathetic and kind. I decided I liked her.

I did what she told me, feeling cold and vulnerable. I pulled the gown tightly around me like a shield, as a light knock came from the hall and the door opened. A woman in a long white coat stepped in; Julie followed.

"Sophie, I'm Dr. Thayne," the woman announced.

I looked at her and then to Julie, who smiled and nodded, giving me some comfort. Dr. Thayne did what the others did, stared at me oddly. She cleared her throat and asked me to 'hop up' on the table that looked like a hard leather bed. The strange paper sheet rustled underneath me as I followed her instructions.

"Dr. Thayne is going to check you to make sure that you're healthy." Julie offered a comforting smile, so I allowed her to continue.

The doctor listened to my chest and back. I started to panic.

"It's okay, Sophie." Julie turned to Dr. Thayne. "I don't think she's ever been to a doctor."

She nodded. "Sophie, I won't do anything that you don't like. I'm just checking your heart and lungs. It won't hurt, so just breathe normally."

I tried, but I found myself forcing each inhale and exhale.

"Sounds good," she announced.

She tapped my knee with a little hammer, giving it a tingle and making it jump. It gave me the giggles; I tried to muffle them, but found Julie and the doctor both smiling. She had me open my mouth wide and pressed a wooden stick in my mouth. She shined a light in my eyes and stuck a small tube in my ears as she looked closely inside.

"Looks good so far," Dr. Thayne announced. "Have you had a period?"

I looked at her strangely.

"What the doctor means is, have you started menstruating?" Julie moved closer. "Menstruating, or having your period, is when you have blood." Her eyes fell. "Down there."

"Blood?" Then it came to me. "You mean the curse."

She flinched. "Curse?"

"Yes, the curse of Eve. It comes every month to remind us that we are sinners."

Julie looked at Dr. Thayne. Her eyes and forehead looked strained.

"How old are you, Sophie?" asked Dr. Thayne.

"I'm almost seventeen."

"When was the last time you had the curse?"

I admitted the curse was on me as we spoke. I was certain it had something to do with all the trouble I was causing.

The doctor smiled and then turned to Julie. "We're fine. She's good to go. Will she be seeing a counselor?"

"I'll recommend it highly."

"That's good."

I looked back at Julie, who put a hand on Dr. Thayne's arm as she opened the door to leave.

"Good luck to you, Sophie. It was nice meeting you," she said, giving me a smile.

"Yes," is all I said back. I liked the doctor.

Julie stayed in the room with me.

"Why did she ask me about the curse?"

"It's a normal thing that happens to all girls, especially when they're your age. She was just checking to make sure you're okay. It's not really a curse."

"Papa says it's a sign from God. Bad things will happen if you disobey God. Eve did and she was cursed, so all her daughters are cursed, too. That is why we bleed every month. It's to remind us."

Julie looked nervous. "I know what the Bible says, but menstruating is something that simply means you are becoming a woman. It's what happens to all women. I don't believe it's a curse."

"Don't you believe in God?"

"I do, but it's all a part of nature. Get dressed. We're going into a room and talk for a while, okay?"

"Talk about what? When am I going home?"

Julie looked pained. "We'll talk about that after you get dressed. I'll wait outside the door until you're done."

"Where's my father?"

"He's with the officers in another building."

"Is he okay?"

"Yes. Sophie, everything will be all right. You're safe now."

How could I be safe when Papa wasn't there to protect me?

I was ushered into a small room. There were easy chairs with worn padded seats, a large coffee table in the center, and a huge mirror that made my skin prickle when I saw it. Carpo and Ellen were waiting in the room. I heard them whispering.

"She's facing away from us," Carpo said in a frustrated whisper.

"Be careful what you wish for," Ellen mumbled.

"What the hell is that supposed to mean?" Carpo asked with a huff.

They were talking about me as if I weren't in the room.

Ellen sighed. "It's strange, but I can't explain it." She held a tattered flyer in her hand and looked at the picture. She turned to Carpo.

He shook his head. "You're kidding, right? That flyer is a joke. It was a source of humor and probably hindered this investigation more than anything."

They were referring to Callidora's "Missing" poster. I learned later that it had been age-progressed from a day-old baby picture with the help of old photos of my mother. The image was scattered all over the state and most of the country. When people saw it, they saw what Carpo did…an unrealistic idea of what the baby had grown into. The poster had become fabled, and so it often was shuffled to the back of the missing children files.

Julie took her chair and placed it at the side of the coffee table. "Sophie, come sit over here so we can talk."

As if on cue, Carpo and Ellen leaned forward, straining to see my face.

I sat beside Julie. My hair was in my face, so I raked a hand through it and moved it aside. The table was scratched and worn. My lips were dry and I needed water, but I waited for Julie to speak.

A light tap was heard and the door opened, revealing a small man in a tan suit. "Sorry I'm late. Have you started yet?" He was pleasant looking, carrying a notepad and smiling at Julie.

Julie stood up to greet him. "No, we were just about to begin." She turned to me. "Sophie, this is Officer Degraw. He is going to talk with us. Is that okay?"

"If I said no, would it matter?"

The same stare spread across his face, wiping the smile from it. I quickly realized that what Papa said was true. He rid our house of mirrors for a reason, and now I was appreciative of that.

"Sophie," Julie said softly. "Officer Degraw is a friend of mine, and he helps children like you. He just wants to ask you some questions about what happened this morning."

I felt my chest heave from the stress of the day. Again, I felt an overwhelming desire to go home and be with Papa. "If I answer the questions, can I go home?"

Officer Degraw took a seat across from me. "Sophie, there's a lot that's happened to you and we'll try to do everything we can to get you somewhere safe."

"What does that mean? Can't I go home?" I turned to Julie. "Where's my father?

"That's what we want to talk to you about. We need to know what happened. So, Sophie," Officer Degraw said, as he scooted his chair closer. "Tell me what happened early this morning at your home."

I shrugged, not knowing where to start. I felt ill from guilt and kept wondering if I was in trouble for causing the incident. Had my father told them what I did, how I disobeyed? "I didn't know Papa was going to shoot him," I said, defensively.

"Why *did* your father shoot that boy?"

Julie sat close, with her arm around the back of my chair. I wondered if that's what my mother would be doing. I started to talk and then bit my lip.

"Do you know that boy?"

"Yes."

"Is he your friend?"

The word hit me like a cold slap. Damien was brilliant and strong, and he was in love with me. He talked to me and made me laugh. Papa had told me often that I wasn't to talk to strangers, or to venture from our small fenced-in yard, but I didn't listen. I had to be with Damien. I felt tears rush to my eyes and a thick ball of emotion welled up in my throat. "Why are you doing this? What have I done wrong?" I cried, burying my face in my hands.

Julie wrapped her arm around my shoulders and pulled me close. "You haven't done anything wrong."

"Then why can't I go home?"

I could tell she had no answer, or at least no *good* answer that would calm me down. "It's important that we find out what happened today. That's why you must try and answer Officer Degraw's questions."

"I don't know what happened. All I know was Papa caught Damien and me at my window. He yelled at him to stay away, then I heard a gun right behind me and something whiz by my ear. I saw Damien running from the house, holding his arm. There was blood on the snow." Then the most horrifying thought struck, and I let out a high pitched moan. "Is Damien dead?"

Julie pulled me tighter. "No, sweetheart. He'll be fine."

I felt my body collapse into her. For several minutes, we just sat in silence. "I need a tissue," I said.

"Sure," she said. "I'll go get you one. Officer Degraw, please come with me. Ellen and Officer Carponelli, let's all talk for a moment outside."

There I sat, trying to avoid and forget about the mirror, the thing that was luring me to stand up and find the answers to my questions. I had seen my reflection in dark windows and the shiny metal of the toaster, but I had never viewed my image in a mirror. I wanted to know what they saw, what made their eyes widen and their faces flush. I walked carefully around the table, keeping an ear out, hoping they didn't return and catch me in my act of vanity.

Chapter 3

Early Spring, Malad, Idaho, 1991

The town of Malad is nestled in a valley at the southernmost border of Idaho. It's a small village made up of less than three thousand people. Everything from the old houses to the hospital to the cemetery has the stamp of early Latter Day Saints influence. Schools are extensions of the Church. Each Sunday, the townspeople make their way to one of the many ward houses to take the sacrament.

On Wednesday nights, teenagers attend youth activities called Mutual, in which adult members of the ward oversee games, service projects, or lessons to reinforce what is taught on the Sabbath. The workings of Malad's culture and society have gone unchanged for decades. Without some updates in photography and a few changes in clothing and hair styles, pictures taken in the late 1800s don't vary much from present day.

Being a teenage boy and Greek Orthodox in this solitary village was like being a piece of coal dropped in the center of a snowfield.

Luke Theotokis was seventeen and the only boy at Malad High School who could grow a full mustache. It was just another thing on a long list that made him feel like an outsider. With his olive skin and straight black hair, he was often mistaken for the Mexican migrant farm workers who worked at numerous farms in Eastern Idaho. But the name Theotokis removed any questions about his ethnicity.

It wasn't his choice to move to the small Oneida County valley. The land was rolling and fertile. And his father Thomas was an efficient ranch manager who also raised sheep, another reason for the snide whispers at school. But the valley gave the small Greek family a stretch of land to graze their flock.

Gene Richardson, owner of the large ranch that Thomas managed, gave Luke's father free rent and use of a small house in exchange for his work and some simple chores on his homestead. The chores ended up being Luke's contribution to the family. He didn't mind, because he was able to escape the small confines of his family's isolated home in the hills and spend his afternoons at the immense and lavish ranch of the fifth generation Richardsons.

Luke worked hard, and he enjoyed garnering the attention and praise he sought from Mr. Richardson.

"I think you're hoping to take over the place," Mr. Richardson chided, as Luke worked even harder. "I better watch my back or you'll steal it out from under me!"

Luke only smiled and continued spraying off the circular drive. He loved the ranch and took pride in his upkeep of it, but his real love was the ranch owner's youngest daughter Vee. If Mr. Richardson had any idea of the thoughts and emotions that welled inside his heart for his precious girl, Luke would be banned from the ranch and probably the county. So Luke kept his feelings hidden.

Vee was short for Veronica. She had an independent streak. Her mother had admitted that she found the streak to be humorous and part of Veronica's will to be something more than just the baby of the pampered and affluent Richardson clan. However, she also admitted that as her young daughter grew and matured, the stubborn independence was becoming a concern. The precocious, apple cheeked little miss had sprouted that year into a svelte and fiery-eyed young woman. She wasn't mouthy or defiant, but something that Molly Richardson feared even more. She was inquisitive.

Vee's questions had started early and now, as a teenager, her queries had turned toward the very things the Richardsons lived for and lived from. She questioned their very beliefs. They feared she might turn, throw her salvation to the wind and become an unbeliever. They had begun regular meetings with their bishop to help find the answers to her questions and hopefully keep her faith from veering off course.

Vee was angelic in Luke's eyes. Her beauty bubbled up from her very soul every time she laughed or even sent a glance his way. He kept back when anyone else was present, but in the long corridor of the indoor arena, she appeared one afternoon looking contemplative and distant.

"You're walking in the water," Luke pointed out as he held the hose, spraying out the stalls.

"I don't care. These are my old shoes," she called over to him, as she continued to stroll along, running her hand over each of the oiled wooden gates.

Luke found himself looking at his own shoes. They were permanently scuffed and the soles were worn crooked.

Vee realized what effect her comment had made and tried to correct herself. "I mean, these are the shoes that I wear when I'm working outside."

Luke smiled at her and raised an eyebrow.

"What?" she asked, stopping near him.

"What work do you do? Outside…"

She looked at the muddy mess on the path. "I work with the horses. I ride English."

Luke smiled again.

"Why do you keep doing that?"

"Doing what?"

"That smile. What does it mean?"

Luke grinned. "Riding a horse isn't working. It's playing."

"It's not just riding. I take care of my horse."

"What do you do?"

Vee scoffed. "I do a lot. I brush it and I train it."

"Do you scoop its poop?"

Vee looked at him with disgust. "No."

"Do you feed it?"

"I give it oats."

Luke smiled again.

"Why does that matter anyway? Just because I don't shovel out the stalls or pitch hay doesn't mean I'm lazy."

"I didn't say you were lazy."

"Yes, you did."

Luke wondered if making her angry was a smart thing to do, but he was enjoying just being able to speak to her. "I said you don't work...at least outside."

"Most women don't work outside."

"So do you work inside?"

Vee threw her shoulders back. "What's it to you what I do? You're *supposed* to be working and you're wasting time bothering me."

Luke shrugged. He pulled a pack of cigarettes from his pocket. He flicked the top of a shiny metal lighter with a green clover on the front, and lit the cigarette. "I'm sorry. Did you have other plans besides wandering through the arena?"

She stared at him, incensed. Her long blonde hair was perfectly pulled back with a pink and white headband that matched the pink in her sweater. Luke was transfixed on the smoothness of her face and the color of her eyes. They weren't just blue, they were the color of the sapphire in his mother's wedding ring. So deep and rich, they were almost violet.

"What now?" she asked, shaking her head.

Luke blinked, realizing he was in a daze. He flicked the ashes from the cigarette and ran his fingers through his mop of thick black hair.

She pointed to the ground. "You missed a spot."

Luke gave her the same mocking smile as before, then pointed the hose and shot a loud and full gust at the ground beside her.

Shocked, Vee jumped to the side with a shriek. "You're crazy," she said, and walked off.

"Wait," he said, trying not to laugh.

She stopped, but didn't turn around.

"Will you get me some water?"

She turned, staring down at the running hose in his hand.

"To drink?" he replied. "If it's not too much... work."

She huffed in exaggerated frustration, and headed toward the house. She turned back to find him staring at her, the hose still hanging at his side. She quickly gave him another exasperated glare, but turned back.

Luke sprayed the corral with fervor, but kept looking over the rail to see if she had returned. After fifteen minutes his hopes were crushed, and he simply continued with his chores. He lit another cigarette after he filled the troughs with hay and sat on a stool, next to one of the stalls. A voice of forced friendliness startled him.

"Luke, you are sure a hard worker." It was Gene Richardson holding a glass of water in his hands. "But I wish you wouldn't smoke on my property. It's your free agency to do that, but your free agency stops here."

Luke snuffed it out quickly and stood up, facing Mr. Richardson. His heart dropped, knowing that his adoration and sometimes inappropriate desire for Vee were blazoned across his forehead like a sign. His face went hot and he stood straight, wishing he could drop the pitchfork and run. "Thank you, Sir."

Richardson smiled and calmly set the glass on the wooden stool next to the stall. He was a tall man with thick graying hair, neatly oiled and combed back. He had unruly eyebrows, but the rest of his face was docile. Luke wondered where the blue of Vee's eyes had come from. Richardson's eyes were a mousy brown; his cheeks weren't the same peachy hue, nor was his skin as smooth.

Luke waited as Richardson went to the next stall and stroked the neck of the horse that stood waiting its turn for hay. His jeans fit snug on wiry legs and were belted with a large silver buckle; his shirt was pressed and tucked in tightly.

"This is a Barr Colt."

Luke nodded, acknowledging the young horse.

"I have had three horses that came from the Barr line and all three won races that made me a lot of money."

Luke just watched and nodded.

"It's breeding. This is Kreios Barr Ditto. Do you know what that means?"

Luke shook his head.

"Kreios is Greek." He nodded at Luke.

Luke looked him in the eye and wondered where this was leading.

"It means, 'lord and master.' Alcippe Barr Dayton over there is his mother. Alcippe is Greek for 'mighty mare.' You see, Luke, I admire the Greek people. I lived around them in Pocatello for half my life. It's how I met your father. I've known Thomas for years. Did he tell you how we used to ride through Yellowstone?"

Luke shrugged. His father didn't say much about his past. Frankly, he didn't talk much about anything anymore.

Richardson cleared his throat and Luke felt the stale, uneasy pause of reproach about to begin. "Like horses, people have different paths in life." Richardson ran his hand down the length of the horse's back. "They may all be horses, but there are differences. That's why I paid fifty grand for this colt. It's in his blood to be something great. Do you understand?"

Luke knew there was a point about to be made.

"Do you know why it's so important for Barr horses to be treated a little differently?"

Luke looked at the ground, searching for the right answer.

"Take Marty over there," he said, waving at a large and ragged draft horse. "He's hard-working and certainly pulls his weight around here, but we certainly won't be letting him get close to Alcippe, now will we? Even with her good bloodlines, the foal wouldn't be worth feeding. A mule would be better." He laughed loudly, eyes wide. He turned to Luke and laughed again, encouraging Luke to join him.

Luke tried to laugh, but his throat was dry, and all that emerged was a fake, mumbled chuckle.

Richardson leaned over the rail and gave Luke an intense gaze. "What I'm trying to say is I'd do anything to keep the things that are valuable to me safe and untouched. If a cougar came down from the mountains and tried to hurt one of these babies, I'd be out here with my rifle, no questions asked." He lifted his eyebrows. "I wouldn't even think twice." Lifting his hand with the finger pointed and the thumb bent up like a pistol, he smiled and aimed it at Luke. "Boom!"

Luke flinched, which made Richardson laugh. He put his hand into an imaginary holster, holding their gaze. "Don't look so scared, son. You'd think I was talking about you."

Luke knew that he was. He looked at the water glass poised on the stool.

Richardson caught his glance. "You need some water?"

Luke shook his head.

Richardson gave a forced, "Hmm." He put his hands on his hips and furrowed his brow in thought. "I thought that's what you asked for. Didn't you ask Veronica to bring you a glass of water?"

Luke stood numb.

"I thought that's what she said. I figured I'd bring it out here so she wouldn't have to walk through all the mud and manure." He looked around the corral and then back to Luke. "I wouldn't want her in this mess, would you?"

"No, Sir."

"Good. Well, I can see I'm boring you with all my stories. I'll let you get back to work so you can get home. Please tell your father I think you're doing a great job. I keep a close eye on my place, and even when you don't realize it, I see what you're doing." He looked at Luke and nodded.

Luke had enough innuendos, and as he watched the lanky, polished cowboy walk off down the long arena corridor, he started to spray the hose toward him. He pressed his thumb down onto the flow and made it hit the concrete with a steady stream. His temper boiled and pushed his sensibilities aside. With each solid click of the man's boots, Luke aimed the jet of water closer. He stood transfixed, wishing he could knock him flat.

The veiled threats started his heart pounding with a mixture of anger and insult. Then the clicking stopped and Richardson started to turn back. Lines of water dripped from his boots and Luke turned quickly to the side, the hose followed. He had let his emotions go too far, and his forehead burned as he tried to act as though he were fully engaged in his work. He felt the stare bearing down on him, but he stayed still, hoping the man would give up and leave.

Luke felt the weighted tingle of regret. Then his rile boiled up again. He put the hose down on the floor and still, without acknowledging the boss he'd been goading, walked to the stool and picked up the glass of water. He looked at it and smiled before taking several long, deep gulps. He let out a loud "Ah," as though it was the most refreshing and enjoyable glass of water he had ever drank. He put the glass back on the stool, picked up the hose and continued with his chore, adding in a whistle to let the boss man know that he'd won.

The clicking of Mr. Richardson's boots began once again. As the sound grew distant, Luke turned and watched him leave the arena. Luke gave him a disgusted huff. He was no second class mangy horse. He might not be blond and blue-eyed, but he refused to be treated like an ill-bred animal.

Luke spent the next hour going over his work and making sure there wasn't a speck of manure or debris anywhere. He patted the horses and gave an extra flake of hay to Marty, stroking his chest and telling him what a fine looking horse he was.

He had to flip on the lights as he coiled up the hose and placed the pitchfork in the shed. Night had come upon him quickly, but he felt invigorated in the cool breeze that came with it.

As he walked from the arena back to where he had left his bicycle, Luke cut through the patio area and around a large spruce tree next to the house.

Out of the darkness came a whispered, "Hey."

He looked back toward the house and saw nothing.

"See you tomorrow," said the soft voice.

Luke knew it was her, and took a cautious step toward the house. "Where are you?" The glare of the porch light came on and Luke backed up quickly; squinting, he expected to see the looming figure of Gene Richardson. His heart pounded, but he stood waiting. When nothing happened he asked into the night, "Is that you? Where are you?"

He strained to hear a reply. When nothing came, he walked slowly to his bike, turning back with each couple of steps he made. He aimed the bike toward the road home. He took one last look back to where the voice had come from. The porch light went out.

When he arrived home, Luke told his father of his desire to quit, but was shot down.

"You would have us kicked off this land. Is that what you want?" his father asked.

"How can you let him treat us like this? He threatened to shoot me if I talked to his daughter."

"What daughter?" his mother broke in. "A girl? This is caused by a girl?"

His mother Theta was short and round with a mass of black curls tied back at her neck. She looked much older than her forty-two years. Her eyes were dark and large, but the lines around them told the story of a rough life.

Luke moaned in frustration. "It's not just a girl. He thinks we're not as worthy as his family. He compared us to his horses. As far as Richardson is concerned, his family is comprised of expensive racehorses and *we* are nothing but dirty mules."

"You don't need a girl from this town. You need a good Greek girl," his mother continued without notice of what he'd said.

"There are no Greek girls here."

"There are Greek girls in the upper county. If you went to church, you'd see."

Luke threw up his hands. "That's over an hour away! I won't find anyone unless I move away from this place."

"What?" his mother shrieked. "Thomas, don't let him talk like that!"

"Why do you make your mother worry?" his father said softly. Luke knew that Thomas had spent much of his time keeping the peace and controlling the things that would send his wife into 'death mode;' this involved panting, moans, waving of a handkerchief in front of her face as she collapsed on the floor, absolutely convinced her life was over.

"Well, it's true."

His father shook his head. "You have less than a year before you graduate. Then you can leave and work for the railroad in Pocatello. There are Greeks there. Right now, this is what we must do. We need to pay off our debt. It won't be long. Keep to yourself and do your work and troubles won't come."

Thomas carried a weight that was obvious in his tightened neck and the slumping of his shoulders. The once jovial risk-taker was now a hunched over, droopy-eyed shell of a man. Luke didn't understand the family's quick departure from their home in the northern part of the state, but knew it was urgent and not a topic of discussion. What he did understand was his father's unwavering appreciation for Richardson, even though he was now working for a man who referred to him as "the boy."

Luke shook his head. A year seemed endless, but he knew what his father said was what had to be.

His mother placed a large plate of stewed tomatoes and roasted lamb in front of him. "You'll meet Talia soon. She's strong and smart, a good Greek girl. Then you'll see."

"See what, Mama?" Luke picked up his fork and waved it as he spoke. "Do you really think I'm going to fall in love with a girl I've never met? It doesn't work that way. This is the nineties. People don't have arranged marriages anymore. I don't want to meet this girl and I'm sure she doesn't want to meet me."

"She does so." Theta leaned in and looked him in the eye. "It's not an arranged marriage. Parents just know what is best. Look at us," she waved a hand at Thomas. "Twenty-five years and we are still married. Your Aunt Mary and Uncle Don are married almost thirty years. All our parents, brothers, sisters--they are all married and still happy. All of us listened to our parents and married right."

"How can you marry someone you don't love?"

"What? I love your father."

27

Luke smiled and shook his head. "You didn't even know Dad when you married him. How could you love him?"

Theta stood up straight. "The love comes later. Marriage is the vessel used by God to put children here, to make families, and have a life. The love comes later."

"What if it doesn't? What if you marry and have children and never end up in love with your own wife or husband? Or don't have *any* children? What then? I don't want to take that risk. I want to be in love when I get married. That should come first."

Theta rolled her eyes and sighed. "You don't talk of love. You talk about passion. Passion turns to trouble. Men fight and kill each other over passion. Life isn't a fairytale, Luke. Love comes because of what you have in the marriage. You make children together, you have a home together and you take care of each other. In God's eyes, *that* is what is important."

God? Luke tried not to flinch. In his eyes it was God that was the fairytale. From the time he was young, he hated attending church. And once he could stay home alone, he refused to go. He saw it as a bunch of odd chants, folk tales, and superstitious nonsense, and he sure as hell didn't want it influencing his decisions when it came to marriage and love.

Then his mind was filled with one thought, the soft whisper of, "See you tomorrow." It made him smile as he ate. His eyes gleamed and he let his mind wander. He knew he would be prodding the bull by even talking to her again, but the hormones coursing through him pushed rationality aside, allowing that gush of foolish passion to overtake him. There was no way he would enter a marriage without this fervent stir.

Chapter 4

Malad, Idaho, December, 2008

Julie returned to the room.

Officer Degraw came in and took a seat, trying not to make eye contact with me. "Sophie, how old are you?"

"I'll be seventeen next March."

"Do you go to school?"

"Yes."

Officer Degraw looked puzzled. "Where do you go to school?"

"At home...Papa is in charge of my schooling."

"Do you know how to read?"

"Of course. I've known how to read since I was four."

"Really? That's very impressive. What books do you read?"

"I've read all of Jane Austen's novels. I love them. Papa had me read Shakespeare. And I'm currently reading *Charlotte's Web*."

"Shakespeare?" he asked surprised. "Do you watch television?"

"Not really. Papa watches the news sometimes, but he says it isn't something that I should see."

Officer Degraw nodded. "When's the last time you left your house?"

"You mean outside?"

"Yes."

"I was outside this morning."

"What were you doing?"

"Feeding the chickens."

"When was the last time you went to town?"

I hadn't been to town in years. The last time I remember going was at night. I sat in the car and waited while Papa went into the store and got what we needed. He parked away from the entrance and told me to stay down and look away if people walked by.

The last time I saw the town in daylight, I was very young. It was a warm day, but Papa still made me wear a hat that almost covered my eyes. Even though it was so many years ago, I still can see the anxiousness in his face as we drove, and the worry in his eyes every time someone glanced at us. It made me feel that going there was scary and uncomfortable. Although the outside world fascinated me, I was also afraid of what I would find.

"I don't remember."

"Has it been longer than a year?"

"Yes."

Officer Degraw bit his bottom lip. "How long have you lived in the house in Arbon Valley?"

"Forever."

"Is that where you were born?"

"I was born in a hospital."

Officer Degraw chuckled. "What I meant to say is, were your parents living there when you were born?"

"No."

"So you really haven't lived in that house forever."

I realized he was right. It was where my earliest memories came from. The crowds of cottonwoods and spruce trees behind us and the willows that lined the creek below had always been my view of the world. In the spring, green spread over the hills and pastures, and the pink and whites of Morning Glories twisted their vines around our fences. In summer, the ground crunched when I walked, because the grass had dried in the arid Idaho heat. In the fall, the valley turned orange and yellow, and sunsets were vivid pinks. In winter, snows covered the land, and hoar frost transformed the brush and bare trees into sparkling ice palaces.

"I don't remember living anywhere else, but I know we moved there after my mother died."

Both Julie and Officer Degraw looked at each other before Officer Degraw continued, "Were you happy at that house?"

"Yes."

"Then why did you want to leave?"

"I didn't."

"You had a suitcase packed. And what about Damien? Wasn't he trying to rescue you?"

"Yes, but..."

They nodded toward me, coaxing me, waiting for my response.

"Papa didn't mean to shoot Damien."

"Why did he have a gun?" Officer Degraw asked.

"He wanted to scare him. It's dangerous to be near us."

"Near who?"

I knew I'd said too much, so I stopped and sat back.

"Why is it dangerous to be near you?"

"Papa said not to tell."

"Why did he do that?"

"He is worried about me."

"Is that why he kept you in that house away from everyone?"

I nodded.

"Sophie, do you know that you have a family that has been looking for you for years?"

My family was Papa. *"Your mother died when you were a baby," he'd said. "Her family doesn't like us and will tear us apart. I no longer have any family left...you are all I have."*

"I don't want to see them."

"Why? They've missed you."

"They don't miss me. They just want to hurt me."

Officer Degraw sat up, looking concerned.

Julie leaned in and took my hand. "Why do they want to hurt you? They've been looking for you all these years because you're part of their family. They never gave up looking. They are your grandparents and your aunt and uncle. They're so happy to hear you're alive."

I felt the walls of the room starting to squeeze in on me. "When can I go home?"

Julie furrowed her brow, confused that I wasn't excited to meet my long lost family.

"I don't want to be with them. I want to be with Papa." I looked over at Julie. "Why can't I just go home and be with Papa?"

Julie's eyes told me my life would never be the same. She stroked my hair with her hand. "Sophie, your father did a bad thing when he shot that boy. He won't be able to go home, because he broke the law."

"Ever?" I asked, feeling my eyes start to sting and my heart ready to burst. "What's going to happen to him?"

"He'll stay in the jail and then go to court where a judge will decide."

"Decide what?"

"The judge will decide how long your father will have to be in jail."

"And then he can come home?"

Julie looked frustrated and sad. "I'm not sure. It's up to the judge. But it won't be for a long time. You'll need to stay somewhere, and your mother's family wants you to stay with them."

I was exhausted. "What if I hate it? What if they hate me? Do I have to stay if I don't want to?"

Julie tried to smile. "Let's see how it goes. If you really don't want to stay, we'll see what we can do, okay?"

Her answer really wasn't an answer. I shrugged my shoulders as a sign of indignant agreement, and then felt a wave of timid curiosity set in as I thought about the family I would soon meet.

"You'll get to go to school and meet some new friends," she blurted out.

Fear washed over me. I had seen the looks I received from just the few people I had seen face to face. I was troubled at what I would find out in the world.

"Don't you want friends?" she asked, smiling.

I didn't know how to answer. I wanted friends, but I didn't think I was capable.

Officer Degraw cleared his throat. "Is Damien your friend?"

The question was pointed and struck to the core. Then I nodded, not wanting to give too much away. I wasn't sure what role I played in what was happening to Damien.

"Do you have other friends?" he asked.

I thought about what he said. I rubbed my hands together in my lap and then scooted them under my legs, palm side up. I bounced my knees together nervously. "No."

"Why not?"

"There isn't anyone around to be friends with."

"How did you meet Damien?"

Damien was part of me that was sacred. The day I met Damien was like being reborn. It was the beginning of what was so precious to me. I didn't want to talk about him. My encounters with Damien were what I lived for. I thought about each of them constantly and remembered every sight, sound, and nuance.

I closed my eyes and shut Officer Degraw and Julie from my mind. I let my thoughts of Damien, of peace and love fill the room, blocking out everything else.

Chapter 5

The Arbon Valley, Summer, 2003

I was eleven years old and completely unaware of my peculiar life. It was early morning and I was sitting on my front porch waiting for Papa to finish his coffee and come out to see the chalk drawing I had made on our driveway. I wore a blue and yellow sleeveless cotton sundress, and the cement stairs were cool on my legs. I noticed a small plume of dust far down the valley. It was followed by a car that slowly made its way up our lonely hill.

Our home was an old homestead surrounded by trees and hidden away from the only road that led up the canyon. It was small, but fit us perfectly. There was a living room and kitchen area that were connected. The kitchen had yellow and orange vinyl floors and the living room was covered with dark brown carpeting. The walls were white, except the one with the fireplace. It had white wood siding, and halfway up was red brick that also was part of the fireplace mantle. The room had two large windows that gave us a view from the back into the woods.

My room was at the front of the house. Papa's room was at the back and had a porch where he could sit at night and read. He didn't notice the car heading our way, until they were in our driveway. From the back seat of a pale yellow Buick, two young faces stared out at me. I stood up and stared back. A woman emerged from behind the wheel.

"Hello!" she called. "I'm looking for…"

Then Papa appeared in the doorway. "Hello," he responded in forced friendliness. I could see that he was disappointed and scared.

The woman was dressed in lightweight jeans and a white collared shirt with short sleeves. She wore white sneakers and no socks. Smiling brightly, she had her hair pulled back in a blue and white scarf. As she walked to the porch, Papa put a hand on my shoulder.

"Miguel, I didn't know you had a daughter," the woman cooed.

"Yes, she normally lives with her mother in California. She spends some time here in the summer when she doesn't have school." He squeezed my shoulder and I knew it was a sign to stay quiet. The entire story amazed me, including the strange name that the woman had called him.

She walked to the porch and bent at the waist to greet me. "I'm Mrs. Graham. I work with your father at the dairy. We live just down the road." She leaned in and pulled her sunglasses down. Her face was close to mine and her brown eyes stared. "My goodness," she said, and then looked up at Papa. "She's stunning."

My father pursed his lips and simply nodded. He shooed me into the house. I didn't want to go, but I did. Once inside I ran to my room and looked out the window at the two boys in the back seat. They noticed me perched on the sill and kept watching, as their mother continued to talk with Papa. I heard Mrs. Graham discussing the dairy, but I kept my eyes on the car. Then the car door opened and one of the boys stepped out.

"It's hot in here," he whined to his mother. "Can we get out for a while?"

Mrs. Graham looked back. "Sure. Can you bring the papers on the front seat?"

The boy wore jeans and a blue t-shirt. His brown hair blew in the breeze and he looked to be about my age. As he walked with the papers to the porch he shot me a look. Then the other boy exited the car and walked slowly behind his brother. He was older and taller. He, too, wore jeans and a t-shirt. His hair was sandy-colored and a bit longer. When he reached the porch, I noticed his large dark eyes that were filled with boredom. Both boys intrigued me, and I stayed at the window watching their every move. They shuffled impatiently as the younger boy continued to cast looks my way.

"This is Donny," Mrs. Graham said, introducing the younger boy to my father. "And this is Damien."

I immediately memorized both names. I said them under my breath, excited that they were there and wishing I could spend the day studying them.

"I'm sorry," said Mrs. Graham. "I didn't ask your daughter's name."

"It's Sophie," Papa said grudgingly.

"That's beautiful. Do you think she could come out and sit with the boys while we go over this?"

I watched as my father looked at the ground, trying to find a good reason why I couldn't.

"It'll give these two ruffians something to do while I explain this to you. I thought it would be better here than at work, don't you?"

Papa nodded, then reluctantly came into the house. I fell back onto my bed so he wouldn't discover me peeking out the window.

He was soon at my door. "You are going to come out here and sit on the porch and talk to these boys. Tell them that you are leaving to go to California on Friday and you won't be back."

"Why?"

He offered me a truly troubled look. "Just do it."

Nodding, I followed him to the front door.

"It's very nice to meet you, Sophie," said Mrs. Graham. "This is Donny and Damien, and you all can sit out here and talk while the adults do some boring work stuff, okay?"

Papa led me to the porch. He made sure he caught my eye and gave me an imposing lift of his eyebrow. I knew what he meant and took a cautious seat on the porch steps, facing away from the boys. I heard the screen door close and Mrs. Graham's voice inside the house.

For several minutes we sat in silence, until Donny piped up. "What do you do all day way out here?"

I looked at him, seeing his suddenly startled eyes. "I draw or read. Currently, I'm reading *Black Beauty*. It's a marvelous book."

He stood up, gave me an odd look, and walked around, facing me. "Do you have any friends?"

I couldn't decide if his question was meant to be mean, so I just shrugged and looked at the ground.

He walked back around to his brother and I heard him whisper. Donny punched Damien in the arm and then declared, "See?" He motioned toward me.

Damien pushed Donny back and rubbed his arm.

I felt insulted, even though I wasn't sure why.

"How old are you?" Damien asked.

" How old are *you*?"

"Thirteen."

"How old is *he*?" I asked, looking at Donny.

"I'm almost twelve," Donny answered. He walked back to the porch and the two boys watched me.

I stood up.

"Where do you go to school?" asked Donny.

I didn't know how to answer, knowing Papa was already worried about what I would say. "California."

"Why don't you live here?" Donny asked.

"Because my mother lives in California." I wondered if I would go to hell for all the lies I told. Papa had taught me many times about the fate I'd suffer if I lied, but I felt that because he ordered me to do it, somehow I'd be spared.

I heard Papa and Mrs. Graham at the door. They had finished their meeting, and she was saying her good-byes.

"Okay boys, let's go. It was nice meeting you, Sophie. We hope to see you again before you head back to California."

"Can we come back here, Mom?" asked Damien, his dark eyes pleading.

I looked up, completely surprised.

"We'll see," she said. "Thanks for helping me with this, Miguel," she called back to my father.

I watched as they pulled out of our drive and headed back down the long dusty lane. Donny looked out at the hills, but Damien kept his eyes on me, even turning around in the car and looking out the back window until it disappeared in the distance.

Papa walked into the house and I followed. "Why did you tell that lady I lived in California?"

"I had to."

"But Mama's dead. She doesn't live in California."

My father put a gentle hand on my head. "I'm sorry I made you lie. I don't like to do that, but I must in order to keep you safe. If they found out I left you alone up here while I worked, they would take you away. Do you understand?"

"Yes."

"That's why we don't go out. I don't want to lose you, and they would take you away."

"Who?"

"The outsiders. Remember, we talked about this."

"Why did she call you Miguel?"

"Sophie, there's a lot I can't tell you. You need to trust me. I'm trying to protect you."

"Can I be friends with those boys?"

Papa shook his head. "No. They will tell."

"What if I told them not to?"

Papa smiled at my innocence. "No one can be trusted, Sophie. If even one person knew the truth we'd be torn apart, and I don't want to lose you."

I sadly agreed with him and went to my room. I gazed out the window with my chin on my hands, thinking about the encounter with the boys. I wanted so badly to see them again, and I cried softly to myself, knowing I wouldn't.

For two weeks I went about my life, doing my chores, reading, and drawing. I had tried to sketch the faces of the boys so I could remember that day, but I wasn't happy with my attempt and crumpled the paper, vowing to try again.

At seven every morning, Papa left for work. He often returned around noon for lunch, and then at five thirty for dinner he was home for the night. I had always spent my days alone, but I never felt alone until after I met Donny and Damien. It was then that I realized I was missing something. I loved Papa, but I wanted friends my own age. I wanted to hear about their lives, their thoughts and then compare them to my own. I wanted to know that I was like them. I often thought about the boys, making up conversations in my mind and laying out games for us to play. Each night I prayed I would see them again.

Early the next morning, I had finished feeding the chickens and folding the wash. I was in the garden watching a ladybug make its way across the leaves of a pepper plant, when I saw something move in the distance. At first, I thought it was a bird or stray dog. I stood up and shaded my eyes from the sun and there, standing in the field watching me, was Donny.

My first instinct was to run into the house and hide, but instead I stood up and stared back, wondering why he was there. As he walked, I noticed another form just up from the brow of the hill. My heart leapt as I realized it was Damien. They had come to see me. I was afraid after Papa's warnings, but pushed the fear aside and walked toward Donny. I knew my boundaries and glanced back at the hill, knowing I was being watched, and making sure I stayed inside the invisible but distinct line that Papa had drawn. I kept looking back at Damien, wondering why he lagged behind. When Donny and I met, I was farther away from my house than I had ever gone, and I felt a rush of anxiety and excitement.

"I thought you were going to California," he said.

I just stood looking at him, still surprised that he was there.

"Why are you still here?"

"Because." It's all I could say. I hadn't prepared my web of lies and my mind raced, trying to come up with something else.

He started to talk, but I interrupted him. "Why are *you* here?"

"We wanted to see if you had left."

I looked behind him to see Damien finally coming to within earshot. "Why?"

He shrugged. Donny turned back. "I told you she would still be here."

Damien simply stared at me. He was handsome with his shirt fluttering in the breeze and his thumb hanging casually from the belt loop of his pants.

"Do you want to go with us?" Donny asked.

"Where?"

"We have a fort over at the dump."

I knew anything away from the house would be risking too much. There was a vivid reminder of why I stayed close. I looked up toward the fluttering red warning perched atop the hill – the constant warning signal that only *I* knew the reason for – and shook my head in disappointment. "I can't."

"Okay," he said, turning away.

I became frantic that he might leave so I blurted out, "Do you want to see my garden? I have caterpillars."

He turned back and looked over at Damien. "Do you want to?"

Damien nodded.

I smiled and we ran back to my house. I was overjoyed to have them there. I showed them the green hairless bugs slinking around rows of plants growing in cool dark rows of dirt, and giggled as they crawled over our fingers. We drew tick-tack-toe boards on the cement and played several games; then we swung on the clothesline pole while they told me what they were going to be when they grew up. Donny was going to be a fireman like his uncle, and Damien a writer, to which Donny started mockingly reciting a story. "Once there was a cowboy who had a horse…"

Damien pushed him off the pole and started wrestling him on the grass until both boys were sweating and laughing. It was enthralling to see the energy and aggression that emanated from them. It was so new and strange, and I wondered what else I was missing by being shut off from the rest of the world. Until then, I hadn't really noticed the full scale of my isolation.

"Let's go into the hills," said Donny, pointing up the mountain and panting.

"No," I answered, adamant.

"Why not?"

I hesitated, wondering if I should tell them.

"Are you afraid?" Donny teased.

"Yes," I said, emphatic.

He laughed, surprised at my honesty. "Why? Are you afraid of the cougars?"

I shook my head.

"Then what? There are no bears up there. There is nothing to be scared of," he insisted.

"Yes, there is. There are ghosts there."

He burst out laughing and Damien gave a small smile. "Ghosts?" Donny yelled. "There is no such thing."

"Yes, there is," I said defiantly. "Papa knows."

"Really? How does he know?"

"He put them there."

Donny's jovial face suddenly looked disturbed. "What do you mean by that?"

I knew I had said too much. With my fists at my side, I stood tall and simply stated, "They're out there. I'm not going into the hills."

"I think he told you that so you won't go up there and get lost. He's trying to scare you so you'll stay here in the yard," Damien said. "That's what parents do. They scare you to get you to do what they want."

"But I know they're out there," I told him. And I did. A blood red reminder was visible in the bright light. It wasn't there the first time, but I witnessed everything the second. There were two ghosts in those hills. When the wind swayed the trees and made the windows on our house bow and sigh, I could hear them warning me to stay away.

He smiled. "Then we won't go into the hills. We can go other places."

I smiled back, feeling closer to him for giving my supposedly 'silly' fears credence.

The morning quickly turned into the heat of the day, and I realized Papa would soon be home for lunch. As much as I hated doing it, I tried to shoo them away.

"Can I come back tomorrow?" Donny asked, still panting from our game of tag.

"Yes, but my father can't see you."

"Okay."

"Are you coming too?" I asked Damien.

He shrugged, but then smiled. It made me tingle and I smiled back.

I was happier than I had ever been just because they wanted to come back. I enjoyed being with my new friends. Donny, with his happy brown eyes and easy laugh made the hours go swiftly, but there was something about Damien that was captivating, and I couldn't wait to see him again.

The next morning I raced around the house doing my chores. I tried to complete my reading assignment, but that was in vain. The words blurred as my thoughts turned to Damien and if he would come again. I finally gave up on my reading and went through the kitchen and out the back door. I saved my outdoor chores for last, so if they were there, I wouldn't miss them. The warm summer air was inviting as I took in the wide span of the fields looking for my new friends, but there was nothing.

I stepped off the porch and went to the hen house. Before opening the latch on the wire gate, I again took a long look around, but all was quiet. I went in with my basket and started collecting the morning's eggs. When I took my harvest into the house and placed them carefully in a bowl in the refrigerator, I looked at the clock. It was nine twenty-three. The morning would be gone if they didn't appear soon.

Going back to the porch, I looked out over the pasture toward the boys' home. That's when I saw them. Like a gift from God, my friends arrived. Donny's tousled hair bobbed just above the ridge as he jogged along, with Damien again walking behind. I was so relieved and excited that I jumped off the porch, through our back gate, and ran at them, the tall, dried grass swiping my arms as I passed through the field.

They saw me running and picked up their pace. When we met, we embraced, and then giggled at our silliness.

We spent the morning much like the previous one. I found myself studying them, watching Damien's eyes dance when he laughed, and noticing dirt under Donny's fingernails and scars on his elbows. When Donny talked, he added noises to his stories — the sounds of a car, the neigh of a horse — it was fun to listen. I encouraged him to keep talking. Damien often shook his head, as though embarrassed at his younger brother's juvenile ways.

We lay in the grass in the shade of a currant bush, our heads close and our bodies spread out like the hands of a clock. We stared at the cloudless sky and talked and talked. It was blissful. I wanted to memorize every story they told, so I rarely interrupted. It was that day I realized we had cut it too close to Papa's lunchtime. We heard the crackle and crunch of tires on gravel.. I jumped up, heart racing, and told Donny and Damien in a panic-stricken whisper to hide.

When I was inside, I tried to greet Papa without the look of terror I felt.

"Were you out back?" he asked, unaffected.

"I got six eggs today," I said, going to the fridge and pointing to the bowl.

Papa nodded his approval. Then his brows furrowed. His deep brown eyes looked me over and he cocked his head sideways. "Why are you sweating? Is it that hot out today?"

"I was playing on the clothesline." Still no lies, I thought.

"Hmm." It was all he mumbled as he went to the cupboard and pulled bread and peanut butter from the shelves.

I knew the more I stood there the guiltier I would seem, so I went to my room and tried to calm myself.

"Sophie," he called from the kitchen.

I jumped up. "Yes?"

He was standing at the window and looking out over the fields. He didn't answer me.

"What is it?"

He stood very still, glancing from side to side, then he turned to me with a look of bewilderment. "Nothing."

I had to tell myself to breathe. Then I went to the fridge and opened it. The cold hit my hot skin and helped to relieve the burning heat that raced through my veins. "Do you want milk?" I asked.

"Yes, thank you."

I poured a glass for him and placed it on the table next to his newspaper.

"How did your reading go today?" he asked.

I paused.

"Sophie?"

I sighed. "I haven't finished it yet."

He gave me his stern, fatherly look of disappointment.

"I'll do it after lunch. I promise."

He smiled, and I knew I had made it through the ordeal unscathed.

When he left and went back to work, I watched his car disappear in the distance. Then I ran out back and searched for the boys, but they were gone. That night I wondered if they would return after our frantic near-miss.

Each day I waited, but I never had to worry, because as the sun spread across the entire valley I would see a mound of sandy hair bounding up the hill. And the one I loved, his smile always beamed like a bright beacon of hope, even before I could even see his eyes. It became a happy pattern in my life. But when Friday came, things didn't go as planned.

That morning didn't start any different, but as I watched the crest of the hill, only Donny appeared. I kept looking for Damien, but he never showed. When Donny reached our yard, I tried to hide my disappointment. "Why didn't Damien come with you?"

"I told him I was going to the baseball field. I didn't want him to know I was coming here. I wanted to come alone."

"Why? Doesn't he like me?" I felt heartbroken.

Donny rolled his eyes. "We both like you. That's why I didn't want him here."

"Oh," I said, wondering what he meant. All I could think about was my impact on Damien. Knowing he liked me made my heart swell. I completely pushed aside what Donny had revealed about his own feelings. The discussion didn't last long, and eventually we went on with our day, and even without Damien we had fun.

We picked seeds out of a huge sunflower head. We held the chickens and I admitted I had named each of them. And he helped pick corn for the dinner I had planned that night. I enjoyed Donny's hearty laugh and chatty personality, but I felt something was missing. Being alone with Donny made me realize even more the intensity of the feelings I had for Damien, but my time with friends my own age was priceless, so I reveled in it.

When it was time for Donny to leave, I realized I wouldn't see him the next day because it was the weekend and Papa would be off work. I felt my heart sink and he noticed my smile fade.

"Is he home on Sunday, too?" he asked.

I nodded.

"Then I'll come back on Monday."

I tried to smile, but my sadness was obvious. I hoped he meant Damien would come, too. I started to tell him that, but he interrupted.

"Do you love me?" he asked.

I looked up at him, astonished. *Love?*

"Well, do you?"

I blushed and looked away. He was my friend, and the word love was something I held close, only peeking at it when I thought of Damien.

"I love you. I want to marry you some day," he said, matter-of-factly.

"You do?"

He took my arm, pulled me to him, and before I knew what was happening, he kissed me. "I think you love me, too," he said.

I watched in stunned silence as he ran back across the field. It was my first kiss, and while I didn't watch much television, I saw the passion and feeling people had during those moments. Their eyes fluttered, and they were dreamy with delight, yet I felt little more than a tingle.

I did love him, but I knew that what I felt wasn't the kind of love he professed. He was my friend, and that was what he'd always be. I worried about what he'd say and do if he knew Damien was the one I truly loved.

Donny stopped at the top of the ridge and turned around. He yelled back, "I'll see you on Monday!" He jumped up and down so I could see him.

I waved, still bewildered as a small dust cloud began to spin on the ridge beside him. He noticed it, too, and shielded his eyes from the dirt. It then moved quickly toward me, as if it had purpose. I saw it coming and put my arm up over my face as the grit and wind spit and twirled around me. When it stopped, I put my arm down and blinked my eyes, trying to focus.

My hair was tousled and full of dirt. I looked to where Donny had been standing, but he was gone. At the top of the hill, set away from the trees, the tiny red flutter caught my eye as though laughing wickedly. I suddenly felt cold and wretched. Feeling as if I were being chased by a brutal monster, I ran into the house and hid in my room.

That night, after Papa and I had dinner, a knock came at the front door. Papa looked up with annoyed and questioning eyes. Normally, the mailman, meter reader, or other visitors came in daylight. No one came at night. He signaled for me to stay hidden, then Papa walked to the door with purpose and opened it. I heard the voice of a boy. I went to the hallway and peeked around the corner. There stood Damien on the porch, looking frightened. He was staring into Papa's eyes. His hands were thrust into his pockets as my father held open the screen door.

The floor creaked and Papa shot a glance over his shoulder, freezing me in mid-stride. He directed Damien into the house and I felt my stomach start to roll.

Papa looked at me. "Sophie, this boy is looking for his brother. Have you seen him?"

I knew I was going to hell now. What possible answer could I give that wasn't a lie but would still keep me from giving away our secret? I just lifted my shoulders, in a sign of uncertainty. I looked at Damien, feeling as though I had betrayed him by being alone with Donny. His eyes were wide, filled with worry, as he nervously stepped toward the door looking for an escape.

"Sophie," Papa said, sternly. "Have you seen his brother, or not?"

I looked at the floor and nodded. I could tell Papa was floored by my admission, and he grabbed me by the arms and made me look into his eyes.

"What do you know? Was he here?"

I felt my fortitude melt, and I started rambling. I told him how the boys had surprised me the first day, and how they had come back every day since. I told him we had simply played games and talked. I explained that Donny came alone yesterday and that he didn't stay long because of a baseball game. I said that for Damien. I pleaded with Papa not to be mad or to cause trouble for the boys, but I didn't say a word about what Donny said...or about the kiss.

"So he was here today?" Papa asked.

"Yes."

"When?"

"He left before you came home for lunch."

Papa looked at me with sheer anguish. *How could you?* He accused me with his eyes. "Where did he go after he was here?"

"I told you, he was going to the baseball field. He walked through the pasture."

Papa looked at Damien with distress. "I hope you find him safe. We'll let you know if we see or hear anything else."

Damien nodded, knowing that was all the information he'd get from us. As he walked to the door, he looked back. I saw distress in his face. Donny and I had betrayed him. As he walked out, I felt my life being pulled from me. Would I ever see him again? I couldn't bear the thought that this might be our final goodbye.

When the door closed, Papa turned around slowly. His shoulders hunched forward and he glared. I immediately started to cry, but he refused to let me escape his interrogation. "Why, Sophie? Haven't I told you? You don't listen to me."

"I'm sorry," I whispered through tears. "They are my friends. I want to have friends, Papa."

Papa shook his head gravely. "I know you do, but there are things you don't understand and I am only doing what's best for you...*and* them."

I sobbed at the thought of no longer seeing Damien or Donny. "Why is it for the best? Why can't I have friends?"

"Sophie, it's dangerous. Bad things will happen."

"Nothing bad happened!"

Papa sighed. "I hope nothing bad has happened to that boy. I pray that he's okay."

I shook my head, confused. "We just played games."

"Sophie, you're too young to understand. Someday I'll explain why you must be careful...when you're older."

"Careful? I'll *be* careful. I *was* careful! I can have friends. I promise." I begged him not to keep me from them. My eyes welled up again, when I saw he wasn't listening. Papa had made up his mind.

Papa picked me up and went to his large recliner. He settled down into the cushioned seat, nestled my limp and shaking body into his lap, and started to rock.

Chapter 6

Malad, Idaho, December, 2008

"Sophie?" Julie's voice brought me back from my daydream. "What is it?"

I wondered how long I had been sitting in a stupor. "Nothing," I quickly blurted. "I was just thinking."

"About Damien?" she asked.

It was then I remembered their line of questioning and what had brought on my trip down memory lane. "Kind of," I mumbled.

"I know this isn't easy for you, but we need to find out some things."

"Why?"

"We need to find out why your father shot Damien."

I took a deep, exhausted breath. "He didn't mean to hit him, just to warn him. He was trying to keep him away from me."

"Why did your father want to keep you away from a friend?" she asked.

"To protect him."

"To protect your father?" asked Officer Degraw.

"No, to protect Damien."

Officer Degraw gave me a look that made his forehead crinkle and his eyes turn into thin lines of color. "You mean to protect *you*, right?"

Julie leaned her head toward me, encouraging me to answer. "No," I said. "He was protecting *Damien*."

"From whom?" asked Julie, completely disconcerted.

I felt my heart fill with sadness. My voice grew cold as I tried to answer. "From me," I said clearly. "Papa was protecting Damien from me."

A light knock came at the door and then it cracked open. A young officer in a suit and open collar leaned in. "The family's here," he whispered.

Julie nodded. My stomach lurched when I heard the words. *Family? They aren't my family.* Julie saw my angst and tried to use her soft eyes and kind smile to calm me. It didn't work. I started to fidget, my mouth was dry. I was also very hungry, but didn't say anything.

"I'll be with you," she said, making me keep eye contact. "When you meet them, I'll be with you."

"Who is it? How many of them are here?" I asked.

She looked at Officer Degraw who shrugged, and then turned to the door. He went to find the answers.

Julie patted my hands as I rolled them in my lap. "I know this is scary for you," she said. "But you'll see how much they love you and it will be fine."

"Papa says they think I killed my mother."

"*What?*" she asked, horrified. "Why would he say such a thing?" This question she asked more to herself than to me.

I sat with my shoulders slouched, wishing I hadn't said anything. I could see from her long and sorrowful face, she thought Papa was a horrible person. I wasn't just being timid; I had a real motive to fear these people she called *family*.

No amount of talks or preparation could keep my anxiousness from filling every pore. I expected the worst.

After all, what would *I* do if faced the person who had killed someone I loved?

"Are you ready?" Julie asked.

I steadied myself, wondering how I could ever be ready for what lay ahead. "What's going to happen?"

Julie smiled, seeing my angst. "They're waiting in another room. I'll take you in and introduce you. It will be like reuniting with old friends. It will be good." She kept nodding, even when she opened the door and led me out.

Officer Degraw was in conversation with Carpo, who looked angry, yet when he saw us, he stood up straight and tried to smile.

"Officer Carponelli is one of the first people who tried to find you," Julie said. "He's friends with your family."

Carpo bent down, with a horrid little smile. "It's nice to finally meet you, Callidora."

I felt my spine stiffen. "My name is Sophie." I looked at him, and with a fervor I hoped carried into the room full of my *supposed* family, I proclaimed it even louder. "My name is *Sophie*."

"Of course," said Carpo. "My mistake." He put his arm across his waist and bowed. "Nice to meet you, Sophie."

Julie put her hand on my shoulder. "I'll introduce you, so everyone will know."

"Thank you," I whispered, as my head pounded.

As the door opened I saw four faces looking weary, but hopeful--an old man with gray hair and a long thin nose; an old woman with brown curls and soft, pillow-like arms; a woman who was thick-waisted with blonde hair, big eyes, and lots of make-up; and a man with thinning reddish-brown hair, small eyes and a bulbous nose. Their

55

faces turned absolutely white, as they gasped at my entrance. I saw the mixture of sorrow and awe and I wanted to turn and run.

Julie cleared her throat. "Everyone, this is…"

Before she could finish, the older woman started to wail, "Oh, Callidora. Oh, Callidora."

The old man tried to calm her by putting his hands on her shoulders, but she brushed him aside and walked toward me.

"It's you." She wept, looking at me as if I were an angel coming down from heaven. "You've finally come home."

The younger woman stood staring with edgy eyes. The man with her also gawked at me, but his gaze seemed far more accepting and a tad bit curious.

The old woman took both my hands in hers. "You look like your mother." Tears rolled down her round, spongy cheeks. "Doesn't she?" she asked the others, who all just nodded their reply.

Hearing the word *mother* made my own eyes start to tear.

Julie spoke up, "This is Sophie. That's what she wants to be called."

The old man's voice was stern as he replied, "Her name is Callidora. That's what I named her and that's what we call her."

I glared at him.

"You're home now," the old woman continued. "We'll never lose you again." She leaned in to kiss me and I broke loose of her grip.

I pushed her aside. "No! Don't!" It was then the emptiness of my stomach mixed with the immense exertion of emotion, and my body simply gave up the battle. The room began to buzz and rotate, and soon my world went black.

Chapter 7

Malad, Idaho, Early Spring, 1991

Luke waited at the trough, hoping it really was she who had called out to him the night before. The soft lilt still filled his head. "See you tomorrow."

He had finished his chores with vigor and hoped to spend the last bits of daylight talking to her. Minutes dragged on and his anticipation grew. He could see light coming from the house, but nothing that indicated she would emerge. Over thirty minutes passed before he heard a door open. His heart leapt, but he tried to keep his excitement hidden while pretending to wash off the sill of a corral window.

"You still here?" asked Richardson, as he rounded the corner.

"I'm almost finished. I got a late start," answered Luke. His heart filled with both shock and dismay.

"Okay. Well, see you tomorrow."

Luke cringed as the words that had kept his emotions aloft now felt like a crushing blow. He watched as Richardson climbed into his pickup truck and pulled out of the drive onto the main road. Luke heaved a deep, defeated sigh and began to gather his things. He closed the corral door, and when he turned back, she was there. It startled him, and she laughed.

"Where were you?" he asked, somewhat annoyed.

"What do you mean?"

"I waited here for almost an hour."

"Waited for me? Why?"

Luke rolled his eyes. "Last night you said, 'See you tomorrow'."

She smiled slyly. "I did. And I've been watching you most of the day from my window."

He looked at her, exasperated.

"I said, 'See YOU tomorrow.'" Then she giggled. "I didn't say you'd see me."

Luke shook his head. "You're crazy." He gathered his tool belt, as if leaving.

"No, you are," she insisted.

"Me?"

"Hey, I'm not the one playing Russian roulette with my father. If he were to see us, you'd be sent packing."

"I'm not afraid of him," Luke said. He looked at her and saw her eyes sparkle as moonlight shone through the branches of a willow tree. "I'm just talking to you. There's nothing wrong with that. It's not like we're making out in the barn."

She gave a surprised gasp, but then smiled.

"So why are you out here?" he asked, with a swagger.

Vee answered with a shrug.

He took her hand and she pulled it back instinctively, looking around. He laughed. "You're the one that's afraid."

"No, I'm not."

He lifted his eyebrows. "I think you're afraid of me."

"What?" she asked with a giggle.

"You are. You're afraid you're going to fall in love with me."

She laughed out loud and then covered her mouth, worried that she would be overheard.

Luke smiled at her, enjoying her laughter. "Don't deny it," he said.

She shook her head. "I have to go in now."

"Why?" he asked, with a devilish gleam in his eye. "Because I'm right?" He took her hand again.

This time she let him. They stood, both smiling broadly looking at each other. But then as the cool breeze of late spring crept into the evening, smiles faded, and a profound feeling encircled them. He pulled her to him with one hand while his other lightly brushed her hair back from her face. For a moment he just stood holding her hand and taking in her beauty.

"You are the most stunning girl I've ever seen."

She looked away, embarrassed.

"No!" he ordered, making her look back into his eyes. "You are. I could stand here and look at you for the rest of my life." He didn't care if it sounded reckless and he didn't worry about her reaction. All his desires and urges were focused on her with the intense yearning and unabashed hope that she felt the same.

She stepped closer to him and studied his face. She nodded her agreement and then let him kiss her.

Luke dropped her hand and wrapped his arm around her waist. He wanted to feel the entire length of her against him. Her lips were soft, and she had the faint scent of lavender wafting from her hair. He stopped and took a deep breath, but kept her close.

She waited for him to say something, but instead he just stared. He was full of emotion and had no desire to keep it in check.

Vee started to step back and he pulled her to him once more. "Say it," he said, softly.

"Say what?"

"That you'll see me tomorrow."

She smiled. "Okay. See you tomorrow."

He shook his head. "Say it like you mean it."

"See you tomorrow?"

"Yes, say it like you mean it. It's our code now. When you say it, I'll know what you really mean."

"And what's that?" she asked.

He kissed her again, this time letting his desire for her swell in his chest, erasing any sign of restraint. He caressed her back and slowly moved from her lips to her cheeks to her neck, tasting her beautiful smooth skin.

She leaned back and gave in to him, which allowed his inhibitions to disappear as he picked her up and carried her back inside the corral.

"Wait," she said, in a hesitant whisper. "We can't. I have to go back inside."

He stepped forward and tried to kiss her again, but she pleaded with him. "If we get caught I won't get to see you anymore. We must be careful."

Even though he was being turned away, her words said she wanted to be with him. He felt contentment rather than rejection.

She looked him in the eye. "Understand?" She was still breathless.

Luke was breathing hard, and simply nodded.

Vee walked to the corral door and opened it. She stepped out and looked back at him. His shirt was open, exposing his tanned, muscular form. She smoothed her hair and licked her lips. "See you tomorrow." Passion filled her voice.

"Yes, you will. And I'll see you."

As she disappeared into the darkness of the house, Luke buttoned his shirt and closed the large gate of the corral. As he walked toward his bike, he saw the light of her father's pick-up truck appear down the lane. Luke's heart fell, knowing he wouldn't be able to leave without being spotted. He scrambled to hide his bike. Luke quickly slipped into the corral. He stood by the window, peeking out to see when Richardson entered the house so he could escape. His plan worked, and when Richardson closed the door behind him, Luke let out a sigh of relief.

The click of a flashlight startled him and he turned to find Vee's older sister, Elise, standing in the corral behind him. "I thought I was the only one to hide out in here." She held an unlit cigarette behind her back.

She walked to him and stood close. "So why are *you* hiding?"

"I'm not. I'm waiting."

"Waiting for what?"

"Nothing. I need to go now." He picked up his tools.

"What's the hurry? Stay." She lifted her hand with the pack of cigarettes. "Want one? I know you smoke."

He looked at the pack and contemplated the offer.

She waved it in front of him. "I know you want it."

He studied her feathered hair, stiff from the hairspray that held it in place, and her heavily-shadowed eyes. Her lips were bright red and one of the corners of her mouth was smudged. She wore a tight, low cut t-shirt and denim shorts. Elise was pretty in a plastic and primped manner, but she didn't have the pure beauty of her younger sister and certainly lacked the sexual draw he felt for Vee.

"You aren't supposed to smoke," he quipped.

"Good Mormons don't smoke. I'm a bad Mormon."
She giggled, then again offered him a cigarette.

"No. I need to go," said Luke.

Elise grabbed his arm as he turned to leave. "Can't
you at least give a lady a light?"

He relented and pulled his lighter from his shirt
pocket.

"Can I see that?" she asked, snatching it from his
hand. "Cool. Where'd you get it?"

"I found it at the baseball field."

"It's a good luck clover," she said, flicking it on and
off. "Do you carry it for luck?"

"No."

"What, don't you want to get lucky?"

He went to take it from her, but she put it behind her
back. "Fine, keep it. I need to go."

"You didn't seem eager to leave earlier when Vee was in
here."

He wondered if she had witnessed their encounter.
Luke stood tall, wanting her to know he wasn't ashamed of
kissing Vee.

"My dad would crap his pants if he knew," she said,
walking around so she could face him. "I won't tell. We all
have our little secrets. I have a question."

"What?"

Elise smiled at his irritation. "Why Vee? She's only
sixteen."

Luke struggled with his response. Elise had made
her intentions known since the day he started working for
Mr. Richardson. She strutted through the arena, smiled at
him while lying on the back porch in a bikini, and pointed
him out to her friends at school. But Luke had no interest. It
was Vee who intrigued him. He saw through Elise. Her

attempts at arousing him fell flat, and what amused him at first, now was a source of irritation.

"Wouldn't you rather have someone who won't make you stop?" she said, leaning into him. "I won't tell."

Luke had enough. "I have to go."

The rejection landed like a slap across her face, and instant rage filled Elise's eyes. "Fine! Run home to your sheep ranch. Maybe you can screw one of them!"

Luke shot her a fiery look.

"That's all you are. You're some poor Greek who shouldn't even be in this county. That's why you work for us."

Luke shook his head and turned to leave.

"You're dreaming if you think Vee will ever really want you. She is young and stupid, but she'll learn."

Luke kept walking. He pulled his bike from its hiding place, adjusted his tools and rode off quickly. He peddled hard, trying to purge the words she said. Vee was better than that, he told himself. She wasn't like her sister or her father. But as he rode on, the doubt seeped further under his skin.

Vee was young and surrounded by those who saw him as an animal. How could she not eventually view him as nothing more than a peasant? When he reached home, tears streaked through the dust that had settled on his cheeks. He wiped them clear before he went in, but his parents both turned and saw the anguish on his face.

"What now?" his mother called.

"It's nothing, Mama," Luke snapped. He walked past her to his bedroom and shut the door. He let the tool belt fall to the floor and sat on the bed. A knock followed.

"Luke," his father called.

"Papa, I'm fine. I'll be out in a minute."

His father opened the door. "Did you have a problem with Mr. Richardson?"

"No," Luke huffed. "My job is fine." He wondered if his father cared about anything more than that.

Thomas gave a satisfied "Humph." and started to close the door. "Dinner is ready. Come out."

"I'll... I need to clean up."

"Clean up good. We have guests coming."

"Guests? Who?"

His father gave him an apologetic smirk.

"Oh, God!" Luke protested. "Why did she do it?"

Thomas stepped in the room and closed the door. "You're almost eighteen. You'll be done with school soon. You need to find someone."

"I will. I don't need my mother arranging dates for me. It's humiliating."

"It's the way things are done." Thomas was older than his age. Life had beaten him down so many times, that he rarely tried to stand up straight anymore.

"I don't *care* about the old traditions."

Thomas nodded. "You don't have to marry this girl, but for your mother's sake, be polite. It's important for her. These are people from the old country. We don't know them well, so they don't know about the past."

Luke sighed sadly. He knew what his father was saying, but felt it was futile. "She's going to be disappointed eventually. I won't marry someone I don't love." He stood up and looked his father in the eye. "I won't."

"We can't force you, but you *will* show respect. You may be living in a different time than we did, but you still must respect your parents."

Luke was surprised at his father's insistence. It wasn't like him. Normally it was Theta who was demanding and outspoken. Thomas typically sat silent and only spoke when asked a question or when someone said something about the price of gas or talked of politics.

That was the extent of Thomas's passion. He preferred instead to work hard and keep his thoughts to himself. He did enjoy socializing with their Greek friends, but there wasn't much of that in their small home in the hills. The family once made it a point to travel north to Pocatello where they attended church and parties on a regular basis, but as they aged and the price of gas went up, their trips to the city became less frequent. As a young boy Luke had to go along, but when he hit his teens, he found the drive long and drab and preferred to hike the woods and create his own adventures.

Luke relented. "Okay, I'll meet her."

Thomas put a hand on his son's shoulder. "You don't want to stay here. You need to go somewhere else."

"What do you mean?"

"There is no life for you here...no future. Don't be foolish with your feelings. You need to be with your own people."

Luke was stunned by his father's perceptive statement, but also angered by it. "Things will never change if everyone keeps treating us like we're not worthy."

"We're not like them, Luke. You'll never be accepted here and it will only bring you trouble." His gaze was solemn. "You already know how they feel. Stop it now or it will ruin everything."

Luke brushed by his father and opened the door. "I need to get cleaned up."

"Did you hear me?" Thomas asked.

Luke turned back both weary and incensed. "Yes, I heard you."

He splashed water on his face and decided he needed a shower. He let the steamy water pour over his body as he tried his best to relax." When finished, he dressed, but made no special attempts to look exceptional. He combed his dark hair into place and tucked in his shirt. The shower had cleared his mind and he felt better and somewhat empathetic towards his parents. He walked to the stove where Theta was intently watching a large pot simmer. The scent was heavenly, and Luke kissed her on the cheek, making her jump.

"So when does my dream girl get here?" he asked.

Theta slapped Luke playfully on the arm. "You be nice!" she ordered.

He set his jaw and took the silverware Theta had set out. He started to place it around the table just as a knock came at the door.

"They're here," Theta said, brushing her hair back and straightening her skirt.

When the door opened, Philip and Agnes Katsilometes stood smiling. Theta gave a cheery laugh and kissed them both.

They looked up at Luke who stood still, holding the remaining utensils, and then pulled their daughter—a shy, dark haired girl--from behind them. She looked horrified. She offered a meek smile at the others in the room. It was obvious that she, too, wasn't a willing participant in her parents' plan for matrimony.

"This is Talia," said Agnes, beaming.

"Ah, Talia," Theta announced, running toward the girl. "Look, Luke. It's Talia."

"Yes, Mama," said Luke kindly. He walked to the girl, as four sets of eyes followed, and put out his hand. "Hi Talia, I'm Luke...nice to meet you."

She shook his hand timidly. She had deep set brown eyes and thick dark hair. "Nice to meet you, too."

Luke was pleasantly surprised. "I'm setting the table. Would you like to help me?"

The others hung on her answer. "Sure," she said. She followed him to the table, as the parents gave each other knowing smirks.

The table setting went on in silence, but the dinner was filled with hearty laughs and loud announcements about the qualities of each intended betrothed.

"Talia is a wonderful cook. She can already feed twenty people and she leaves no mess when she is done," spouted Agnes.

"Luke works for a wealthy ranch owner. He can build and fix anything," Theta added. "And he is *so* strong."

Luke looked at Talia. "Do you want to go for a walk...outside?"

She smiled and her eyes lit up. As her mother put a hand to her chest, Talia stood and followed Luke out the front door. When they were away from the house and hidden from the porch light, she looked at Luke shyly. "Thank you."

"I thought I would save us both from the sharks in there. Can you believe they think they can just set us up like that?"

She laughed in agreement.

They walked through dry grass and weeds surrounding the small home. They talked about school and life in their different towns. The conversation was friendly but tame. When they went back inside, Luke felt he had done his duty for his parents and also helped Talia survive the evening. When they were getting ready to leave, Agnes and Theta spoke in whispers as they hugged each other on the porch.

Back inside, Theta's eyes were huge. Filled with questions, she prodded Luke about her obviously correct choice of girls. "You see?" she sang with an 'I told you so' lilt. "She is beautiful and smart *and* she can cook!"

Luke shook his head. "She is nice, but that doesn't mean I'm going to marry her."

"You should come to church. She goes to church and you can talk more. Talia is a good girl," Theta said with excitement.

"Just because she goes to church doesn't mean she's a good girl," he said, with an image of Elise in his mind.

"If you went to our church you would meet good Greek girls."

"I've been to your church and seen those girls."

Theta threw up her hands. "Why do you want a pale, weak girl? Why do you think that will make you happy? They are tramps."

"Mama!" Luke was both surprised and a bit humored.

"They are! Who marries and then lets other women marry their husband?"

Luke knew this argument could never be won, but he was irritated enough with the evening that he let his exasperation flow. "Those are polygamists. Those are the *old* Mormons. The new ones don't do that anymore and you know it."

"Old. New. It's the same church. They believe crazy things and you want to marry one of them?"

"All religion is crazy, Mama. You believe in all this hocus pocus, too. It's not real and I'm not going to church."

Theta's once happy face had grown long and distressed. "You need to go. It's part of who we are. Our family has always gone and good things happen. Only bad happens when you don't go."

"Nothing bad is going to happen to me if I don't go to church. I haven't gone in years and nothing bad has happened."

Theta gasped. "Don't say that. You'll bring misery on the family with your words. You should pray. Thomas, make him stop talking down to God. Make him go to church." She put a shaky hand to her chest.

"Mama, where are your pills? Did you take them today?" Luke asked with concern.

Theta brushed him off. "The death of me you'll be," she mumbled.

Luke continued to place dishes into the sink. "Why do you think that Talia wants to date me? She was miserable here tonight. You and her mother need to butt out."

"Agnes says Talia has wanted to meet you. She saw you at the Greek Fest last year." Theta's eyes grew large and she clasped her hands together on her chest. "The Greek Fest is coming up! You can take Talia."

"Mama, no."

"Why not? You'll be going anyway."

Defeated, Luke turned away from his mother. "The only place I'm going right now is to bed. Good night."

Chapter 8

Early Summer, 1991

Luke and Vee's love grew swiftly. It played out in hidden spaces all around her family's homestead, except for the arena where Luke worried that Elise might be silently watching. Some days they had hours to flirt, kiss and push their limits. Other days they were only given minutes to keep their spark kindled because of Vee's riding lessons, or church activities. It was on these days that the fire burned the hottest.

Not having time to relish in their affair, these short days led to quick sultry stares and multiplied desire. Kisses were fierce and remorseless. Luke lay in bed on those nights and felt as though his heart was swelling. Theirs was a bursting passion that only grew more intense over the weeks of those late spring days.

What happened one afternoon in the hay loft of the old barn was an eventuality. Even at their young age, the need to consummate their love overwhelmed them and neither held back or worried what would come of it. It was a day they didn't have to fear being caught, because the rest of the family had gone to church and Vee had feigned illness. Luke wasn't expected to work on Sunday.

"Sunday is the Sabbath," Richardson had told Luke years before. "We believe it is a day of rest." Luke saw it as a day to sleep in and rarely was at the ranch on the weekends. No one would suspect a thing. Therefore, they had an entire afternoon to savor their love and delight in their bodies.

They stole away in the old barn at the far side of the arena. Luke helped her up the rickety ladder into the loft and was pleased to see a bed of straw perfectly hidden from view, but speckled by the warm afternoon sun spilling in from the large loft's transom. As they lay together, Luke knew that Vee wanted him, but was still careful not to rush her. Vee felt this and took the initiative. She leaned her head back as he kissed her neck. Wrapped in an old quilt with straw as a pillow, Luke loved her with his entire being.

Vee reveled in his touch. The emotions felt novel, yet true. Neither had regret. After a light nap and soft kisses, Luke made love to her once more.

"I love you," she said. He tucked his face into the crook of her neck.

He leaned up so he could look at her. "I've loved you from the first time I saw you."

"What are we going to do?" she asked, her face turning sad.

"What do you mean?"

"I don't want to keep hiding and only being together once in a while. I want to be with you always. I want to live with you."

Luke was surprised, but he also felt the same. "We should get married."

She smiled. "My father would never allow it."

"Then we should run away."

She looked at him to see if there was any sign of sincerity in his statement.

He thought a moment. "We should. We can go to Salt Lake City or Pocatello, and I can get a job at the railroad. It's what I was going to do after school anyway. I'll just take you with me."

"Really?" she asked hopefully.

He looked down at her and felt sure it could work. They would be together, and that was all that mattered.

"When?"

"I graduate in May of next year. It's still over..." he counted the months in his head, "eleven months away. It sounds like forever, but if we can wait I know it'll work."

"I don't think I can wait," she said, pulling his face to hers and kissing him softly.

"We'll try to be together every chance we can, and we'll make it work."

She bit her bottom lip and nodded.

He sat up and looked out across the ranch. Moving to the loft opening, Luke lit a cigarette with a match, silently cursing Elise for taking his lighter, and thought about their plan.

"When I'm your wife I'll make you stop smoking."

He smiled back at her. "All you'll have to do is ask. I'll do anything you want."

She giggled, "Then come back here and kiss me."

He did as she asked, but before he went much further, he sighed. "They'll be home shortly and I need to help my dad with the animals at home."

In the still warm solitude of the loft, the sound of their contented breathing combined with the soft lilting of blackbirds in the trees. Luke and Vee lay exhausted and spent, but joyous.

Luke kissed her cheek and Vee purred, "Don't leave me," she mumbled, sleepily.

"Never," he whispered.

When Luke knew that they were past pressing their luck, he stroked her hair from her face. "We really have to get up and get going. They'll be home soon."

She reluctantly agreed and combed through her hair with her fingers. The sun lit her face. An aura of contentment was everywhere. When they were both ready to present themselves to the outside world, Luke pulled her close and gave her an earnest embrace. He held her tightly, never wanting the moment to end. When he released her, his eyes were wet and red.

She sighed. "I love you. I'll miss you."

They climbed down the ladder, and at the heavy barn door they parted. As Luke walked off toward the trail to his house, he turned back and called, "See you tomorrow."

"And I'll see you!"

The sun had just begun to set as Luke threw grain to the chickens and hay to the sheep. The pinkish-gray of the sky above Elkhorn Peak made Luke stop and reflect on the day. It was wonderful and beautiful, and the sunset was the pinnacle of what he wanted to remember for the rest of his life.

The squeak and clank of the screen door alerted him to his father's presence. "That lamb has really grown," he said, pointing at one of the black faced babies.

"Yes," Luke agreed, barely noticing.

"Where were you all day?"

Luke knew he would be missed around the house, but hadn't stopped to concoct a story to keep his secret hidden. "Just hanging out."

"With who?"

"A friend."

Thomas stepped off the back porch and walked toward him. His shoulders were their normally rounded bow and his large calloused hands were shoved deep in his trouser pockets. "I don't agree with everything your mother says or believes, but when it comes to you and Mormon girls, I know it will bring trouble."

"Pop, you too?" Luke asked. "This isn't about being Mormon. She's just a girl. She's wonderful. Mom's only upset because she's not Greek."

"Sometimes it's better to stay with your own kind."

"You sound like Richardson," Luke said, shaking his head. "We're not that different. Why do you all think being your way is better?"

"I didn't say that, but the two cultures are different. No one will get along, and everyone will want the other to change, to fit their ways. It'll cause fights and you don't need that."

But I need her, thought Luke. There was no truer statement. He needed Vee like he needed breath in his body, and nothing was going to keep him from loving her. He knew he'd never change his parents' minds, so he pretended to listen to the rest of his father's lecture and then swept the porch as an excuse to stay outside a bit longer after Thomas had gone in.

As he brushed off the small concrete slab with the old straw broom, he relived the afternoon. He felt her in his arms, smelled her skin and heard her breathing. His body tingled at the thought. Luke gazed off into the dusk toward Vee's home and wondered if she was daydreaming about their time together, too.

A dark plume rose from above the hill and Luke watched it for a moment, wondering if it was really smoke or a cloud that was darkened in the twilight. Then he noticed an orange glow at the bottom and realized there were flames.

"Fire!" he called, as he jumped from the porch. "Fire!" he yelled toward his house. "Call the fire department."

"What?" Thomas said, leaning out the door, watching his son run off toward the ranch house. He saw the plume of smoke growing large in the sky. "Luke, wait!" He turned back to Theta and told her to call for help. Thomas pulled on his shoes and starting running after Luke.

Luke imagined the house on fire as he ran frantically down the lane. His worst fear was that Vee was in the house, trapped and injured. When he rounded the toe of the hill and up the small plateau he stopped, terrified by the flames dancing in the evening air. But it wasn't the house that was on fire, it was the arena. He gave the scene a quick scan and noticed Vee and Elise pulling hoses toward the flames.

Luke ran down the hill, yelling to them to stay back. When Vee saw him, her face went from determination to dismay. He hugged her quickly, but then he directed both Elise and her where to put the hoses, as he worked his way through the smoke toward the burning arena.

The fire looked to be confined to the corral and he knew the horses were in grave danger. Luke pulled off his shirt, dunked it into the water trough, and held it over his face as he pushed his way into the smoke-filled arena. By memory, he plodded around to the stalls. He kept his arm outstretched, reaching for the gates so he could set the horses free. He felt around the wood of the stalls, found a latch, and opened one of the gates.

Luke could feel panic coming from the horse inside. It huffed and stomped, and he wondered if it was going to trample him once it realized it was free to escape. There were five, including Marty, the old draft horse Luke felt akin to.

The horse followed Luke as he led it from the corral and toward the open gate. When the smoke cleared, the horse bolted, and Luke looked up to find Vee, Elise and Thomas standing, completely terror-struck as they watched the scene play out. Luke gave them no time to talk him out of going back, and he again followed the path into the corral. He crawled to the next stall and opened the gate; unlike the first, this horse bolted out.

He crawled to the next gate and popped the latch, hurriedly leading the horse to safety. When he emerged from the smoke, he saw Richardson holding the halter of the horse that had bolted. Luke turned, but Richardson ran to him and pulled him back.

"No," he demanded. "It's too dangerous. We have what we need out."

"But there are more in there," Luke said, his eyes and lungs burning. He looked around and counted four horses walking around the yard being calmed by Vee and the others.

"Only the old one, it isn't worth it." Richardson shook Luke's arm to make his point.

Luke realized that Marty was still inside. "No, I need to get Marty."

"Don't be stupid, boy."

Luke's ire rose. He broke away and ran to the arena once more. He knew that Marty's stall was on the far side and hoped that it wasn't already engulfed in flames. He heard timber crackling in the heat above his head and

77

realized the smoke had dropped lower. He crawled quickly, coughing and gagging from a combination of smoke and dust. As he made his way to Marty, he felt small pebbles and pieces of wood piercing his hands and knees, but he pressed on.

When he reached Marty's stall, he quickly unlatched the gate. The horse was lying down, and Luke gasped in horror. "Come on, old guy, we'll get you out," Luke assured him. He stood and yanked hard at the horse. He yelled, "Yah! Yah!" hoping to get a response...and he finally did. Marty rocked and lumbered and then rolled up to a standing position. "Yes! Good boy!"

He knew their only escape was at the far end, and he hoped that the fire hadn't spread. The horse trotted heavily behind him, and Luke found himself silently praying to a God he claimed didn't exist. He coaxed Marty along, knowing that they would soon be free.

When they reached the door, Luke released Marty's halter and yanked at the heavy sliding wood door. When it opened, a rush of smoke spilled out and the last bits of the day's sun rushed in. Marty galloped out, and when Luke turned the corner to see the others huddled, watching, he ran to them. The wood splintered, and the roar of fire meeting the oxygen caused a huge explosion. Seeing that all the horses were safely outside, Luke attempted to take a deep breath. Suddenly, his lungs seized; he bent over hacking and gagging until sooty phlegm spilled out on the ground.

"Thomas!"

Luke looked up to see his mother running toward him.

She grabbed his arm and with frenzied eyes, she cried out. "Where is Thomas?"

Luke felt his stomach heave and he shook his head unable to speak.

"When you didn't come out, he went in!" she cried.

Then he saw Richardson dragging the limp body of his father across the lawn.

Theta screamed as she ran to them. "No God, NO!"

Luke stumbled after her, and then felt Vee's presence. She lifted his arm to stabilize him as they hurried to his father's side. Paramedics pushed them away and quickly kneeled next to Thomas, who was flaccid and ashen. They opened large tackle boxes and screamed orders at each other. They listened for breaths and heartbeats, starting chest compressions as Theta wandered in a circle, hands in the air and talking to the sky. Luke watched through the tears that streamed down his blackened face. He felt Vee being ripped from his side. He peered up to see Richardson leading her off and glaring at him.

"It was a worthless horse. You stupid fool," he grumbled.

Vee's face was a mask of devastation, as she was pulled away.

Luke began to cough again. His body shuddered and heaved and he vomited blood.

Theta witnessed this and ran to him.

"Oh Mama," he cried in despair, collapsing to the ground.

Her face hovered over him, weeping.

Luke kept trying to breathe but his lungs were tight and painful. The coughing began again and then the dark blue sky above him turned black.

Chapter 9

Arbon Valley, Summer, 2003

I sat with my legs folded on my favorite spot on the sofa. It was worn just right, so I could curl up and read my book that was perfectly cradled in front of me. As I finished chapter fourteen, I heard tires on gravel in our driveway. I sprung up in alarm. I looked at the wall clock as I hid in the hall, wondering who it could be. Papa wasn't due home for another hour. I heard keys jangle and the lock turning. I ran to my room, but before I closed the door, I heard my father's voice loud and frenzied.

"Sophie!" he called.

I stayed silent and frozen, sensing an aura of anger and dismay.

"Sophie, where are you?"

He turned the corner and saw me standing, mouth agape. His face was a mixture of fury and fear. Stomping down the hall, he made me cringe. Papa had never struck me before, but I flinched, feeling as if he were about to. He dropped to his knees and pulled me down with him. With his hands on my shoulders, he made me look him in the eye.

"A terrible thing has happened," he announced.

I felt like crying but didn't know why. "What is it, Papa?"

He inhaled loudly, hesitating, licking his lips and shaking his head. With tears in his eyes he told me my precious Donny was dead.

The words struck me like a slap. "What? How?" My voice cracked. I felt my chest heave and tears pour from my eyes.

"He was playing in a tunnel he dug out in the landfill. The dirt was too heavy and collapsed on him. He couldn't breathe."

"Damien?" I asked, worried that somehow he was gone, too.

Papa gave a sorrowful sigh. "I heard that he found his brother. He's blaming himself."

I stared at the ground, trying to take in what he said. Then I sobbed, knowing what he told me was true. Donny and Damien had talked many times of their adventures at the dump and how much they wanted to show me their creations and playground amongst the dirt and trash. "Sophie, tell me what happened that day he was here."

Through sobs and sniffles I wiped my stinging eyes and tried to make out what he meant. "I told you, we played in the yard."

He held my shoulders and squared me up. "Sophie, tell me everything that happened. *Everything*."

"I told you..."

"Sophie!" He was desperate. "What happened between you two? What was said?"

"We're just friends, Papa."

"Did he touch you?"

I looked down, wondering how he knew.

"Sophie, did he touch you?" He emphasized each word.

He shook me again. I wriggled free and complained. "Ouch," I said, rubbing my arm.

He didn't care and grabbed me again. "Don't lie, please. Did he touch you?"

"Why?" I asked, defiant.

"Sophie, don't disobey me. Tell me right now what happened."

At this point, his grip and elusiveness angered me. "Yes, he touched me.'"

"Where?"

"On my arm," I said, pointing to my wrist.

"Anywhere else?"

I shook my head.

"Sophie, you must tell me. It's important." For the first time since he'd come through the door, his face was tender.

I broke down. I told him about the kiss.

"Oh dear," he said, sounding grief-stricken. He hugged me tightly. We both cried for a moment as we held each other. "There's something I must tell you," he said, still holding me to his chest. "I wanted to wait until you were older, but you need to know now."

He told me to go to the couch. Sitting down beside me, he turned so he could see my face. He tried to find the words to tell me about my fate and future, but the horror of it all kept tripping him up and leaving him speechless.

His large brown eyes were red from tears and, despite his young age, his skin seemed more creased and leathery than usual. His hair was black but had a warm glow that didn't make it seem as dark as it was. He was my father, so I didn't appreciate his strong, angular features and handsome face. I saw him as paternal and protective. It wasn't until I was much older that I realized what he had sacrificed. He gave up being a man and having the companionship of not just a woman, but of any social interaction whatsoever. For someone with his good looks and equally good intentions, it was tragic that his life was so solitary and vexed.

"It's my fault this happened," he finally muttered.

"What do you mean? You said Donny was killed by the cave-in."

"Yes, but there's more to it."

"You didn't kill Donny, did you?"

"No, but…"

"Then why are you saying it's your fault?"

Papa lifted his hand to hush me. "Let me talk, Sophie. There's a terrible cloud that surrounds us and hurts others. That's what killed the boy. It was a consequence of something I did long ago."

"What?" It was all I could muster, hoping he'd explain what he meant.

"Sophie, you're so young but you must understand. I don't want this to happen again. If I tell you why, will you promise me you'll do what I say?"

My head felt heavy with everything he said. It made no sense, but I felt the magnitude of its meaning and so I nodded. "I promise."

"And promise me you won't hate me for what I've brought upon you. Someday I'll be able to set you free, but until then you must listen to what I tell you and obey."

What had brought so much pain to Papa? Why did he feel responsible for Donny's death? What he prepared to say both intrigued and scared me, and I knew that when he was finished my life would never be the same again.

He rarely looked at me as he spoke. I saw and felt the magnitude of his guilt and pain. "A long time ago, before you were born, a terrible thing happened to our family. It caused much anger and hate. From that came a terrible curse that fell on us."

The more he talked the more his words stacked like weights on my shoulders, and I was in disbelief at what he had carried silently for all those years. "We stay up here alone and away from the rest of the world because we'll bring the same pain and tragedy on others. That boy died because of you. That's why I keep us up here away from everyone. When people love us, it's a bad thing. It's why I lost your mother, too. It has to stop." The burden and sadness he bore was overwhelming, and my love for him was even stronger because of it.

When our talk was over, I sat numb. Papa went to town and returned with several large racks of steel bars and a tall chain-linked gate. He spent the rest of the day attaching the bars to my window, and securing the gate, effectively replacing my bedroom door.

"They'll want to get to you, but you must keep them out...protect others."

He told me to lock it from the inside and to hide the key somewhere in my room. I did as he said, and then sat inside my new caged room while he took a shower. The sun still came through my window but made clear prison-like patterns on the floor. I knew it was for the best and tried to accept why it was necessary. But even though I had never been to another person's house or seen another girl's bedroom, I knew in my heart that this wasn't right...that I wasn't normal. My isolation was even more apparent, and for the first time in my life, it mattered.

Chapter 10

Malad Idaho, December, 2008

The lights above were bright and I blinked fiercely, trying to focus. When I tried to sit up, a gentle hand held me down. I turned to see who it was and could make out a young woman standing beside me.

"Can you hear me?" she asked.

I blinked some more, and my eyes started to clear. She was thin, with short brown hair and mischievous eyes. Her skin was freckled and her lips were rosy.

"Who are you?" I asked.

"I'm Stephanie. We're cousins, kind of."

I tried to sit up again.

"Whoa," she said, urging me back down. "You aren't supposed to get up yet."

"Why? Where am I?"

"You're at your grandparent's house."

I felt my head throb and I put my hands over my eyes. "How did I get here?" Small bits of memory started rolling in my head. They started slowly then the scenes raced through my mind. Women screaming when I fell to the ground...bright sunlight hitting my face as they walked me to their car...pictures of homes and snow-covered hills that were a complete blur as we drove past...and then a woman's voice saying she was only removing my shoes, as she tucked me into the bed.

"You passed out!" she said it with zeal. "Everyone freaked." She started to laugh and then put her hand over her mouth. "Sorry. I guess that's really rude of me, but they were all going crazy about finally finding you and then, 'BAM!' you faint right in front of them."

The magnitude of the day sank back into my consciousness. I moaned from the weight of it. I pulled my hands from my eyes and looked at her.

She studied me. "You're quite a legend around here."

"What's that mean?"

She laughed. "It's all over the news. They thought you were dead. Now you're here. It's crazy!"

I sat up, even though she tried to hold me down again. "Stop pushing," I said.

"Keep it down or they'll all hoard in here again," she whispered, looking at the slightly open door.

"Who?"

"The family. They've been standing around here staring at you ever since they got you home. They finally went out to the kitchen, so I stayed in here to watch you and tell them when you woke up."

"I'm awake."

"Yeah, but I wanted to talk to you first."

"About what?"

"I want to know what it was like."

"What do you mean?"

Stephanie sat on the bed beside me. "What was it like living in a cage for all those years?"

"I didn't live in a cage."

"They said you had bars on all the windows and your door was a big gate that locked."

What she said was true, yet, such a lie. "I didn't live in a cage."

"Then why didn't you just run away from him?"

"From who?"

"From your kidnapper. Your dad."

"My dad didn't kidnap me!"

Stephanie's face turned sullen. "Then why did he shoot that kid for trying to rescue you?"

"Damien wasn't trying to rescue me." I was annoyed with her questions. I crossed my arms in a show of defiance.

Humored, she lifted an eyebrow. "No one will believe what you look like. I can see why he hid you from the world."

I couldn't believe what she said. I felt so hurt, my eyes welled up.

"Wait," she said, putting a hand on my arm. "What's wrong?"

"Why would you say something like that?"

"What did I say?"

"I can't help the way I look."

She sat back down. "I'd love to look like you. Anyone would."

We both sat in silence, staring at each other for an explanation.

Stephanie's eyes suddenly grew big. "You've never *seen* yourself. They said there were no mirrors in your house. I heard he took them all down so you couldn't see what you really looked like. You have *no* idea how beautiful you are. Holy crap! That's crazy."

I felt the eerie hesitation of distrust creep in.

Stephanie smiled. "This is the most bizarre thing I have ever witnessed. You're the only pretty girl I know who's clueless about it. Most girls think they're prettier than they actually are, but you don't even *know* you're pretty." She continued to erupt in spontaneous giggles.

energy and candor. The incredible sense of anticipation and my yearning for Papa started to flutter again in my chest, but her statement about the two of us spending time together soothed my fears a bit.

I smiled at her. "Are you really my cousin?"

She shrugged. "Well, step-cousin." She sighed. "My mom died when I was little."

"My mom died, too," I said, somewhat excited at our having a common tragedy.

"Yeah, I know. When I was about seven my dad married your aunt. She tries to act like she's my mom around everyone, but she's really a crazy lunatic. When people aren't around, she's always yelling and wanting me to be like her, all churchy."

"What is churchy?"

"It's what most of the people are around here. Very religious. But my step-mom, she's like the evil step-mother in Cinderella."

I had read that story and knew what she meant. "Why did your father marry her?" I asked.

Stephanie laughed. "I have no idea. Probably because she has big boobs."

"What are boobs?"

Stephanie laughed even louder. Then she cupped both hands in front of her chest. "You know — boobs."

"Why would he want that?"

By this point Stephanie was giggling hysterically and so loud that the door opened and two women and the man came into the room. Their faces were quizzical and anxious. It was an awkward and palpable silence that made me so uncomfortable that I looked to Stephanie for guidance.

"She's awake!" she announced, mockingly. She sat next to me, as if protecting me from the others.

The older woman came closer. "Hello…Sophie. I'm your grandma."

"Hello," I said, softly.

"We're all so glad you're here," she said. She came to the bed and started to sit next to me. I leaned away and she immediately stood up again. I didn't mean to offend her, but I was worried about letting her get too close.

"I'm your aunt Elise," the woman with blue eyelids and red lips said, stepping forward.

"Hello," I whispered.

"Well I can see you two have become fast friends," Elise said, with a hint of displeasure.

The man had a genuine smile. "I'm your Uncle Lonny."

"That's my dad," said Stephanie. "And that's my stepmom," she said, pointing toward my aunt.

Aunt Elise scoffed. "That's ridiculous, Stephy. I've told you a hundred times there are no *steps* in our home."

Stephanie ignored her, and held up the mirror. "I was showing Sophie something she's never seen before… herself. She actually had no idea she was pretty."

"Pretty? You're beautiful," said Uncle Lonny. He looked around awkwardly as though what he said wasn't meant to come out.

"She has a lot to learn about herself and the world," Stephanie said, "and *I'm* going to teach her."

"That's ridiculous," my aunt huffed. "You're no older than she is. What are you going to teach her…that won't get her in trouble?"

Stephanie rolled her eyes and looked at me. "My stepmom is a probation officer, so she thinks she's a cop. This makes her a know-it-all."

I was stunned to hear anyone talk like that, let alone to her parents.

My grandmother stepped in. "Do you need anything? Can I get you anything?"

I was tired of having everyone stand around while I was in bed. "I'd like to clean up a little."

"Of course," she said. "The bathroom is just around the corner. I'll get clean towels and there's plenty of soap and shampoo in the shower."

"I'm also..." I felt funny asking, but my hunger was unbelievably strong.

"Yes, dear?" she coaxed.

"I'm hungry."

"Oh," she said, pleased beyond belief. "What would you like? Anything, just ask." I was to learn that my grandmother loved to cook. It was her calling in life to feed her family, and she did so much of it that no one ever had to tell her they were hungry. Telling her I wanted her to feed me was like telling her I loved her.

She took over, scooting everyone from the room. When we were alone, she closed the door and sat on the end of the bed.

"I like eggs," I said, already missing my chickens. Then I realized they hadn't been fed and there was no one there to do it. I put my hand to my mouth in fear.

"What is it?" she asked.

"My chickens. They'll die. They need to be fed."

"Your chickens?"

"Yes. They're in the hen house in our backyard. I was supposed to feed them this morning and I didn't." A wave of guilt hit me. I had put off my chores that morning to see Damien, and now my beloved pets were in peril because of my selfishness. "I must go," I insisted, sliding my legs from the covers.

"Wait," she said. "Don't worry. I'll have your grandfather go and get them. We have a chicken coop and we'll bring them here."

I looked at her skeptically. "You will?" Then I realized that the man they called my grandfather was nowhere in sight. The last I saw of him was when he had called me Callidora. I wondered if he was mad that I had yelled at him.

She patted my arm. "Yes. We'll take care of them and we'll take care of you."

"I must go with him. He won't know how to get there," I insisted.

My grandmother smiled. "You don't need to go. We'll get directions. Stop worrying. He'll find it and take care of everything."

"But it's hidden."

"It was, but the officers know how to get there. That's how they found you, remember?"

I thought about the day. It was hard to believe that it was just this morning when I'd been at my house. I pictured Damien's face at my window as the early morning sun was just starting to wake-up.

Even through the screen I could look into his eyes and see the intense feelings he harbored, as he begged me to let him in. It was the hardest thing I've ever done to tell him I couldn't. He saw in my eyes how much I loved him. He kept yelling at the sky and pulling at the bars trying to break them from the window.

"I'm trying to save you!" he kept yelling. "I know you love me, Sophie. Why are you doing this?"

I wanted to tell him, but he wouldn't have believed it. How could he? What I knew about myself was inconceivable. It was something I had to live with in silence.

"When will he go?" I asked.

"I'll tell him to go now while you're getting cleaned up. It will take several hours, but the chickens will be just fine."

I felt a great relief.

"Okay," she said, as though taking an order. "What about some toast with those eggs?"

I nodded.

"Take as long as you like to get cleaned up. I'll have your food ready when you're done. Then we'll take a little walk around and I'll show you where your mother grew up. Sound good?"

The word *mother* still hit me as odd. I was incredibly curious, but also hesitant about knowing more. She was the connection I had with these new people, and I worried that if I got to know more about her my ties to them would become stronger. I was sure that I didn't want to stay with them, and knew that getting back to Papa was what I wanted and needed to do. Any comfort and enjoyment I had with these people would just get in the way.

My grandmother saw my hesitation. "Is something wrong?"

"Will I ever be able to go home?"

Her face was both sad and disappointed. She went to speak, but a low voice interrupted her from the doorway. We both jumped.

"This *is* your home." It was my grandfather. I couldn't tell if he was being kind or insolent. "You are going to live here now. This is where you should've been for the last seventeen years."

I stayed silent. He was old, but stood tall and strong. His shoulders were straight and his eyes were determined. He wore jeans, cowboy boots and a cream colored western shirt that made him look like some sort of southern gladiator.

"I know it's not what you're used to," my grandmother said, trying to ease the tension in the room.

"It's better than what she's used to," he spouted.

I felt as though he was trying to talk me out of loving my father, and it angered me.

"Gene, please."

"She needs to know the truth," he said. "She's almost an adult and if we keep pussy-footing around she'll never have a normal life."

"Why do you want me here?" I asked him.

He looked surprised. "Because you're our granddaughter and we're your family."

"But you don't even know me."

"It doesn't matter," my grandmother jumped in. "We love you."

I turned to her with skepticism, and then looked at him for confirmation. It caught him off guard that I was challenging them.

"She's right," is all he said.

I raised my eyebrows. "How can you love someone who hurt you?"

He stepped into the room. "What are you talking about?" he asked, sternly. "What have you been told?"

"Papa said we had to hide because of what happened to my mother. He said you blamed us for her death. How can you love me if I'm the reason your daughter is dead?"

My grandmother gasped and put her hand to her chest.

"That's a fool talking!" my grandfather raged. "He's filled your head with lies."

"We never blamed you for her death," my grandmother insisted. "*Never*! It was an accident."

"Then why did Papa say it was because of what he did? Why did he say he was to blame?"

"Because he's a coward and a scoundrel." My grandfather's lips were curled and he barely opened his mouth as he spoke. "He ruined your mother's life and refused to leave her alone. He took you to punish us for trying to keep her away from him. And now he's turned you against us, too."

"Gene, you're scaring her," my grandmother scolded.

His furor didn't scare me as much as it intrigued me. He spoke as though he knew Papa, and I found myself curious as to what had happened in their past. Papa rarely spoke of my mother, and I had never heard him say anything about my grandparents, except that they blamed us for the tragic end of my mother's life.

My grandmother took my hands in hers. Her round face was intense, but genuine. "Sophie, we love you and we have *never* blamed you for what happened to your mother. We know you've been gone a long time, but we never stopped loving you. You always were and always will be our granddaughter."

"But you hate my father," I said, not comprehending how they could love me and hate him.

My grandfather didn't speak, and looked away.

"No, we don't hate him," my grandmother said. "But we don't like what he did." She pulled my hands toward her, so I'd look in her eyes. It was then I realized how blue they were. I have her eyes, I thought. For the first time, I felt some connection to my strange new family. "There *is* a difference. We don't hate. It's not what we're taught."

What she said made sense, but my grandfather's stance didn't mesh with her words.

"I'm going to go and get the chickens," he said. He quickly left the room.

I could tell he wasn't happy. I wondered how the kind and endearing woman that was stroking my head could be married to such an ogre.

"He loves you," she said, seeing my obvious reluctance. "This has all been so hard for him. I know that he's glad you're back with us."

"He doesn't seem glad."

"Don't worry. You'll see. How can anyone not be glad you're here?"

My aunt walked into the room. "We're heading home now. I'll talk to you tomorrow about the school stuff, okay?" She was talking to her mother, but shot a quick look at our clasped hands. She seemed anxious and had obviously overheard the raised voices.

"Are you sure you don't want to stay for dinner?" my grandmother asked.

She looked at me. "No thanks. We'll come by tomorrow." She flashed me a quick, stiff-lipped smile. "It was nice to meet you Sophie," she said, leaving the room.

Stephanie popped her head in quickly and waved. "See you soon, Cuz!"

I smiled back at her, knowing she would be my only harbor from the storm I was about to face. Her frankness and wit were refreshing among the dramatic roller coaster of emotions that everyone else was showing.

My grandmother went to the door and saw them out. Then she returned. "I've kept you from doing what you wanted. I'll go get your food and you get cleaned up." She smiled down at me; her billowy arms were wrapped in front of her as if she were giving herself a hug. "I have a hard time taking my eyes off you. I'm afraid if I do, you'll disappear again."

I didn't know how to respond. I was beginning to trust her and I already liked her. I started to talk, but then stopped.

"What is it, dear?" she asked.

I bit my lip and hesitated, wondering if I really wanted to ask what had been on my mind all day. I finally pushed forward. "How did my mother die?"

Her face fell and she sat on the bed quickly. She straightened her back, as if gathering all the strength she needed to muster in order to reply. "I'll tell you anything you want to know and I'll tell you the truth. But first, you must eat and take care of yourself. You've been through a lot today, and we have plenty of time to answer all your questions."

Chapter 11

Malad, Idaho, June, 1991

It rained all day; the sky was exceptionally gray. It was as if the weather was scripted for a day of sorrow.

Theta Theotokis buried the man she was married to for twenty-five years and now the family was reduced to just two. Was two a family? No, thought Luke, which made him ache inside, as he watched his mother become nothing more than a shell. He turned inward, too, blaming himself for their plight.

Thomas had run into the flames to save *him*, and now Luke stood at the front of the Greek Orthodox Church in Pocatello, greeting people he had never met, and watching his mother slowly die inside. He was now the man of the house and he had no idea how to support the two of them. He had planned on graduating next spring and then looking for an apprenticeship with the railroad. Now, he knew school would have to end, and work would be his focus, and his plans with Vee had been destroyed.

She had come to the house the day following the fire and brought dinner. She was alone and looked uncomfortable when Luke invited her in. Theta was in bed, and as the two quietly stood in the small living room, all Vee could say was, "I'm so sorry."

Luke wasn't sure if she was offering an apology for his father's death or for their future together. He tried to hold her but she stepped away. It killed Luke, and he ended up thanking her and sending her back home, because it was harder for him to be near her and have her reject him.

After she left, he sat at the table in the kitchen and wept for what he had lost. He felt completely alone in the world...without a plan or purpose. Even with his mother still physically there, mentally she was absent. The day of the fire she shrieked when the paramedics stopped CPR on Thomas, their solemn faces telling her he was gone. She'd flung herself on to his chest and cried. Then she stopped and, without speaking or acknowledging anyone else, she walked the half mile up the hill to their house, took off her shoes at the door and climbed into bed.

The day after the funeral, Gene Richardson called Luke and his mother to the house. With Vee and Elise in the room, he revealed the charred cloverleaf lighter and announced that the fire inspector had traced the source of the blaze to it. Luke looked to Elise, who kept her eyes forward. Vee looked at Luke and started to cry.

"What do you know?" Richardson asked his youngest daughter.

She didn't speak, but covered her face with her hands and sobbed.

"Luke, is this your lighter?" he asked.

Luke started to answer, then again turned to Elise, wanting to scream out that she was to blame, but instead he just nodded.

Theta moaned and slumped into a chair behind him.

"I didn't start that fire." Luke said it with resolve.

"No one in this household smokes," Richardson calmly explained. "If you didn't start it, who did?"

Luke again looked to Elise.

"Why are you looking at Elise," he asked. Then he turned to his older daughter. "Elise, do you know who started this fire?"

She looked at the ground and shook her head.

"Where were you that morning? You weren't with us at church," Richardson pressed her.

"Neither was Vee," she accused. "Why aren't you questioning her? Ask her where *she* was." She turned to Luke and glared.

"Vee was home sick," Richardson answered. "Luke, where were you? Your mother said you were gone all morning. Where did you go?"

Luke felt his stomach heave. He knew what torture would befall Vee if her father knew they had been together. "I was out with a friend."

"Really. What friend?" he asked.

"Just a friend from school."

"You say you didn't start the fire, but you said this was your lighter."

"Yes, but I lost it and I haven't seen it for weeks."

"I know you smoke. I've told you before not to smoke around my house."

Luke nodded. "I swear, Sir, I didn't start that fire."

"You swear?" Richardson asked with deliberate cynicism.

"Yes."

Richardson walked closer to Luke. "What does that mean? Does it mean you're not lying?"

"Luke is a good boy," Theta called from behind.

"That's good to know," said Richardson, his gaze never wavering from Luke. "Do you *swear* everything you told me today is the truth?"

Luke's body went cold and knew he was caught. He either had to take the fall for the fire and for his father's death, or reveal his relationship with Vee and possibly ruin her trust in him forever. She knew the truth and that's all that mattered to him now. "No," Luke said, barely above a whisper.

"No?" Richardson said loudly.

Elise flashed a heated and fretful glare his way.

"I was lying. I was smoking in the corral and I accidently dropped a cigarette on a pile of straw. The fire got out of control before I could stop it. It was an accident." He looked at his mother. "I'm sorry, Mama." His eyes still held the perpetual scars of grief, and with this terrible revelation they would forever harbor regret.

Theta looked like she wanted to die. "No," she moaned.

"That's not true!" Vee yelled out. "Why are you doing this?" she screamed at her father.

She gave Luke the most sorrowful look he'd ever seen. He wanted to run to her, hold her and push the pain away, but instead he shook his head in defeat. His heart broke as she ran out of the room, sobbing.

Richardson told Theta he wouldn't press charges against Luke after all they'd been through, but that they would have to leave his property. He gave them a week to find a place and pack their things.

The members of the church in Pocatello had already offered them temporary rooms. Without telling Luke, in one of her rare lucid moments, Theta had called and made arrangements for them to stay with Philip and Agnes, probably hoping to seal Luke's fate with Talia and relieve Theta of the constant worry about his future.

Each night, as Luke tried to arrange and sort the boxes of their belongings, he tried to keep Theta from slinking back into her bed. He needed her help, but also her comfort. The only thing that kept him going was the knowledge that he was truly innocent. His heart told him that someday the truth would be known. He only hoped Vee would forgive him for doing what he did. He wondered if she understood he was only trying to protect her.

It was the night before their move and Luke had finished putting all their things into the back of his father's old pickup. Other than a few items Luke viewed as being part of Thomas, the rest was put into a large box and marked for Goodwill.

Luke looked around the small house making sure he was really finished. The house looked smaller than ever without the bits and pieces of a cherished life strewn about. He went to Theta, who was still in bed.

She was curled up and facing away from him. He could tell that she was awake, but knew it didn't matter. She wouldn't answer him with any more than moans and sighs. His mother's loss was overwhelming, and he hadn't realized it until he sat there seeing her alone and broken. He put his hand on her shoulder. "Mama, please be okay. I need you."

He waited for a response as tears welled in his eyes. When she said nothing, he broke down. Through his sobs, Luke confessed that he had lied all along. He told her he did it for Vee. Luke told her everything about his powerful love, and what had really happened with his lighter.

The mothering instinct of a woman is strong and with her child in such horrendous pain, Theta was stirred from her own despair and turned to him. Through wet eyes, he saw her reach out. He fell into her arms and she stroked his head as he cried.

When his sobs subsided and his breathing calmed, she wiped his face with the bed sheet and made him look at her. "It hurts to love," she told him, with her voice still filled with mourning. "Sometimes I feel it's better never to love, but that's not true. It is always better to love. The hurt will leave...someday." She gave him a weak but genuine smile. "And I still have you."

The next morning with the truck filled with their belongings, and they passed by the regal Richardson homestead, Theta turned away. Luke searched for any sign of Vee, but the cover of the dim morning sunrise made it hard to distinguish much, and his eyes were still puffy and sore from the night before. He stopped the truck and sat for a moment taking a last look at the burned out arena...a monument to his father's courage.

"What are you doing?" Theta asked.

"Remembering. Someday, they'll know the truth." Luke took a deep breath. "You know the truth and so does Vee. That's all that matters."

"No! They are making us leave. And now people think you did this."

"Like I said, Mama, the people who matter to me know what really happened. Someday Elise will get what she deserves."

Theta huffed. She turned to the immense estate. She sat studying it.

Luke turned to her in wonder. He watched as her eyes went thin and her brow lowered in a deep stupor.

"You hurt my child and now I hurt yours." Her voice was a strange and unfamiliar monotone. "Any child that is born to you will forever feel the pain of loss." She mumbled words in a language Luke didn't understand. It wasn't Greek.

"Mama, what are you doing?"

She sat for a moment in silence. Her eyes were closed and she was still in a trancelike state. Then she opened her eyes. "Drive away," she said, staring straight ahead.

Exasperated, Luke put the old truck in gear. It lurched forward, rocking the towers of boxes in the bed. They turned onto the highway.

When they were on the interstate, coasting at a constant speed, Luke turned to his mother who stared out the window. She looked tired and blank. "Mama, what was that back there? I've never seen you act like that before. Are you okay?"

She looked down at her hands. "I am imposter."

Luke was tired from the events of the past week and his patience had left him long ago. "What are you talking about? An imposter of what?"

She brushed her prematurely gray hair from her face and sat up straight. "I am not Greek," she said softly. She sounded as if she had been burdened with this horrific secret for so long that she was grateful to shed her lie.

"What?"

"I am Romani."

"Romani? What is that?"

Theta sighed long and loud. "Romani is Gypsy. I am Gypsy."

A short burst of laughter exploded from Luke and he had to steady the truck. "*Gypsy*? What the hell does that mean?"

She seemed even sadder by his reaction, and looked at the floor of the truck.

"Mama, how can you not be Greek?" he asked, thinking about her broken English and strong Greek accent. "You've talked about it all my life. If you're not Greek, then why did you always say you were?"

"I lied because I am Gypsy. We have no family because I am Gypsy. Thomas's mother..." her lips began to quiver and she hesitated on her words. "She disowned him because of me. She thought I was Greek when we married, but then she learned the truth. Thomas wouldn't leave me, so they sent us away."

"They sent you away from Greece?"

Theta shook her head. "No, Utah."

Luke chuckled again. "Utah. There are Gypsies in Utah?"

"Gypsies are everywhere, but they live in the mountains. They stay away from people and only come down to... work. My family was Gypsy family. They sell me to a family who was Greek. They meet at a street market. They tell their friends and other relatives that I am Greek and that my parents are dead. It was secret to everyone that I was Gypsy. They raise me as Greek. But I'm not Greek. I am really Gypsy."

"How old were you? My God, Mama, why didn't you ever tell me?"

"I was ashamed. I was twelve years old. I was so worried people would know. I am still worried."

Luke shook his head. "Good hell, they *sold* you? What did they sell you for?"

"I work in the kitchen for my new family."

"Who sells their own kids?" asked Luke, horrified.

"Gypsies. I tell you they terrible."

"It doesn't matter. You are who you are regardless of whether you're Greek or Mexican or Gypsy... whatever that means. Why did you decide to tell me now?"

"Because what I did was Gypsy curse."

Luke threw his head back and laughed. "You put a Gypsy curse on the Richardsons!" For the first time in a week, he felt a spark of glee. "That is the funniest thing I've ever heard." Luke reached over to her and pulled her to him. He kissed her head. "I love you, Mama, even if you are a Gypsy."

She frowned, angry that he made light of her terrible predicament.

He laughed again. "A Gypsy curse. I had no idea what power you had. I can't wait to see what anguish this brings to poor old Mr. Richardson."

Chapter 12

Malad, Idaho, Early Spring, 2009

Even in the face of losing his freedom, my father still tried to protect me. He pleaded guilty, waving all rights, eliminating exposure for me. He didn't want to see me testifying in court with cameras and questions. His only concern was keeping me as far from his fate as possible.

Due to the high profile of the case, he was sentenced to at least fifteen years in prison for attempted murder with additional time imposed for use of a deadly weapon. He'd be close to fifty before he'd even be considered for parole. His only request was that my whereabouts be sealed and that I not be interrogated any further. The court agreed, which angered the press, so they were especially severe in their coverage of his sentencing. He was to serve his time at the Idaho State Penitentiary in Boise, a five hour drive from where I was living

I slowly adapted to my new home and my new grandparents. They did everything they could to make me feel comfortable and wanted. Even my grandfather talked more kindly and smiled as time went along. His gruff persona had melted and he called me Sophie.

My grandmother was warm and cheery and bought me several new outfits during our first and only trip to the mall. It happened the weekend after I'd been brought to their home, and the stares and whispers that surrounded us that day as we shopped were enough for both us to decide we'd wait awhile before attempting it again.

I spent most of my days reading, learning how to cook, and brushing or riding the horses. My grandfather used this activity to engage me in conversation, and it worked. I loved my time in the arena, and even though the size of the horses was intimidating, especially at first, I quickly learned to be confident around them. He told me about their unique bloodlines, and I was surprised that they had beautiful and meaningful Greek names. I felt closer to them, and to him by having that connection.

My aunt was the most distant of my new family and made me uncomfortable. Elise always smiled and asked how I was doing, but the curve of her mouth and twitch of her brow made the words seem like they were laced with venom. I stayed away from her as much as I could, and that was easy since she worked a lot. Her job required her to wear a gun. It seemed her position gave her both status and flight, and I think she enjoyed being away from us and her life at home. Stephanie annoyed her constantly.

During the weekdays, I attended school at Stephanie's house. I arrived at 8:15, just after I watched my aunt drive down the lane on her way to work.

It was a small home just up the hill from my grandparent's large ranch. It was old with worn carpet in the bedrooms, velvet patterned wallpaper in the living room and a chandelier that twisted above the dining table in the small kitchen. In the bathrooms, rust stains trailed from the faucets to the drain, and the yellowed vinyl floor was curled up on the sides. It was a stark contrast from my grandparent's home. I assumed my aunt's surly ways were due to her disappointment of having to live in the small, decaying home rather than the immaculate estate that she was raised on.

At the side of the house was a large room used as our classroom during the day and a family room any other time. It had a long sofa, two dilapidated recliners and an old dinette set that was used as our lesson area.

Stephanie's father, my new Uncle Lonny, was our teacher, except on Tuesdays and Thursdays when a woman named Sister Meyers came to teach us history. Stephanie had been suspended from public school for reasons I hadn't quite learned, and because of the drama my so-called rescue created, it was decided that I should attend home school, too. I was relieved with this and enjoyed my time with Stephanie, regardless of what we were doing. She was funny and smart, and I was in awe of her free spirit.

I was still getting used to all the new people in my life, and often longed for my simple days of solace. After six months, I still felt like an intruder, and only when I was alone, or in the arena with the horses, did I feel content.

One morning, we were in the middle of our English lesson and Stephanie was bored, giving her father sarcastic answers when defining words. The word that day was "ironic" and she was asked to use it in a sentence. After several offensive and unacceptable answers, Stephanie became annoyed and blurted out, "Ironic. It's ironic that after keeping his daughter in a cage, now Sophie's father lives in one."

"That's just great," Uncle Lonny admonished her. "Does it make you happy to hurt people? This is why we're in this mess. You don't think." He was usually very tolerant and at ease with us. He made the hours of study go by quickly with his kindness and wit. Even Stephanie's antics rarely shook his calm demeanor.

I put my hand on his arm. "Why does everyone think they need to hide my father from me? I miss him and I need to know he's okay."

I saw Uncle Lonny's eyes soften. He told both of us to go to the kitchen for a snack. We made peanut butter and jelly crackers in silence. I felt my energy weaken, and Stephanie put a caring hand on my shoulder.

"I don't understand why people think Papa's so terrible," I said. "He isn't. He loved me and I was happy living with him. Now I feel like I'm lost."

I could see sympathy and confusion in Stephanie's face. "Were you really happy living like that?"

"It's not what you think. I wasn't in a cage. He was protecting me. No one understands."

"Tell me. I'm your best friend. We're supposed to tell each other everything."

"Do you tell me everything?" I asked, knowing she hadn't.

She rolled her eyes and smiled back at me. "No, but I will if you want me to."

"Promise?"

"Yes. Do you promise to tell me everything?"

"I do."

We smiled at each other, as though we had sealed a best friend's contract.

The next day, when Uncle Lonny entered the room I could tell that he was torn. He asked me to sit with him on the sofa. "I'm going to answer your questions but you need to promise something first."

I nodded, "Anything."

"Before you say that, you must swear that anything we say between us is our secret. You've got to swear on your life that you'll never say a word about what we talk about to anyone, okay?"

"I swear."

He told me about my father. I was unaware of what prison really was and what my father's life would be like. When we were finished with our talk, I was convinced Papa was miserable and that I'd never see him again. I was crushed and felt hopeless. I cried hard and Uncle Lonny hugged me and rubbed my back. I felt my head would burst from the weight of my tears.

"I miss him so much," I sobbed. "I don't want to live if I'm never going to see him again."

Uncle Lonny took my wet face in his hands. He looked down into my eyes and I could see he was determined to help me. "I don't know if I can do it, but I'll try to find a way for you to visit him."

"Really?" I suddenly felt the dark clouds parting.

"Don't get your hopes up," he said. "I said I'd try. It may take months or even years, but if you do your school work and do what I tell you, I'll try my best to help. You mean a lot to me, Sophie. We'll work on it together."

I hugged him tightly. "Oh, thank you, Uncle Lonny. I love you."

He hugged me back then stood up quickly. "I'll go get Stephanie. Finish your lesson. I expect you to have chapter seven finished when I get back." He raised a finger. "And remember your promise. *No* talking to anyone about this. It's just between you and me. Otherwise I won't be able to help."

"Uncle Lonny, I promise. I'll never say a word."

I watched him walk out and felt incredible joy and appreciation. He was my champion and I wanted to do everything I could to make him happy. Then I remembered my talk with Stephanie. If she was my best friend, how could I keep all this from her? I had sworn on my life with Uncle Lonny, yet, I also promised Stephanie I'd tell her everything. I had to do my best to keep my promises to both and hoped I wouldn't go to hell for failing.

Chapter 13

The Arbon Valley, Late summer, 2003

After Donny died, I spent most of my time inside the house. For the first week, I didn't even feed the chickens or collect eggs. Papa did it before he left for work. I became so stir crazy that I started leaving the gate unlocked and going about the house as I had before. When Papa came home for lunch, or at the end of the day, I hurried back to my room.

I missed being outside, but also felt from Papa's demeanor that it was for the best. From my window, I watched him leave for work each day and noticed that he always spent a moment on the porch scanning the entire valley before walking to his car and driving away. I wondered if he was searching for the thing I still longed for.

I hadn't seen Damien since the night he came looking for Donny. I missed him terribly. Even though I kept to the house, I walked from the front window to the back regularly during the day, hoping to catch a glimpse of him waiting for me in the field. A month had passed, and nothing.

One evening, Papa said it was okay for me to go back to my normal chores. He made special mention of the 'watchers' on the hill, but seemed fine with me returning to my routine. I found his change of heart odd, but was grateful.

It was hard at first to be in the yard and not spend hours gazing off to where I last saw Donny standing. It made my heart ache when I tried to imagine Damien, his hair blowing in the breeze and his handsome face smiling back. I longed to be near him, and as the months passed my desire for him deepened. It took a long time to break my habit of waiting and hoping, but after a year passed, I finally stopped looking.

It was early Spring in 2008 when I turned sixteen on a sunny Wednesday morning, and Papa had placed a small box wrapped in pink paper on my nightstand. There was a note promising me pizza for lunch that day. I opened the package and found a dainty silver bracelet with glistening blue gemstones. It was beautiful, and the only piece of jewelry I'd ever owned except for the tiny gold cross I always wore around my neck.

I was both shocked and elated at the gift. It was difficult to unlatch with just one hand, but after struggling for several minutes, I was able to clasp it around my wrist. It fit perfectly and I sat admiring it for a long time, moving my arm to make the stones sparkle in the sunlight. A tiny folded note was placed inside the box. It was handwritten in Papa's precise, box-shaped printing.

To my daughter, Sophie. Happy 16th Birthday. This bracelet is to remind you to always do what is right. Love, Papa.

I smiled and continued to admire my gift. I had never owned anything so beautiful; I never wanted to take it off.

I dressed and had breakfast while I continued to give it glances. I debated whether I should take it off while doing my chores outside, but since I'd had such trouble getting the bracelet on I decided to keep it there, and ended up feeding and gathering eggs one-handed.

Then I saw a familiar sight in the distance. I felt it before I realized it was real and my heart yearned for it to be true. I waited and prayed before I looked up and when I did, I thanked God for answering. It was Damien. He was far off, just above the crest of the hill, but I knew it was him. He wasn't walking, just standing, as if reluctant to move closer. Joy burst from my heart, and without hesitation I ran straight to him. When he saw me running, he smiled. We met and hugged; he picked me up and twirled me around in a circle.

"Where've you been?" I asked, breathless.

"We moved to Pocatello." He still held me, turning me in a circle.

"Why?"

"When Donny died, my mom couldn't stand to live here. She got remarried about a month later and we moved to my stepdad's house in Pocatello."

"Why are you back?"

"My grandparents are here. When we were here, we lived with them. We're only here for a couple weeks, but I'll be back for the whole summer."

I hugged my head to his chest. "I am so sorry about Donny. I still get so sad when I think about him."

"Me, too."

My delight of having him back was tempered when I started walking with him toward the house.

"Wait," he said, stopping. "What about your dad?"

"He's not home. He won't be here until lunch, just like before."

He looked at me with a glimpse of sorrow. "When will it be okay for me to see you?"

I didn't have an answer, because I wasn't sure if it would ever be okay.

He could see my distress and decided not to push the issue, deciding instead to walk with me to the garden. He opened the gate and my stomach tingled as I walked through. He was the Damien I remembered, but things were different. He was taller, he smelled heavenly, and he looked at me in a way that made me feel like he could read my thoughts. At times his stares were so intense that I felt my face flush and I had to look away.

That week we tried to go back to the way things used to be. We met at the same time each morning. We sat in the backyard and talked, but we rarely played any of the silly games like before. Part of me felt it was because Donny was no longer there, but the more time I had with Damien, and looked into his eyes when we talked, the more I realized nothing was the same.

As the days passed, we talked less about us as individuals and more about us and the future. He touched me in tender, affectionate ways as we spoke. While sitting on the garden bench he held my hand, or ran his fingers along my arm. It often stopped me in mid-sentence and made me want to ask what he was doing. But in my heart, I already knew.

There were days where we rarely spoke and we simply lay in the grass with the sky bowing high above us. He traced his fingers along my face and over my lips, studying each feature before always coming back to my eyes. I often felt awkward having him look at me so closely, but I loved his touch and didn't want him to stop.

"Hold still," he said, one morning, as he peered into my eyes. He went to reach for something near my eye and I sat up, wondering what he saw.

"What is it?" I asked.

"You have an eyelash that's about to fall into your eye." He tried to brush it away. He tried several times and finally shook his head. "You'll need to do it. It's too close to your eye. I'm afraid I'll knock it in."

I started to try and find it with my hand.

"The light is too bright out here. Let's go in," he said, directing me toward the house.

Once inside, he looked around. "You need to look in a mirror."

I stood stunned.

He looked perplexed. "What is it?"

I didn't know how to tell him. He walked toward the hall and I was frozen, fearful of what he'd find. He kept going and then I took several steps, following him hesitantly.

He opened the door to the bathroom, looked around and then turned to me confused. "There is no mirror." He started walking around the house opening doors with a pinched brow. When he stopped at my room, he looked at the gated door, completely baffled. He opened it and stepped inside.

My body felt weak as I watched him look around, horrified. He came out quickly and ran to me, grabbing my arm.

"My God, Sophie, you have bars on your windows and a cage door. He has you locked up like a slave."

"No." I wanted to explain that it wasn't what he thought, but I knew he would never believe me. "I'm not locked in. See?" I showed him the door. "It's to keep people out."

"To keep *who* out?"

The web of lies got larger and stickier as I tried to explain. But how could I ever convince him that I wasn't a slave or a prisoner. The bars on the windows and the lock on the door were for protection, not imprisonment. "It's not what you think," is all I could muster.

"Why are there no mirrors anywhere?"

This I could answer. It wasn't a decision of Papa's, but of God's. "Mirrors have no place in God's world. They are only for the vain."

"What?" he looked as though I had sprouted another nose. "Sophie," he said, pulling me toward the back door. "This isn't right. We must get you away from here."

"What are you doing?"

"You're coming with me. My grandparents will help you. We'll get you away from him."

I stopped and shook my arm free of his grasp. "No."

His eyes were pleading. "Please, come with me. I love you Sophie."

I knew then that I had not only disobeyed my father, but had put Damien at risk. He was my world, and I stood torn over what to do. I had put everything I loved and cared about on the line, and now I saw it all slipping away. "You can't tell anyone I'm here. If you tell, they'll take me away."

"That's good!" He took my arm again and tried to lead me out.

"I can't go with you. I'm begging you not to tell. I won't be able to see you anymore if you tell."

"Do you love me?"

I looked at him, horrified that he didn't already know the answer, and stayed silent. He leaned down to kiss me, but I pulled back.

"What's wrong?"

I bit my lip, knowing I couldn't tell him, especially with what he had already seen. "He'll be home soon."

Damien scoffed. "I want to punch him in the face for what he's done to you."

"No, Damien! You don't understand."

"Do you want to be with me?"

"Yes."

"Then we must get you out of here."

"But I can't."

"Are you planning on living like this forever?"

Then it dawned on me that I'd never considered what my future would hold. I had no plans past the day ahead, and had never imagined any other life than the one I had with Papa. But I knew I had to end it with Damien or the same terrible fate that befell Donny would take him, too. I stood tall and nodded.

"You don't mean that."

"I do. I can't see you anymore. You must leave now." My heart was being ripped apart, but I knew I was doing the right thing. I twirled my bracelet, remembering my father's note that came with it.

Damien shook his head with a face that was both hurt and bewildered. "Why are you doing this?"

"Because I have to."

"But you said you loved me."

I shook my head. "No, I didn't. You said you loved me."

His face turned to stone. He tried to talk but failed. His eyes welled up and he turned away. Before I could see him cry, he tore through the house and slammed the back door.

I ran to him and stood on the porch, my entire body aching as he walked off toward the field. I stood alone feeling scared and tormented. I had done what I knew was right, but the pain I felt was so overwhelming I couldn't understand how it could possibly *be* right. I loved Damien more than anything, and now he was gone.

If this was my destiny, I thought, why would I even *want* to continue this life?

Chapter 14

Malad, Idaho, Early Spring 2009

Spring had spread across the fields and pastures. Cottonwood trees fluttered their newly sprouted green, and purple asters covered the rolling hills. The snow had melted and Stephanie and I started taking the horses on rides up the valley. It was incredibly liberating to roam and wander without fear.

The sound of hooves on early spring dirt was solid and steady. The breeze was still crisp, but the sun reached down and warmed our shoulders. For almost an hour we rode in silence. We both were in awe of the day and the splendor that was ours alone to enjoy.

At the top of the hill, the trail opened up to a small plateau and a blue mountain lake. I gasped at the incredible beauty of it. I smiled at Stephanie and she nodded in acknowledgement. Her eyes were bright and her freckles seemed to glow in the sunshine. The horse she rode was a black mare my grandfather was going to sell. Stephanie loved the white diamond-shaped patch on her forehead, and scolded him for even thinking about selling Black Bean. My horse was an old buckskin gelding named Clyde. He lumbered along and rarely went faster than a slow trot, but for a beginner like me he was perfect.

Stephanie turned her horse down the hill and toward the lake. "Do you want to go swimming?" she called back.

"I don't know how," I answered.

She giggled as she reached the water's edge. "You don't need to. The horses do it all." Her hair was pulled into two short pigtails and they bounced with each step of her horse.

I waited and watched as she urged Black Bean into the lake. As the water got deeper, the splashes became larger around her legs as it pushed forward, and soon they were floating along smoothly.

"Come on!" she yelled, waving me in. She waved so hard she almost fell off the horse, and started laughing as she steadied herself.

It looked like fun, but I was terrified. The water was immense and dark. I wondered what would happen if I fell off in the middle.

I gave Clyde a slight nudge and he walked to the shoreline. The water lapped as I waited and watched Stephanie continue to beckon. Clyde seemed unconcerned as he clopped loudly into the water. I told myself to keep looking forward and it would be okay. Clyde had no hesitation, which helped my fears.

As the horse rhythmically propelled us along, I began to feel a sense of buoyancy and freedom. When we crossed the center point and were on our way to the other shore, my confidence turned to elation. I sat up straight, closed my eyes and imagined I was flying, gliding along on my winged unicorn, soaring through clouds and racing the wind. When the horse's hooves made contact with the lake bottom and we started to emerge from the water, I wanted to burst from relief and joy.

"That was the most wonderful thing ever!"

Stephanie was sitting on a large tree limb that had fallen while her horse munched on fresh new grass beside her. "I didn't think you'd do it. I'm proud of you."

"It was so scary, but then it was *so* amazing."

"I'm glad you liked it, because that's how we're getting back."

We led the horses to a shaded area and tied them loosely to a tree so they could rest and graze. Stephanie leaned back against a tree and looked out at the incredible view of mountain-lined lake and clear blue sky.

"This is where I go when I can't stand life anymore. The first time I came here, I tried to kill myself. I stole my dad's gun and had it all planned out. Then I sat here and looked around at all this and thought…who would care? I'm nothing and no one will miss me, so why do it? That's when I decided to live for me. I do what makes *me* happy now and screw the rest of them."

"You were going to kill yourself. Why?"

Stephanie heaved a deep, labored sigh. "I didn't see the point in living. My mom was dead and my dad married that crazy bitch." She shrugged. "I don't really fit in anywhere. Even at school, the kids hate me."

I shook my head. "I don't believe that. There is no reason to hate you."

Stephanie scoffed. "You say that because you don't know what normal is. That's why we get along. I'm a freak, but you've never had any friends, so you don't know how weird I am."

"I've had friends," I protested.

"Really? I thought you were kept alone at that house all the time."

I nodded.

Stephanie raised an eyebrow. "So, did your dad kidnap kids and bring them home for you play with?"

Stephanie laughed and I realized she was joking. I paused for a moment, trying to pick my words carefully.

"Don't worry about me telling anyone," she said. "Remember, we're best friends, so you should be able to tell me anything. I've never told anyone that I was going to kill myself."

I looked at her with a mixture of love and concern. "I had two friends. I met them when I was eleven. Their mother worked with my father and they came to our house one day. That's how they knew I lived there. They lived over the hill from us and they sneaked up while Papa was at work and we played in my yard." I stopped and smiled at the memory.

"You had to hide them from your father. Why?"

"He was afraid that if people knew I was home alone all day, they'd come and take me away."

"Didn't it drive you crazy to be alone *all* the time?"

I shrugged. "Not really. When I met Donny and Damien I was much happier. I didn't know what it was like to have friends before I met them, so I didn't realize what I was missing."

She studied me. "Isn't Damien the kid your dad shot? Why'd he shoot him? Did he catch him with you?"

"Yes."

"Why didn't you just tell him that you two were friends and that it was no big deal?"

"I tried to convince him, but... there is a lot you don't understand."

Stephanie gave me a disappointed curl of her lip. "And I won't be *able* to understand if you keep everything a secret."

I stayed silent.

"Sophie, I've already told you something that I never told anyone. I trust you because we're friends. That's what friends do. They trust each other and they tell each other things. Do you think I won't believe you?"

"No, it's not that. And I do trust you, but there are things that will sound strange, and I don't want you to think I'm a monster."

She laughed. "You are the opposite of a monster. You're friendly and kind. So, what is this big dark secret? You say your father didn't kidnap you or treat you badly, so why did he keep you locked up in that house hidden away from the world?"

"I'll tell you, but you have to swear you'll never tell anyone else."

"I swear. I swear on my step-mother's grave," she giggled.

I looked at her, worried that she wasn't in the right mind frame to hear what I had to say. My face must have showed it, because Stephanie quickly lost her smile and leaned forward. She put her hand on my shoulder. "God, Soph, I was just kidding. You look like I just cursed her dead."

I gasped and put my hand to my mouth. I felt an icy chill go down my back and my heart jumped.

"What?" she asked.

"It's what you said. That is why I had to hide all those years."

"What I said? How could that be? I wasn't even around."

I put my face in my hands and rocked back and forth, trying to steady my nerves and my thoughts.

"Sophie, what's wrong with you? You're not making any sense. I can't help you if you don't talk to me."

I stopped rocking, and looked up at her. "I'm so afraid to say anything."

"You have no reason to be afraid. I'm not going to tell anyone. You're my only friend! You'll go crazy if you keep it all inside."

"But what if you don't want to be friends after I tell you?"

"That's crazy." She sat up on her knees and squared her body to mine. She held my shoulders and made me look at her. "Here, think about this. Imagine I'm the one telling you this big secret. If that were the case, would we still be friends?

"Sophie?"

I suddenly realized that I had no idea where to start. It struck me as funny, and I stopped and smiled to myself.

"You're a tease!" she yelled. "Come on, out with it."

"I don't know where to start. There is so much to tell."

She leaned back against the tree and put her arms behind her head. "We have all day. They don't expect us until dinner and I brought food in my backpack. Spill it!"

I took a deep breath. "There is something terrible that happened a long time ago and it's the reason Papa and I had to hide all those years."

"Did he kill someone?" she asked, both horrified and intrigued.

"No," I said firmly. "It's not something we did, but something that was done to us."

Stephanie lowered an eyebrow. "What?"

"A curse."

Her eyes shot wide open, but she gave me a sideways grin. "A curse?"

"Yes. We had to hide away because Papa says we are a threat to the people who love us."

125

She cocked her head to the side. "How?"

I looked at the ground and felt my face flush. "I'm not sure, but some of them have died."

Stephanie reeled back. "They died? How?"

"Papa says it's the reason my mother died and Donny. He says *we're* the reason."

"You said he didn't kill anyone."

"It's not us. It's the curse that kills them."

"How did they die?"

"Donny died when a dirt cave collapsed on him." I felt a heavy lump in my stomach. "I don't know how my mother died. Papa never talks about it."

Stephanie gave a 'humph.' "Sounds to me like your father gave you a line to keep *you* in line. There is no such thing as a curse."

I felt rejected and embarrassed. It had taken every ounce of trust I could muster to tell her and now she brushed it off. "Yes there is."

She furrowed her brows. "Did you push that kid into the cave?"

"No!"

Stephanie sat up straight. "Do you think that other kid was shot because of this curse, too?"

I lowered my eyes. "Yes."

She sat in silence, looking as if she were deep in thought. Several times she began to talk and then stopped. She stood up and walked in a circle. "That doesn't make sense. If you say the curse kills people who love you, then why am I still alive? And what about your grandparents? Why aren't we all dead?"

"I'm not sure. Sometimes it scares me. I don't want to hurt people, but I don't want to be alone. Papa was trying to explain it, but then we got caught. I've tried to figure it out, but without Papa, I can't. There's more to it, and he's the only one who knows."

"Who put the curse on you?"

"Papa said it was done a long time ago, before I was born."

Stephanie lowered her brow. "If you weren't even born, why would anyone want to curse you?"

"It was placed on our family for something Papa did. He said it was done out of anger. He said he didn't believe it at first, but when my mother was killed, he knew we had to hide or more bad things would happen. He said if anyone found out about the curse, I'd be taken away. He hid us for our own good. He didn't want the curse to hurt anyone else. I didn't know about it until after Donny died. Papa felt it was his fault for not warning me sooner."

Stephanie looked at me in awe. She hadn't moved a muscle or changed her facial expression in the slightest. Then she took a seat beside me and put an arm around my shoulder. "So, what are you going to do? If you think you're cursed and you're putting other people at risk, how are you going to live?"

I thought for a moment. "I don't know."

"That's crazy, Sophie. There is no such thing. I think he told you that just to keep you from running off. He knew that if people saw you they'd find out who you are. That would threaten him. He made it sound very convincing."

She sat back with a start. "He must have seen the newspaper article that ran the sketch. That's why he took all the mirrors out of your house. He didn't want you to discover who you really are. On the other hand, this is so strange, because if he really thought you were cursed, a lot of this stuff he did makes sense. That's totally wild."

I thought about the mirrors. I remembered the expression on Damien's face when he realized all the mirrors in my house had been taken down or destroyed. I still had aversions to them, and rarely gave in to the temptation. They were everywhere at my grandparent's home, but I did my best to avoid them, knowing that God watched and judged what I did.

"When I tell you that I love you, does it scare you?" she asked.

I contemplated her question, knowing I had thought about it many times before. "It used to, but for some reason I'm not worried anymore."

"I think I know why."

"Tell me."

"Sophie, I don't believe in curses or superstitions. I think the more you're out in the normal world, you'll realize all the stuff you've been told is not real. You're not cursed."

What she said completely deflated me. I had trusted her with my deepest, darkest realities and now she said that what I harbored and lived with my entire life was just a lie.

"You'll never be happy if you live in fear like this. You'll have an awful life if you never let anyone love you. I think it's terrible what he did. He's the one that's cursed you with stupid superstitions."

I was shocked at what she said and felt the need to scoot away, fearing God would strike her down with a bolt of lightning. "You don't believe in God?"

"No. And I don't believe that how I live my life will determine how I spend my death. I believe that you do the right things for *this* life, not for some afterlife. When my mom died, people actually told me that God needed her in heaven and that's why he took her home." She smirked.

"My mom died because cancer cells overtook her body. It had nothing to do with God, and it had nothing to do with curses or prayers or any other hocus-pocus that everyone tries to fill your head with."

I was still uneasy.

"You were worried about telling me your secret because you thought I would be afraid of you. And it turns out, you should be afraid of me."

"Why?"

"Because I am a bad influence. That's why I'm not allowed at the school. I asked questions and talked about things that made everyone nervous. The other kids told their parents that I didn't believe in God and that I attacked their precious religion." She smiled and pulled me close. "I'm worse than you. You may lure them in with your beauty and then kill them off, but I threaten their beliefs and their chances at eternal life. We make quite a pair."

Being close to her was a comfort, even though I was still concerned about what she said. I cared about her and felt her statements against God would come back to haunt her

"I know you aren't going to believe everything I say, but I want to show you something that will hopefully help you get over this. We're going to do an experiment so I can prove that there is no such thing as a curse."

I didn't like the idea and was apprehensive.

"You don't have a choice," she said, with a defiant lift of her eyebrow. "You are my best friend, my *only* friend in this world. I love you like a sister. Nothing fatal has happened to me yet and nothing will. I'll prove to you that you are not cursed."

I felt funny having her tempt fate for me.

"I was planning on killing myself anyway, so this isn't a big sacrifice. Quit looking like that," she chided. Stephanie put her finger to her mouth and feigned deep deliberation. "Hmm. If you have the power to kill people, then let's work on how we can use it to bump off my step-mother!" She fell back against the soft forest floor in wicked laughter.

"Stephanie!"

She giggled with delight.

I couldn't help but smile, even though she had made me out as toxic. Stephanie was intriguing and confusing, but I had no reservations that she was loyal and trustworthy. She had the power to destroy my world by exposing my enigma, yet I felt assured she would guard it, regardless of her own doubts about its truth.

She stopped laughing and leaned over to her backpack. She pulled out a bag of chips and a bottle of soda, and offered them to me. I took a handful of chips and we sat in silence for awhile as we passed the bottle back and forth. "I think you saved me," she said.

I looked at her strangely.

She smiled back. "You did. Now the hard part is going to be saving you."

Chapter 15

Carpo came to the ranch often. At first, my grandparents were happy to see him and talked about my progress. I felt awkward and uneasy in his presence. I made it a point to not be alone with him ever. My grandparents spoke well of him, but when he started showing up on a weekly basis and talking about the book he was planning, they became reluctant and apprehensive about his visits.

After he left for the last time, I waited in my room pretending to read. When my grandmother finished cleaning up after dinner and went to her room to watch television, I slinked out of my room and found my grandfather alone in the living room. With the exception of his reading lamp, he sat in his recliner simply staring into the dark, with a book across his lap.

My presence roused him from his trance and he smiled, motioning me over to him.

"I thought you'd gone to bed," he said.

I took a seat on the edge of the sofa next to him.

"Is there something wrong?" he asked.

"Why does that man continue to call me Callidora?"

My grandfather smiled. "Because that is your name. It's what you were named when you were born."

I thought about it for a moment.

"I picked out your name," he said with a sad smile. "It is Greek for beauty."

I furrowed my brow. "Why did my father change it?"

His face went from serene to agitated in only a matter of seconds. He tried to keep his composure, and hesitated before he spoke. "I think he changed it to keep you hidden."

"Why would my name keep me hidden?"

"Everyone was looking for you and your name was in the newspaper and on TV. Callidora isn't a common name, so if someone heard that your name was Callidora, they would realize who you were."

I thought about what he said and it made sense, except that I wasn't ever around anyone else except for Damien and Donny. "Why does that man want to ask me all those questions?"

My grandfather's breath quickened. "He wants to write a book about you."

"About me. Why?"

"He thinks it will make a lot of money."

I was disturbed and felt violated. "What would he write about?"

My grandfather sat up in his chair. "The fact that you were found after all these years is something people find interesting."

"When he asked me all those questions about Papa, my room and Damien, was that for his book?"

My grandfather bit his lip and looked at the floor.

"He's going to write about all that and let people read it. Why did you let him in here? Did you know that's what he was going to do?"

He looked up at me.

"*Did you?*"

"Sophie, we were grateful to him for getting you back to us. We know now that what he's doing isn't right."

"But it's too late." I quickly walked back to my room. I felt exposed and vulnerable. I had missed Papa ever since we were torn apart, but at that moment I ached for him. I needed him to hold me and make it all go away.

A light tap at my bedroom door made me wipe my tears. As the door opened, I turned away.

"Sophie, please don't be upset," Grandfather said softly as he stood in the doorway. "I didn't realize what was happening until it was too late. I want to protect you and help you…and I *will*. I will make sure he never comes back here again. Okay?"

I stayed facing the wall, but nodded. When the door closed, I turned back to it and wondered what would happen now. I wondered if I would ever have a normal life, and questioned if there even was such a thing.

Months passed, and as Stephanie and I flipped through magazines as we sat on the porch swing on the long veranda at my grandparent's home, I asked her what it was like to be around all the kids at school and what she did when they stared at her.

She laughed. "They don't stare at me, in fact, most of the time they don't even act like I exist."

I smiled in envy. "You go to your classes and they don't whisper or point at you?"

"They act like I'm invisible." Then she became quiet. "Good hell, that's all you're used to, isn't it? People always gawk at you. I bet you've never been able to go anywhere without it." She pointed at one of the photographs in the magazine. "It's like you're one of these people. You're a celebrity, but not really. It's weird. You're living a scandal you had no control over and you can't go anywhere because of who you are." She laughed to herself. "All my life I wanted to be famous. I wanted to have people stare at me when I walked in the mall and whisper to their friends when they saw me."

"Why do you want that?"

"A lot of people want that. No one wants to be part of the crowd. They want to stand out and have people notice them. If you're famous then everyone wants to be around you."

It made no sense. "You've never met these people. Why do you want to be around them?"

"They're celebrities. You feel like you know them because there is so much stuff written about them. I know how old they are, what they like to eat, where they hang out, who their friends are. I know more about them then I do about the kids at school."

"That man wants to write about me."

"It's kind of the same thing," she said. "People want to know about you."

I sighed. "I don't want them to know about me. I don't want Carpo to write that book. I want my life to stay a secret."

"I hate to tell you this, but I don't think you have a choice."

I was deflated and felt helpless. "What should I do?"

She shrugged and thought a moment. "What do you want? I mean, what would make *you* happy?"

"I want to be with my father."

She lifted her eyebrows and looked at the ground. "That isn't going to happen and you know it."

I nodded sadly.

"Start thinking about what's going to make you happy. You're supposed to graduate from high school next year. What will you do then? You don't want to live here with your grandparents forever. Are you going to college? Do you want to be a nurse, or a teacher, or an astronaut?"

"I don't know. What are you going to do?"

"I'm going to be an actress. I want to be a movie star."

The only movies I had seen were those shown on daytime television. When Papa was at work, I sneaked into his room, and took his small TV from the back of his closet, and watched whatever I could find. I did see several movies, even though I rarely saw them in their entirety. The picture was usually grainy and the sound was erratic, but for an hour or so I was able to lose myself in another life.

"I think you'll be a great actress," I told her.

"Thanks," she said, smiling. "So what about you? What do you want to be?"

"I've never thought about it before."

"What do you like to do?"

"I like to read."

Stephanie tipped her head and scrunched her nose. "That's good, but it isn't something that you can do as a career. What else do you like to do?"

"I like to draw."

She nodded. "Okay. Are you any good?"

"Yes," I said, boldly.

She laughed at my childlike confidence. "What can you draw? Show me."

"I'll be right back," I said. I stood up from the swing and ran to my room. I pulled my secret drawing pad from beneath my bed. When I got back to the swing, I held

135

it out to her. "I have more at my house, but I had to leave before I could gather them all."

She took the pad and looked at the first drawing. It was the view from the back porch of my old house. I remembered how much I loved the contrasting colors of the alder bushes against the snow, and how I had toiled to recreate the tiny sprigs of green on the juniper trees that dotted the hillside.

"Did you do this with colored pencils?" she asked.

I nodded.

She started flipping quickly through the pages. "My god, Sophie, these are amazing. Where did you learn to draw like this?"

"I don't know. I've always drawn pictures, even when I was really young. It's what I did all day when Papa was at work."

She turned the page, took a quick glance, and then stared up at me. "Who is this?"

I looked over the pad and smiled. "That's Papa."

She studied it a bit, turning her head from side to side. "Hmm, he doesn't look like a creepy kidnapper."

"He isn't."

"He has really dark hair and eyes."

"Yes. He's Greek."

"You obviously got your eyes from your mother." Stephanie saw my distress. "Do you miss her?"

I was painfully aware that I was without a mother, but my sadness wasn't for her specifically, and that made the absence even more profound. I sighed and shrugged. "I didn't ever know her."

"That's right. You were just two days old when your dad took you. It was right after she died."

I wondered what she knew, knowing that she was aware of a lot more than she usually let on. "Do you know how she died?"

"No," she answered quickly.

I watched her face to see if she was telling the truth.

"I swear, Soph, they never say much about her. When they do, they talk like she's a saint. I think that's why my stepmom hates her."

I reeled back in shock. "Hates her?" I asked. "Why does she hate my mother? They were sisters."

Stephanie cringed, and I knew she had again said too much. "I don't know if she hates her. I think she's jealous because her parents seemed to love her more. She gets weird every time her name comes up."

"I asked my grandmother how she died, and she said she would tell me, but she never has." I wondered if they were aware of my role in my mother's death. I thought about what had happened before my father took me and why he felt it was necessary to leave. They must have suspected something and that's why he felt it was better to take me away. I wanted so badly to talk to Papa and find out the answers to all the questions that crowded my head.

Stephanie continued to look through my drawings, making comments and compliments as she went. Then she stopped and studied one for quite a while. "Who's this?" She looked like she'd eaten a lemon.

It was a self portrait. The eyes were large and dreary looking, the head oddly shaped, and the face distorted. "It's me," I said, awkwardly.

"What?" she asked shocked. "*You?* No way."

"It's what I saw before…in the toaster."

"In the toaster? What are you talking about?"

"It was the only way I could really see myself. It's what I saw in the reflection of the toaster."

She laughed and looked at the portrait. "Good hell, no wonder it looks like that." She ripped it out of the pad. "Get rid of this. Do a new one. This is the old you."

I agreed, taking the portrait and stuffing it into my jacket pocket.

She continued to flip through as we talked. When she was almost to the end, she turned a page and then went back to it. "Whoa, who is that?"

I smiled, shyly. "That's Damien."

She gave me a wicked grin. "*The* Damien?"

I nodded.

"He's gorgeous. Does he really look like this?"

I nodded.

"Where's he now?"

"I don't know," I answered sadly.

"Don't you want to see him? Sophie, you can't tell me you don't want to see him. I can tell you love him."

I looked at the ground, feeling heartbroken. "I do, but I can't see him."

"You're not thinking about that curse stuff, are you? That's crap."

"Even so, I don't think he'd want to see me."

"Why? I bet we can find out what school he goes to."

I shook my head. "After what happened to him, he's probably angry."

"Yeah, I'm sure he's not happy about being shot, but that isn't your fault. You didn't shoot him, your dad did. Besides, he's fine. I heard it barely did anything to him."

"You did? Who told you that?"

"I hear a lot of stuff. The point is we should find him so you can see him again. Don't you want to see him?"

"I love him, but it was my fault that he was shot. I should've told the truth from the beginning but I didn't. I hid what I was doing from my father and because of it, Damien was almost killed and Papa's in prison. I want to see them both, but I feel so guilty and responsible. I wouldn't blame them if they hated me and never wanted to see me again."

"I think the only way you're ever going to realize you're not to blame is *if* you see them. They're the ones who know what happened. Find out for yourself. I'll help you. Somehow you need to get the truth from your father."

I stopped short of telling her what her own father had promised.

Stephanie continued, "I also think my stepmother is hiding a bunch of stuff. She's guilty of something. I can see it in her eyes every time she looks at you. Something happened a long time ago, and it's like you've come back to haunt her." She smiled. "She's got a big secret and I would *love* to see it spill out all over the place."

I saw the glee in her eyes, but I knew that whatever joy Stephanie found in seeing her stepmother squirm would be at my expense, and the thought made my stomach turn.

Chapter 16

It was a cold for a sunny spring morning. Spires of sunlight streaked through the blinds in my bedroom as my mind came out of a deep sleep. A sharp metal clanking had roused me on that Saturday, and I wondered where the noise was coming from. It was rhythmic and constant and I wondered what ranch chore was so important that it had to be done so early in the morning.

I pulled on my robe and went into the kitchen. My grandmother stood looking pensive, as she stared out the window above the sink. She heard me plodding across the carpet and immediately put on a forced smile.

"Did the noise wake you?" she asked, taking a folded newspaper and slipping it stealthily into a drawer. She moved away from the window and motioned for me to sit at the table.

Instead, I went to the window and looked out. I saw my grandfather supervising the pounding of tall metal posts into the ground by a ranch hand with a large sledge hammer. "What's he doing?"

My grandmother came to my side, her hands fidgeting. "He's building a fence," she said, softly.

"I see. Why do we need a fence around the front of the house?" I asked, watching him wiggle the stake to see if it was secure, and then pick up his tape measure and start plotting out the next pole.

She didn't answer.

"Is there something wrong?" I asked, feeling her worry.

"No!" she exclaimed. "You know men. They always have to be working on something. Can I get you some breakfast? I can make you pancakes, or eggs."

"Maybe later." I looked at the clock. It was just after eight. "Is it supposed to be warm today? Stephanie and I plan on taking the horses up to the lake again."

Grandmother took the chair beside me. "I think it will be a perfect day for that. I'm glad that you and Stephanie are friends."

I was too.

"I think it may be time for you to meet some new friends as well. Would you like that?"

I thought about it for a moment and gave her a half-hearted shrug.

"I was thinking you may want to come to church with us tomorrow. There are some very nice girls your age there, and I am sure they would love to meet you."

The thought of venturing outside the ranch was both exciting and terrifying. She had talked about taking me to church before, but had never mentioned meeting other girls my age. I had enjoyed my friendship with Stephanie so much that I had started to wonder if meeting other friends would add to my enjoyment.

She saw my hesitation. "It will be safe. It won't be like what happened at the mall. These people are kind, with sweet spirits,"

"Will Stephanie be coming, too?"

"I'm not sure. We can ask."

"I'll ask," I said, feeling as though I was helping her out. "We are supposed to meet after lunch today."

She patted my hands. I went to get dressed, but before I could reach my room Stephanie barged through the side door of the house.

"Did you see this?" she asked, looking frenzied. She thrust a newspaper at me.

Before I could uncurl it, my grandmother took it and gave Stephanie a look of rage. "There's no need for that," she scolded.

I stood agape at her show of anger. It was so out of character that I knew it was genuine.

"Why are you hiding it from her?" asked Stephanie. She tried to grab the paper, but my grandmother swung it behind her back.

"Hide what?"

Stephanie looked to me and shot my grandmother a defiant glare. "There's an article about you on the front page. They even have a picture."

I felt my heart sink. "Oh no."

"They had no right to come out here and do this." Grandmother tried to comfort me. "They were trespassing. Your grandfather has already called the sheriff about it."

"Give me the newspaper. I want to see it."

"Don't do this to yourself, darling."

"She's got to get used to this crap. You're not helping her by hiding her away," Stephanie argued.

"You don't know what's best!" Grandmother snapped back. "We're trying to protect her."

I heard the words and cringed at their meaning. It's what I had heard ever since I could remember. Papa hid me away and kept me from the world to protect me. Now the people he was protecting me from felt the need to do the same. My mind spun with the irony of it all. I heard blurred sounds of voices quarrelling, as I felt my head spin.

"Stop!" I yelled, fed up. "Give me the paper, now."

With pained eyes, Grandmother handed it over.

I unfolded it to find a large photograph of me outside near the stables. I was leading Clyde, with the reins over my shoulder. I wore a pink t-shirt and jeans and my hair was pulled back into a ponytail at the nape of my neck. On the top of the photograph in large bold lettering it read, "Callidora the Cowgirl," and then in smaller letters, "Life is still a mystery for this former kidnap victim."

I read on as the reporter detailed my past, my rescue, and how everything from that point was sealed and kept a secret. The article said that reports had been filed with the state child welfare office and that an investigation would be initiated.

I looked from the paper into my grandmother's red and weary eyes. "Are they going to try and take me away?"

Grandmother straightened her shoulders. "We worked too hard to get you back. No one is going to take you away."

I went to the window and watched my grandfather diligently building the fence around us. I knew that he was aware of the article, and felt this was not only something he deemed necessary to keep probing eyes and cameras away, but was a form of therapy to keep his anger and anxiety from tearing him apart.

As he continued to measure the fence, I felt a closeness to him that surprised me. I saw the determination in his face. He would make sure that nothing was going to get past him.

"He's building the fence because of me," I said, as I watched.

Both Stephanie and my grandmother stood quietly.

"Is it ever going to end? I don't understand why anyone cares. What have I done? Why do they think I'm some kind of freak?"

Grandmother put her arm around my shoulder. "Oh sweetie, you've done nothing. They're curious because they don't understand."

"They don't have a life," said Stephanie. "These people are pathetic. If you lived somewhere else, you wouldn't have to deal with this."

"Don't say that!" my grandmother snapped.

"It's true. If she lived in New York, or Denver, or L.A., no one would even know who she is or what happened in her past."

"I don't want to move," I said, feeling exhausted even at such an early hour. "I want to be here."

Stephanie huffed. "That's only because you don't know what's out there. You've been stuck here just like you were stuck in the jail cell you called a bedroom before they found you. Now your grandfather is out there putting up bars around this place. One of these days you're going to wake up and realize you've gone from one cage to another, and that's no way to live."

"Stephanie, I want you to leave," Grandmother said sternly.

Stephanie shrugged. "Whatever. I'll be at my house, Sophie. If you want to go riding, call me." She turned to my grandmother. "And I'll try not to corrupt her. God knows, I wouldn't want her to be happy." She let the door slam behind her.

"You're still young," said Grandmother, hugging me. "You don't need to move away. Things will calm down and people will see you for who you are. Stephanie is a very unsettled young lady. Don't let her unhappiness affect you."

"Why do you feel she's unhappy?" I asked. I saw Stephanie as fun-loving and carefree. I admired her fearless attitude and candid personality.

My grandmother hesitated as her strong Mormon upbringing kept her from talking ill of others. "Stephanie is strong willed. It's not always a bad thing, but for a girl it isn't very becoming. I believe she knows what is right and true in life, but sometimes it's harder to do the right thing. I feel that Stephanie would rather take the easy way out."

What she said didn't explain much, and I didn't have to say a word for her to see that I didn't understand.

"We have certain beliefs and values, and when Stephanie came to live with her father here on our land, she struggled to understand our way of living. Her new mom was raised in the Church and has tried to teach her what is the true path to happiness, but Stephanie is still unwilling to accept it. I think she feels if she does, she's not being loyal to her mother. What she doesn't understand is that the only way she'll be able to see her mother again is through faith."

"She told me her mother was dead."

Grandmother smiled. "She is, but we believe in the teachings of the *Book of Mormon* and that if you do the things we know are true, then you can be with the people you love for all eternity. We know the way to heaven and that is why we live our lives the way we do here on earth."

I thought about what she said and felt a welling up of joy fill my entire body. "Will I get to see my mother again?"

Grandmother's face widened to fit her smile. She was overwhelmed that I was interested in what was the basis of her entire being. "Yes. We know that we'll see her again and if you believe and do what the Church teaches, so can you."

Later that day, as Stephanie and I reached our favorite sitting place up by the lake, I told her about my plans to attend church the next day.

"Good hell!" she moaned

I laughed at her performance of feigned death. "Why do you think it's so awful?"

"Faith will suck every last ounce of common sense from you."

"What my grandmother told me sounds wonderful. She said I'll be able to see my mother again."

Stephanie rolled her eyes. "I don't think you need to be Mormon to go to heaven, if there really is such a place."

As we made our way back down the valley, the sky that had already been a hazy gray all morning turned to a sideways snowstorm. What we had been enjoying as a sunny and anticipated spring day was being halted by a late season flurry. It matched the damper on my hope that life would be again filled with joy and optimism. I felt like I was being told to keep my bliss in check.

We spurred the horses to a canter and I was thankful for the wetness on my face when we arrived. Stephanie knew I had been crying, but stayed quiet as we put the horses back in their stalls. I took a seat on a wooden stool next to the corral and watched as the snow came down in waves.

"You're strong and will get through this," Stephanie said, as she stared out at the storm.

"What do you mean?" I asked, trying to act as though nothing was wrong.

She scooted a tree stump that was being used as a doorstop and used it as a seat. She leaned forward and looked at me with the most mature and serious face I'd ever seen on her. "You've gone through hell in the last few months. Your whole world has been blown up in front of you. I can't believe how well you handle it. I'd be a mess."

I felt like a mess. I worried about Papa and wondered if I would ever see him again. I never stopped thinking about Damien and where he was now. Did he think of me, too?

"I don't have a choice."

"Yes, you do."

"I can't change what happened, or where my father is. I have to live here and make the best of it now."

"That's true, but you also have choices that will make a difference later. When you turn eighteen you're an adult, and you can do whatever you want. Don't let them talk you into becoming a Mormon who never leaves this valley. You have the choice to believe what you want, do what you want, and be what you want. Don't waste it."

I loved her and the way she made me feel. I felt like I had someone who really cared and was looking out for my well being. "It seems so far off. I wish I knew what to do. Part of me wants to go and see what's out there, but part of me just wants to stay in my room and read."

"I can understand that. It's not like you haven't been treated like a freak when you have gone out." She looked at her hands. "You must get away from here."

"Why?"

"Just promise me you will. You must learn that this isn't all there is, see that there are other people out there."

"You don't seem to like anyone here."

She shrugged. "It's not that. But there are things you don't understand and don't know that..." she stopped short. "Sometimes the people you think you can trust are the ones you should run from."

"Who are you talking about?" I was scared by what she said.

"I'm not going to say anymore. I get in trouble every time I talk. But make sure you don't let people take advantage of you. Be strong. Don't hide away here and think these are the only people who care about you, or *will* ever care about you. One of these days you've got to just go for it. Hold your head high and don't care about what people think or say." A huge smile spread across her face. "We should do that!"

"Do what?"

"Get out. We should go somewhere and just throw it all in their faces. Walk down the mall and let them stare. What could happen? If you don't start doing normal things, you'll never be normal. We'll go together."

I felt my courage sink. "I hate it when people stare."

"You'll have to get used to it, it's not going away. They stare because you're news. Most people would kill for that." Stephanie turned to me with a gleam in her eye. "It may be the only way you'll get to see Damien again."

"What do you mean by that?"

"Sophie, do you really want to go through life never seeing him again?"

My heart ached for him.

"This is no way to live. Your grandpa is fencing in the house. Your grandmother won't take you with her to the mall, or even the grocery store. You're barricaded in here even more than you were before. If you want to have a life you'll have to go out and find it yourself, because there is no way it'll come to you."

She was right. I was contented with my new surroundings. I had my chickens, my books, and my drawing pad from my old house; I had horses, a new family and Stephanie at my new home. But I was still hidden away, shut off from the rest of the world. And just like before, Damien was kept out of my life. "I want to see him, but I'm scared."

She smiled. "That's because he means something to you."

"What if he doesn't want to see me, and he hates me for what happened?"

"Then he isn't worth your time. It's a risk, Soph, but that's life. You have to take risks or you'll never know."

I imagined Damien's face going from a smile to an angry scowl and then seeing him walk away.

"If you think something bad is going to happen to him, stop it. Bad things happen all the time. That's life and it's scary, but you'll never know unless you take the risk. It's like the first time you took the horse across the lake. Remember how amazing you felt when you made it across? What if you had never taken that risk? It's worth it."

"How will I find him?"

"I bet he still lives around American Falls. I'll start looking around. What's his last name?"

I had no idea.

"Don't worry. Damien isn't a common name. I'm sure people know where he is. There's Facebook and YouTube, MySpace and Twitter...believe me, we'll find him." Stephanie walked over to the open corral door and watched the snow. "Tell me if you want me to help find him, otherwise I'll stay out of it."

I didn't believe she would ever stay out of it. But I wanted to know where my life was going. If it wasn't with Damien, I needed to adjust to that sorrow and move on. I felt a new spurt of energy and suddenly wished I could face him at that very moment. "I want to find him."

She gave me a satisfied smile. I walked to her and stood staring silently out at the snow. From inside the dry shelter of the corral, the storm seemed to gain in strength.

"It's a good thing we came back when we did," she said. "It would have been hell to get caught in that."

I motioned to my drenched jeans and jacket.

She mussed my hair. "It could've been worse. It can always be worse."

Chapter 17

Pocatello, Idaho, Early Fall, 1991

After being cast out of the Malad Valley, being branded an arsonist—and possibly his father's killer—Luke Theotokis felt lost and even more of an outsider. Even though he knew Vee was aware of his innocence, he wondered what good it would do him now. Her father would never allow him near her, and now they were almost a hundred miles apart. His plans of marrying her come summertime had turned to a pipedream, and what made it worse was having no idea how she felt.

Theta and Luke were taken in by Talia's family, which was unbelievably awkward for Luke. He knew what plans his mother and Agnes had for the two of them, and seeing the women whisper together and coo over each of them, made him miss his old life even more. Their house was a split-level, with beige siding and a large backyard. It was in a nice neighborhood that was near the city golf course.

For their first few months in Pocatello, Luke tried to avoid Talia, but living under the same roof made it impossible. He and Talia saw each other with morning faces at the breakfast table, bumped shoulders passing in the hallway, and were embarrassed as they were coming out of the bathroom. The house wasn't small, but when trying to avoid someone, it felt like a shoebox.

Theta was in good health and good spirits. She had kept up her medications and they were working. The day Theta told Luke she had found a job cleaning the house of a wealthy family on the outskirts of town was joyous, especially when he learned they were moving to a tiny single-wide trailer near the estate. It was old and rundown, but he could use the bathroom without worry and wouldn't have to be fully dressed before leaving his room. Even though the trailer was south of the city, in a small town called Inkom, Luke attended the same school.

Talia became a familiar and warm face in a crowd of strangers, and he secretly was glad that he had been forced into her life. When he and Talia saw each other in the halls in between classes, Luke smiled and offered her a ride home. She always accepted and they found themselves talking the entire way, and usually continuing their conversations while sitting in her driveway.

Luke joked that they talked more now than when they were living in the same house. Talia had become his closest friend. He enjoyed her wit and was impressed at her determination to get good grades. It seemed to spur him on, where before he had little interest. Talia was pretty and her big brown eyes were always warm and inviting, but his feelings for the blue-eyed beauty he had left behind was still the only romantic interest he had. She was still in the forefront of his mind and had lost none of the intensity in his heart.

Luke could tell that Talia longed for more than mere friendship, and he didn't want to give her reason to believe there was more. He never held her gaze or touched her, but his presence and eagerness for friendship was enough to give her the wrong idea.

One night as they sat in his truck in the school parking lot after a career fair, she reached over and took his hand. He pulled it back and she looked at him with shocked disappointment.

"I'm sorry," he said. "It's just..."

She looked away, rejected and hurt.

"I don't want to hurt you. You're my best friend."

Talia looked back at him, surprised.

"I don't want to lose that. Do you understand?"

She nodded. "But we won't. It will be better because we're friends."

Luke shook his head. "No. It always ends up where one person gets hurt and then they both hate each other. I don't want that."

"So what do we do? Just be friends?"

"You say that like it's a bad thing. It's the best thing. How many girls do you know who have a guy for their best friend? It's like having a big brother who actually likes being around you."

Talia looked at him with appreciative and understanding eyes.

Luke saw her mind working. "See, it will be really great."

Talia nodded. "I just wish you weren't so cute. I'll be jealous when you like someone else."

Luke grinned. "And I'll be jealous when you do. But the difference is when you break up with him, I'll still be here. I'm not going anywhere and I'll tell you if he's a jerk."

"And I can tell you if I don't like your girlfriend?"

"Yep. And when she dumps me, you'll be the one I call."

"Promise?"

"I swear on my father's grave."

"Luke!" Talia said, horrified. "You shouldn't say stuff like that." She looked around as though lightning would strike.

Luke laughed. "And you'll have to put up with me being a pagan."

Talia shook her head. "You are not a pagan."

"Yes, I am."

"Luke, a pagan doesn't believe in God."

Luke looked at her and lifted his shoulders.

"You don't believe in God. Why?"

"I think it's all folktales and myths."

"Then what do you believe?"

"I believe we're all born, we live our life, and then we die. No heaven, no hell, no God."

She was aghast. "But what about love and nature and...miracles? Do you really think things just happen?"

"Yes."

"I think it's sad. Knowing there is a god who loves me and watches over me is what helps me through the tough times. I know that there are things that He's helped me with. I can't imagine a life without believing in God."

"I think it's a crutch. People need religion because they need something to blame terrible things on, or give credit for the good. It's used to make people feel guilty so they'll do what's right. "

"Do you think I'm stupid for believing?" she asked, with a lift of a dark eyebrow.

"No. Do you think I am, for not?" he answered, giving her the same quizzical expression.

She laughed. "So, I guess my plan to invite you to church this Sunday is a bad idea."

He laughed, too. "I wouldn't want to risk an earthquake or lightning strike."

"Really? I thought you didn't believe in that stuff."

"I don't. So I don't want to risk being proven wrong."

"You're crazy," she said, giving him an affectionate push on the shoulder.

"Yep, and I'm your best friend, so what does that say about you?"

The two sat and stared at the school as other students, some alone and some with their parents, came through the doors and found their cars in the parking lot.

"Do you see anything in there that you'd want to do?" Talia asked, referring to the dozens of different booths and displays with pamphlets and smiling faces of all the possible careers they could choose.

"Not really," he said, disappointed. "I've always thought I would work for the railroad, but it wasn't really my choice. It was my father's."

"What do you want to do?"

He sat, contemplating her question. "I don't know. The only thing I've ever dreamed about is how I'd get out of here. I guess that's why I didn't have a problem with the railroad, because at least it would get me away from here once in a while."

"Why do you want to leave so badly?"

He thought a moment. "It's mainly the people around here. Everyone is Mormon and if you're not, they treat you like you're different. Don't you feel that way?"

Talia tipped her head to the side in a slight show of agreement.

"It's not as bad here in Pocatello, but down in Malad it was tough. I was the only kid in school that wasn't Mormon."

She gave him a skeptical smirk.

"No, really," he said. "Everyone *was* down there. There are things I love about this place—the mountains, going fishing, even the snow—but I don't want to live around such religious people, and I certainly don't want to raise my kids here."

"Kids?" asked Talia, humored.

"Well, someday I'm going to have them and I don't want to be stuck here when I do."

They drove back to Talia's house, and in the driveway they embraced.

"Are you sure you're okay with what I said tonight about being friends?" he asked.

"Yes."

When Talia left the car she smiled back at him and waved before going inside. She had lied when she agreed they would just be friends. She loved him, and the only reason she didn't tell him was she didn't want to push him away. In her heart she felt that in time their love would grow.

She was aware of his love for this girl in Malad. Talia never talked to Luke about her, or let on that she knew, in the hopes it would eventually fade and die. There were phone calls that came to her house during his stay there. Talia knew it was her, but lied and said he was gone or that he was out with friends. The final call came after Luke and Theta had moved out. By then Talia had her own plans for Luke and wasn't about to let a girl from his past get in her way.

"What is your name? Can I take a message?"

"My name is Vee," said the soft voice on the line. "I need to talk to Luke about something very important."

"Can I tell him what it's about?"

"It's personal."

Talia felt the spark of jealousy grow inside her soul. "Luke no longer lives here. He got married and moved to another part of town."

At first there was only silence on the line, but then a trembling voice asked, "Married?"

"Yep, married," Talia said firmly.

"To who?" Vee asked, her voice still quivering.

"His girlfriend, Talia. They've been together for months."

Again, silence on the other end.

"So what was it you wanted me to tell him?" Talia asked, confident her charade had worked.

Vee's voice barely registered in the receiver. "Nothing. Never mind."

When Talia hung up she knew what she did was wrong, but also knew Luke would never be free of his misguided feelings if she hadn't stepped in. In Talia's mind she had done him a favor. He'd be much happier with someone who was like him, who understood his culture and who believed as he did. She was his perfect match and it wouldn't take long for him to realize it.

This was reinforced when Luke asked Talia to the Christmas cotillion. Both Theta and Agnes jumped into the planning stages of tuxedos and dresses, as if they were arranging a wedding.

When the night of the big event arrived, Theta put her hand to her mouth when Luke entered the kitchen where she was busy washing dishes.

"You look so handsome. Talia is a lucky girl," she said, almost in tears.

"Mama, we're just two friends having fun. Don't get all weepy on me."

"She is the one for you," she said.

Luke sighed. "I'm leaving now. I'll be home late. We have a party at a friend's house afterward."

"Be careful, and tell Talia I wish I could see her in her beautiful dress."

When Luke arrived at Talia's house, he straightened his hair in the rearview mirror and popped a piece of gum into his mouth. He smiled, reminding himself that this was Talia, but he still wanted to make a good impression.

"Oh my!" said Agnes as she let him in the front door. "You look so handsome."

"You sound like my mother," chided Luke.

"Someday, I hope!" she said back.

Luke stood in the living room with corsage in hand and waited. Slowly, with measured and careful footsteps, Talia appeared. In a winter white satin gown, she was glistening like an angel's wings, as she came down the stairs. Her dark hair was piled in loose curls, and her skin was radiant against her sleeveless, form-fitting dress.

"Wow, you look amazing," said Luke. He handed her the corsage of white roses and silver glittered leaves; she slipped it on her wrist.

Agnes made them stand together so she could take pictures. Finally Talia said, "Enough." And they left the house and headed for the school.

"Do you think they'll ever give up?" asked Luke.

Talia gave him a questioning look. "What do you mean?"

"Do you think our mothers will ever accept the fact that we're just friends?"

Chapter 18

Malad, Idaho, Spring, 2009

I parted my hair on the side and slid a comb through the tumble of long brown curls. I turned to the mirror and wondered what they would see and how I should react. I practiced my smile and spent more time than usual studying the face staring back.

I slipped on a long floral print skirt and light blue blouse. My grandmother had guessed on the size, and it fit perfectly. My shoes were shiny, with a thin strap and buckle on the side. I had never worn clothes like this, and I considered going to church more often if I was able to dress up each time.

As we drove off toward church, I looked down the lane and wished that Stephanie was coming. I wanted her there to help me cope with the unknowns I'd soon be facing.

I looked out the window at grass covered hills, wishing the drive would be long enough for me to muster some confidence. Grandfather slowly pulled into a large parking lot that encircled a huge white brick building with one tall spire on top.

"Okay, we're here," Grandmother said nervously. "Everything is going to be just fine. You'll see."

Dozens of people clad in suits and dresses held leather bound books and small children, as they made their way into the church.

"Come along, dear," Grandmother chirped, putting a hand on my back and leading me up to the building.

Several people smiled and waved, many did double-takes and gave approving head nods. I felt as if I were on display, but I was prepared for it, knowing too well what to expect.

The chapel was a long, large room with pews and two aisles. The front had a stage-like pulpit with a modest pipe organ on one side, and a white-cloaked altar on the other. Women chatted and tried to control their children, who climbed on and around all the pews.

Grandmother led the way, offering raised eyebrows and head nods in response to the numerous stares. Grandfather stayed behind as though making sure their gawking was kept to a minimum.

The meeting started with one of the men in the rows behind the pulpit standing and welcoming the congregation. Then everyone sang a song from a hymnal. As they all sang, it gave me a chance to look around at the faces.

There was a group of boys my age near the covered altar. I also saw a girl that looked to be my age. She had light hair and eyes, and looked taller than me. She glanced over and caught me staring, but I turned away quickly before I could gauge her response. When I looked back she was still staring, with a face that looked both uneasy and curious. I should have smiled, but I was surprised, and instead turned away. I wondered what she thought of me.

When the hymn ended, people from the congregation stood and walked to the podium. Others took to the pulpit with messages and stories that all talked about the truth of the Church and their feelings of being blessed simply by being a part of it. As I sat and listened I felt more at ease, and began to enjoy being around other people. The stares started to subside and I even garnered several genuine smiles.

Then my grandmother stood up. I almost stood up with her, but she put a hand on my shoulder. "I've never felt the spirit more than I do right now," she said, scooting by me.

In her simple wool suit, with her hair curled tightly and her sensible shoes barely visible under the hem, she pulled nervously at her jacket. She made her way to the podium and quietly cleared her throat before looking out over the audience.

"This isn't something I do often, but it doesn't mean my testimony isn't strong. Today, the spirit spoke and I couldn't sit there any longer without sharing my blessings with you."

I peeked up, hoping that she wasn't going to single me out.

"As you're aware, our prayers have been answered. For years we were heartbroken with the loss of our daughter and then our granddaughter…"

I felt my heart pulsate in my throat, horrified that I would be set out on display for all these strangers to scrutinize.

"I must admit there were times when I questioned God. I felt like I was losing my faith, but I pushed doubts aside and prayed. The Lord answered our prayers and brought her home."

As she continued to speak, I thought about what she said. My grandmother felt her prayers to God were what brought me to them. What about the prayers Papa had said, asking to keep us safe and hidden?

When she finished, she walked back to the pew and heaved a relieved sigh as she sat back down beside me. "You have blessed my life," she said in a whisper.

The meeting finished, and before I realized what was happening, the girl who had stared at me was ushered over and introduced. Her name was Linda and she was sixteen.

"Where do you go to school?" she finally asked, breaking the silence.

"I go to school at my cousin's house. My Uncle Lonny teaches us."

I was handed off to Linda to take me to the next meeting. I looked back at my grandparents as she led me away. We entered a small room with folding metal chairs and walls of plastic accordion dividers. Three other girls were already sitting in a huddle talking. They stopped when they saw us and looked to Linda for direction. Linda took a seat and pointed at a chair. "This is Callidora," she said.

I gasped as the girls stared. I shook my head and, as politely as possible, corrected her. "No. I'm Sophie."

She flipped around. "*Sophie?* I thought you were that girl who was kidnapped by her father and then found all caged up in Arbon Valley. That's what my mother said."

I wanted to run from the room. My face went hot with embarrassment and fear. "My name is Sophie and my father didn't kidnap me."

"But you are the one they've been talking about, right?"

The other girls started whispering, and Linda turned to them in anger. "Stop talking like that." She turned back to me. "I didn't mean to embarrass you. It's just what I heard. Are you okay?"

I didn't know what she meant. Okay with life, okay at that moment. I sat thinking, would I ever be okay? I nodded.

"No wonder you don't go to school. I wouldn't want to if I had everyone talking about me like that. You're pretty brave to even come to church." She smiled, and I could see that it was kind and sympathetic.

I sat up and tried to smile back.

"I like your shoes," one of the other girls with long straight hair said. The other two nodded as a show of friendship.

"Thank you," I said. "My grandmother bought them."

The girl with the long hair smiled knowingly. "Yes, you're lucky. Your grandparents probably buy you all kinds of things."

Linda scoffed. "Not everyone cares about how much money people have, Marcy."

"I know that. But it's not like everyone doesn't know they're rich. I'd rather have money than be poor," she quipped back.

An older woman with dark glasses and lots of dark brown hair shuffled into the room. "Good morning, ladies," she called out. Then she looked at me. "You must be Sophie."

I was so relieved she knew my correct name. She introduced herself as Sister Beeson and quickly started a discussion about modesty and dressing with respect.

After the lesson was over, Linda turned to me. "Let's go to the restroom real quick, okay?"

Inside, she took my arm and looked around to make sure we were alone. "I'm sorry if I made you feel bad before. I really didn't mean to."

I liked her. I felt her honesty and was warmed by her genuine concern.

"I have to kind of warn you about our next class."

I felt my heart sink, and it must have showed on my face.

"Don't worry. It isn't a bad thing. I just want to warn you that the boys in this class will be annoying."

"Boys?" I asked.

"Yes. Most of them are dorks, and they'll be totally gawking at you because you're beautiful. Just ignore them and stay with me, okay?"

I nodded and followed her from the restroom to our next class. Before we could take a seat, I heard a group of boys talking loudly as they entered the room. When they saw me they stopped their discussion, and the tallest of the group flashed me an interested smile. He turned to Linda. "Who's your friend?"

One of the other boys gave him a shove. "Didn't you listen during testimony meeting? This is…" then he whispered loudly. "…that Callidora girl."

The tall boy stood up straight and studied me even more. His name was Eric; he was handsome, with light hair and blue eyes. His shoulders were broad and he carried himself with confidence. "That makes sense," he said.

I turned away, uncomfortable with his gaze and angered that they didn't respect my correct name.

"Her name is Sophie," Linda piped up. "Come on," she ordered and led me to a seat. "I told you they were dorks."

Chapter 19

Pocatello, Idaho, Early Winter, 1992

Elise Richardson had reluctantly agreed to drive Vee to Pocatello. The only reason she said yes, was because of her wicked desire to see Luke's face when Vee confronted him with the news. She hadn't gotten over his rejection of her and was already reveling in the fact that he had also dumped her little sister. The vision of him standing there with his little 'wifey' as Vee revealed she was carrying his baby was just too juicy to miss.

As they drove, Elise tried to hide her smile, and acted as though she was concerned and appalled by her little sister's predicament.

"I don't know why he even needs to know," Elise said. "He doesn't deserve to know. After what he did, I don't know why you'd even want your baby to know he's the father. And staring out the window won't bring us there any faster, so talk to me."

Vee sat in the passenger seat and stared out over the vast empty fields. Some were charred after the post harvest burns. "Focusing into the distance helps the sickly stirring in my gut." Her shoulders were tight. "I'm exhausted from being up at night worrying and wondering what I should do. He needs to know because he's the father. I know what you think of him, but I know he didn't start that fire."

"Well, who else could have?" Elise asked.

Vee shrugged. "It doesn't matter now. Besides, even if he had started it, he's paid a terrible price."

"You act like you still love him," Elise sneered.

"Why wouldn't I?"

Elise let out a disgusted grunt. "How can you say that? He gets you pregnant and then leaves, and is already married to someone else. I wouldn't be surprised if he was two-timing you with the other girl months before."

Vee sighed sadly. She knew what her sister said could be true, and it hurt. The thought of Luke with someone else was the worst pain she ever endured, and now that she was alone and pregnant she felt helpless and defeated.

Her attempts to call him on the phone were discouraging, but there was something in the voice on the other end that gave her reason to doubt Luke had really forgotten her. There was still a tiny spark of hope that smoldered intently and gave her reason to make the trip North and find out for herself.

As they rounded the bend into the Portneuf Gap Vee's heart jumped, knowing they would soon be there.

"So what are you going to say when you see him?" Elise said. "What if his wife is standing right there? I'd just slap him and tell him what an ass he is and then walk off. His wife will probably kick him out." She giggled.

Vee tried to tune her out. She had gone over her meeting with Luke a dozen times in her head. She had practiced what to say and how to react, whether he accepted or rejected her. She prayed that his face would turn from surprise in seeing her to joy after discovering what she carried, but she knew even with this ideal situation his being married would surely cause pain for everyone. She had done more planning for the opposite reaction.

Elise interrupted her thoughts. "Dad should have had him thrown in jail when he had the chance."

"Please stop it!" Vee piped up, having enough. "He's still my baby's father. I don't want you talking bad about him when this baby comes. I don't care what he did or what happens today. This baby is not going to think he's a terrible person."

"You better have the same rule with Dad then. You've heard what he has to say about him."

Vee sat up straight. "I'll move out."

"What?" Elise asked with a laugh.

"I will. I won't raise this baby around people who are going to make her feel like she's some type of cancer."

"Where will you go? You don't have a job and you're only seventeen. You can't even take care of yourself."

Vee started to cry. "I don't care. I'll be poor and live in a box before I'll have you making this baby feel like she's a monster. It's not her fault. She's innocent. She is a tiny little baby and I love her already. I won't let anyone hurt her or make her feel like she's unwanted."

Elise raised her eyebrows and stayed silent. For the remainder of the drive, the two sisters looked out opposite windows.

The city of Pocatello spread out through the narrow valley. The snow-covered peaks of Scout Mountain towered in the west, and houses lined the hills in the east. The sun was just setting and an incredible pink and orange sunset glowed on the horizon.

Vee took a long deep breath. She shut her sister out and thought back at the lazy, carefree days she and Luke had spent together on the ranch. She wondered how her life could have changed so drastically in just six months. Was he really over her? Unless he was a completely different person than the one she knew and loved, it couldn't be possible. She put a hand on her bulging stomach and rubbed it slowly and softly.

Vee counted out numbers on the houses as they drove slowly up Highland Drive. "Twenty-one fifty... That's it," she said, pointing to the redbrick home of Talia and her family.

Elise pulled the car into the drive. "Are you sure you want to do this?"

"Yes," said Vee, confident. She pulled a small envelope from her purse and opened the door before she lost her courage.

"What's that?" asked Elise.

"Just a letter, in case he isn't here, or I lose my nerve."

"Why didn't you just mail it?"

"I did. I've mailed several and still...nothing. I'm not sure he even got them."

Vee heaved her swollen and awkward shape out of the car. Elise opened the driver's side door and started to follow.

"No," Vee ordered. "I want to do this on my own."

"I don't think you should."

"I don't care." Vee struggled up the steps of the porch and pushed the doorbell. It gave two distinct tones. Then she heard footsteps. Her heart pounded and she felt her stomach turn with each throb. The door opened and there stood a stocky, older man with dark skin and hair and a thick mustache.

Yes?" he asked, taking a quick glance from Vee's pretty face to her obvious protruding belly.

"I'm looking for Luke Theotokis."

"Oh," he said, and then smiled. "He is not here. He doesn't live here anymore. They moved." His strong Greek accent reminded Vee of Luke's father.

Inside Vee cringed at the word, *they*. "Do you know how I can find him?"

"Yes, they live south from here, in Inkom. You take Tudor Road past the old Sinclair station..." then he noticed Vee's furrowed brow. "Do you know where that is?"

She shook her head. "No. I'm not from here."

"Oh!" he exclaimed loudly. "Here, come in and I'll draw you a map." He led her into the living room.

She turned back, giving Elise a quick look before following him. Inside, there was a large red sofa and ornate tables, with thick shag carpet and the smell of dinner cooking.

"Stay here and I'll go get a paper and pen."

He left the room and Vee stood still, feeling a bit relieved that she wouldn't be facing Luke just yet. She heard Philip in the kitchen, rustling through drawers. She studied the living room; it was filled with trinkets and books. A large cross hung on the wall and Vee felt uncomfortable seeing the ceramic Jesus attached to it with pained face and bloody palms and feet. Vee wondered why anyone would want that image in their living room.

She looked away and saw photographs in dark wooden frames sitting on one of the tables. Vee decided to risk being snoopy and walked toward it. In the center of the cluster was a large photograph of Luke and a pretty dark haired girl. He was stunning in a black tux and she was gorgeous in a long white satin gown. They both had wide smiles and their eyes danced with happiness.

Vee's knees buckled and she almost fell to the ground. It was obviously their wedding photo, and she was too late. Her heart broke. Tears filled her eyes, and she felt like she was going to faint. She heard the old man coming back from the kitchen. She gathered her strength and made her escape.

As she burst through the screen door and down the steps of the porch, she heard the man call to her. She couldn't speak, and instead just shook her head and held her hand up to stop him. Vee sunk into the seat of the car, and cried, "Drive away, quick!"

"What happened?" Elise asked, as the man stood at the top of the stairs looking perplexed.

"Just drive!"

Elise did as she was told. As she pulled the car away, she passed a car with a woman inside who looked horrifyingly familiar. The woman stared back with eyes that were large and stunned. It was Luke's mother. As their cars slid by each other, it was if they were in slow motion. Elise and Theta's eyes met and both had faces of fear. Elise looked over to see if Vee had seen her, too, but was relieved to see her sister with face in hands, crying and unaware of what Elise had witnessed.

"What happened in there?" she demanded.

"Leave me alone." Vee wept, clutching the letter in her hands.

"No. Tell me."

Vee's sobs grew louder. She pulled tissues from her purse and wiped tears from her eyes and nose. "He's married. I saw the picture of them. It's too late now."

"So, you're not going to tell him...ever?"

"What good would it do? He's married and happy. I would just mess up his whole life."

"Well, he messed up yours."

"I want to go home. Please just drive and get me out of here."

Elise nodded and then sat in thought. She sighed, and turned to her sister. "What if that man tells him you were there and he tries to call you?"

"I told you it doesn't matter. He has probably read all my letters and doesn't care. I should never have come here." The baby rolled in her stomach and Vee put her hand to it, trying to adjust the seat.

"I hadn't realized until now that I had counted on Luke to embrace me and my pregnancy. I believed that once he knew about it, he'd throw caution to the wind and sweep me and my problems away. Now all of my hopes are gone and I know the baby I'm carrying is a mistake.

"I'll have to live with our parents and endure disappointed glances from Dad and condescending lectures from Mom. My beautiful dream of a family with Luke is over." She wept uncontrollably the entire way back to Malad Valley.

When Theta made the turn onto Highland Drive she noticed a young woman coming out of Philip and Agnes's house, but it wasn't until she was much closer that she recognized the car and the girls in it. Theta stopped and watched for a moment, stunned at who it was and piecing together what the bulging belly of the girl Luke once loved could mean.

The car backed out of the driveway quickly and started towards her. She pressed on the gas and slowly continued up the hill. As they passed, Theta saw it was, in fact, the Richardson girls and knew they had come with a purpose. Her heart sank, knowing her plans for Luke were in jeopardy, and wondered what Philip had been told.

Pulling the truck into the drive, Theta tried to concoct a lie to counter what might have been said. As soon as she knocked on the door, Philip answered with a look of confusion and concern. He told her about the pregnant girl who was looking for Luke.

Theta shook her head as he spoke, offering him a look of calm befuddlement.

"Why would she be looking for Luke? And why did she storm out of here?" he asked her. "Did Luke have a girlfriend before he came here?"

"No," Theta insisted. "Never. He has always been true to Talia. There were no others."

Philip looked at her skeptically. "What about the letters that were sent here? You took them. Were they from her?"

"No," Theta answered, worried that he had noticed her concern and stealth in hiding them from Luke. Then she lowered her head and relented. "Yes, but the baby isn't his."

Philip ran his fingers through his hair. He looked like he didn't believe her and saw clearly what was happening. "My Talia is in love with Luke."

"Yes," Theta said robustly. "Luke loves Talia, too."

Philip paused and paced a moment. He heard a noise outside and went to the window. "They are here," he announced sternly, as though needing to control the tone in the room.

Theta looked anxious.

"I'll not have Talia hurt," he said.

"No, no." Theta was begging him to keep their secret safe.

"I don't ever want to hear or talk about this again. Don't tell anyone. Not Luke, not Agnes. Do you hear?"

Theta nodded and tried to smile as Luke and Talia bounded into the house. Luke gave Talia a friendly push on the arm to signal he'd see her tomorrow and went to the door. Theta gave Philip an appreciative glance and followed behind him.

Molly Richardson was wiping her hands on a dish towel when Elise and Vee arrived home. Vee looked relieved that her father's truck was not in the drive. He had already made his intentions known concerning Luke, and made it clear he should have nothing to do with either Vee or the baby.

"Where've you been?" she asked with a hint of concern.

Vee turned away and started to cry again.

Molly ran to her and took her hands in hers. "What is it?"

Elise shook her head and blurted, "We went to tell Luke about the baby."

"You *what*?" asked Molly, horrified.

"He has a right to know!" said Vee.

Elise butted in, "When we went to the house, Vee learned that Luke is married."

"He told you that?" asked Molly, surprised.

"No," continued Elise, as Vee just continued to cry. "She saw a wedding photo. We didn't see him...or anyone," she emphasized.

Molly hugged Vee and tried to stop her sobs by rubbing her back. She took her to the bathroom and told her to wipe her eyes and blow her nose. Elise gave her mother a disgusted look and left the room.

When Vee came back out, she sat on the sofa looking helpless and sad. Molly sat on the couch with her and held her silently, tormented at the secret she possessed. She put her hand down and felt the square, thick envelope in her apron pocket. Luke had sent several letters since he'd been sent away. They had been intercepted by Mr. Richardson, since he was the one who stopped at the mailbox each evening when he came home from work.

When Vee had not responded to Luke's notes, he must have known what most likely was happening and had decided to address a note to the one member of the house that might have some compassion, or at least a conscience. His letter to Vee was placed into a larger envelope addressed to Molly in smooth, flowing, feminine cursive. It was his last attempt to reach Vee, and he only hoped that Molly would pass his note on.

Vee sniffed and tried to stop her tears, but it seemed fruitless.

"You can't tell your father you went up there. He'll be furious."

Vee sighed. "I don't care anymore. Nothing matters."

Molly hugged Vee tightly. "That baby matters and you've got to stay positive for it. All this crying isn't good for you, or your baby."

"But everything I hoped for is gone. Mom, I thought he loved me. I know how you and Daddy feel about him, but I love him and now I've lost him. I don't know what I'm going to do." She put her hands to her face and started to cry again.

"It's not over," said Molly softly.

Vee's breathing was choked, but she managed to ask, "What?"

Molly knew she had to tell her daughter the truth, but also knew it could ruin both their lives. She bit her lip and sat silently, wondering how to start.

Vee turned to her. "Mom, what is it?"

Molly pulled the letter from her pocket and handed it to her. "I should have given this to you weeks ago. I am so sorry."

Vee looked at the letter addressed to her mother, and then stared at Molly with questioning eyes.

"It's from Luke. He wrote others, but your father destroyed them. This one got by him because he sent it to me."

Vee still held the letter she had intended to give to Luke. With both letters in her hand, she sat terrified of what she would find inside.

"He still loves you," Molly said, with anguish.

Vee gasped at the words.

Molly lowered her head, feeling ashamed. "If it's too late then it is my fault, and I'm so sorry, dear. We were only doing what we felt was best for you."

Vee unfolded the pages of the letter and started to read.

That night, Theta waited for Luke to go to sleep. After making sure his door was closed, she carefully removed the letters sent to Luke from Vee from the bottom drawer of her dresser. She sat by the small wood burning stove in their kitchen and rocked back and forth in a weary trance. She spoke in soft chanting whispers as she burned each letter, watching the sides turn black and curl until it disappeared into the flames.

Her knowledge of the girl carrying her son's child was more than a problem that would ruin her plans for his betrothal. It was the beginning of what she had started the day they left the ranch, and she had allowed her vile and wounded emotions to unleash a destructive hex.

Theta was unaware at the time that the curse she had placed on that family would end up haunting her own. As she sat and watched the evidence of her betrayal turn to ash, she begged her god to give her strength to live with the knowledge that she had condemned her own flesh and blood.

Chapter 20

Malad, Idaho, 2009

"So how was the big day at church?" Stephanie asked, as we sat across from each other doing a geography assignment. She had her hair parted to the side and wore blue eye shadow. I wondered if she'd let me wear some, too.

"It was okay," I answered, not wanting to say much more. I was used to seeing her gloat when what she told me came true.

Stephanie smiled. "So when is the big baptism?"

"Stephanie!" Uncle Lonny scolded from across the room.

Stephanie giggled and continued to write. After several minutes, Uncle Lonny came over and checked our work.

"Not bad," he said, giving me a smile and putting his hand on my shoulder. He handed back the paper. "Keep going. You can start on the next chapter if you'd like." He turned to his daughter. "Finish up so we can get you back to school."

When they left, I snuggled down into a beanbag chair in the corner of the room and picked up where I'd left off in, *To Kill a Mockingbird*. I was just about to turn the page when I heard a knock at the door.

My old ingrained habits of wanting to hide when someone knocked had started to subside, but the instinct was still strong. I peered out of the large living room window and noticed it was Eric, one of the boys at church the day before. Before I could step out of view, he saw me and waved. I awkwardly waved back and decided I should open up and see what he wanted.

"Hi," he said. He looked down at the ground and then tried to make eye contact but failed.

"What do you need?" I asked, wondering why he was there and not at school.

He looked up surprised. "I wanted to talk to you."

"To me?"

"Yes."

"What about?"

He shuffled and seemed uneasy. "What are you doing?"

"I was reading." I stood, holding the door open and watching him fidget. "How did you know I was here?"

"Your grandmother said you were up here. I came through the gate when your uncle was leaving with Stephanie. I didn't know you went to school here, but your grandmother told me how to find you."

I cringed with the thought that everyone knew Eric was up here. I groaned, realizing Stephanie knew. Her questions would be unending.

"So are you going with anyone?" he asked, still looking at the ground.

"Going where?"

He looked up with a smile and for a moment I saw an attractive young man with bright eyes. "What I meant is…are you dating anyone?"

Dating? The thought of being courted was one I dreamed of often, but never discussed with anyone. There were so many nights that I lay awake imagining Damien picking me up in a car and taking me out on a date.

He stood silent for a moment. "Sophie?" he asked.

"Yes," I answered.

"Is that, 'yes, you're dating someone?'"

"No."

"No?" he asked, encouraged.

I felt like running away.

"Can I come in?"

I knew the consequences I had faced by giving Damien access to our home, and I had been willing to risk everything for him. I closed the door, leaving just enough space for me to stand in. "I can't."

"Why not?"

"I'm not supposed to. There's no one here but me."

He smiled. "Then I'll come back later. I'll stop by tonight at your grandparent's house."

"Why?"

"Because I want to talk to you more. I don't bite," he said, with a smile. "Come on. I want to be friends. I'll come to your grandparent's house tonight around seven. We'll just talk, and then you'll see that I'm okay."

I didn't understand what he meant or why he was so persistent but I nodded, hoping he would leave before Uncle Lonny returned.

"So, I'll see you tonight?" he asked, walking back toward his car.

When Uncle Lonny returned he smiled knowingly as he entered the room. I gave him an uninterested look as I glanced up from my book, and then continued reading.

"What did Eric have to say?" he said.

I shrugged. "Nothing. Why did you let him through the gate?"

He walked over and pulled a chair in front of the beanbag. "I thought you two had become friends. He said you met yesterday at church."

I bit my lip.

"What happened?"

I started to tell him and then guarded my words. "He wanted to talk and I told him I was reading."

"You don't like Eric?"

"I don't even know him. He asked about dating," I cringed as soon as the word came out.

"Dating?" Uncle Lonny asked with a lifted eyebrow. "That's a big step. I bet that made you feel uncomfortable."

I nodded. "It did. I tried to get him to leave but he wouldn't until I agreed to let him come to the house tonight. I wish he wouldn't."

Uncle Lonny took a deep breath. "Dating is a normal part of life, Sophie, especially for someone your age. Most of the girls around here aren't allowed to date until they're sixteen; you're seventeen…and so pretty."

I winced.

He laughed softly. "It's not a curse, Sophie."

"What did you say?" I asked, dismayed at what Stephanie may have told him about my plight in life.

"Being pretty is not a bad thing. It's a blessing. Someday you'll see."

I hoped Stephanie hadn't broken our confidence.

"Don't you want to go on a date someday?"

I lifted my shoulders. I wasn't about to tell him about my dreams of Damien. "Someday," I mumbled.

"It's completely normal. It's how you meet people and fall in love."

I sat up with interest.

He noticed. "Someday you'll fall in love—maybe get married and have kids."

"I'm already in love."

Uncle Lonny's eyes grew big and he leaned back in surprise. "Really?"

I didn't want to say anymore, so I just nodded.

"Why do you think that?" he asked.

"I know."

He smiled and relented, seeing that I was not interested in talking about it. "I have a surprise for you. I got the information about how we can request a visit with your father."

I dropped the book. "When?"

Uncle Lonny put his hand up to temper my excitement. "It may take a while, but at least we can start the process. I have the papers in my bedroom. It's important that we don't let anyone know, or your grandfather may try to stop it."

My excitement turned sour. "Why would he do that?"

"He's just worried about you. Going to the prison is not something for a young girl. A lot of awful people are there and he wouldn't want you around all that."

I thought about what he said, and realized it made sense.

"Do you want to see the papers?"

I jumped up. "Yes!"

"We have to make sure that no one knows about this, remember?" he said, walking me to the back of the house. He led me into a large room with a queen-sized bed covered by a muted floral bedspread. Uncle Lonny sat on the bed and motioned for me to do the same. I looked around before I took a seat. "Where is it?" I asked.

"Patience, my dear," he said. "I want to talk to you first."

"Okay," I agreed, wondering what rules I must follow before he continued to help in my quest.

"You've done a good job in your studies and I'm proud of you. You're very special to me. We've been together almost every day for the last six months and I feel we can talk about anything. We trust each other, don't we?" He took my hand.

I was confused and worried that I may have done something wrong. I nodded, trying to convince him that I was trustworthy and deserved his help.

"Sometimes when people spend a lot of time together they become more than just friends."

I kept listening and wondering when he was going to show me the papers. I wanted to fill them out quickly and do what was needed to visit Papa. Then, before he spoke again, I heard the click of the front door of the house. I turned toward it.

"What is it?" he asked.

"I think I heard something."

"Crap," he mumbled, jumping up. "Quickly, go to the classroom." He pushed me towards the bedroom door.

I hesitated, wondering.why he was frantic.

"Sophie, classroom," Uncle Lonny ordered.

I did as he said. Then I heard more noise in the kitchen. I turned to see Aunt Elise standing with two brown bags in her hand, packed with groceries. She threw her car keys on the counter and set the bags down, as Uncle Lonny tried to help her.

"What happened?" he asked, obviously wondering why she was home at that hour.

"My car died. I had to have some guy jump start it for me. I tried to call here but no one answered." She looked down the hall, and noticed me standing there watching them. She looked back at her husband with squinted eyes. "Where were you?"

"I must have been taking Stephanie to her session at the school," he answered quickly.

"What, *she* can't answer the phone?" she snapped, motioning to me. "Why weren't you in the classroom?" she asked.

"She was," Uncle Lonny said loudly. "She was just using the bathroom down the hall."

I knew by the tone of his voice something was terribly wrong, and it was time for me to go. I hated being around Aunt Elise and knew she felt the same way about me. I quickly went to the classroom and disappeared from view. I quietly left through the door nearest the classroom.

Outside, I immediately felt the air clear and I inhaled deeply as I walked quickly down the lane toward the ranch. I went over in my head what had happened, and wondered why my stomach felt uneasy and my mind confused. I kept thinking how happy I should be. I was one step closer to seeing Papa, but for some reason I felt unstable and defiled.

I waited before going inside, knowing my grandmother would wonder why I was home early, and for some reason I felt the need to hide what happened from her. I walked slowly through the arena, stopping at each of the stables and talking to the horses. I went to the shed and filled a bucket full of chicken scratch. I wanted to talk to someone about what had happened, but I knew if I did, I would ruin my chances of ever seeing Papa again.

Chapter 21

Grandmother served a delicious roasted chicken for dinner, but I had a hard time enjoying it because I found myself constantly staring at the clock. I could literally hear the 'tick-tick' of the seconds and my stomach kept churning with each clank of someone's fork on a plate, or scoot of a chair.

"Is there something wrong, dear?" my grandmother asked.

I wanted to tell them both what was going to happen, but I was secretly hoping Eric wouldn't come and I could forget about the entire incident. "No."

A knock came at the door. My instinct was to tell them not to answer it, but instead I sat stunned as Grandfather placed his napkin on the table and walked with long, loud steps to the door. He opened it, and there stood Eric.

"Hello, Brother Richardson," he said with a smile.

Grandfather ignored him and looked out the door. "How did you get in here?"

"I climbed the fence. My car is parked up a ways. Sophie knew I was coming, so I thought the gate would be open."

I felt my heart sink.

Grandfather turned back to me with a strange frown, but then shrugged. "Come in," he grumbled.

Eric hesitated. "Would it be possible to open the gate? I left Linda in the car."

Linda? My dread turned to happiness, and I stood up from the table. Eric saw me and smiled, giving me a half wave. I didn't wave back but lifted the corner of my mouth in acknowledgment. My grandfather grumbled, grabbed his keys and walked out the door – with Eric following behind.

"Why didn't you tell us Eric was coming to visit tonight?" Grandmother chirped happily.

"Because I was hoping he wouldn't."

"Why? He's such a nice young man. I spoke to his mother this afternoon and she said he was talking about you. I hoped he would come."

I looked up at her mischievous smile with skeptical eyes. I was annoyed that I was the center of a plan.

When Grandfather came back into the house, he was alone. "They'll be here in a minute. He has Linda Stevens with him. Why did they come?"

"I don't know," I answered.

"They came because they want to be friends," my grandmother called from the kitchen. She had placed cookies on a plate and walked around the corner toward the living room.

"Humph," Grandfather said. He walked off toward his bedroom. "Remember, you have school tomorrow."

A light tap at the door had my grandmother eagerly running to answer it. Linda rubbed her arms and shivered as she walked in, but she smiled when she saw me. Eric greeted my grandmother, calling her Sister Richardson, and she giggled when he told her the cookies looked wonderful.

We all sat at odd angles on pristine sofas, as Grandmother set the plate of cookies on the coffee table closest to Eric. When she was gone, Linda scooted toward me.

"So how's it going?" she asked.

"Fine," I answered, wondering what *could* have gone on since we saw each other at church just yesterday.

"This is a great house," Eric exclaimed, chomping on one of the cookies as crumbs went everywhere. "We didn't get a lot of time to talk to you yesterday, so we thought we'd come by and see if you were interested in hanging out with us this weekend."

Linda's eyes sparkled as she spoke. "There is a regional stake dance on Saturday. We thought it would be fun. Do you want to go with us?"

"A what?" I asked.

Eric laughed. "It's just a big dance, and people from all over come to it. It's at the stake house near the college in Pocatello."

"What's a stake house?" I asked.

"A big church," Linda tried to explain. "Yesterday we were in a ward house. The stake houses are bigger because a whole bunch of the wards meet there. It's easier if you think of it as just a bigger church. Besides, this isn't a church meeting, it's a dance. It really is fun and there will be a ton of people there." She said it as though that would encourage me to go, when it actually terrified me.

"Isn't Pocatello far away?"

"It's about an hour," Eric piped up. "But I'll drive."

I looked at Linda.

She smiled and nodded. "I'll be going too, so will Brad."

"Who's Brad?"

She smiled. "He's my boyfriend."

"Oh," I whispered.

"So what do you say?" Eric asked, leaning toward me.

I leaned back. "I'm not sure. I'll have to ask my grandparents."

"Your grandmother already said it was okay," said Eric.

"Eric," Linda said, glaring at him.

His eyes went big, realizing he had spoken out of turn. "What I meant is…we asked her if we could come and ask you. But it's up to you, of course."

"Can Stephanie come?" I asked, feeling that was the only way I would be comfortable venturing out.

Strange glances passed between them. Eric cleared his throat. "Well, I'm not sure I'll have room in the car. It's pretty small and we'll already have four people in it."

I didn't answer, but kept looking at him as he fidgeted and reached for another cookie.

My grandmother entered the room. "Do you need anything else? Some milk, maybe?"

Eric smiled at her. "No, thank you. But maybe you can convince Sophie that this dance will be fun and she should go with us."

"Oh, you *should*," she said, clasping her hands together. "You can meet a bunch of other people your age."

"But there will be so many," I told her, anxious.

"Yes, but Eric and Linda will be with you. This is a church dance. These kids will be kind, and want to be friends. There's nothing to worry about."

She sounded so comforting and convincing, I nodded. "Okay."

She reeled back, with a look of surprised joy on her face.

Later that night, after Eric and Linda left, Grandfather came out of his room and found Grandmother and me talking at the kitchen table.

"Why a big dance?" he asked. "They could go into town and get pizza some Saturday. A huge crowd like this is just asking for trouble."

She shook her head, disagreeing with his words.

"You saw what happened the day you went shopping at the mall. They practically mobbed her. Why do you want to put her in this situation?"

"She'll be fine," Grandmother said. "That was when everything had just happened. Things have settled down now. She'll be with Eric and the others. She *needs* to live a normal life, Gene."

He shook his head. "I still think we should take it slow. Letting her go all the way to Pocatello is too far."

"I want Stephanie to go with me, but they said there wouldn't be room in the car."

"This is one situation where I'd prefer she was with you," he said.

Grandmother huffed. "You need to make other friends besides Stephanie. She's a nice girl, but you should have other friends, too. This will be a good thing, you'll see."

Grandfather walked off, putting a hand to his chest. "Where are my pills?"

"They're on the table next to your chair," my grandmother replied.

He picked up the bottle. "Not these. I need my nitro pills."

"What?" my grandmother said, standing up. "Do we need to take you in?"

He grumbled. "Not if we can find my pills."

She went quickly to the bathroom and came out holding several bottles, reading the labels. "Here it is— nitroglycerin."

"What's wrong?" I asked.

"Nothing," my grandfather barked.

"He'll be fine, dear," my grandmother said. "It's his heart. It doesn't work the way it should. These pills keep it going."

The next day while Uncle Lonny corrected our assignments, I told Stephanie about the visit from Eric and Linda and about the dance. I was surprised when she wasn't repulsed that I had agreed to go.

"At least you'll be getting out of Malad for a night," she said, pulling her ponytail to make it tighter against her head.

"I wish you were going," I said.

"Been there, done that, no thank you."

"Why?"

"It's a dance with a bunch of 'churchy' kids. Everyone stands around and talks about everyone else. Even the music is lame."

I sat back, suddenly worried.

"I'm not trying to burst your bubble here, but you asked, so I told you." She leaned toward me. "It will probably be fun for you. You've never been to anything like this. I'm kind of jealous because I wanted to be the first person to take you out into the great big world."

"Then come with us."

"No. It isn't for me." She went back to reading a Judy Blume book. It was one my grandmother had refused to let me read.

I felt anxiety creep into my gut. Hearing her say there would be crowds and talk, I envisioned only horror. "What do I do when I get there?" I asked.

She giggled and looked above the pages. "It's a dance. You dance."

"I don't know how to dance."

"Neither does anyone else at those things. Don't worry about it. I'm sure Eric will teach you."

"I don't want Eric to teach me."

Uncle Lonny finished our assignments and handed them back to us. "It's about time for us to leave, Stephanie."

She nodded, closed her book, and went to grab her jacket. "Quit worrying about this. I'll try to teach you a couple of things when I get back. It's not a big deal."

The night before, as I lay in bed, I stewed, not about the dance, or the visit from Eric and Linda, but about the afternoon and the way the air had turned thick and sour the moment my aunt had entered the house. It was a tension I could physically feel, and the way Uncle Lonny reacted was unsettling and curious.

That morning, as I walked up the hill to their house, I wondered if that heavy smothering feeling would still be in there. It wasn't. My aunt was gone and it was class as usual. However, Uncle Lonny's normally cheery greeting wasn't as animated, and was almost apologetic. Stephanie, too, was muted but seemed to be herself once our studies began.

When I finally had relaxed into my book, and Stephanie had been delivered to her sessions at the school, Uncle Lonny returned. He walked to me with his coat still on. "Spring is sure taking it's time to get here," he said, unzipping it and hanging it on the back of a chair. He nervously wrung his hands and walked to me. "Sophie, I'm sorry about yesterday. I hope you're okay."

I wasn't sure how to react, but I had questions about why I felt troubled. "Did I do something wrong?"

"No!" he answered emphatically. "You did nothing wrong."

"Then why does she hate me?" I asked.

Uncle Lonny raised his eyebrows. "It's not you. It has nothing to do with you. It's me. Your aunt is a very angry person and I think sometimes she hates everything and everyone."

"Why did you marry her?"

He let a quick burst of laughter escape him. "That is a very good question I have asked myself many times. People sometimes act one way when you're dating, and then things change once you're married."

"She always looks at me funny, like she sees something that isn't there. I always feel like she knows what I'm thinking and can see inside me. I don't like it."

Uncle Lonny smiled sadly. "I'm sure there's a lot that she feels guilty about when it comes to you and your mother. I don't know a lot because I didn't come into this family until years later, but I do know that she doesn't like to talk about either of you."

"What do you know about my mother?"

"Not much. She died long before I came around. I've seen pictures and she was beautiful, just like you."

I nodded. My grandmother had pulled out a huge assortment of photo albums and scrapbooks the week I was brought to the house. I leafed through the pages often. My mother always wore a vibrant smile in the photographs. She had large eyes and brilliant blonde hair. It drove me crazy wondering what she was like. Papa told me she loved me very much and that I reminded him of her, but even he didn't say much more. His eyes turned red and filled with unshed tears whenever I asked about her, so I learned early on to keep my questions to myself.

Uncle Lonny gently took a strand of my hair. "Your father must have very dark hair and skin. Your mother and everyone else in this family are so blonde and fair." He studied it. "Everything about you is unique, even your hair color. It's not just brown, but a caramel color."
He twirled the piece in his fingers.

"Papa says I have my mother's eyes."

Uncle Lonny nodded in agreement. "They are very pretty." He dropped my hair and put his hand to my face, cupping my chin and lifting it to him. "You are beautiful."

He suddenly stood up and rubbed his hands together. "We need to get you started on your math. We didn't get too far yesterday."

"Are you still going to help me see Papa?" I asked him, fearful of his answer.

He dropped down to eye level and put one knee on the floor. "Of course. Nothing's changed. I'll do whatever it takes, and I think it will work."

I hugged his neck and he stood me up, still in his embrace.

"I love you, Sophie," he said without looking at me.

I was so thankful to have him in my life, I immediately returned the words. "I love you, too, Uncle Lonny."

He let me go and said quietly, *"Uncle* Lonny. How about you just call me Lonny? We're friends, right? Uncle Lonny is so formal sounding. You can call me that when everyone else is around, but when it's just you and me call me Lonny, okay?"

"Okay."

When he returned later with Stephanie, I quickly talked her into showing me how to dance. She went to her room and brought out a CD player. After shuffling through a packet filled with CD's she picked one and put it in the player. The music made me smile, and I felt like my chest was pounding along with the beat. She took my hands and stood facing me.

"Okay," she said, over the music. "Do what I do."

I nodded, watching as she stepped back and forth and rocked with the beat. I watched intensely at first without doing anything, until she shook my arms and widened her eyes with a look of command. I tried to follow her steps and felt awkward and goofy as I swayed my hips and shoulders. She bent over laughing, which made me stop and fold my arms in injured defiance.

"I'm sorry," she said. "Let's try something else. Don't try to do exactly what I do. You're just supposed to move to the music. Dancing is supposed to be how *you* feel when you hear the beat." She started bobbing her head with the song. "Just move with the music."

Listening to what she said, I closed my eyes and felt the notes and sounds whirl around me. I started to turn and sway and become one with the beat. When the song came to an end, I opened my eyes and found both Stephanie and Uncle Lonny watching with surprised, but satisfied faces. "That was fun," I said, beaming.

"Now *that's* dancing," said Stephanie.

When the next song started, I began to sway again, but the melody was slow and I looked over to her and shook my head.

Stephanie put my hands around her neck and put her arms around my waist. "This is a slow dance. Pretend I'm the boy…"

Uncle Lonny came over and picked up one of my arms, stepping in between us. "Let's try to remember you aren't a boy," he said. "I'll be the boy." He put my arms around his neck and carefully placed his hands on my lower back. He smiled and danced me slowly around the room.

Stephanie resisted at first, but then stood back by the wall and gave us apprehensive and anxious looks. Then she went to the CD player and turned it off. "I think she gets the picture," she said. "You'll be fine, Soph." Stephanie picked up the player and her CD case and went back to her room.

Uncle Lonny released me and stood watching her walk down the hallway. My elation quickly fell and I felt the suffocating presence from yesterday begin to fill the house again.

Chapter 22

Pocatello, Idaho, Late Winter, 1992

Philip Katsilometes knew what he had to do. He wanted Luke out of sight, and hopefully out of reach of a young girl that could certainly ruin Talia's plans.

That night he called in some favors with a man who worked with the Union Pacific Railroad, and also owned several large dairies in the adjoining counties. He secured Luke an entry level job with the railroad and some side work at one of the dairies as payment for the position. It required that Luke leave school, but this was the fast track to what he was planning anyway. Luke would be out of sight, and with any luck the pregnant girl would give up and leave them alone.

When he first told Talia, she was angry. She didn't want Luke so far away, but eventually she saw the benefit to her and what she had planned for their future.

"I don't want to owe him anything. I already feel like we're in debt to him for letting us live with them," Luke complained, when Theta told him of the news.

"This is what your father had planned. It is what's best. You can't say no," she told him with a face that showed both urgency and insistence.

Luke knew he had no choice. The only thing that wasn't part of the plan was Vee. She was always in the picture, and now all other dreams and intentions seemed irrelevant without her. The job *was* different and that *is* what he longed for. As much as he didn't want to feel obligated to Talia's father, at least his new job would be a new beginning and a possible first step into his new life as a man.

Luke stood brushing his teeth in the small bathroom of the trailer house and imagined how his life would change. He tried to clear the anxiousness and worry from his mind. Luke rubbed the stubble of his cheeks and chin. It was coarse and a lighter color than his hair, and was filling in fast. His shoulders were broad and his arms and chest had grown large. He'd grown another couple of inches, as well. Luke stared at himself in the mirror, hoping that the wealth of fear he felt inside was hidden by the strong façade staring back.

American Falls, Idaho

Luke's first day was a disappointment. He was told to arrive early at the dairy. It was a large operation nestled at the base of a canyon in the small city of American Falls. Inside, he found Pete McGill, a large man with thin red hair, wearing thick brown coveralls and talking to a quartet of Hispanic men dressed in a variety of worn flannel shirts, weathered jeans and heavy boots. The room had a table, a refrigerator, and counter with a small microwave and coffee maker on top. The floor was wet with mud and muck, and the entire place smelled like manure.

"Can I help you?" Pete said with a gruff but kind voice. He snuffed out a cigarette in a glass ashtray.

"I was told to come here for a job."

Pete directed the other men out of the room; he took a red handkerchief from his back pocket and wiped his

197

hands before offering one to Luke. "Yes, I was told you'd be here. I'm Pete."

Luke nodded as he shook Pete's massive calloused hand.

"You done this type of work before?"

"Kind of. I worked some with horses."

"No dairy work?"

"No."

"So, did ya lose a bet?" he asked with a laugh.

Luke smiled, but inside he cringed with worry.

Pete slapped him on the back and walked him toward a door at the back of the room. He directed one of the other men to come forward. "Gerard will show you what you'll be doing. Are these the only clothes you have?"

Luke looked down, wondering what wasn't appropriate.

"Here," he motioned, handing Luke a heavy coat from a line of hooks along the wall. He pulled some filthy leather gloves from a box on the floor. "I'll get you some boots, but it may be a couple of hours before I can get them to you."

Luke nodded, suddenly wanting to hide his canvas athletic shoes.

For the next four hours, Luke was back to shoveling manure. When he went back to the room for his break, Pete was sitting at the table marking in a large three-ringed binder; an empty coffee cup sat nearby. When he asked how it went, Luke shrugged.

"What? Not your dream job?" Pete said under his breath.

"Not what I was promised," grumbled Luke.

Pete closed the binder and watched as Luke took off his grungy shoes and put on the boots Pete had dug up for him. "What? Were you expecting a desk job? This is a dairy."

"I know that, but I was told I had a job at the railroad and that this was only a side job."

Pete took a long and labored breath. "All Mr. Strickland told me was that you'd be working here and that I was to let him know what kind of worker you were."

"Who is Mr. Strickland?"

"He's the owner of the dairies. He works as one of the 'big wigs' on the railroad, too. He said he was doing a favor for your father-in-law in hiring you."

"What?" Luke said with a huff. "I don't have a father-in-law."

"Settle down, man." Pete put up a hand in defense. "I meant, soon to be father-in-law."

Luke shook his head. "Is that what you were told?"

Pete shrugged. "That's what someone told Mr. Strickland. He's the one who does a lot of the hiring at the railroad. He owns this dairy and two others. I just manage this one for him."

"So I have to kiss up to this Strickland guy by working here, just to get a job at the railroad?"

Pete grunted. "You don't have a chance in hell in getting on there if you don't know someone or, better yet… are related."

"I am not marrying Talia just to get a job."

Pete raised his eyebrows. "Then you may end up like me—knee deep in cow poop with the only women interested in you being the heifers wanting hay."

Luke slunk down in one of the plastic chairs and groaned.

"Oh, come on now, I'm just giving you a hard time," said Pete. "Do your best here and I'll tell Mr.

Strickland you're worth a lick." He leaned an elbow on the table. "So, what's the problem with this guy's daughter?"

"There is no problem. She's a good friend, but she's *only* a friend."

"Not too good to look at, huh?"

"No, it's not that. Talia's very pretty and very nice, it's just…"

Pete cocked his head, waiting for Luke to finish.

Luke envisioned Vee in his mind and wondered if he was a complete idiot for continuing to devote his entire heart to her. It had been months since he'd seen her and he had no idea if she even thought about him. He noticed Pete studying him and sat up. "I don't need the trouble right now. What I need is money."

Pete nodded. "Well, this ain't half bad for that. You won't get rich, but at least you won't be making minimum wage like the kids in town flippin' burgers."

"So how long do you think it will take?" Luke asked.

"For what?"

"For me to prove myself to Mr. Strickland?"

Pete sighed. "You won't be seeing much of Mr. Strickland. He rarely comes by, which is a good thing. You're here to prove yourself to me."

Luke sat up straighter. "So how do I prove it to you?"

Pete went to take a sip of coffee and realized the cup was empty. He grumbled. "After less than one day of work you shouldn't be asking me that. Learn patience. I'll decide if and when you deserve any type of reference." He stood up and went to the coffee maker. "Now quit gabbin' and get back to work. You have my old boots, but you can keep them. I have a better pair of gloves at home. I'll bring them tomorrow."

Luke gave Pete an appreciative nod, pulled his coat closed and left the room. As his face hit the frigid breeze of the dark Idaho morning, he wondered how long he'd be at the dairy before Pete gave him the 'foot in the door' he needed. The entire situation wasn't what he'd hoped for or even imagined, but there was something about Pete that made it tolerable. He was genuine and real, and Luke knew that regardless of what he was scooping, hauling, or cleaning, he would feel good about the time he spent working for Pete. He needed this break to physically survive and to keep him sane. For months he had felt like an outcast and a criminal, and even though he knew the truth, the weight of shame that he bore was too heavy to carry much longer.

At the beginning of the third day, Luke shielded his face from the cold as he stood on wooden planks of the chute and prodded cows down the lane. At the other end of the chute waited a veterinarian who vaccinated and checked them for pregnancy. Luke was almost dizzy from lack of sleep and he gazed off, daydreaming. He had gotten a chuckle over the doctor ordering him around in Spanish, apparently assuming that with Luke's dark skin and hair he was Mexican like the other workers. Luke didn't correct him, and even though he wasn't fluent in Spanish he knew the routine and did what the vet asked without problems.

At the end of the day, Pete called him in and sat him down. "I should have done this on day one, but I'm not much when it comes to paperwork. I need you to fill this out for tax stuff."

Luke took the papers and quickly filled in the blanks. He handed it back to Pete and sat quietly as Pete looked them over.

"This can't be right," Pete said, looking up. If you were born in 1975, then you're not eighteen."

Luke shook his head in agreement.

"Crap!" Pete said, pounding a fist on the table. "I knew this would screw me over somehow. We were told you were eighteen."

Luke felt anxious, as though he had done something wrong, but knew he had never been asked his age by anyone. "No one told me I had to be. Besides, it's just a matter of weeks."

"It's not your fault. But you can't work here unless you are."

"But..." Luke started to speak, and then stopped. He wanted to beg Pete to keep him on, but his pride refused to allow it.

Pete paced. "Do you need this job?"

"I do."

Pete paced some more, mumbling with each step. "Not offended by people thinking you're one of the Mexicans out there?"

Luke shrugged. "No."

"Here," he said, taking Luke's forms and tearing them up. "You're now Miguel—Miguel Sanchez—the Mexican migrant worker. Just keep quiet and don't let anyone know you're out here, okay? And start learning Spanish."

"But, what about Mr. Strickland?"

"He has no clue who's out here. He won't even ask."

"I don't have a chance in hell of getting on at the railroad, do I?"

Pete slapped him on the back. "If you keep quiet and work hard I'll take care of that. When you're eighteen, I'll tell him you did a fine job and I'll send you over to the rail yard as an apprentice. You won't be able to get on there until you're eighteen anyway. He won't know the difference."

Luke was still a bit confused, but appreciative that Pete hadn't sent him on his way.

"Just remember, tell no one that you work here. There will be no paper trail and no one will be the wiser. I don't want any trouble from the labor department. If anyone comes around, just hang with the other Mexicans and keep quiet."

Luke nodded. "What about Mr. Katsilometes…and my mother?"

"Hmm," Pete grumbled, as he figured out just the right story to use. "If they ask, just tell them things are fine and leave it at that. I'll pay you in cash. And remember, you are now Miguel if anyone shows up here."

On the drive home that evening, Luke felt exhaustion sink into his shoulders and thighs. He started to miss the carefree life of high school and hanging out with Talia and his other friends. But his life as a boy had ended, and there was no going back.

Just like his father, Luke's life would now be filled with long days of labor and very few moments of the lazy contentment he had felt while at the ranch. Sometimes he missed those days so much he ached and even cried. It felt like another death of a loved one, and the loss was so profound it often made him wonder if he even wanted to continue living. He dreaded his long drives to and from work, because they gave him the solitary time that allowed his pain to fester and his fatalistic thoughts to grow.

On an unusually sunny day, Pete sought Luke out during his break. "You look rough. What's up?" he asked.

Luke took a deep breath. "Nothing. Just tired."

"Where do you live? Pocatello?"

Luke shook his head, "No, we live just outside of Inkom."

"Good hell, kid, that's over an hour drive."

Luke nodded, knowing he spent a good hour and a half each way.

"I've got an extra room at my place in the Arbon Valley, why don't you stay there?" said Pete, with a look of fatherly concern.

Luke quickly shook his head, hating to hear the condescending tone.

"Really," Pete said. "I'd love the company. It's just me and the chickens. It's a lot closer than Inkom."

Luke sighed.

"Let's go up there and I'll show you. You don't have to decide right now, but at least take a look and then you can see that it wouldn't be a problem."

Luke agreed, and after work he followed Pete over the freeway bridge and up the canyon to Arbon Valley. The land was rolling with Aspen and Spruce trees. Several farms spread out over the fields with lone houses nestled in the trees. Pete slowed down and turned onto a hidden lane that wound its way up into the hills and back into a secluded plateau surrounded by gigantic cottonwood trees and alder bushes. A small house with white siding and a black roof sat in the center with a fenced garden area and a gravel driveway.

Luke got out of his truck and walked to Pete. "This is great," he said, looking at the view and the woodsy solace.

Pete smiled proudly. "I bought the land years ago. I built the house myself. After my wife died, I wanted to hide away."

Luke looked up at a large windmill twirling in the breeze.

"I'm completely self-sufficient; I pump my own water and generate my own electricity. I answer to no one up here. Someday I'll retire and when I die, no one will even know. At least, not till the wind blows in the right direction." He laughed. "Let me show you inside."

Luke took the tour and felt welcomed and comfortable in the little house.

"What do you say? Ready to be roommates?" asked Pete.

Luke's happy grin faded. "I am not sure I can leave my mother. She's a widow and shouldn't live alone."

Pete frowned. "I can't see having a woman up here, kid."

Luke shook his head. "I wasn't asking, Pete. I just don't know if she'd be okay alone."

"You're a good kid. You do whatever you want. If you want to stay here during the week, or even on days you're just too tired to drive back, the invitation is open." He handed Luke a key. "It's my only spare, so keep it safe."

Luke put it in his wallet. As he drove down the gravel drive and back on the main road leading to the freeway, he let his mind drift, wondering what life would be like secretly hidden away from the pain and shame of what was solidified in the minds and on the tongues in the valley below. He made it his goal to one day have his own place of solace, and hoped his life would eventually give him back his freedom from condemnation he didn't deserve.

For the next month, Luke worked under the guise of a Mexican migrant worker. He hated living a lie, but in many ways he enjoyed the anonymity. As he got to know the other workers and began to hear their stories and understand their lives, he started to realize his life wasn't so different. They smiled at his attempts at Spanish, but understood what he meant. He cringed at first when they called him Miguel, but after a while it grew on him and Luke soon answered to it as though it were a nickname. His Spanish improved immensely.

Theta pestered Luke about the job at the railroad until he finally conceded and told her he had gotten the job. She couldn't say anything because of his age, or it would be over. When she heard this, she was elated. Luke didn't have the heart to tell her the truth, especially when he saw her demeanor was so bright. Luke felt so good about her change in attitude that he felt confident about staying at Pete's for several nights during the week. He told her he had early shifts and was staying at the bunkhouse at the railroad.

On a frigid early morning, Pete was already at work doing the books. He grunted a good morning and Luke returned a similar sleepy greeting.

"Come sit down for a minute," said Pete. "I want to show you something."

Luke did as he said.

"I'm going down to Salt Lake City at the end of this week. I want you to take care of this place while I'm gone."

"Me?" asked Luke, surprised.

"Yes. I don't want Mr. Strickland's office people coming in here and getting in the way. He won't even know I'm gone. It's not that big a deal."

"Why are you going to Salt Lake City?"

Pete sighed and exhaled loudly. "I'm dealing with some crap in my lungs. The doctors here don't do this type of work, so they're sending me down there."

"Are you okay?" asked Luke, feeling a shot of fear and concern for his friend.

"Heck, yes. It's going to take more than some gunk in my chest to shut me down." He flipped open the binder and explained to Luke what needed to be recorded and monitored each day.

Luke followed along and tried to listen, but the thought of Pete being sick was the only thing he could concentrate on.

At night, he paid closer attention to the hacking cough coming from the other bedroom. He woke when footsteps went into the bathroom, and he lay awake hearing guttural and vile noises of mucus being coughed up and spit into the sink. Sometimes the sound was so disturbing, Luke felt the need to go to Pete and help him. But he knew it would only embarrass his burley boss, so he stayed quiet and listened to the horrid effects of the disease that was slowly killing the man he had grown to respect and love.

"It's when you're dying that you realize what's really important in life," Pete said one evening, as they both sat on the back porch of the house looking out over the moonlit tips of the trees. "If only we realized that before we start grasping at those last precious moments. I guess that's what makes us human. We have to learn things when it's too late."

"Or we can learn from others," Luke said softly.

Pete smiled and took a long drag off his cigarette. "I hope you've at least learned this," he said, holding up the cigarette. "I hope you never start. It's a wicked and vile habit."

Luke looked down at the ground.

"Have you ever smoked?"

Luke nodded. "Yeah, but I quit."

"You're awfully young to have already started and quit."

"I had a good reason."

Pete raised his eyebrows. "Did someone you know die because of this?"

Luke gave a weary smile and looked up at Pete with red eyes. "I guess you could say that."

"What happened?" asked Pete.

Luke wasn't sure if he was up to sharing his painful tale, but he felt Pete deserved an answer. He had been so good to him and Luke wanted to let him know he appreciated and trusted him. "I lost my father."

"He was a smoker," Pete surmised.

It killed Luke to continue, but he wasn't about to lie to Pete. "No. He was killed in a fire that was started by someone smoking." He paused, realizing how much sorrow he still had inside. "He was trying to save me."

"That's rough, kid. I'm sorry. When did this happen?"

Luke sighed. "It was just a few months ago. That's the reason we moved to Pocatello."

"You have family up here?" asked Pete.

"No. It's just me and my mom, but we had nowhere else to go and Mr. Katsilometes let us live with them until we found a place."

"You had nowhere to go? Didn't you have a house in Malad?"

"We rented a house, but..." Luke was unsure how to continue. He took a deep breath and struggled with the words.

"No jobs there?" Pete asked.

Luke shook his head. "We were kind of forced to leave. There was some stuff that happened and..."

"*Forced?* Why?"

"They think I started the fire that killed my father. My lighter was found in the area."

"If they thought that why weren't you arrested?"

"They couldn't prove it because I wasn't there. I was with Vee."

Pete gave a knowing and sad smile.

Luke nodded. "She's the rancher's daughter."

Pete sighed. "So, you not only lost your father but your love, too. So, why not stand up for yourself and tell the truth?"

Luke stood up. He picked up the two empty beer bottles with one hand. "Do you want another?"

Pete looked at him. "Sounds like I might need several for this."

Luke gave a jaded laugh. "You got that right."

Chapter 23

Malad, Idaho, Spring, 2009

Carpo stared at the letter from the publisher and felt as though his years of work and patience had just been snuffed out with nothing but a three paragraph note. The manuscript they had agreed to publish that fall was not 'meeting their expectations' and the contract was being broken. It was his lack of insight into what the girl had experienced and who she had become that changed their minds and squashed his dreams of being a true crime writer.

It was the grandparents who stood in his way, and he swore under his breath that they would pay for stealing his dream. It was he who kept the investigation going and made sure the "missing child" posters stayed at the forefront of everyone's mind. Without his persistence, the girl's identity might have gone unnoticed, even when she was found in such a sensational and scandalous way. He needed to get to her, gain her confidence and entice a story from her. The publisher would still be interested if he could get the juicy details of her life.

He needed a guise that would allow him uninterrupted access, but without drawing suspicion. But even if he figured a way to entice her into talking, since she was still a child, the Richardsons had complete legal control over where she went, what she did and who she spoke to.

When Stephanie left for her counseling session at the school, she gave me a look of concern before closing the door. I could tell that she was disturbed and knew it had something to do with her father cutting into our dance.

I contemplated how to ask him about the progress he had made toward my visit with Papa. He hadn't mentioned it since that terrible day when my aunt came home early. I worried that he had decided not to help and desperately hoped that wasn't the case. I paced in front of the window until I saw his car coming up the dirt road. I went to the chair and pretended to read.

"Did you finish the assignment?" he asked, hanging his coat on the rack.

"Almost," I said, glancing at the table. I was having problems with the equations and needed his help.

He frowned. "You need to take this more seriously. How can you expect to graduate if you don't do what I say?" His face was oddly serious and I felt my heart drop in my chest.

"I'm sorry. But I didn't understand it and was waiting for you to come back and help me."

"Well, then let's get to it," he grumbled, walking to the table. He pulled out a chair and motioned for me to take the seat next to him.

I did as he directed and showed him the problem on the page that had me perplexed.

He nodded and started to explain. Uncle Lonny turned to me and looked into my eyes. He stopped talking and sat staring.

He took my hand. "I'm sorry," he said, squeezing it gently. "I can't stop feeling the way I do and I think I'm going crazy. I know it's wrong. I feel guilty about it, but..."

I felt a sharp stab of worry that he wasn't going to help me. "You're not going to help me see my father, are you?" I said, distraught.

"What?"

I lowered my head, about to cry.

He gently raised my chin. "Don't cry. I told you I would help you and I did. I sent in the papers and now I'm waiting to hear back. Don't lose hope yet."

A buoyant elation filled me and I sat up with an appreciative smile.

"My beautiful, Sophie. One day I hope you'll understand." He continued to gaze at me. He leaned closer and with his hand guiding mine, placed it on his leg. "Will it make you excited to see your father?" he asked, pressing down on my hand and moving it up his thigh.

"Yes," I answered, so relieved and thankful.

"How excited?" he asked, sliding my hand, so my fingers were moving up and onto something hard on the inside of his leg. I was naïve but wasn't stupid. I suddenly knew what he was doing.

A vile crushing repulsion hit me and I jerked my hand away, giving him a disgusted glare.

He jumped as though being knocked out of a dream. "I'm sorry," he immediately blurted. "I didn't mean to do that." He walked off down the hall.

I sat stunned. In an instant I had gone from joy about seeing Papa to complete upheaval.

Lonny returned with a red face and panicked expression. "This is another one of those things that's just between you and me, okay?"

I started to answer but he interrupted.

"If you say anything, the meeting with your father is off. Do you understand?" His voice was thin and urgent.

I nodded, dismayed at his change in mood. I stayed silent, not wanting to do anything to reverse his decision to help me. Inside I felt queasy and troubled.

He left me alone until he went to retrieve Stephanie, but gave me a final warning when he was halfway out the door. "Remember. Don't say a word."

When Stephanie returned, we left the house to go to the arena. We led the horses to their stalls and removed their saddles and bridles. As we toweled them off, Stephanie looked deep in thought.

"Did your father show you he loved you?" she asked.

I looked at her surprised. "Yes, of course," I answered.

"How? What did he do?"

"What do you mean?"

She stopped her brushing. "How did he show you he loved you?"

I had to think for a moment, because I hadn't thought of it before. "He took care of me. He made sure I had the things I needed. He read to me. He taught me things." I stopped and looked to her for a response.

She squinted as though studying me. "Did he ever touch you?"

It was an odd question and, as I pondered it, I realized Papa rarely touched me. "He did, but not a lot. Why?"

"I was hoping you knew the difference between someone loving you and someone who just wants to touch you."

Why was she questioning that?

Before I could ask, she blurted out, "I've been thinking about this curse thing. You said that your father told you that the people who love you are the ones in danger, but there are a bunch of people who love you now and no one is dead yet."

I knew that she didn't believe in the curse, so I was skeptical to take what she said seriously.

"You said your mother died, but you aren't even sure how she died and you don't remember any of it because you were so young."

I nodded.

"Your friend Donny was different though. You *do* remember what happened with him."

"Yes. He died in the cave."

"When did he die?" she asked.

"When I was eleven."

"How long did you know him?"

"Just one summer."

Stephanie shook her head. "That's why this doesn't make sense. Why do you think you or this curse had anything to do with his death?"

I stood silent.

"Your mother obviously loved you, but this Donny kid was just a friend. What makes you think he loved you?"

I felt myself blushing. "He told me."

"When?" She leaned over the stall partition.

"That day."

Stephanie lifted her shoulders, unconvinced. "I tell you I love you. I know your grandparents love you. What was special about his love?" She lifted an eyebrow. "Do you see what I mean?"

I relived my last moments with Donny. "He kissed me."

214

Stephanie leaned back. "The kiss of death?" She smirked. "This is getting ridiculous, Sophie."

I reeled back as though she'd slapped me. "Why are you doing this? I already know you don't believe it."

She licked her lips. "I don't, but you do and I want to find out why. I want to find out what makes you believe in it."

"Why?"

"Because I'm going to get to the bottom of this and show you that it's not real."

I bit my lip and sat on the stool. "You're trying to make me feel stupid because I believe."

Stephanie smiled. "No, that isn't it at all. I'm doing this because I want you to be happy. You can't be happy if you go through life with this hanging around your neck like a noose. You saved me and now I'm going to save you."

Chapter 24

Arbon Valley, February 28, 1992

Pete left for Utah and Luke was left in charge of the dairy. The other workers went on with their duties as though it was any other day and this surprised Luke. He was at least fifteen years younger than any of them and had the least amount of experience, but his direction was taken with smiles; they even seemed happy to have him holding that clipboard. The days were bitter cold and Luke was happy to have his beard and face sock as he walked the corral outside. The sock was thick wool and covered everything except his nose and eyes.

While talking to one of the men as they explained a problem with one of the cow's hooves, he heard a commotion near the main building.

"Oh no," the man said quietly. "It's Mr. Strickland."

Luke turned to see a man in a thick coat and jeans standing with a young woman, and signaling him over. The man's hair was blowing in all directions, exposing a bald top that was normally covered by the wisps that he was trying to control.

Luke walked to him, but before he was able to greet the two, the man bellowed out, "Where's Pete?"

Luke pulled the face sock down as he spoke. "He had to go to Utah."

"What the hell for?" asked Mr. Strickland.

The young woman stood shivering by his side, even though she was covered from head to toe in winter clothes. She smiled apologetically when Mr. Strickland raised his voice. She had kind eyes and looked to be not much older than Luke.

"He had an appointment with…"

Mr. Strickland cut him off. "Who are you?"

"I'm Miguel Sanchez."

Mr. Strickland nodded. "Yeah, he told me about you. How long will he be gone?"

Luke hesitated, not wanting to get Pete in trouble by telling Mr. Strickland he would be gone for a week. "I'm not sure, but I'm in charge while he's gone."

The woman's eyes grew big and she looked over to Mr. Strickland as though she expected trouble.

"*You're* in charge?" Mr. Strickland bellowed. "You work for me! That means I'm in charge."

Luke nodded. He smelled the odor of coffee and morning breath as Mr. Strickland spoke. It made Luke want to back up, but he stood his ground.

"The steers I have in the far pasture are supposed to be shipped out next week. I tried to call Pete to find out if they've been vaccinated and signed off, but of course I got no answer." He spoke with an air of disappointment.

Luke directed the pair back into the building. "It was done last night."

"By whom?" Mr. Strickland asked, skeptical.

"I had Dr. Bardwell here. Pete had said the steers needed it done, so I scheduled it last night. Everything is good to go."

Again the woman looked to Mr. Strickland for his response.

He huffed.

She looked at Luke with a humorous glint in her eye.

Mr. Strickland looked at the mud and manure. "Well, someone needs to clean this up." He looked up for a reaction.

"I'll take care of it," Luke said.

Mr. Strickland tapped his finger as though looking for something else to criticize. "You tell Pete I don't appreciate him going on these little jaunts of his. I need someone here watching over these...these people." He looked at Luke. "You speak really good English. How come?"

Luke smiled to himself. "I'm a fast learner, I guess."

Mr. Strickland gave another huff and turned to leave. "Mandy, get whatever paperwork you need. I'll be waiting in the truck." And without further acknowledgement, he left.

When the office door closed, Mandy turned to Luke. "Usually I just come and pick up the reports each quarter, but when he can't reach Pete, he makes a point of coming along. I think he does it to keep Pete feeling like he's on the bubble."

Luke was surprised at her open frustration with her boss. "What do you do for him?"

She looked up and smiled. "I'm his assistant. Technically I work as his secretary at the railroad, but he pays me on the side to take care of the books for the dairy."

Luke nodded. She was a friendly face—something he had missed in the months since he'd been isolated at the dairy. "How long have you worked for him?"

"I started when I was still in high school. It's been about three years now. I got married two years ago and I have two baby boys. It's been a good job because he lets me set my own hours."

"You already have two kids?" Luke asked, surprised.

She giggled. "I better get the reports, or he'll be back in here."

Luke pulled out the binder and she leafed through it, removing the papers she needed. When she was done she thanked him and started to leave. Turning on her heel, she gave an exasperated gasp. "Oh, I almost forgot," she said, reaching into one of her coat pockets and pulling out an envelope. "Is there a guy named Luke out here?"

Luke's heart jumped, but he tried to hold his face intact. "No. Why?"

Mandy walked back to him with a look of wicked glee. "Well, this girl came into the office about a month ago looking for some guy named Luke. She was kind of upset and *very* pregnant. She thought he worked for Mr. Strickland at the railroad, but I told her he didn't. Anyway, I remember Mr. Strickland hiring some kid at the dairy named Luke as a favor for one of his friends, so I told her I would try to get this letter to him."

She flashed a mischievous smile. "I opened the letter and it's a long love note; it says that he is the one who got her pregnant!" She giggled. "The poor guy is probably trying to hide out. I thought maybe it was one of the guys out here."

Luke was stunned and wanted to grab the letter from her hands and run. "I can ask," he muttered. "Some of them don't speak English."

"Well, I don't think he's one of the Mexicans. This girl was blonde and beautiful, but who knows."

"Well, that's all we are out here, just us Mexicans," he said, teasing.

Mandy put her hand to her mouth in horror. "I'm sorry. I didn't mean you. Oh dear…you know what I mean, right?"

"Yeah, it's no big deal. There are some others who come in part-time. It may be one of them." He reached for the envelope, desperate to read its contents.

"Let me know if you find him and what he does when he reads it," she said, handing it to him. "Let Pete know I'll be back in to get the payroll numbers next week."

A horn blared from outside and she jumped. "Crap! Hang on old man," she said with disgust.

Luke watched her walk out the door. He slumped down at the table and, with heart racing, opened the envelope and unfolded the letter. The first sentence let him know it was Vee, and by the time he finished the first page, he had to stop as tears clouded his eyes. The joy and elation he felt knowing she still loved him and was carrying his child was more than he could contain. It wasn't just the relief that she still cared, but also the surprise and wonder of being an expectant father.

Luke went to the phone and dialed Vee's number. It was something he had done many times, only to hang up when he heard a voice other than hers. He knew the trouble he would invoke by trying to contact her; he had kept his distance after what had happened, hoping that the shame would one day fade. But now he had a reason to call…he had a right! He was the baby's father, and that was his ticket to reuniting with Vee.

His stomach churned and his heart throbbed with every ring of the phone. "Please let it be Vee. Please let it be Vee," he whispered.

"Hello?" It was Richardson.

Luke winced and put his hand over his face.

"Hello!" He demanded.

Luke knew it was what he had to do, so he took a deep breath and tried to sound confident. "I need to speak to Vee."

There was silence.

After a while Luke wondered if he was still there. "Hello?"

"Leave her alone."

"No. You can't do this. That baby is mine."

There was silence again.

"It's my right as the father."

"*A father?* You're no father. Leave her alone."

"But I love her."

"Then leave her alone. If you care at all, you'll stay away."

Luke felt his blood course through his body and fill his face. "Let me talk to her!"

"She's not here. I won't let you do this. She's had enough crap in her life." Richardson's breathing was loud and angry on the other end of the line. "I said, leave her alone. I'll have you arrested if you come anywhere near her."

Luke felt his breath being ripped from his body. "Has she had the baby?"

"Leave us alone!" And the line went dead with a loud crack.

Luke stumbled back, the phone still in his hands. The load of information that had been dumped on him was overwhelming. Clutching the letter in his other hand he hung up the phone and looked at it. Vee *had* tried to find him; she *had* tried to tell him. Luke paced the grimy wet floor. The letter was over a month old and he tried to calculate the due date in his head. He couldn't imagine what Vee was going through, not knowing he loved her and wanted to be with her. He had to get to her!

Luke refused to let Richardson continue to stand in his way. He thought about leaving the dairy that minute and making the hour and a half drive south, but then he stopped and his mind cleared. He had no idea what Vee was thinking and feeling now. She probably thought he had abandoned her and he knew that her father would make good on his threat to have him arrested. If he wanted to be with Vee and have time to talk to her, it would have to be without anyone else around. He thought back on his life at the ranch and what opportunities there would be to get her alone.

Luke visualized the schedule of the family that he still remembered. Then his mind cleared. It was as perpetual as the sun rising and setting. Every Sunday—no matter what—Richardson and his wife left the ranch for church.

It would give Luke at least three hours without the worry of being caught. The only risk he took was that Vee would go, as well. She had strayed from the Church while Luke was there at the ranch, but he didn't know if that was just for the sake of being alone with him, or if she really wanted to distance herself from religion. It had been months since they had been together and he wasn't sure what her thoughts were now. His heart warmed, thinking about the many afternoons they spent together, and especially of the day when they stole away in the barn hidden in the hayloft and made love...a child.

It was Friday, which seemed a tortuous amount of time to have to wait, but then he realized that Richardson would probably be expecting him to show up soon, so the days in between may be enough to let his suspicions subside.

Luke spent the evening with Theta. He wanted so badly to tell her his news, but didn't want anything to come between him and his quest to see Vee. He wondered what his mother's reaction would be when she learned she'd be a grandma.

A smile spread across his face as a vision of her rocking and singing to his child filled his mind. It may be the one thing Theta needed to bring her back to life. He knew she would worry because of his age as well as Vee's. He also knew that she would be disappointed that his betrothal to Talia would never come to be, but how could she not be thrilled when she learned that a baby was coming into their family?

"Why are you so happy? You're grinning like a donkey," Theta exclaimed, with an air of annoyance.

He just smiled bigger. Luke was buoyant with joy over what he had learned and the effect it would have on those he loved.

The next morning he was at the dairy early and was surprised to see Pete wasn't there. He looked around and saw no signs that he had been, and when he asked the others if they had seen him, everyone shook their heads and looked puzzled.

During a lull in the day, Luke decided to drive up to Pete's house and see if he was home. He sighed with relief when he saw Pete's old red truck in the drive and hoped that Pete wouldn't be upset that he was checking up on him.

Luke went to the door. He tapped the door lightly at first, but when no one answered, he knocked harder. He looked around the back to see if maybe he was in the yard, but saw nothing. A sickly sensation came over him, and Luke began to worry. He pulled his spare key from his wallet and unlocked the door. "Pete?" he called, as he walked through the living room and into the kitchen. Pete's keys were on the table.

"I'm back here, kid." It's was Pete's voice, but it sounded weak and low.

Luke found Pete lying in bed. The room was dark, but Luke could see that Pete was up on one elbow and his face looked drowsy.

"I didn't mean to wake you," said Luke, apologizing. "I was just seeing if you'd made it back okay."

"I made it back. I'm not so sure I'm okay."

Luke went to him. "What can I do?"

Pete gave a weary sigh. "There is nothing anyone can do."

"What did the doctors say?"

"They told me I'm dying, but I already knew that, so I just spent a week away from work and a bunch of money for nothing." He lay back against the headboard. "I'll need a day or two to get back on my feet. The stuff they shot me with won't let me keep anything down, but it should be out of my system soon. I need you to keep up on things at the dairy until then, okay?"

Luke nodded.

"Everything been okay so far?" he asked.

"Uh huh." Luke couldn't help staring at how thin and frail his friend had become in just a few days.

Pete put an arm behind his head. "What's up, kid? You don't look right?"

"I have had some stuff come up in my life."

"What kind of stuff?"

Luke took a seat on the bed and leaned over with his elbows on his knees. "Remember I told you about the girl at the ranch where I worked before?"

Pete nodded. "This is the same place that had the fire you were blamed for?"

"Yes. Well, I found out today that she's pregnant with my baby."

It wasn't a word but a low whispered, "Ah."

"I have a letter from her that says she still loves me, but it was written a while ago, so I'm not sure how she feels now."

"Have you called her?"

"I tried," said Luke. "Her dad answered and told me I'd be arrested if I came near her."

"It's your baby. You have rights."

"I know. But until I can talk to her, I don't know what I should do."

Pete tried to adjust himself in the bed and winced in pain.

Luke stood up and bent over to help him sit up. "Do you have pain pills or something?" he asked.

"They're out in the kitchen."

Luke started to go retrieve them, but Pete grabbed his arm and made him sit back down on the bed.

"Stay here."

"I'm not leaving. I'm just going to get the pills."

"No, I mean live here. When you and this girl have the baby, I want you to live here."

"What?" asked Luke, surprised.

"I want you to have this house when I'm gone. I'm giving it to you."

"Don't talk like that," said Luke.

"It's what will be. The doctors were surprised I've lived this long."

Luke felt his eyes start to tear and wondered if he could take yet another heartbreak in his life. "Don't talk about dying."

Pete patted Luke's arm and sighed. "It's God's plan. I'll be fine."

Luke reeled back. "God's plan?" he said, with venom.

"Yes."

Luke pulled his arm away.

"What's wrong, Luke?" Pete asked.

"Why do you say it's God's plan? Do you really think *God* has anything to do with taking your life?"

"God didn't take my life, I did. But it's God's plan that we all live and die, some of us sooner than others."

"That isn't God's plan, it's just life. God didn't start that fire in the arena, Vee's sister did. It was her recklessness that killed my father, not God. Why does everyone think that God is hovering around making a difference?"

"Why are you so bitter? We can't understand everything that happens because God has His own reasons for giving us the challenges we have in life."

Luke shook his head.

"Luke, I believe with all my heart that God brought you to me. In just a few short months you've become like a son to me. I feel like God gave me a gift in you and that's why I'm giving you everything I have. Now that I hear you're going to be a father, I know what I've worked for all my life. I know now that the things I've done were for a reason. I feel blessed and happy for the first time in years."

Luke listened to Pete skeptically. He wondered if the disease hadn't affected his mind, but he knew how Pete felt about him and it was a comfort for Luke to know he had Pete in his life. However, he worried about losing yet another person that he loved. He stayed with Pete, giving Pete his pills and making him dinner. Pete thanked him, but Luke heard him vomiting in the bathroom later that night.

In the morning Luke dressed quietly in his room and then went to check on Pete before he left for the dairy. He found the man in his t-shirt and underwear, sitting on the edge of the bed.

"Do you need something before I leave," Luke asked quietly.

Pete looked up with a face that showed both exhaustion and fear. He shook his head slightly.

Luke pushed the door open and stepped inside. "Are you okay?"

"I'd rather die than feel like this for even one more hour."

Luke picked up one of the bottles of pills. "Aren't these working? Do you want me to call a doctor?"

"No. I don't want any more doctors." He took several deep, pain-filled breaths.

"Maybe I should stay here today…"

"No," Pete interrupted. "Go take care of things." He swallowed. "Sit down for a minute."

Luke did.

"When are you going to see this girl?"

"Tomorrow. I'm hoping I can get to her while her parents are at church. If I leave here by eight, I should get there in time to make sure they have left."

Pete listened intently as he stared at the ground. "Then what?"

Luke thought for a moment. "I'm not sure. I hope I'll have the chance to tell her that I love her and that I want to be together and raise our baby."

"What if she says no?"

Luke shook his head slowly. "I believe with all my heart that she won't."

"And what if she says yes?" Pete smiled.

It made Luke feel good to see him smile and he beamed in response. "Then I'll be the happiest man alive."

"Treat her as though she is the greatest gift in the world."

"I will."

"And don't ever let a moment go by where you don't thank God that she's with you."

Chapter 25

Malad, Idaho, Spring 2009

The drive was incredibly awkward. I hated the fact that everyone kept calling it my first real date. Stephanie said it tipped with sarcasm, and my grandmother made the word sound sweet, like a fairytale. "It's what all girls dream of," she cooed. "You'll remember it forever."

Linda and her boyfriend, Brad, sat in the back. I heard them giggling and whispering. I had my hands carefully placed on my lap. Before we pulled out of my grandparent's drive, Eric had quietly told me how nice I looked. My hand was on the seat next to me and he laid his on top of it, giving it a squeeze to emphasize his compliment.

When we pulled into the parking lot of the large brick church house, I had never seen so many people my age. There were girls gathered in groups around the double glass door entrance. Young men lingered in the parking lot leaning on cars and laughing.

"They obviously got the word out," said Linda. "I can't believe how many people are here."

As we walked toward the building, Eric kept looking at me and smiling. He stayed close and made sure that he was in between Linda and me. I needed her to lean on, in what was sure to be an anxious and challenging first experience. I could tell that Eric was using that to his advantage and hoping I would look to *him* for security.

We reached the doors of the church house. Eric stepped forward and opened them with a grand sweeping wave. I stepped through, and a girl walking by said the name I dreaded but had expected to hear..."Callidora."

I heard it again, "Callidora. You know the one..." With every step we took, more faces turned to me, offering looks of bizarre curiosity and awe.

Finally, Linda stepped in. "Her name is Sophie. She doesn't like being called the other name."

"That's enough," Eric called, pulling me toward him.

Eric walked beside me with a look of pride. He put his hand on my back as he directed me through the foyer and toward the large dance hall. Loud thumps and distorted sounds of music filled the entire building and people had to yell to be heard.

"Do you see how everyone is staring at us?" he asked with glee.

I nodded sadly as we continued through the crowd. Once inside the hall I felt a bit relieved, even though it was twice as crowded as the rest of the building. The lights were dimmed; it was so dark and congested, I was able to become a bit more anonymous.

Eric found a cleared space and stopped. Brad and Linda weren't far behind and when they reached us, Linda's eyes grew wide. "This is crazy. I can't believe how crowded it is. There are usually a lot of people, but this is the most I've ever seen. Are you okay, Sophie?" she asked, seeing my apprehension.

I tried to smile, but before I could do anything Eric butted in. "Of course she's okay. She's with me." He laughed. "Let them stare. I don't care."

I could see that Linda felt guilty for being part of it. "If it's too much, we'll leave. We can go get ice cream or do something else."

"We're not leaving," said Eric, stepping between us. "We're dancing, and we're dancing out there for everyone to see. They can eat their hearts out." He took my wrist and pulled me to the dance floor.

We dodged other couples and made our way into the middle of the dancers on the floor. Right when he found the perfect place, the song ended.

"Just hold on, another one will start," Eric said, glancing at those around us. They stared, clumsily, after realizing who I was.

Another song began. "Sweet!" he exclaimed. "A slow one." He took me in his arms and placed my hands around his neck. He started slowly rocking back and forth. Eric held me much too close. Other couples were in similar bear hugs, and all were shooting glances in time with the music, back and forth between Eric and me. Some whispered to each other, but most just stared.

"This is great," Eric said with delight. He was enjoying the scandalous limelight.

I sighed, baffled at what anyone found enticing about being squeezed tightly and shuffled around in a crowded, stifling pandemonium.

As the song continued along with our awkward two-step, I felt an eerily cool breeze float around us. It was out of place in the stuffy hot room and I wondered if anyone else noticed. My shoulders tingled. I looked up into the space above the bobbing heads and saw a cloudy murk, swirling above the crowd. It was enticing and lured me in. It wasn't smoke or haze but a churning energy that I felt was searching me out. Whispers and murmurs of my identity floated along and carried across the length of the large room. I looked at Eric, wondering if he saw the cloud, too, but he just continued to revel in the stares of others.

Then I heard a hum come from across the dance floor. It started quietly, but grew as voices carried it in a spinning, spiraling force that became like a swarm. Soon it was all around us and the crowd seemed to get closer and thicker as the whirling strength turned the individual bodies into a single rotating mass, controlling where we moved.

"What the hell," said Eric, annoyed at how we were bumped and jostled about.

Eric was pushed away. I was separated from the swarm, but still being pushed by it. I felt scared and helpless, but as I looked up at the swirling mist above, I noticed it was starting to calm.

Suddenly, I was thrust out of the mob and into a small open space, still surrounded by faces in the crowd. They looked perplexed, but relieved for the chaos to be over. Then, out from the throng, stepped a tall, sandy-haired young man with dark eyes. He looked as mystified as the rest of the crowd, as he stood alone and looked over at me. In the dimly lit room, surrounded by the buzz of the crowd, I studied him.

"Look, they're together," I heard a voice call from the group.

He took a step forward with a warm and astounded smile.

I was so stunned at what I saw I barely realized who he was until I said his name out loud. "Damien." The moment I heard it leave my lips, I wanted to fall into his arms. I went to him and he hugged me.

"Sophie," he whispered into my ear. The sound of his voice and the tickle of his breath made me weak. "I can't believe it's you."

I looked up through my tears. "It's me. I've missed you so much." He felt heavenly in my arms, and I let the crowds and noise vanish as I clung to him. I closed my eyes and relished my body touching his. Damien's chest was broad, and I could feel the strength and tone in his back. He had become a man in the months since I watched him flee from my window.

"I didn't think you wanted to see me again," he said, looking into my eyes as the music blared in the background. "You told me…"

"It was a lie. I was trying to protect you. I love you, Damien. I always have."

For a moment I thought he was leaning down to kiss me. I felt my heart expand and my stomach tighten.

"Hey!" A voice yelled. "Look at the two love birds!"

"Didn't he already get shot once for being with her?" another voice called out.

A roar of laughter erupted.

Damien looked at them and his face turned to worry. "Let's go," he said, trying to walk us away.

I felt a hand grab my arm and rip me from his embrace. It was Eric. "What are you doing?" he growled. "You came with me."

I tried to shake free, but he yanked hard. A flash lit up the darkness and then another. Cameras were going off everywhere.

"Damien," I said, reaching for him, as Eric tried to pull me away.

"Let her go," said Damien, taking my other arm and pulling me toward him.

Eric stopped and lunged at him. "Lay off! She's mine."

Damien looked at me for a response. I shook my head and tried to release my arm from Eric's grip, but he was strong and able to pull me back into the crowd.

"Did you come with me, or not?" Eric demanded.

"Yes, but..." I tried to explain.

"They're going to fight over Callidora!" a girl cackled.

Damien started to back off, looking confused and bewildered.

"Damien," I called, as Eric dragged me through the mass of onlookers.

Damien looked around as the group taunted and laughed. Someone pushed him back into the crowd. I saw the angst in his face as he flinched against his sudden notoriety. I wanted to go to him and make him see it was still just me, the same girl that he spent his lazy summer days with, and not the scandalous sideshow he now witnessed. I pulled against Eric's grip only making him tighten it further.

"Stop," I said, finally digging my heels in and ripping my arm away. Before he could grab me again, I stepped away quickly. "Don't touch me!"

He stood up defiantly. "If you don't leave with me right now you can find your own way back to Malad."

I didn't even answer him, but turned and went to find Damien.

The crowd had closed in and I looked over the sea of faces trying to find his. The music was still loud and someone pushed me into the middle of the floor. I searched for Damien and found him looking over the masses, but getting farther away as the crowd formed a barrier between us. I tried to keep eye contact with him, but it was impossible, as I was being bounced around the dance floor in a wicked game of pinball. I tripped and flailed – listening to the mocking laughter all around me.

"Stop!" I tried to yell, but the dizzying jostles had me concentrating on trying to stay upright. I felt my breathing grow rapid and my face begin to sweat. I worried I would pass out and be trampled by the mob. Then I felt my foot kicked out from under me and I fell forward, skidding on my hands and landing face down. I turned to see Eric standing over me, seething.

"I don't care who you are or what you look like, no one leaves me," he said, lifting his arm as though to backhand me. I put my arm up to guard my face, as the taunting shouts filled my head. I felt my legs being stepped on and I tried to curl up and protect what I could. Then I was pulled to standing. As I tried to break away from what I was sure was Eric's grip, I heard Stephanie's voice over the noise.

"Come on, let's get you out of here," she said.

I looked over to see Eric on the floor, rubbing the side of his head. He pushed himself up and shouted, "Lesbian!"

The crowd settled in a startled hush.

"Look at the lesbian lovers!" he yelled. "Everyone already knows Stephanie Dunford is a dyke. Look at the two of them. She came all the way up here to save her from being with me." He pointed at us as we huddled together. The crowd stared and whispered. I was so relieved to have Stephanie there that I clung to her, wanting nothing more than to get away.

"See!" he shouted, adding an obnoxious guffaw. "Lesbos."

Stephanie ignored him, turned, and walked us out of the dance hall. The crowd parted like we were contagious, as we made our way through and outside. The cool, fresh air made my sense of freedom even more pronounced and I gasped.

"You'll be fine," she said, directing me to the car. It was my grandfather's Cadillac and I looked at her apprehensively before I got in. "I, on the other hand, may be spending even more time in juvie."

"Did you steal Grandfather's car?" I asked, shocked.

"No. I borrowed it."

As we drove away, I looked out the back window and started to cry. "That was the most terrible thing ever."

"I told you they were a bunch of pricks."

"It's more than that," I tried to explain. "I lost him again."

"Who?"

"Damien. He was there. I got to see him and he hugged me; I told him that I love him, but that was it. They started taking pictures of us and pushing us around. Then Eric pulled me away and that was the last I saw of him."

Stephanie put on the brakes. "Do you want to go back?"

I shook my head, then sat and cried. I couldn't believe I had lost him again. I wanted to die if I couldn't be with him. Every time I saw his face looking down into mine, my tears became stronger.

Stephanie didn't say a word, but just kept driving.

I wondered why she wasn't talking to me or trying to comfort my pain. I felt exhausted and I rubbed the palms of my hands where I had landed. They were red and still stung from the skid when I fell. I sat, feeling unsettled, wondering if she was mad at me for what happened. "Thank you," I muttered, hoping to at least get a response.

She didn't look at me, but gave a soft grunt.

I stayed silent in my seat, watching the streetlights pass and kept playing out what happened over and over in my mind. I couldn't wait to tell my grandparents what type of person Eric really was. I made a vow that I would never be out in a crowd again. My heart sank with thoughts of what might have happened if Stephanie hadn't been there. "You saved me. You said you'd save me and you did."

Stephanie slammed on the breaks and swerved the car to the shoulder of the road. "This isn't what I meant by saving you. This is what a best friend does when her friend makes a dumb decision. I helped you. I didn't save you."

I didn't understand what she meant. I started to ask her but she held up a hand for silence.

"Do you still believe in that stupid curse? *Do you?* Or is that all for show so you can be 'Little Miss Innocent Callidora' for the rest of your life?"

"What do you mean?"

"Answer me. Do you still believe you are cursed and that anyone who loves you could die?"

I hated her tone and felt attacked. I tried to talk, but all that I could muster was a weak "Yes."

"You do?"

"I said, yes."

I saw a vile look in her eyes. "But I thought you loved Damien. Isn't that what you said?"

"I do."

"Really? You must not love him very much. Maybe it's just lust." She laughed mockingly. "Poor little

Callidora. What? Don't you know what lust is? Or are you too pure for all that?

"Lust is when you want to rip his clothes off and climb all over his body. It has nothing to do with love. I think your hormones are raging and you're using all this curse stuff as an excuse to keep him at arm's length because you don't understand your own body."

I felt violated with the way she talked about Damien and me. "I love him."

"How much? How much do you love your precious Damien?"

I felt like she was mocking my feelings, but I answered her anyway. "More than anything."

"I don't believe you."

"I do. I love him more than anything in the world." I said the words with vengeance, hoping she'd see my resolve.

Her face went from livid to sullen. "Then why do you want him to die? If you love him so much and you still believe in that stupid curse, why would you want to hurt him? Why do you want to be around any of us for that matter?"

The words were like a stinging slap.

"Do you really believe in this curse? Think about it, Sophie. It wasn't your fault that the people you loved died. They died because of accidents. It's what happens in life. The only way you'll ever be happy is if you can push that aside. You can't go on living if what you believe, and what you feel, are at war with each other."

"But Papa said..."

She scoffed. "You can't believe in everything he said. You aren't even really sure what he told you. You can't trust him."

"But he's my father."

She inhaled deeply as she sat back against the seat. "I know this is hard for you to understand, but just because he's your father doesn't mean you can trust him. Fathers aren't supposed to hurt you."

"He didn't," I said, trying to defend him.

"He made you think that you're the reason people are dead. A father who loves you would never say that."

"He didn't say it to hurt me. He was trying to explain things, but then the police came."

Stephanie looked over with weary, sad eyes. "Stop this insanity. Someone said once that, if you live with someone who's crazy long enough, you start going crazy yourself. Your father is crazy, and you will be, too, if you let his insanity affect you. Love Damien, live a fun life and start thinking for yourself. Remember what I said. You can't trust people."

"I know that."

She looked over her shoulder and pulled the car back onto the road, a sign that our conversation was ending. "I told you before and I'm not going to tell you again. I'm your best friend and you're supposed to tell me everything. I can't save you if you don't let me."

Chapter 26

When we arrived at the ranch, Grandmother was waiting in the doorway. Even though she looked tormented, I sat for a moment before getting out. "What's going to happen? I don't want you to get in trouble."

Stephanie finally smiled. "When you are constantly in trouble, one more thing isn't going to make much of a difference. You better go before she comes running for you. She's probably worried that I kidnapped you away from those 'nice kids' at church."

"I am going to tell her exactly what happened. I can't believe I agreed to go with them."

"Live and learn."

I reached for the car door but then sat back, remembering what I had wanted to ask her the entire drive home.

"What?" she asked, seeing me hesitate.

"Why did they call you a lesbo? Don't you like boys?"

Stephanie smiled. "You can't tell anyone, but I'm not a lesbian. I just tell everyone I am."

"Why would you do that?"

"I want to be left alone. It was an easy way for me to get out of a bad situation. When you're a pariah no one wants to touch you. You won't be bothered if you're repulsive."

I sat and thought for a moment.

"Don't get any ideas," she said. "Everyone knows you love Damien. You'll have to find another way to avoid your problems. This lesbian thing is my gig." She looked at the house and I turned to see what she was looking at.

My grandfather stood next to my grandmother. I was surprised that he hadn't already pulled me from the car and had Stephanie arrested.

"He loves you. I've told you not to trust anyone, but you can trust him."

I looked back at her shocked. "I thought you hated him."

"I did. But sometimes people prove you wrong. If anyone does things to you that you know aren't right and you don't want to tell me, tell him."

"Why wouldn't I want to tell you?" I asked.

She shrugged, but stayed silent.

We both stood in the glare of the security light of the gravel driveway. I walked toward the house, but Stephanie stayed by the car.

My grandmother put her hands out. "What happened? Where are the others?"

I shook my head and walked around her and into the arms of my grandfather. The minute my face was buried in his chest, I began to sob.

He put a hand on my head and one on my back.

"What's wrong?" my grandmother continued. "Gene, what's going on?"

"It's okay," he said to me, rubbing my back. "Go to your room and I'll be there in a minute. I need to talk to Stephanie."

"She helped me. Please don't be mad at her," I pleaded with tear-filled eyes.

"Don't worry. I'm just glad you're home safe."

My grandmother became indignant. "What's going on here?"

My grandfather released me and directed me toward my room. "I knew this was a bad idea. That kid wanted nothing more than to bring attention to himself. I don't want that Eric anywhere near this house again."

"But they're nice kids. What happened? I just wanted her to get out and meet people. She needs to be normal."

Grandfather turned on her. "She needs to be *normal*? She doesn't need to prove that to anyone. She *is* normal." He left her standing with mouth agape and walked out the door toward Stephanie, who was still standing at the car.

I watched through my window as he took the keys from her and then put an arm around her shoulders. He directed her to get into the car and then he drove her home.

My grandmother came to my room. "I'm so sorry, dear. I really thought it would be fun for you." She walked to me and took my hands. "I truly love you and only want you to be happy."

I nodded.

"I would never do anything to hurt you. I want you to have a happy and full life. I don't want you to be trapped inside here. I want you to have friends and be able to see the world. Do you understand?"

Again, I just nodded.

"I don't see how being here all alone with us will make you happy. I feel like your grandfather wants to keep you all penned up. I know he worries, but that's no way to live."

My grandfather came to me. "Stephanie had called me and told me what happened. I'm so mad I feel like killing that boy, Eric," he growled.

"I'm okay," I assured him.

"She also said that the boy your father shot was there."

I wasn't sure if I should be angry or relieved that Stephanie had told him. I felt tears fill my eyes again.

Grandfather hugged me, this time with even more vigor. We went to the sofa and sat down. "I should have listened to my instincts. I knew something bad was going to happen."

"How did you know?" I asked.

He exhaled loudly. "I know how people are. I can see the way people react to you and look at you. They'll take advantage of you and it scares me."

"It's just like Papa," I said softly, not realizing my words could be heard.

"What did you say?" Grandfather asked.

I looked up at him, worried I'd made him mad. I shook my head, trying to erase what I'd said.

"It's okay. Tell me what you said," he assured me.

"Papa said he kept me in the house because he was scared of what would happen if I was around people. Damien and Donny were my first friends." I lowered my head. "And Papa didn't know the boys were my friends. I kept them secret because I didn't want him to worry and keep them away."

"I don't want to keep you locked up," my grandfather said. "That isn't what is best. I don't know what to do."

"Papa always said he was protecting me."

243

My grandfather sighed. "That's ironic, because that's what I thought I was doing with your mother. I thought I was protecting her." His face turned to a daze and I saw an incredible sorrow creep into his eyes. "I miss her so much. I feel doubly responsible, like I not only have to protect you, but also do everything I can to make it up to her."

"Is that why you let me live here?" I asked.

They both turned to me in shock. Grandmother let out a breathy, "No!"

"You're our granddaughter. You're our family. That is why you are here," my grandfather said with verve.

"But you didn't even know me."

"That doesn't matter," he continued. "We loved you all these years because you are a part of us. You have our blood. No matter what, you'll always be our family."

I felt warmed, but also confused. What they were saying conflicted with what I had been told most of my life. "What about my mother? How can you love me after what happened to her? I thought I killed her."

Grandfather gave my grandmother a stare that silenced her, and she looked as though she would explode. "That's not true. You didn't kill her."

I sat up away from him and squared my shoulders with his. I wanted to look into his eyes and see the truth. "Then why won't anyone tell me how she died?"

For the first time, my grandfather looked to my grandmother for support. She leapt at the chance. "You asked me that question the first day you were here and I was afraid to tell you, but I think it's time you knew the truth."

I expected to learn my accountability and how it shaped my entire life.

She looked at her husband and he gave her an approving nod. "I'll tell you everything you want to know, but I can't do it here."

"Then where?" I asked.

"I want to take you to her."

I felt a sting of horror, but my grandmother tenderly placed her hand on my head. "I think she's been watching over you all this time. It's time you know."

For perspective I looked to Grandfather, but he cast his eyes to the side, giving me reason to worry.

"You need your sleep. In the morning we'll talk," Grandmother said.

Grandfather went to the kitchen table and picked up the newspaper along with his glasses. They both busied themselves, but it was obvious years of pain—an empty hole in their hearts—permeated the house. I didn't press for more, seeing the sadness in both their faces. Their obligatory joy at my being found and returned to them was tempered by the vast somberness I saw hidden behind insistent smiles.

I had gone to bed feeling anxious, but woke feeling good. However, the sensation left quickly when memories of the horrid night before filled my head. I walked out to the kitchen and my grandmother greeted me as though it were any other morning.

"Eat and get dressed so we can leave. I want to take you somewhere. It's a place I should have shown you a long time ago."

I did what she said, and without explanation we got into the car and drove off toward town. I enjoyed being out and seeing the different buildings and landscapes of the valley. My grandmother looked awkward and uncomfortable behind the wheel and I couldn't help smiling.

She noticed me watching her. "Would you like to learn to drive?"

I was floored. "Me?" I asked.

"You're seventeen. Most kids around here start driving at fifteen. I'm sure your grandfather would teach you. He taught your mother and aunt."

I smiled to myself at the thought. I imagined being behind the wheel and the enormous sensation of freedom it brought. "Yes. I want to."

"Okay. I'll let him know."

We drove through the main part of the city and then took a road that led to the outskirts of town, and up a solitary hill. As we hit the crest, I could see acres of headstones. I turned to my grandmother in horror.

"This is where your mother is buried."

I felt my heart tighten and I wanted to bolt. "We need to leave."

"What?" she asked, surprised.

"Hurry. Turn the car around."

She put the car in park and placed a hand on my arm. "Sophie, there is nothing to be afraid of."

"There are ghosts here. We need to leave, now." I was sweating and looking around for signs of 'them' coming to get us. I couldn't understand why she brought me to a place that would surely kill us both.

"Sophie, listen to me. There are no such things as ghosts. This is a cemetery. People come here every day to remember the ones they've lost. Nothing is going to hurt you."

I shook my head frantically and tried to breathe. "But there are ghosts. There were ghosts in the hills where Papa buried them."

My grandmother shook me and made me look at her. "What did you say?"

"There are ghosts, and if you go into the hills they'll kill you."

"That's ridiculous. There are no such things."

My breathing became less intense the longer we sat in the car. After a while I realized we were okay and I took a cautious scan of the area.

My grandmother waited patiently for me to calm down, and then she took my hands. "Whom did your father bury?"

"My grandmother and his friend. He buried them in the hills behind our house."

She furrowed her brow and bit her lip. "Did he kill those people?"

I shook my head. "No."

"Why are you so scared of them?"

"They are the watchers. They'll get you if you go into the hills. Ghosts are out there." I looked out at the rows of tombstones.

"Sophie, you must stop saying that. It's not true. Your mother is buried out there."

"Papa said that she died because of me."

"That's terrible," she said still holding my hands. "I still can't believe he said such a thing."

"I thought you knew. That's why I thought you hated me. I thought that's why you never explained how my mother died."

Grandmother leaned back and closed her eyes for a bit. "No dear, you are not the reason she died. I don't ever want to talk badly about your father, but what he told you is awful. It's all a lie. You didn't kill your mother and we certainly don't blame you for her death. He was wrong for telling you that." She stopped and gave a loud 'humph' of assertion. "Come on," she said, opening the car door.

I flinched.

"It's okay. Come with me so I can show you where your mother is. Nothing is going to happen. I want to tell you the truth about how she died so you'll know it wasn't you."

Chapter 27

Arbon Valley, Idaho, March 2, 1992

Luke woke feeling anxious but invigorated. He knew there was a risk Vee could turn him away, or that she was not there at all, but just the possibility of seeing her and knowing she was carrying his child was exhilarating. His love for her had only grown over time, and with that on his side, he was confident the day would go well.

He went to check on Pete and found him already dressed and looking revived. "You look like a new man," he said.

"I am. Good luck today," Pete said, handing him his keys. Luke had asked to borrow his truck for a better disguise. "My prayers will be with you,"

Luke accepted Pete's good will and felt that, regardless of what he believed about God and prayer, he would take whatever help he could get. He packed some food, knowing he might be sitting and waiting for hours, and then headed out. "I don't know when I'll be back," he said to Pete, as he stood in the doorway. "Hopefully, sooner than later."

Pete gave him a smile. "You'll be fine. I'll leave the key on top of the door jamb."

Luke waved and set off on his quest. It wasn't until he was down the long lane and out on to the dirt road that he realized what Pete had said. Why would he leave the key, when Luke had one of his own? Luke shrugged, writing it off to Pete's illness and the fact that he was probably still tired from the medication and lack of sleep the last few days.

Luke turned the radio on and daydreamed about Vee's reaction when she saw him. It was something he had done many times, and in just a couple of hours it could become a reality.

As he drove through the Portneuf Gap and down through the open valley of Mink Creek and Arimo, the weight of what his new life could be began to settle in. It made him think about his own father and the struggles he had endured in his life. It gave Luke strength, having seen Thomas sacrifice to take care of his family. It's what it would take, and Luke was ready and willing. With Vee by his side, he knew he could do anything.

The more excited he got the faster he drove, but the road seemed to stretch out even longer than he remembered. His stomach started roiling the closer he got, and the tingle of both excitement and fear traveled up into his chest. When he saw the sign for Malad, he started to catch his breath and steady himself, knowing he needed a plan.

The drive through town and up the narrow road toward the Richardson ranch was heart-wrenching. Luke knew driving straight up to it was a huge gamble, but there was no other way. He sighed as he looked out over the rolling hills and pastures that he had explored for years before life had become so trying. What he wouldn't give to have just a few hours like it was before.

The morning had started out with a brilliant sun show, but as the day wore on the clouds turned dark and the sky became thick with what was to come. Luke turned the heater to low and was grateful he remembered to bring along a wool blanket. It would come in handy if he had to sit in the truck and wait.

As the truck made its way up the hill, he took a deep breath and knew that as soon as he hit the summit, it would dip down and he'd be able to see the ranch spread out in the basin below. He smiled in anticipation.

When Luke hit the peak of the hill, the valley opened up and he paused for a moment to take it in. Regardless of what had happened, he still considered the ranch and its endless acres of fields his home.

From his vantage point he could see the sprawling house and the narrow dirt lane that led to the small caretaker's home. It was just over the hill, so the little house itself was still hidden from view. And then he noticed the arena that sat just to the side of the large house surrounded by a clean white fence. The section that had burned was repaired, but the distinction was obvious due to the newness of the siding and shingles. It was a clear reminder of what had happened, and Luke wondered if the pain of that day would ever fade away.

He picked out a spot along the road that ran in front of the house, but was blocked from view by a large snow drift. It was just far enough away to park the truck and hide from view while watching the house. He was able to see if their cars were still there and then decide his next course of action.

There was no movement from the house and the cars were gone. He made it to the spot without incident. He parked and turned off the truck, investigating the area. Could he be this lucky to have them already gone? He decided to wait until ten thirty just in case there were stragglers. He pulled the wool blanket around his shoulders and waited as the storm began to churn and fill the valley.

The cold quickly took over the truck cab and Luke swore at its harsh and bitter bite.

When his watch told him it was time to act, he started the truck and slowly eased it back onto the road. Cautiously, he made his way to the house. It was a path he had taken a thousand times, but this one ripped at his gut as though it were a death march. He talked to himself, giving pep talks and telling himself that it would be the first day of their new life together. But he knew deep inside the possibilities were endless—both for success and for failure —and the knowledge that he risked being arrested kept throbbing in the back of his mind.

Luke saw no point in not pulling straight into the drive. He needed the truck close if he required a quick getaway. It was time for him to make his move and he turned off the truck and looked down at this clothes. He tucked in his shirt and straightened his hair in the rearview mirror.

The wind had picked up and pushed against him as he made his way to the ranch house door. It was so cold he could hardly focus and didn't waste time with the doorbell, quickly knocking on the heavy wood.

Luke pulled his jacket up around his face and waited. After several seconds he pounded again. Then the door opened, and as if his daydreams were playing out in front of him, there stood Vee.

She squinted up at him as the harsh wind rushed into the house, "Can I help you?"

Luke smiled at her round belly, knowing what she carried was his. He caught her gaze and for a moment Vee looked scared. She put a hand to her belly and took a step back. Her face seemed pained and she bent over slightly.

"Vee," Luke said, his voice cracking with emotion. "It's me."

She studied him and blinked several times. Then her eyes shot open and she put a hand to her mouth. "Luke," she cried.

He stepped into the house, closed the door and without worry of anyone else being there, took her in his arms and held her. "It's you. I love you."

Vee relented and sank into him. Even her large round belly didn't keep her from holding him close. Feeling his warmth and strength, and knowing it was really him, she started to cry.

"Don't cry. I'm here to take you away. We're going to be together. I won't let anyone get in the way."

She tried to answer him, but her voice faded into a groan and she had to wipe the tears from her face.

He stepped back from their embrace just enough to look down at her belly. He put a hand to it, and then his own tears came. "You're beautiful," he whispered and then kissed her.

She held him close. She gave a small laugh and ran her fingers through his dark hair, putting a hand to his face. "I didn't recognize you. Your hair is so long and..." she giggled. "You have a beard." She smiled. "It looks good." Then her joy faltered. She pulled back and swallowed hard. "But what about your wife?"

Luke face turned stunned. "*Wife?* I don't have a wife. I would never be with anyone but you. I've never stopped loving you."

"But when I tried to find you, to tell you," she looked down at her large belly. "I saw that picture of you and her. And when I called, a girl told me you were..."

253

"That I was married?" He grimaced in disgust, realizing how things had played against him. Luke gently took her face in his hands and looked down into her large blue eyes. "I'm not married; never have been and never will be unless it's to you. I love you and only you." He kissed her softly. "We're going to be a family."

Vee gave him a sad smile. "Why didn't you tell the truth about what happened with the fire? Why did you let Elise get away with it?"

Luke nodded, understanding her quandary. "I knew that no matter what I said, your father wouldn't believe me. I didn't want him to know about us because I didn't want you to get in trouble." He laughed and touched her stomach. "But I knew that someday he would know the truth."

Vee lifted an eyebrow. "I think he already does. It wasn't long after you left that he caught her smoking in the barn. I don't think he'll ever come out and admit it, but I think he knows. Elise, of course, is still denying everything."

Luke laughed. "My mother put a Gypsy curse on all of you as we were leaving."

Vee looked at him with shock. "A curse?"

He nodded and laughed again. "Yep. So I'm sure Elise will get what's coming to her."

Luke pulled Vee close and kissed her. When he leaned back, looking into her large blue eyes, he knew his life would finally be right again.

Then, like a curtain being closed between them, Vee slowly shut her eyes. Her body went limp and she sunk down into his chest. He put a hand to her belly.

"What is it?" Luke asked.

She looked up at him and her eyes had turned to fear. "Something's wrong."

Luke took her shoulders and kept her from sinking to the floor. "The baby? Is it coming?"

"I..." Vee tried to speak but then a low and awful moan replaced her voice.

He pulled an afghan from the end of the sofa and wrapped it around her. Cradling her in his arms, Luke lifted her up and carried her to the door. She cried out in pain as he reached for the knob.

Luke whisked Vee out of the house and went quickly to the truck. He carefully placed her on the passenger seat, and she bent over with a loud wail. The blanket came undone and as he went to wrap it back around her, he noticed a smear of blood. His heart leapt and he quickly secured the seatbelt around her, running to the driver's side. He pulled out quickly and drove as fast as he could, trying not to jostle her as she screamed and wept.

"Something's wrong," she cried again. "Luke, I don't want to lose the baby. I'll die if I lose her."

"You're not going to lose her," he encouraged. "Everything will be fine."

She leaned forward and groaned. Vee took arduous and intentional breaths. "It's a girl. We're having a girl." Her voice trailed off as she spoke, but Luke kept trying to engage her, to keep her with him.

"She'll be beautiful, just like you," he said.

She smiled weakly. "That's what Daddy said. Her name is Callidora. It's Greek for beauty. Daddy named her." She grimaced as another contraction hit.

He reached over to her and put a hand on her shoulder. "There won't be a person alive who won't fall in love with her."

255

Vee's head bobbed. "I already do love her, more than anything," she whispered. Her eyes were heavy and her voice started to slur.

"Stay with me, Vee. Oh, God, please hang on." He shook her shoulder and she opened her eyes. "I love you Vee."

"I love you, too," she said in a half whisper. She leaned forward and cried out in pain.

"We're almost there."

They cleared the top of the hill, and Luke swerved the truck as it barreled along. In town, he dodged cars and sped through stop signs, reaching the small rural hospital. A pool of red had formed on the seat and was dripping onto the floor of the truck.

Vee wept and cringed as pain overtook her.

Luke ran through the doors with Vee in his arms, straight into the receiving area. A nurse saw the blood and immediately directed him through the swinging double doors and into a large open area where people in white coats and scrubs were busy working. The nurse called out to several of them and, in a matter of moments, Vee was swept out of Luke's arms and out of his reach. He stood feeling numb and alone as she was carried away.

The nurse took him to a room down a hall and directed him to a bathroom. He looked down at his shirt and realized he was covered in Vee's blood. She handed him a smock to change into and told him what floor the emergency crew had taken Vee.

Luke quickly did as she directed, stripping off his shirt and cleaning up as best he could. He ran down the corridor and to the elevator. When the doors opened at floor three, he went to the reception desk. A young woman directed him down the hall to Vee's room. People were running in and out of the door so he stayed back, not wanting to hinder their efforts. Instead he wrung his hands and paced. He felt like crying, but his anxiousness was so pronounced that his body couldn't relax enough to relent to his emotions.

"Respiratory therapy to room three eleven," a voice boomed overhead.

Luke looked up from his pacing. It was Vee's room. The door opened, and a nurse walked quickly toward the nurses' station. She gave Luke a surprised and horrified look. It made Luke's heart freeze, and he bolted through the door. Inside, the doctor was at Vee's head, his body blocking Luke's view. In a small, clear, plastic basinet, a nurse was working with the baby, but she watched the doctor, her eyes fearful and her mouth taut.

"What's happening?" Luke demanded.

The nurse turned to him and just shook her head.

From behind, three men came through the door, rolling a large machine. They pushed by Luke and began to set up. The doctor talked to them in quick mumbles and then stood back and let them go to work.

Luke squeezed through the crowd and saw Vee's face. It was covered with an oxygen mask, but he could see her eyes; they were half closed and she looked pale and groggy. Her hair was sprawled across the pillow and some was glued to her forehead with sweat. For a moment it looked as if she caught his gaze. He opened his mouth to tell her to hold on, but he saw her sinking away, as her breathing went from raspy and loud to nothing but a soft hiss. Then she closed her eyes.

Luke felt his life go with her. All his plans were sucked from him, like the blood from his face, when he saw her go. He leaned on the bed, as the technicians slowly

257

cleared the room. Their faces were sullen and apologetic. As the baby was wheeled by, Luke looked over and marveled at her perfect pink face.

The nurse put a hand on his arm. "I'm so sorry."

"Did she even get to see the baby?" Luke asked in a choked voice.

The nurse nodded. "She did. She got to hold her for a moment. She kissed her and told her she loved her." She patted Luke's arm. "It happened very quickly. I don't think she suffered." It was meant to comfort Luke, but instead it stabbed at his heart. "Are you the husband?" the nurse asked.

Luke was numb. "I'm the father," he mumbled.

The nurse left him alone to grieve.

When he was alone, Luke bent down and kissed Vee's forehead. "This can't be," he whispered. "Vee... please let this be a dream." He found a chair against the wall, slumped down into it, put his face in his hands and sobbed.

He found a restroom down the hall and grabbed a handful of paper towels after trying to clear his eyes with cold water. As he dried his face, he stared into the mirror above the sink at a truly unrecognizable image. His mind blurred with pain, and when it sharpened back into focus, the face of his dead father had replaced his own. Luke's heart clenched and he tried to turn away, but was paralyzed at the vision. Thomas' eyes were sad and Luke's skin turned cold when he saw a look of dread fall over his father's face. He started to call out to him, to ask what he saw, but then the restroom door swung open and jarred Luke out of his trance. A young boy hurried in and ran urgently to one of the stalls.

Luke took a deep breath and reached for the door. He turned for one last look in the mirror and found nothing but his own reflection…weary and vacant, staring back.

"Amniotic embolism," is what the doctor tried to explain. There was nothing anyone could do.

Luke stood out of sight, around the corner of the hallway of Vee's room. He listened and tamped down the sobs he felt rising in his throat.

"Nothing?" raged Richardson, red-faced and tear-stained. "In this day and age of artificial hearts and total hip replacements, there is *nothing* you could do to save a woman in childbirth?" He used anger to fill the intense sorrow.

The rest of the family stood with him outside the room and cried. It was extremely rare, the doctor said. No way to predict it and no way to prevent it.

"Who was with her?" Richardson asked.

Luke peeked around the corner, hearing the question.

The doctor looked back to the nurse, who brushed a strand of hair from her sullen face. "It was a man. Dark hair…"

"Luke," Richardson growled. He looked at the nurse. "Did you get a name?"

The nurse shook her head; her eyes were large and she swallowed hard.

"I know he had something to do with this." Richardson said, pacing. "Only bad follows that little creep. I know it was him."

The nurse piped up. "He was disheveled looking, older. He had long hair and a heavy beard. He said he was her father." She shrugged.

"*I'm* her father!" Richardson spewed.

The nurse stepped back quickly.

"It doesn't sound like Luke," Molly said softly.

"Where is he? Where is this man now?" he asked. "I want to know what happened to my daughter!"

Luke felt his composure falter and he fell back against the wall. His precious Vee was dead, and now Richardson wanted to blame him. He felt the fury rise with his tears as he broke and ran.

He believed Vee's father would do anything he could to point the finger of guilt at Luke and again he had no one to prove he was innocent. As he drove back home, he cried hard and hit the seat with his fists. How could this be? He had planned on making a life with Vee. He finally learned she still loved him and they were going to be a family. Now all his hopes and plans were gone. Oh, God, how could she be dead?

As he sobbed and drove, his mother's face came to him in a blurry fog. She was summoning him home. It wasn't a comfort, or motherly assurance he felt as her presence drew him in, but an urgency that chilled his heart and made his mind feel like it was on fire. The sensation pulled at him as though it were steering the truck for him. Strange repetitive words and noises filled his head.

He leaned forward and purposely struck his head on the steering wheel, making the truck swerve chaotically. He yelled, "I hate you!" out through the windshield and into the sky. It was for no one and for everyone. His sorrow grew into anger and rage and was so strong he felt his veins throb with every heartbeat.

By the time he reached his mother's small trailer, his body was exhausted and his emotions were numb. He sat,desolated, in the truck, feeling like the shell of a person his mother had been for the past year.

He walked into the house without knocking and found her sitting near a wood-burning stove with a blanket over her lap. She looked like an elderly woman, even though she hadn't reached fifty.

"Luke, where've you been? We've been looking for you. We called your work and they say they've never heard of you. What's going on?"

"Sit down," he told her. "I need to talk to you."

"Talia has been so worried."

"I don't care. I want nothing to do with her."

"What?"

Luke fidgeted a moment. "I don't want to talk about her. Mom, something terrible has happened. I feel like my life is over." His lip began to quiver.

"What? What?" Theta cried out in her thick Greek accent.

"It's Vee."

Theta leaned back.

"She's dead. Everything was going to be perfect and it turned terrible."

"How?"

Luke shook his head, weary at the thought of explaining everything that happened that morning. He tried to speak and his tears began to fall to the floor.

Theta put a hand to her mouth. "The baby?" she asked.

"The baby is fine." Then Luke looked up, shocked. "You *knew* about the baby."

Theta's eyes turned to fear.

"Oh, my God...you knew," he said, stunned. "How? *Why?*" He stumbled with his thoughts. "You knew and you didn't tell me. How could you?" Luke stood up and paced, throwing his arms up and down in fury. "When did you find out? I should have known. She tried to tell me. You all kept it from me and now look what happened, I've lost her!"

Theta cowered in her chair.

"Why Mama? *Why?*" He kneeled in front of her, shouting.

"It's my fault," she said timidly.

"Yes, it is," he said back.

"It's all my fault. What I did, it is now happening."

"What are you talking about?"

She couldn't look at him. Her hands grabbed at the blanket and she bit her lip.

"What!" he demanded.

"It's the curse," she whispered.

"Oh, good hell!" Luke roared and stood up. He turned back to her. "Why are you doing this? There is no curse. Vee is dead and all you can say is that a curse killed her. Why did I even come here?" he yelled at the ceiling.

"Luke, you have to listen," she begged. "It'll get worse. You have to stop it."

"Get worse! How could it get worse? The girl I love is dead and now her parents are blaming me and want me arrested. And they have MY baby." He went to the sofa across from her and sat down. He glared at her and shook his head. "I don't want you talking to anyone about me, what happened, or anything. Do you understand?"

Theta gave a hesitant nod.

"No, I mean it! I know that Talia and her family lied to Vee about me. I'll never forgive them, and if you ever want to see me again you had better keep your mouth shut." Luke stood up and pulled his coat closed.

"Where are you going?"

262

Luke had no idea what his plan was at that point, but he knew he needed time and space to think. With what whirled through his mind at that moment, all Luke could say in response was, "Hell."

Chapter 28

Luke pulled the truck into the drive and marveled at the amount of snow that must have fallen just that morning. There were no other tracks in the drive and none leading from the closed garage. He went into the little house, wondering if Pete had decided to stay home, but found him nowhere. Luke figured Pete had made it to work and was relieved that his friend was well enough to go in on a Sunday. It was also nice that Luke was able to be alone, feeling he needed some time to regain himself before facing Pete and exposing the horrid details of what happened earlier that day.

Luke wandered around the kitchen, feeling hungry but refusing to eat. He took a shower and cried when he removed the borrowed scrub shirt and realized Vee's blood was still covering his jeans.

The sound and feel of the water masked his choking sobs, but when he finished, Luke could feel that some of the morning's misery had subsided. He was ready to talk and prepare for what was ahead. Pete would be home soon and Luke was comforted by that. He knew Pete would have the advice and assurance that he so desperately needed.

He pulled a pizza from the freezer. As he stood waiting for the oven to preheat, Luke looked out the window and up into the hills. The late afternoon sun was just starting to make its way toward the tips of the Albion Mountains.

Against the crystal brilliance of newly fallen snow, he noticed a hint of red fluttering high on the hill. He studied it for a moment, wondering if it was a bird or a stubborn fall leaf. He ruled both out, and was then plucked from his daze from the beep of the oven telling him it was time to put the pizza in. He slid it onto the rack and turned on the timer. It would be ready almost exactly when he expected Pete home. Luke pulled out a beer and sat in the living room...waiting.

The oven timer woke Luke from a shallow sleep. He walked to the front window and peered out, wondering where Pete could be. Luke shuffled into the kitchen, pulled the pizza out and placed it on a tray on the stovetop. He went back to the window, continuing his vigil.

When seven o'clock hit and Luke had already eaten two pieces of the pizza, he began to worry. He decided to go down to the dairy and find out what was taking Pete so long. He knew Pete kept a strict schedule, and if he was still working, then something had to be wrong.

Luke's exhaustion set in as dusk fell over the valley. He had cried and ached so much that day, his body was beginning to shut down.

At the dairy, Luke saw only two cars. One belonged to the ramrod, Gerard, but the other he didn't recognize. He walked in to find Mandy at the table. She looked up and gave an annoyed sigh upon seeing him. Before Luke could say anything, she said. "Do you know where Pete's at?"

Luke shook his head. "I was wondering the same thing. That's why I came down here."

"He's been acting so weird lately. If I didn't hide it from Mr. Strickland, he would have fired him weeks ago." She turned to Gerard. "You can go home now that Miguel is here."

Gerard nodded and quickly left the building.

"Get this straightened out before Mr. Strickland throws a fit. Can you take over until we find out what's going on?"

"Yeah, sure."

She closed the ledger. "Do you have any idea where he is or why he's doing this? And why does Pete pay you under the table?"

Luke's head was still spinning with questions about Pete, but he swallowed and answered her. "Pete pays me under the table because I'm not legal."

"Really? *You?* I didn't expect that. You just don't seem…" she didn't finish.

"Will that be a problem?"

She laughed. "Half the people on these dairies aren't. I'll deal with it. Did he pay you in cash?"

Luke nodded.

"Then I'll pay you in cash. You won't be making as much as he did yet because you don't have the experience, but I'll be able to bump you up soon. Okay?"

"What are you talking about? Why would you bump me up?"

Mandy sighed heavily. "Because if Pete doesn't come back, then you'll be doing his job." She bit her lip. "I swear, after all these years of working with someone you'd think you'd know them better. I can't believe he just took off."

"He is very sick," Luke blurted it out. He knew he was breaking a confidence with his friend, but felt she needed to know Pete was no flake.

She raised an eyebrow. "How sick?"

"Very. I don't know how long he's got. He told me the doctors can't help him."

266

"Do you think he went away to die?"

Luke was stunned at her question, but the more he thought about it, it made sense. Pete didn't want to be a burden, and he knew it was inevitable. Still, Luke couldn't imagine Pete leaving without telling him. "No. He wouldn't just leave. I'm sure there is a reason he's not here. I'll make sure things are okay until he is."

Mandy pulled on her coat and gloves. "I'll need a phone number where I can reach you."

"I've been staying with Pete. I guess I'll stay there."

"I've been calling there all day," she said, exasperated.

Luke put up a hand in defense. "I was gone...at my mother's. I just got in a couple hours ago."

"Oh, okay. So that's where you'll be living? I've never been to his place. Is it up Arbon Valley Road?"

Luke nodded.

"Well, good luck...Miguel. Make sure you call me if you see or hear from Pete, and avoid Mr. Strickland at all costs."

After Mandy left, Luke walked around the office and break area, looking for something to explain where Pete was. He soon gave up and decided to go back to the house.

The drive back to Pete's had Luke dismayed and confused. It made no sense to him that Pete would just disappear. Even with the illness, Pete was mentally alert and certainly cared. Luke couldn't imagine him just deserting everything. And the one thing Luke knew Pete would never do is take Luke's truck. They had switched that morning, and while it was Luke's idea so he could be more discreet, he knew Pete wouldn't leave for good with Luke's truck.

267

When he reached the house, he decided to do a better check of the rooms inside. He checked Pete's closet and dressers. Nothing seemed to be out of place. In fact, the more he looked, the more he realized how clean and organized the entire house was. It was as though Pete had made a special effort to have everything just right.

As he undressed for bed, overwhelming loneliness filled him and again the horrific scenes of losing Vee that morning rushed his mind, making him flinch. It was still like a nightmare he couldn't wake from.

Sleep was arduous. The full winter moon kept the darkness at bay and Luke flipped back and forth trying to clear his mind. It was useless. He knew what he had to do, but without Pete for guidance he was left feeling frustrated and helpless. The more time ticked away, the more his sadness over losing Vee was being replaced by his intense desire to have his baby beside him.

When his attempts at sleep were finally exhausted, he sat up in bed. "What do I do?" he said out loud. "If anyone needs a god right now, it's me. Please help me."

The night rejected his plea and remained silent. Luke went to the kitchen, poured a glass of milk and stood alone, drearily staring at his reflection in the window. What was once a handsome and stalwart young man was now a ragged and weak relic. He tried to see through the window, but the darkness outside refused to reveal it. His image was so glaring and solemn that even when he tried, he couldn't turn away. Something coerced him to keep looking as though the reflection would show him what was veiled but obvious.

The door leading out to the living room framed him, and he stood staring at the image, as tiny snowflakes fell outside, making it look like they were all around him. The wooded jamb was thick and made the entryway stand out from the room.

Then Pete's words whispered to him. "I'll leave the keys on the door jamb." It's what Pete said as Luke was leaving that morning. Luke thought it was odd at the time, but now he felt as though tiny pieces of a giant puzzle were floating down all around him and finding their exact spot.

Luke opened the front door and reached atop the wooden frame where Pete left the spare key to the house before giving it to Luke. Luke felt along the jamb and then he touched the metal, grabbing the cluster of keys. They were Luke's truck keys. He stared at them, bewildered. The air was so cold the perspiration on his shirt made the cloth freeze to his skin. He pulled the door closed and huddled to get warm.

"How could he leave my keys and take my truck?" He asked into the empty space of the house. Luke went to his bedroom where Pete's truck keys were sitting on the nightstand. He picked them up and held both sets of keys in his hands. Pete couldn't have left, at least not in Luke's truck.

He stood up and walked quickly out to the garage. He opened the door, and there was Luke's truck parked inside. "What the hell?"

Monday came quickly, and with myriad questions and horrific scenes fighting for time in his mind, sleep was still elusive. But he got ready for work, keeping his private promise to Pete to keep things going smoothly at the dairy until he returned.

When he arrived, the workers were huddled talking and they looked at him with faces of worry and unrest. Without giving them a chance to increase their concern with queries, he put up a hand and simply said, "We're to keep things going until he gets back."

They stood with skepticism.

"Nothing has changed. Go back to work."

Reluctantly they did, and Luke sat at the table waiting for them to leave before he let his own concern spread over his body. It wasn't the job he feared, but the loss of his confidant and friend. What he was facing in life was so immense he just couldn't bear the thought of dealing with it on his own.

Luke walked the chutes, corral area and through the milking barn, checking for problems and making sure the men kept things moving. Snow was still falling since the night before, but the milder temperature was destroyed by the biting breeze.

Luke's mind raced with what had happened, and he thought about his baby and who would care for her now. The idea of Vee's father naming her, and now *raising* her, clutched at his heart and made his stomach turn. If Pete didn't return soon, Luke knew he would have to do something on his own. There was no way he was going to let Richardson raise his child.

Luke walked back into the building and pulled the ledger from the cabinet. Taking a seat at the table, he envisioned the first time he had seen Pete hunched over and filling out daily reports. His large form and gruff Irish ways were in such contrast to the small Mexican workers he was so kind to.

He went home for lunch, and took some much needed time to think. The questioning looks from the other workers and the signs of Pete everywhere at the dairy haunted Luke, especially when he had no answers.

His exhaustion was evident as he stood at the sink, washing out the dishes he had used and gazing off at the hills in a stupor. Then the flash of color caught his eye again. It was the same red object he had seen the day before. It fluttered in the winter wind and was like a drop of blood on the pure white blanket of snow.

Even in his state of weary grief, his curiosity prodded him. Like a solid punch to the middle of his chest, it hit him. He didn't want to go, but knew he had to. Pulling on his coat and boots, he felt the terror of what he expected to find wash over him. The snow was over a foot deep and he made slow progress as he tried to leap with each step to avoid it. It was like trying to run in water. Each step was a struggle, but he pushed up the hill toward the red flag.

Luke's chest ached, and he repeated the words, "Please no," with every difficult stride. When he was just below the crest of the hill, he stopped. The red flutter was a red handkerchief and it was tied to a wooden handle. Luke walked slowly, panting, to the spot where it was planted. There, lying covered in snow in a shallow grave was the body of his beloved friend. Luke could see a dark pool of frozen blood surrounding his head; Pete's body was curled up, his hand still holding the pistol by his face.

"Oh God, Pete...no," Luke muttered. Carefully, Luke climbed down and brushed the snow away from Pete's body, removing the gun from his fingers. The snow continued to fall and Luke kneeled beside him and shouted up at the sky, "Stop it! God damn it!" His breathing became deep and he started to moan with each throaty gasp.

Then, like a tree losing its battle against the wind, a deafening crack echoed out from him. The snap was audible and made Luke flinch. The moans stopped, and with empty eyes, he stared out over the valley. He crawled from the hole and pulled at the handle revealing a shovel. He took the handkerchief from the handle and noticed a small sodden envelope tied to the handle. In Pete's handwriting was simply: "To Luke." He opened it and read:

Luke,

I am sorry you had to see this and do the horrible job of burying me, but you didn't need a dying old man to look after. This was best for all of us. This is your home now. I have signed over the house and land to you and want you to be happy here with your family. I hope that you will raise your children here. My only regret is that I won't be around to see it. I could find no other way to do this, but my last request is to be with this land forever. I hope that you will feel that I am watching over you and your family and being your guardian angel. I have taken everything from the bank and hidden it in your truck. I didn't know what the baby would be, so I bought something that will be okay for a boy or a girl. Please do everything in your power to protect and cherish your child. I wish you love and happiness. Again, I'm sorry, but I know this is for the best.

God Bless you, Pete

Luke folded the note and placed it in his pocket. Without emotion, he took the shovel and dug into the pile of dirt Pete had left after digging his own grave. Luke started the job slowly, but then his rage took over and with anguishing cries he stabbed at the dirt, filling the hole and burying Pete. When he was done, Luke fell forward in a heap of defeated sorrow. He lay there panting and crying and then rolled over, lying face up toward the white fluttering sky.

Luke stayed there and let the flakes fall on him. Wetness washed over his face, mixing with dirt and tears. So much pain and sorrow…his thoughts turned to blame.

His mother's voice rang out all around him, reminding Luke of his defiance toward God. He had spoken loudly and often of his lack of belief and his scorn for those who had faith. He had rejected God, and now he saw that even with the prayers of others, those he loved didn't stand a chance.

Luke's defiance was what caused it all. Theta was right. It was his rejection of faith that resulted in his losses, and if he didn't regain it, only more tragedy would follow. Luke pulled from the deepest parts of his past to when his parents prayed with him to relieve his fever, woke him from a deep sleep to read the Bible before his chores on the farm, or dressed him in clean black slacks and a white shirt for their Sunday morning services. Now he believed that his lack of faith was what had taken Vee. It was his punishment for his insolence. He loaded every gap and nook of his being with self-reproach for being weak and rebellious.

Luke took the shovel and pushed it deep into earth. He tied the handkerchief tightly to the handle, to be a marker and memorial to his friend, and trudged back to the house, gun in hand, hunched with the overwhelming pain of loss and despair.

Luke put the gun on the kitchen table. He went to the garage and unlocked the passenger door of the truck. Inside the glove box was a paper bag holding a large plastic storage container filled with money. Luke gave a weary sigh. Wrapped in newspaper was a small gift. He tore away the paper. Inside was a tiny yellow nightshirt with a sleepy sheep on the front. Luke smiled, but it quickly turned to grief. He held up the tiny garment, picturing how his baby girl would look in it, and ached inside that he didn't even have her to fill the void.

The things he loved and cared about were gone, and what was left was regret and an overwhelming need for vengeance. He was now a single father at age eighteen, and he wondered if his new daughter could ever forgive him for not being the man of faith she deserved. He knew what he was going to do, and he had the will and means to make it right. If insolence against God took Vee, Pete and even his father from him, then by accepting Him, Luke felt he deserved to take back his family.

He kneeled down by his bed and clasped his hands in front of him as he had done as a child. He let the silence of the house and the vast expanse of the night sky guide his prayers. Luke poured out his heart, his fears and desperate desires. The words were spoken in his mind, but the sound echoed in his head. He talked to God and felt that God answered. Luke heard His voice telling him what to do.

When he finished, Luke calmly pulled on his coat and hat and took the gun from the kitchen table. With God's army on his side, he would battle to take back what was rightly his.

Chapter 29

Malad, Idaho 2009

From the hillside where my mother was buried, I could see the entire town. It was a nice view, and Grandmother said that's why they put her there. I thought about the hill in back of the house in Arbon Valley. That is where ghosts were buried, too. Dead people must spend a lot of time looking out at what is going on without them.

"I love being here," Grandmother said dreamily. "Being on this hill gives me hope." She smiled at me. "I can look down over the entire valley." She turned to the grave.

The headstone read: Veronica Richardson, beloved daughter, sister and mother. I read it and looked up at my grandmother who was smiling sadly. Her story of how my mother died was quick and sterile. There was no mention of my father. In fact, her version made me feel as though my mother was happy to sacrifice her life for me. She was that devoted and selfless.

"She loved me," I said looking at her name on the stone.

Grandmother leaned into me and grabbed my shoulders. "She loved you more than anything. She was so excited about having you and I know she watches over you every day."

"She's a ghost too?"

My grandmother shook her head. "She's an angel in Heaven looking down on us and watching over us."

I looked up into the gray, cloudless sky. "Will you see her again some day?"

"Yes," my grandmother answered, ecstatic at the opportunity to espouse her beliefs upon my pure and green mind. "We believe eternal families will always be together, even after we die. In fact, we look forward to being together in the celestial kingdom."

"Can I come too?"

With a giddy laugh she hugged me. "Oh, yes. We'll make sure you are sealed to us for all eternity."

"What does that mean?"

"It means our whole family will be together again."

My heart leapt. "Even Papa?"

Her smile slipped into a baffled frown. "Well, to get to the celestial kingdom you have to live a life that is worthy while you're here on earth. You have to do what's right."

I thought about what she said. "How do you know you've done enough?"

Her smile slowly crept back. "You know because of a feeling you get. You hear the voice of the Holy Ghost guiding you."

I leaned back and glowered. "You said there was no such thing as ghosts."

"It's not that kind of ghost. The Holy Ghost is like your conscience. It is a feeling you get when you know you're not doing the right thing. It makes you feel funny inside. Sometimes you are confused, but the feeling tells you it's bad."

The image of Uncle Lonny and what had happened the day we talked about visiting Papa popped into my head.

I wondered if that was the Holy Ghost telling me what was happening was bad. I nodded in understanding, and my grandmother gave a satisfied smile.

"If you pray about accepting God and doing those things to return to Him, He'll give you the guidance you need."

"I pray all the time," I said. I wondered why I was still confused about so many of the things in my life.

Again she gave me her grandmotherly smile.

"There are a lot of dead people buried here," I said, giving the cemetery a sweeping gaze.

We stood looking out over the expanse of headstones, half-dead flowers, and other earthly gifts that the dead supposedly appreciated.

"There is someone else from your family who is buried here," my grandmother said, hesitant.

I turned to her. "Who?"

"Your other grandfather."

"Papa's father?"

"Yes. His name was Thomas and he was a very good man. Would you like to see his grave?"

I was a bit disturbed by my enthusiasm to see where my dead grandfather lay, but I was curious. We walked over the hill and down to the edge of the cemetery where under a tall oak tree was a small headstone with simple lettering.

"Thomas Theotokis," I read. Then I paused. I looked back up the hill where my mother was buried. "Why do we have different last names? Why is my mother's name Richardson like yours and mine is Theotokis like Papa's?"

My grandmother looked at the ground. "That's because your father and mother never married."

"Why? I thought they loved each other. That's what Papa said."

"They were young, and sometimes things happen when you don't expect them."

"Do you mean me?"

She was obviously dismayed at what I assumed.

"They weren't expecting me."

"No, but that doesn't mean they didn't want you. We all wanted you."

I didn't believe her. It was all starting to make sense. The hex that surrounded Papa and me wasn't a blight that was just on us. It affected everyone around us. I had plagued my family and anyone else who crossed my path. I was unintended; even my own birth had caused tragedy.

Grandmother could see my mind turning and my face growing with sadness. "Stop this," she ordered. "You're making up things that aren't real. What happened is in the past. It doesn't matter now. What matters is that we love you."

More than ever my desire to see Papa was overwhelming. There were so many questions I needed to have answered and I knew that my grandmother would never tell me the whole truth. I knew now that what Papa had told me made sense and there was more at stake in my life. Simply existing was a risk I placed on anyone I cared about. Their decision to reject the notion of the curse could have grave effects.

I started to check off in my mind the list of those whom I had possibly ruined. It was something I was just starting to see, but knew my father had realized it long ago. I envisioned the day I first saw his expression toward me change. I was so young, but the switch from true affection to trepidation was so clear, even years later I could picture it and it still struck me tragically. I took a deep breath and looked at Grandmother without feeling.

"You love me?" I asked.

She nodded emphatically. "Oh, yes. Very much."

Without emotion, I continued, "My other grandmother told me she loved me, but only once."

"Why only once?" she asked, surprised.

"All I remember is my father coming home and asking me what happened. He looked at me like I was evil. I was still wet and wrapped in a towel. My grandma was lying on the floor dead. I don't know what happened. I remember her hugging me and telling me she was sorry and then she said she loved me. She had never said it before, so it stood out."

"Why were you wet?"

I looked away, wondering why I should tell her the truth. I was so young, and I wasn't even sure if my memories were accurate—the thrusting gasps and blurry view of Theta's face as I had fiercely fought her grip was no delusion. I knew in my heart that the woman I had known as my grandmother had tried to kill me.

It was no coincidence that I had something to do with her death. But I wasn't going to let anyone know that. "I don't know. Papa said I was only four when it happened."

As though she would explode if she held it in any longer, my grandmother tried to swallow her words but failed. "I must tell you about your other grandmother."

"Did you know her?"

"Not really, but I knew Thomas. He was Gene's best friend."

I leaned back in surprise. "They were friends?"

"Yes, in fact they were childhood friends. Thomas and Gene went to high school together, but then Gene went on his mission. A mission is something the young men in our church do. They leave and go teach the Gospel to others for two years. Thomas went to Nebraska."

I nodded, hoping she would tell me more.

"Your Thomas isn't a member. He went to the Greek Church, so when Gene left for his mission they didn't see each other for a while. But when Gene and I were married, Thomas was there. He wasn't in the temple for the ceremony, but he was at the reception.

"We didn't meet Theta until later. Thomas was living in Pocatello and managing a restaurant," she said, with the notion that I should be proud of that. "He met Theta at their church and they married just a few months later. It was a nice ceremony. We drove up from Malad to see it.

"It was years later, when Gene got word that Thomas needed our help. We had just built our house on the ranch, and Gene offered to let Thomas and his family come and live with us on the ranch. Gene gave him a job and let them live in the smaller house over the hill."

It was the question she expected me to ask. "Why did he need your help?"

She nodded as I finished my last word, and then continued. "There were things that happened that made your grandpa lose his job and, well…" she paused, searching for words.

I could see her reluctance and prodded her. "What is it?"

"Theta was…" she hesitated and then pursed her mouth in thought. "She was ill."

"She was sick?"

"Well," Grandmother stammered. "Yes. She had some problems that…" Again, she struggled. "It made her do some things that weren't good. Thomas wanted your father to have a decent life without people knowing, so he let them come and live with us."

"What did she do?" I asked.

Grandmother looked down. "It wasn't her..." she stopped.

"Who was it?"

"No, what I mean is...well, it was her illness that made her do those things."

I became annoyed at her avoidance. "What things?"

"I don't know for sure, but what I was told is she acted funny and threatened people. I guess she would become a different person. She talked to people who weren't there. She thought she saw things. She chanted, talked about things that weren't real. It scared people."

She saw the dismay in my face. "It was the illness. That's what it can do to people."

"Her illness made her chant things? What things? She sounds crazy." The minute the word came out of my mouth, I felt my demeanor melt. I could see my grandmother was shaken, too. I suddenly remembered what Stephanie had said about living with crazy people.

Her face became creased and sullen. "I'm sorry, dear," she said. "It wasn't her fault. We still don't understand a lot of it. One thing I can tell you is your grandfather loved her. He took care of her and your father. When Thomas was killed, Gene wanted to let Theta and your father stay in the little house, but he learned what had happened and worried that Luke was a bad influence on our girls. He had to make a choice, and it was one he questions himself about every day."

"Grandpa Gene made them leave. Is that when Papa took me?" I asked.

"No. That was before you were born." She tilted her head and smiled. "At that point, we didn't even know you were on the way."

I felt a cold blanket of depression fall over me. "Papa was all alone," I said, feeling incredible sadness for my father. "He had no one but me. No wonder he was scared that you would come and take me away." Suddenly, I missed him more than ever.

"There was so much anger. Adults can act worse than children. It seems we all caused you so much pain, when we should have all wanted to help you."

I raised my eyebrows. "I wasn't unhappy. I loved living in that house and being with Papa."

Grandmother's face turned to concern. "Weren't you lonely being there without any friends?"

I thought about it for a moment and then sighed. "I was happier then. Most of the time, I'd rather be alone."

She patted my hands and lifted my chin. "It'll get easier. Young people can act very silly sometimes. Don't let what happened the other night sour you on making friends."

It hadn't. I was already disillusioned about letting people get close, but what that night did was convince me that, no matter how much I prayed, what I did, or how I changed, I would never be treated like everyone else. I would always be the girl who had been raised in a cage.

Chapter 30

Malad, Idaho, Early March, 2010

In all the following months that year, Uncle Lonny submitted the jail visitation form, but it was turned down because I was under age. With his next submission, a corrections officer noticed the request and alerted Carpo, who intercepted it before it was sent back. It was all Carpo could do to keep his elation in check when he called to inform Lonny, who had listed himself as the contact, that he would be happy to make the arrangements.

His plan was simple. He would be my personal escort. He portrayed himself as the 'hero' to me, and without my grandparents knowing or standing in the way, he had me all to himself on the five hour drive to Boise.

His dreams of "Anthony Carponelli, True Crime Author" had been resurrected. And the hours alone in a car were all he needed to make that dream come true. He could get the dirty little details he needed for his book to be the sensational masterpiece he had banked on for years.

It was the day after my eighteenth birthday, and I was still in awe of all that my grandparents had given me; a small compact car, a fancy cell phone, and a laptop computer. They were newly dedicated to opening up my world.

"I'll teach you in the evenings after school, but you'll still have to take the test before you can drive on your own," Grandfather said smiling. "Stephanie will help you with the computer and cell phone."

I marveled at my gifts. Although my grandfather was incredibly kind, he rarely smiled or showed any type of happiness. Oddly, it made it easier for me to be around him. I quickly tired of the overactive enthusiasm of my grandmother, so together they balanced each other quite nicely.

Uncle Lonny returned from taking Stephanie to her counseling session. He took my hand and pulled me to standing. He pulled papers from a folder and presented them like a gift.

"I couldn't give this to you yesterday during the party because it's important that you don't say a word to anyone but...Happy Birthday," he announced, holding out the signed paperwork.

I looked at it and then at him.

"Read it. Just the top," he said.

"Idaho State Department of Corrections Visitor Application," I read aloud. I then looked down and saw a scribbled but official looking signature next to red typed words saying "authorized."

"You did it," I said in a half whisper.

He stood back with his chubby chest sticking out and simply grinned.

"When?" I asked, searching the form for a date.

"Tomorrow," he said.

I gasped. "Papa," I mumbled in a daze.

"Is that all I get?" Uncle Lonny said, opening his arms for a hug.

"Oh," I said, being shaken from my joy. I hugged him gingerly, and he took advantage of the opportunity and kept me locked in his arms. He smelled of burnt popcorn and I felt my stomach heave.

"Detective Carponelli will meet us early and drive you over to Boise. It is important that your grandparents don't know about this or they'll stand in your way. It's a long drive, so I've told them that we're all going on a field trip to Salt Lake City to visit the planetarium."

"Stephanie?" I asked, wondering why she hadn't said anything.

"She doesn't know. No one can. I'll tell her you're not feeling well and stayed home for the day. I'll pick you up when Carpo brings you back tomorrow night."

My heart was racing and I kept stepping on my foot to make sure I wasn't dreaming. It had been more than a year since I'd seen Papa, and now in less than a day I would be with him again.

It was six in the morning when Uncle Lonny drove me north toward Pocatello. Detective Carponelli waited at the gas station near the intersection of the two interstates. Normally I would have avoided him, but today he was my ticket to see Papa.

"I do believe you got even prettier since the last time I saw you," Carpo said, trying to offer a genuine smile that looked more like a snarl.

I slipped into Carpo's car before Uncle Lonny had a chance to hug me again. In a small way, I felt guilty for not being nicer to him after I got what I wanted, but at that point my thoughts and concerns were on one thing—seeing my father.

"Seat belt," Carpo ordered. "You're precious cargo."

The way he talked grated on me and I cringed every time he muttered a word.

"Does this look familiar?" he asked, after we had driven for at least half an hour in silence.

I looked out and was surprised that it vaguely did.

"You were found in a house right up there," he said, motioning to a small dirt road that was just past the freeway turn off.

"I still remember the day you disappeared," he said. "That was a long time ago, but I remember it clearly. It was a horrible thing."

I didn't speak, but sat with my hands in my lap, staring out at the fields and pastures of my past.

"It's hard to believe you were this close all along. I'm surprised no one ever spotted you. Did you *ever* leave that house?"

"Can we stop?" I asked Carpo quietly.

He was surprised I had spoken, but he reminded me of our time constraints. "It's your home. You can visit it any time you want."

I stared at him.

"You're eighteen. The land and house are yours. You're an adult, so you can go and do whatever you want. You can also talk to whoemver you want."

I looked over my shoulder as the route to my home faded into the distance. "I could live there?"

"Sure, if you want to go back to being a hermit. But why would you?"

I sat back against the seat, praying for him to stop talking. I didn't contemplate my future much. In fact, outside of wanting to be with Damien, I had no desires or plans.

Carpo saw my state of stupor. "I'm not trying to upset you. I feel like I've known you for years, and I want to help you. That's why I'm driving you to see your dad. I'm not getting paid to do this. I'm doing it for you."

I nodded, but I didn't look at him.

He tried to engage me again. "I used to call or visit your grandparents all the time. Even years later, I still stayed in touch. I had an artist do a picture of what he thought you might look like when you were older. I took your baby picture and a picture of your mother, and she spent weeks working on it. That picture was in every newspaper in the region."

I closed my eyes as my mind brought back the horror of that day. Carpo's voice faded as I heard loud bangs of a hammer being swung with vengeance and the shattering of broken glass. I was ten years old. Papa had looked at the front page of the newspaper, at me, and then back to the paper. He mumbled words like an angry prayer and then, with folded newspaper in hand, he methodically went to each room and destroyed every mirror in the house.

"I'm doing God's work by keeping you humble," he said. "Mirrors are the devil's portal to the soul, and now that you are tall enough to peer into them, I must remove the temptation to look, and the opportunity for Satan to find his way in."

Carpo tried again to extract the details of my life. "What did you like about living up there?"

I bit my lip and squirmed at the question. "I don't know. It was quiet and..." To explain my connection would never make sense to him. "It was pretty," I said without sentiment.

My words were not what Carpo needed to sell books, and he gradually became more anxious and annoyed at my unwillingness to open up to him. For over an hour we sat in silence.

"I hear you saw Damien Graham," Carpo said, knowing he'd get my attention.

I knew what he was doing, but it still jolted me to hear Damien's name. "Yes."

"Do you want to see him again?"

I looked over at him skeptically.

"I can help you."

I shook my head.

He lifted his eyebrows as a show of surprise. "I hear he's leaving for school back East. He got a baseball scholarship." He paused. "I've been keeping tabs on him, too."

My heart dropped, but I kept my face expressionless. Damien was leaving. Even though I'd only seen him and touched him once since the whole incident happened, the thought of him going off and having a life and a path without me was gut wrenching.

"Your father never did say what happened, but Damien's lucky to be alive. It was pretty brave the way he tried to save you."

I turned to him. "Save me?"

"Well, yeah," he answered. "Damien said he wanted to rescue you after he saw how you were living." Carpo looked over at me. "He almost died. He must really love you to risk being killed."

"Papa wasn't trying to kill him," I said defiantly.

"Really? What was he trying to do then?"

I didn't want to talk to him, but I also felt the need to set him straight. "He was just trying to scare Damien away."

"Why didn't he just tell him to leave? Why did he have to pull a gun?" Carpo asked, thrilled that he was getting his interview.

His question pricked. It was the same question I had asked myself more than once.

"You graduate this year. Do you have any plans for college?" Carpo asked.

I adjusted my seat and took a deep breath.

"You're a pretty remarkable person, especially considering all you've been through."

I kept looking out the window at the passing fields of sagebrush.

"I'm serious," he defended. "Your uncle tells me you're practically a straight-'A' student. It's amazing when you consider you never went to school, or really anywhere, but that little house. When your father took you, you weren't even a week old. He was seventeen. I can't tell you how many dead baby cases I've investigated because of teenage parents who couldn't handle the pressure.

"Even the people he worked with had no idea. He held a job, raised a kid and no one ever questioned him. I don't see how he did it all alone. Did you ever know your other grandmother? Her name was Theta."

My throat tightened as he struck a chord, like a razor piercing my skin. I could hardly keep my body upright and wanted to open the car door and jump out regardless of the speed.

"She went missing the same time you and your father did," he said nonchalantly. "We have proof she was in the cabin at one time, but as of today she's still listed as missing."

I closed my eyes hard. I wondered what he really knew and if this was just a ploy to break my shell and dig at the soft flesh underneath. "Why are you doing this?" I asked, enraged.

He looked over, surprised at my reaction. "Doing what?" he asked.

"I don't want to talk about this."

"Okay, but why?"

My head was spinning and my neck and underarms dripped with sweat. In the dark haunting of my mind, I saw her face clenched and determined as she pressed me down, stiff-armed, under the water. Her eyes were empty and I saw that my pleading and struggles weren't affecting her. I was barely four years old and the echoing in my head screamed out "Why?" but the only noise I made were my chokes and gasps that only sucked more water into my lungs.

I tried to grab the edge of the tub for leverage, but my small arms didn't reach and the porcelain was slick, giving me no traction. The view up at her was watery and blurred as my hair floated, whipping slowly around my face.

As my life began to slip away, I felt my body being ripped from the water and embraced tightly. It was an odd and confusing transformation. At first, I struggled against her, fearful that she was still trying to kill me, but exhaustion took over and I eventually fell into in her arms.

Her voice was frantic and loud. "I can't do it!" she wailed, squeezing me tightly and rocking me back and forth. "I am weak. I can't do it," she yelled up at the ceiling. She wrapped her arms around me and in an eerie and rhythmic murmuring repeated, "I'm sorry. I'm sorry, dear. I love you."

My body was like a limp wet towel in her arms. However the choking and gags continued until my body revolted and I vomited water everywhere.

The smell of Carpo's car heater and the visions in my head mixed dreadfully and took over my body. I felt my stomach lurch. "Pull over!" I urged, leaning forward and dry heaving.

He swerved the car to the side of the road and stopped. I flung open the door and vomited onto the gravel shoulder of the road. The chill hit my face and helped calm my stomach.

I felt better, but the memories still came.

I hadn't talked about what happened that day with anyone, including my father, but I could feel he was aware of what happened. It was something that had always been awkward between Papa and me: the look of horrified despair when he returned from work and found me half dressed and sitting guilt-faced in the corner, and my grandmother sprawled lifelessly in the hallway.

No words had been spoken, no tears had been shed, but he made me hike with him up the hill after he had buried her and told me she was now a ghost that would haunt the hills. He showed me the other grave and explained there were two. Even if one was sleeping, the other would get me if I wandered out alone from the safety of our little yard. It was the last time I ever went up the hillside, and I even avoided looking up in that direction, especially when darkness had fallen.

As my thoughts returned to the present, I realized that back then, Papa had been only twenty-two, orphaned and widowed, with a four-year-old to care for all alone.

Carpo paced near the front of the car until I was finished and leaning back against the seat, exhausted. My body and mind were weary and the stress of the trip overtook me as I started to weep.

"I'm sorry I upset you," he said, frantically. "I didn't mean to. I was only trying to make conversation." He quietly climbed back into the car.

I sat in silence with my eyes closed.

"Are you okay to keep going?"

I hesitated before answering. "I need to keep going. I need to know."

"Are you sure?"

I nodded.

"We can stop in Twin Falls and get some lunch. Would that help? We're making good time, or we can grab something to go."

"No. Keep going." I knew if I didn't press on and face what was waiting, I would never be able to answer the questions that constantly ticked in my mind. Papa was the only one who held the answers.

Chapter 31

March, 1992

Luke found himself driving in the center of the road. Pete's gun was on the seat beside him. Out of an indomitable daze, he realized he needed supplies to do what he planned. He pulled into a large grocery store in Pocatello and searched the aisles for what he needed. The more he pored over the choices of diapers, formulas and tiny clothes, the more he had to push thoughts of doubt and regret from his head. He paid cash and then doggedly drove on.

With one hand, he opened out a small blanket he had brought from Pete's room and placed it on a pillow he had stuffed into a small dresser drawer he had placed in his car earlier. He then headed for Inkom.

When he pulled into the drive of Theta's small trailer, the sun was still high in the sky, but it did nothing to take the edge off the frigid chill that covered the valley. He took the gun from the seat, walked up the wooden steps and knocked.

When Theta answered the door, she gave him an apprehensive smile, but then she looked down at the gun. A thin line formed between her dark brows. "What are you doing?"

"Quickly. Pack your things. You're coming with me."

She shook her head in stunned worry. "Why do you have a gun? Come with you where?"

"No questions, Mama. Just do what I say." He walked past her and went to her room.

She followed, rubbing her hands and watching him. "Why do you have a gun? Luke, what are you doing?"

"Pack, Mama."

"No. Tell me what you've done," she said, her voice quivering as though she were about to cry.

Luke had no time for emotions. "Damn it, Mama! Just pack. You did this to us and now you're going to help me. No questions and no arguments, or I swear I'll..." he raised the gun and looked at it.

"I'll call the police," she threatened in a scared whisper.

He turned to her with dead eyes and a low voice. "If you do anything except what I say, I'll tell everyone that you are a Gypsy and that you put a curse on us and that is the reason Vee is dead."

Theta gasped in horror. "You won't."

"Just try me."

Her eyes filled and tears spilled over her cheeks.

Without sentiment, Luke pointed at the closet. "Pack everything you want because we're never coming back."

Luke loaded several boxes of her things into the back of his truck. Even with over four decades of life, she possessed very little. He made sure she had packed her medications. He needed her well for his sake and his daughter's. Theta held her head low as she allowed him to open the truck door for her. Before he had a chance to get in, Theta had taken in the sight of diapers, bottles, and the drawer he had lined like a bassinet. Her eyes grew huge.

"Luke, you can't do this."

"Mama, I am doing this. She's my daughter and she's going to be with me."

"They'll never allow it."

"They won't have a choice."

For over an hour, they drove in silence. The sky went from sunny to a dark blue that was highlighted in the west by a glowing display of pink and orange. Luke's eyes began to droop as the hum of the truck lulled his worn out body into a sleepy trance. He was aware of his mother's presence but didn't care, when the sorrow again overtook him and soft, low moans of loss filled the cab of the truck.

When Luke's sobs stopped, Theta waited. She didn't say a word until he had gone a full ten minutes without a sniffle or a groan. Then she lowered her head and apologized to him. "I'll never forgive myself for what I've done to you. I'm so sorry, Luke."

"I'm the one who forced you to come with me. Why are you sorry?"

"None of this would have happened if I hadn't been weak and kept my Romani ways hidden."

Luke gave a disgusted sigh. "Good hell, Mama, not that stupid curse again."

She swallowed, wondering if she had spoken too soon. "You have to heed my warning Luke. It's already taken one life."

"It?" Luke asked enraged. "This is my daughter you're talking about, not an 'it'."

"It's the curse, Luke. It follows that family and she is now a part of it. Stay away, or you'll risk everything."

"Like what? I've already lost everything. She's all I have."

Theta shook her head. "Luke, I cursed them. They hurt our family and I wanted to hurt theirs. I cursed their offspring only to find death when they found love. I felt they took that from me, so I wanted them to feel the same pain. I had no idea I was cursing my own granddaughter."

"You didn't. That is all a bunch of phony voodoo crap. My daughter isn't cursed. And she had nothing to do with Vee's death."

"Luke, please," Theta pleaded.

"Mama!" he shut her down. "I won't listen to this. You are not a magic witch who has powers. You are an old woman who's lost her mind. I'm sorry about what happened to Papa, but turning crazy isn't going to bring him back. I need your help. Please be here for me. … Please, Mama. Will you help me?" he asked.

She looked at him with troubled eyes, but simply nodded.

Luke's heart started to pound powerfully in his chest as the truck began the steep climb of the Malad pass. A light snow started to fall and the pavement was exceptionally black against the coating of white flakes. As they crested the hill, a large dark cloud covered the entire valley. The storm had hit and he could hear the wind even from inside the truck. It made Luke dread his mission even more. But his fortitude was unfaltering. He felt it was the right thing to do.

They would be there soon and wait. The sky would turn from gray to black and the house would slowly close up and turn dark. Getting into the house would be easy, because the Richardson's never locked their doors. No one did in the valley. No one had a reason. Luke's only concern, besides making noise and waking them up, was being able to find what room his baby was in. He hoped that she was in Vee's old room. Now that Vee was gone, he worried they might have moved the baby into their room, making it a much more challenging task.

It wasn't worth worrying about. Regardless of where she was, he meant to find her and bring her home.

When they arrived, Luke pulled into the same side-of-the-road alcove where he had hidden before. He remembered his feeling of anticipation and excitement the last time he had sat there waiting, knowing he would see Vee and tell her he loved her and wanted her. Luke closed his eyes and let a rush of joy roll over him, remembering how he held her and knew she loved him, too. A stinging slap of reality hit him and he sat up straight and awake, wondering if he would ever feel any type of joy again. He couldn't think about that now.

Theta wasn't so composed. "Mr. Richardson is volatile and I know he owns guns. He won't think twice about shooting an armed intruder." No answer. She shuffled in her seat. "What happens now?" she asked, when the last light on the property was off.

"We wait."

"Then what?"

"I'm going to drive the truck up closer and then I'll go get her."

Theta squirmed nervously.

"I have a home and that is where we'll live—*all* of us. It will work."

"But they'll come after us."

"They won't find us."

She looked over at him with complete skepticism. "We can't hide forever."

He refused to let her slide any sliver of doubt into his plans. "I'm not letting them win. She is *my* daughter and she is going to be with me. They have already taken everything else. They aren't getting her." He paused, trying to keep the rage from overtaking him. "You should feel the same way. They took happiness from you, too."

"I think it's time," Theta said in a steady voice.

Luke looked at her, surprised, but felt a surge of strength, hearing his mother's acceptance of his plan. He put the truck in gear and slowly rolled out of their hiding place toward the sleeping, unsuspecting house.

Luke kept the headlights off and was able to see the street easily in the moonlight. He stopped just short of the lane and turned to Theta. "When I get out, scoot over. You're driving."

Luke licked his lips and took several deep breaths. Lifting the gun, he looked at it before opening the truck door and sliding out. He closed it carefully and then started toward the house, turning back to make sure Theta did what he ordered. His face was tight with fear, his eyes forlorn.

Luke went quickly and quietly around to the side door. It was the closest to Vee's door and was hidden around a corner, just out of sight of the security light.

The cold air and light snow helped keep his senses alert. Luke could hear the hum of the truck's engine, but even that wasn't enough to keep him from noticing how eerily still the night air was.

Reaching the cement pad by the door, Luke took several small breaths before proceeding. He hadn't tripped the light and felt confident. In several swift and smooth movements, Luke was inside the Richardson's house with the door left slightly ajar for his escape. He kept it that way, knowing his hands would be full when he left.

The house was dark, and he waited for his eyes to adjust. He didn't want a bumped corner of a wall or stray chair to keep his path from being quick and quiet. Luke listened intently, wondering how deep the sleep was, and hoping the house was as at ease as it seemed.

Seeing Vee's door was open, he slipped in and stood at the foot of the bed. Holding his breath, he looked to see if there was a body asleep next to the crib. His eyes said no, but he carefully reached down to softly feel if a foot was under the blankets. When he found nothing but a smooth flat bedspread, he felt relief and went to the crib. Reaching down, Luke immediately felt a soft warm body covered with a fluffy satin blanket. His heart stopped. It's my baby. It's my little girl, he thought. His eyes began to tear, but he pushed back his emotions, knowing it wasn't the time.

He started feeling around the room, and came across a pack of diapers, some plastic containers, and some tiny folded clothes on the dresser. Hanging on the side of the crib was another blanket. Luke carefully swaddled his baby in the satin blanket and then lifted her into his arms. He paused, feeling her warm face against his neck. A burst of love rose up in him and he stood motionless, hugging her as tears rolled down his cheeks. She started to stir and Luke quickly grabbed the second blanket and tucked it around her to block the cold and wind.

He bounced her lightly and she settled. Luke slipped out of the bedroom. With heart racing, he padded quietly back across the living room, through the kitchen to the obscure side door, and escaped.

Once outside, he ran to the waiting truck. He balanced the baby and the gun, as he opened the door and carefully slid in.

Theta's mouth was open in surprise that he had done it, and watched the bundle intently as Luke quietly closed the door and motioned for her to quickly drive off.

She did and they stayed silent until the truck had ducked over the ridge and was out of sight.

Luke laid the baby on his lap and turned on the dome light. "Look at her, Mama. She's so beautiful."

Theta took a quick glance and nodded. The baby started to scrunch her face and bring her little fists up around her head.

"What is her name?" Theta asked.

"Callidora," Luke said.

"Beauty," Theta answered.

"No, wait," said Luke, thinking a minute. "That is what Vee's father named her. I don't want that. What is a Greek name for having wisdom?"

Theta looked at him oddly.

"I don't want him to have anything to do with her. She's already beautiful. I want her to be smart. What Greek name means thoughtful and intelligent?"

Theta searched her mind. "Your father's sister is named Sophie. That means wisdom."

Luke looked at her with approval. "Then that's her name." He bent down and picked the baby up to his face. "You are Sophie Theotokis. You're beautiful and you will have a mind that will move mountains." He kissed her forehead.

Theta gasped.

"What?" Luke asked disturbed.

"You'll make her sick by kissing her. She is too young and you could have a cold."

Luke smiled. "Don't worry. She'll be safe. In fact, from this moment on I'll protect her with my life."

Chapter 32

Boise, Idaho, Early March, 2010

"Your legal name is Callidora Richardson," Carpo explained as we sat in a holding room, and I was about to sign in. "You won't be recognized or let in if you sign it Sophie Theotokis."

Even though I usually put up a fuss about using my correct name, I wasn't going to win this one, so I quickly scribbled the name. He smiled and nodded, pleased with my compliance, and stacked the papers nicely before handing them to the guard.

"Will you be going with her?" the guard asked Carpo.

"No," I answered, sternly.

Carpo shot me a glare, but then relented and turned back to the guard. "No, she wants to go alone."

"I'll be back," the guard said, leaving the room with the paperwork.

"Are you sure you want to go in there alone?" Carpo asked, trying to sound concerned.

"Yes," I said, completely sure.

The guard returned. "Come with me," he said.

I stood and followed him.

"I'll be right here," said Carpo.

The guard talked as we walked down a stark white hallway with bright fluorescent lights. "You are not to talk with the other inmates or visitors. You are not to have any electronic devices or cameras. You'll be searched before you go into the room. You'll have fifteen minutes and must leave when you are told. Do you understand?"

"Yes."

At the end of another long and sterile hallway was another door that led me into a room with a long row of cubby holes, each with a chair and a glass window. A phone was attached to each partition wall. The guard and I were the only ones in the room.

I was relieved to hear I'd be with Papa alone.

"You're going to be timed. Take a seat at the end there and I'll let them know you're ready."

I looked through the glass, and my stomach ached from a combination of nerves and hunger. A guard appeared on the other side of the glass wall. At his side, dressed in an orange jumpsuit looking old and drained, walked Papa. His dark hair was streaked with gray, and the skin around his eyes sagged. He was nearing thirty-five and looked sixty.

I gasped as tears rose up in my eyes and my throat burned. He was in shackles and his hands were cuffed. His eyes caught mine and he gave me a small, sad smile.

"Papa, are you all right?" I asked.

"Sophie, please don't cry," he said.

This only made me cry harder, and I wiped my tears with a tissue from a box on the counter in the cubby.

"Why is all this happening?" I asked. "Why do you have to stay in this awful place?"

He didn't answer but lowered his head. His thick hair fell forward. "It's best, Sophie."

"No," I answered. I sat and waited for him to look up.

With his head still down, he spoke softly. "You are so beautiful. I hope you are well. Are you happy?"

His words were flat and I tapped on the window to get him to look up. He did, but with eyes that were filled with shame.

"Papa, we don't have much time and I need to know some things. Please talk to me."

He looked away and sighed deeply.

"Tell me..." I stopped and looked around. Then I whispered it softly, "About the curse. I need to know what it is."

Papa shook his head slowly, still looking away.

"How did my grandmother die?" I blurted out.

"I don't know." He said it with honesty and heartache.

"I remember that day, Papa. I remember what she did to me. Was I the one who killed her?"

His eyes grew wide with awareness. He saw my understanding and then looked around in fear that the guards may have overheard. "Why do you think that?" he asked.

"Papa, please just tell me the truth. Did I...did the curse kill her? Was it me?"

"It doesn't matter now."

A knot formed in my stomach. He didn't deny it, which meant it was probably true. "It does matter. You told me that a curse was put on our family. You said that love would cause death. Is that why Grandma died? Was it because she loved me?"

His eyes turned red. "Sophie, you must keep this secret or you'll be in danger. I thought the curse died with her. She cursed your mother's family for what they did to us. She didn't realize that your mother was pregnant with you. That's why you carry the curse. When I buried your grandmother on the hill, I thought we were free."

Again, his eyes filled with tears and he leaned closer, trying to shield his voice from anyone else who might be in the room. "For years I thought that one day you'd be able to live a normal life. I thought once you were grown, you could leave and be on your own. But when those boys started coming around, I knew something wasn't right. It was like they were dogs on the prowl, unable to control their attraction. You are my daughter and I could see your beauty, but not in the same way others saw it. They were mesmerized and taken over by it. It scared me, but I felt it was just my instincts as a father."

"You knew they were coming up to play?"

He smiled and nodded. "I was kind of happy because it made me see that one day you could be out in the world and have friends. ...A normal life. But then you received the curse of Eve." He stopped and swallowed hard. "It's when that boy died that I knew the curse was alive in you."

My mind rewound back to Donny, his windswept hair and easy smile, as he took my arm and pulled me to him. "That's when you put up the bars and gate."

He nodded sadly. "I knew it was an awful thing to do, but I knew the danger. I hated keeping you locked away, but it was what I had to do. I had no choice after what happened."

"But why just me? If we were cursed, why were you able to go out and I wasn't?"

He looked up at me with weary but determined eyes. "It was you. It wasn't me."

"It was just me?" I asked. "You mean I was the only one who was cursed?"

Papa licked his lips and stammered, and then he simply nodded.

"Why didn't you tell me?"

"You were young. I didn't want to tell you because I didn't want to hurt you. For years I tried to do the right thing, but I couldn't. I didn't want to believe it was true and then when I learned the truth, it was too late. I was too weak. And look what happened."

"Too weak? Papa, you almost killed Damien. Papa, why not talk to him…or, to me? Why did you try to kill Damien? I was the one who was cursed, not him."

He sat up straight. The face I had always known as strong and fatherly turned weak and sorrowful. "I know that. I wasn't trying to kill him. I was trying to do what I should have done from the start."

"What?"

He furrowed his brows apologetically and raised the phone again. "I wasn't trying to kill *Damien.*"

"I know. You just said that." I sat back and waited for him to respond, but he didn't. He just sat, slumped and broken, with his eyes cast down.

Then it hit me like a frigid, salty wave. He wasn't protecting me from Damien. *I* was the target. I dropped the receiver and felt my chest tighten. I sprung up and stumbled back as the metal chair skidded noisily. The realization of what my life was and what should have happened made me shiver with horror. My own father had tried to kill me, thinking he was saving others from his deadly pariah of a daughter.

I looked at Papa with eyes of grief. *Tell me it isn't true!* My heart screamed at him. But Papa refused to speak. He just sat, looking forward and letting me absorb everything that I was guilty of. His shoulders seemed to relax as though a weight had been lifted. The burden was now mine.

"Sit down or you'll have to leave. Others are coming in now," the guard ordered.

I stood paralyzed and too numb to cry. The immense rumble of metal doors opening made me look up, as a steady stream of orange-clad men walked through and started taking their seats at the other cubbies.

I put my hand to my mouth and turned quickly to the door. One of the last things my father had said to me before the police took him away from the house, finally made sense. *It is up to you now.* My body was rocked by the force of my sobs, knowing what he had meant.

The drive back was nothing but silence. It was as though Carpo knew. The closer we got to Pocatello, the more I yearned for Stephanie. I needed her comfort and strength. I could tell her what I learned, and even though there was nothing she could do, I knew her solid resolve would give me the confidence I needed to survive.

I debated telling Stephanie about what I had learned, for fear she would reveal my reasons and make my secret known, but she never gave me grounds to mistrust her and my need for release was overwhelming. Even knowing she would balk at what I learned about myself, I had to tell her. I wanted to hear the words come out of my mouth and see the look of disbelief. Maybe I secretly hoped that she could talk me out of what I knew. She would at least try. But mostly I needed her. She was my one true friend and her very presence kept me buoyed when so often my soul was sinking.

Chapter 33

Malad, Idaho

When Uncle Lonny pulled into the lane, the gate was already open and a small black car was parked on the large gravel pad near the arena.

"I wonder who's here," Uncle Lonny asked himself as he drove in.

I didn't recognize the car, but didn't think much of it, since people often came to the ranch to talk with my grandfather about the cattle, or church matters.

Uncle Lonny parked the car and turned to me. "Remember, don't say a word about this to them. We were on a field trip. It's our secret."

I moved away and opened the car door. Without looking back, I started walking.

Hearing my footsteps crunching across the gravel, Grandfather emerged from the arena. "There you are," he said.

I looked back at him, wanting to cry. I wanted to run to him, have him hold me, tell him what happened, and have him hug the pain and past away. But I knew I couldn't. And then out of the arena door stepped Damien. I gasped. Even after the gruesome and horrid truths I had learned earlier that day, he was the one sight that lifted me. I was stunned to see him standing there indisputably real. My heart leapt. Even in my sorrow, he was a vision.

He walked to me and reached out to hug me. I was both horrified and euphoric at his presence. His strong hands touched my shoulders and I looked into his familiar eyes. For a moment I felt the wind stop blowing, the chirping of the birds silenced, and the earth come to a halt. My exhaustion overtook me as I fell into Damien's arms. Having him there was right. It gave me the opportunity I needed to say good-bye to the one and only love in my life.

He sighed as we hugged, unaware of the information I possessed.

"We've been waiting for over an hour," my grandfather said. "Stephanie said you told her you were sick today."

I shook my head. "No, I…"

Then Stephanie appeared from the arena. She looked at me and then past, to where her father was backing his car down the gravel path. When her gaze came back to me, I could see the devastation in her eyes and my stomach clinched. She knew I had lied. I was torn between clinging to Damien and running to her to explain. But before I had a chance, she bolted from the arena door and ran behind the dust trail of her father's car up the lane. I watched, feeling what was left of my heart, break.

"You can talk to her later. Come inside. Your grandmother has dinner ready," Grandfather said, noticing my concern. He walked into the house, leaving us alone in the breezeway.

"I like your family," Damien said. "Your grandpa was a little nervous about me at first, but considering how I feel about you that's understandable." He smiled slyly. "And I'll never be able to thank Stephanie enough for telling me where to find you."

Stephanie? I felt even guiltier. He lifted a strand of my hair from my face.

"I can't believe you're here," I said. My emotions were chaotic. The day had been a whirlwind of highs and lows, and I felt both elated and depleted.

"I've wanted to come, but after what happened the other night I thought you'd be mad at me for leaving the way I did. I felt like I'd lost you forever."

I hugged him. He felt muscular and warm in my arms.

He looked into my eyes. "It's cold out here, but I don't want to let you go."

"Don't," I whispered, holding him tighter.

"I'm leaving for school in a few weeks. I should be excited, but all I keep thinking about is you. I don't want to go. I'm miserable without you."

"Me, too."

He smiled. "Come with me."

I raised an eyebrow.

"No, really," he said, seeing my skepticism. "I talked to your grandfather and he said he thought you'd be happier away from all this. You could leave all the crap from the past and we would be like any other two people— go to school, be together."

"Where?" I asked.

"In New York. It's a big city and no one would know who you are or were. Think about it, Sophie, no one would know anything about what has happened."

I loved the thought of being with him anywhere, but along with my exhaustion from the long drive and dreadful visit with Papa, I knew my fate. I felt my head spin and put my hand to my forehead to steady myself.

"I can't be without you, Sophie," he said, holding tight. "If you decide not to go, I'll stay here. I can go to I.S.U. Being here right now, I know I want to be with you." He looked down and caught my eyes. "I won't ever leave you again."

My heart was already full and now his affection made tears rise in my eyes. He leaned down and for a quick moment I lifted my face to kiss him. Then my crushing reality jumped into the forefront of my mind, knocking me out of his arms. What was I thinking? After what I had just learned, I was about to destroy the one thing I adored in this world. Did I want to add his name to the list? I was enraged at myself for letting it get this far.

"What?" he asked, both stunned and upset.

"Oh, Damien," I cried. "I can't."

He stepped back and shook his head. "Sophie, I love you. Why?"

I stood, frantic in my search for the words to explain. My body shivered from the cold air that hit me now that we stood apart. "I love you too." I cringed at the words. I shouldn't have told him. It would be harder now for both of us. "But I can't. I won't."

He reached for me. "I'll stay if it's too much for you to go all the way to New York. I won't care. I'd be happy to stay in Idaho."

"No, you don't understand. I can't be with you... ever." I heard the words and felt them stab.

"I know you've been through a lot in the past, but I'm not going to hurt you. Your father is gone now and can't get to us. Even if he could, I'd still be here just like before. I'd risk my life for you."

My entire body flushed with his words and I hugged him again, this time with so much intensity I could hear his heart pounding. I never wanted to let go. But I loved him so much, I had to. My own selfish feelings and needs must be set aside for me to save him.

Grandfather stuck his head out the door. "You two are going to freeze out here. Come in. Dinner is on the table."

I gave my grandfather a weary smile and nod and then looked up at Damien. His dark eyes were confident as they held my gaze. I wondered what he saw. We had spent so many hours, so many days silently studying each other, talking while lying in the grass on those vivid summer days. I knew each crease in his smile, every eyelash, the strong slope of his chin; I saw the dreamy interest in his face when I spoke and the way his eyes narrowed in thought. As I watched him, I saw past his handsome profile and captivating features, and into his soul. I saw goodness and strength, and I loved him deeply.

"I can't be with you. You must go to New York alone," I said, my voice assertive and sure.

"No. I want to be with you."

I stepped back, knowing it would be the last time I touched him. I started to cry. "I don't want that."

"Sophie?" he said in shock. "You don't mean it."

"I do. I really do. I'm sorry, Damien, but I don't want this. You must leave."

"Why are you saying that? You just told me you love me." He came toward me, but I stepped back and put my hand up.

With every ounce of energy I had left, I gave him a look of calloused certainty. "I don't want this. I don't want you. Leave me alone." I turned and ran to the house, blocking out his calls for me to stop.

Inside, my grandparents sat at the table with faces of stunned concern.

Red faced and eyes blurry, I called to them. "I don't want to talk to him. If he comes to the door, tell him to leave me alone."

"But…" my grandmother started.

"I mean it!" I yelled and ran to my room. The door slammed loudly as I fell onto my bed and a wave of tears and despair rushed over me. Through my sobs, I heard my grandfather and Damien talking. I listened and then heard the door close. I turned off the light in my room and looked out through the blinds. In the stillness of my room, I saw Damien's car drive away. The one thing that mattered, the only true and sure part of my life, was now gone. I felt the emptiness descend and knew it would be with me forever.

"Are you all right, dear?" my grandmother's voice called from the other side of the door.

"Yes. I'll be fine." I waited and listened until finally I heard her walk away.

I kneeled at the side of my bed and clasped my hands. I leaned my head on my folded fingers and prayed to God for strength. With fervor, I begged Him to give me direction. I needed comfort and guidance with the burden I faced. Tears streamed down my cheeks as I mumbled the words over and over. But I knew I was alone in the world, and now I feared even God had deserted me.

Oddly, I fell asleep easily that night. No dreams, just deep and fervent slumber. Even the nudging that went from light taps to hearty rolls didn't wake me.

"Soph!" I heard in my head and wondered if it was real. "Wake up."

I stirred and lifted my head. Through squinted eyes, I found Stephanie standing by my bed. "Stephanie," I said, still tired, but relieved to see her.

"Wake up. We need to talk," she said, taking a seat beside me.

I rolled over to my side. "Yes," I agreed. I was glad she was there, and even though I was still drowsy, my need to tell her what I had learned was still strong.

"Where did you go with my father?" she asked.

"He drove me to Pocatello," I confessed, not caring about my promise to Uncle Lonny.

"For what? Tell me the truth."

I braced myself on my elbows and told her the truth.

"Sophie, why didn't you tell me?"

"I was afraid to let anyone know. I didn't want to be talked out of it."

Stephanie nudged me to scoot over and she crawled under the covers with me. "My God, that's so dangerous. What was it like? What did he say?"

I licked my lips, took a deep breath and told her everything that had happened at the prison. When I finished I lay weeping, wishing I could see her face. In the dark, I didn't see her reaction to anything I said, and now I felt vulnerable to her judgment.

"So, what are you going to do?" she asked, calmly.

"What do you mean?" I asked, wanting more.

"I know you expect me to argue with you and tell you your father is nuts, but I can't keep doing that. This isn't something I can do for you. Sure, there are people who have died who loved you, but I love you and I'm fine and what about your grandparents...what about Damien? There's evidence all around you that what your father says is a lie. He was sick, like his mother. If you don't come to your senses you'll get sick, too. How many times can I try to convince you?"

She knew about Theta.

"But it's different," I said softly. "There is something else."

She shifted in the sheets, but didn't say anything.

"The people that died all told me they loved me and then they kissed me. In less than a day they were dead. It's the last thing Donny did. My father told me that my mother had held me and kissed me right before she died, and even though I was young, I remember my grandmother..." I paused to push her violent attack from my mind, knowing now why she tried. "The last thing I remember is her crying and telling me she loved me and then kissing me." I took a deep breath. "Every person who has shown their love for me with a kiss has died, and died quickly."

I felt her sigh. "What about your father? Didn't he tell you he loved you? Didn't you kiss him?"

"No. The only time he told me was right after he shot Damien. And he never kissed me, ever."

"Really, he never did?"

"No."

"What about Damien?"

I felt my tears come again. I saw his face blocking out the sun in the sky as he bent over me and traced my lips with his finger, smiling. I could feel the warm breeze on my legs and the cold grass beneath me and wanted nothing more than to feel his lips on mine.

My voice cracked as I spoke. "He tried, but I've never let him. I can't. I told him I never wanted to see him again. I had to...for him."

"Jesus, Sophie. I don't know what else to say. So what now?" Stephanie asked, quietly. "If you feel like you're some kind of 'kiss of death,' what are you going to do?"

"I'm not sure. I was thinking about going back to the house in Arbon Valley. The detective told me it's mine. I could live there."

Stephanie rolled up on one elbow. "This is crazy. You can't spend the rest of your life thinking you're about to kill people with a kiss. Do you really want to live like a hermit in the hills?" She shook my shoulder. "Look at me. Sophie, don't do this to yourself. Don't let your crazy father win. You can beat this. I know you can."

I shrugged. "I know you don't believe me, but it's what I have to do."

Stephanie huffed. "So when are you making this move?"

"Soon. I know that Damien will try to come back. I don't want to be here when he does."

She laid back and was silent for a moment. I could hear her breathing.

"What has my father told you about me?" she asked.

Her question struck me as odd. "What do you mean?"

Stephanie hesitated, starting and stopping before blurting out, "Has my dad ever done anything to you?"

The guilt I felt over lying to her about him driving me to Pocatello made me pick my words carefully. "Like what?"

"Has he done anything to you that he shouldn't?"

"No!" I said adamantly. Then the memories of him taking my hand and bringing it up his leg appeared and made my stomach turn. "Why do you ask?"

She paused and laid very still in thought, before clearing her throat. "I see the way he looks at you; the way he talks about you and forgets that anyone else is in the room when you're there. I worry about you. I worry about what he might do." She stopped.

I rolled toward her and put my arm on her shoulder. "Why? What do you think he'll do?"

She didn't answer.

"Have I done something wrong, Stephanie?" I wondered what she had seen or learned about her father's secret pact with me.

"No. It's not you. But promise me something…"

"Anything," I answered, strongly.

"Promise me you'll tell me if he does."

"I will. I wish you'd tell me why." A dreadful thought began to creep into my head.

"I just worry. I think you trust people too much. Just like that Carponelli guy. I can't believe you let him drive you that whole way. Even your grandparents don't trust him anymore. Why did you do that?"

"I had to. I had to learn the truth."

She took a deep breath. "It's just caused you more problems, if you ask me."

I knew where this was going, and wanted now to just sleep and be close to her. "Don't worry about me. For the first time in my life, I understand who I am and why my life is the way it is. Even though it's awful, at least I know."

Stephanie sighed. "I don't want you to leave. At least stay until we can both get the hell out of here."

"Where do you want to go?" I asked.

"I don't know…anywhere. Maybe I'll come live with you in Arbon Valley. We could be the two lesbians living on the hill. Then no one would bother us!" We both burst into giggles.

I was so relieved that she was with me after my horrifying day of revelation. Only Stephanie could have me laughing when inside I wanted to die. As much as I loved Stephanie, I knew a life of solace in the hills was not for her. She needed to find her calling in life and I knew it wasn't with me.

My affliction was my own, and while she would always live in my heart, what I had to do from that point in my life was a journey I had to take alone.

Chapter 34

Arbon Valley, 1992

Luke paused at the door watching Theta rock the baby covered in a delicate receiving blanket. It was to be his first day back at work. He had called in sick the last two days, and while he still wasn't completely comfortable leaving Theta and his new daughter alone, he knew it was what he had to do.

"We'll be fine," Theta scolded him. "Go."

Luke sighed and nodded, but a gloomy chill crawled up his back when he closed the door behind him. He pushed on, knowing he had to work to support his new family. It wasn't ideal. He still longed for Vee and the life he had imagined so many times—her standing at the kitchen sink, the baby sitting on the floor playing with pots and pans, as he came through the door after work. In his mind he could smell Vee's lavender-scented shampoo as he wrapped his arms around her from behind and nuzzled her neck.

The apparition dampened his heart, but even after two days he was already buoyed up just from the presence of his daughter. He was drowsy from being up all night, not because the baby wouldn't sleep, but because he wanted nothing more than to hold her. Luke loved the feel of her tiny warm body lying on his chest, the smell of her breath as she slept, and the soft feel of her head lightly cupped in his hand. He hated having to leave and go back to the cold, dirty confines of the dairy, but he knew it was for her.

When he arrived, Billy, one of the milkers, was in the breakroom finishing a cup of coffee. He nodded at Luke, as he walked in. "Miguel, there were men here yesterday asking questions. They were cops."

"What did they want?"

"They made Gerard take all the books out. They put them all over the table."

"What for?"

Billy shrugged. "I went into the milk barn. I was worried they were going to ask for cards, but Gerard said they didn't."

Luke went to the holding corral and saw Gerard driving a tractor and cleaning out the feeding area. The tractor was loud, and Gerard didn't see Luke trying to flag him down, so Luke walked out to him.

When Gerard finally saw Luke, he immediately turned off the tractor, jumped down and went to him. "Miguel, there were cops here," he said, urgently.

"Yes, Billy told me. What did they want?"

Gerard looked disturbed. "They were looking for someone named..." he paused and pulled a crumpled piece of paper from his back pocket. "Luke Theoto..." he started to pronounce the last name, but then stopped and just showed the paper to Luke. It held a photo of him taken at the cotillion, just his head. He relaxed as he realized it looked nothing like he looked now.

"Why were they looking here?" Luke asked, surprised that they had tracked him to the dairy.

"They didn't say, but said they'd be back. Do you think they're planning a raid?"

"No," said Luke. "Just keep working. It's nothing. We don't know him and he's never worked here, so there isn't an issue."

Luke went home for lunch, telling the other workers he still wasn't feeling well. As he drove he began to panic that when he arrived at the house there would be cop cars everywhere and his daughter taken away. The more he played out the nightmare in his mind, the faster he drove. He turned onto the lane and up the hill, snow and gravel sprayed across the field.

When he parked, he exhaled loudly. There was nothing amiss. The house was sitting just as he'd left it early that morning. He unlocked the door with his key and found Theta in the kitchen washing dishes.

"Where is she?" Luke asked.

Theta turned, startled. "She is down for a nap. Why are you home?"

Luke went to the room.

"Stop Luke," Theta said, following him. "Don't go in there."

Luke felt a jolt of fear go through him. He burst through the bedroom door and over to the little blanket-lined drawer to find his daughter on her side, her little fists curled under her chin, sleeping. His heart raced and he had to take several deep breaths to slow it down.

Quietly, Theta took his arm and led him out of the room. "She's fine. Let her sleep," she said, after closing the door.

Luke stood and studied her. He didn't trust his own mother. Would she call and turn him in? His mind was beginning to ease regarding that, but something else stirred doubt and worry within him.

On the long drive back with the baby in his arms, Theta had stared out at the road with a face of stone. She had changed since she lost her husband, but this was an even more disturbing sight. Theta's eyes were fixed and Luke could see her lips moving in the dim light of the truck cab. It was the same stormy trance that he had seen as they pulled away from the ranch after the fire. However, this time instead of fiery words of blight, she sat mumbling wearily, apologetically into the black abyss ahead.

Luke could see that the attentive, loving and stubborn woman he called Mama was mad. Had he any other option for the care of his baby, he would have taken it. Instead he had to trust that she'd keep up her medications and not only care for his daughter's basic needs, but not let her misguided beliefs drive her to do the unthinkable.

The load of what he faced was immense and he felt the weight of it everywhere on his body. "The cops came to my work yesterday," Luke said, detached.

"What happened?" Theta asked.

"Nothing…yet. They must know it was me who took her."

Theta nodded in thought. "I worry. This is not good Luke."

He turned on her. "Don't ever say that again. This is good. It's what is best. She should be with me."

Theta lowered her head. "But it will never leave us if she's here."

"Shut up, Mama. I don't want to hear about the curse, or anything bad about Sophie. So help me if anything happens to her, I'll…" he clenched his fists, and walked off.

321

She followed him to the kitchen. "So are you going to hide up here forever? Is she?"

"If that's what it takes to keep her, yes."

"But..."

"Stop arguing with me. You're not going to convince me or change my mind. Stop!" he yelled.

"Okay, okay," she said, looking over her shoulder toward the room where the baby slept.

"I'll go to the store tonight and get some more stuff. We must stay away from town as much as possible. If anyone comes to the door, don't answer it. Keep everything locked. Do you understand?"

When Luke arrived at the dairy the next morning the break room was filled with several men gathered around a table studying the newspaper. Luke walked over and looked over their shoulders. The headline screamed out: "Baby Kidnapped from Her Own Crib!" And at the bottom of the story was a picture of him. Again, it was the cotillion picture he had taken with Talia.

"It's the name the officers were looking for out here," said Gerard.

Luke shrugged, trying to act unfazed. "Like I said, he's not here."

Gerard nodded, and then ordered the others to get to work. They scattered slowly. There was no sign of suspicion, and Luke could see they had lost interest already.

The paper said the cops had interviewed Mr. Katsilometes about what he knew. It mentioned Luke's lies about jobs at the railroad, the dairy, and the fact that he had never been seen or hired at either place. This was actually a relief for Luke. He thought about Pete and was even more thankful for his help in hiding Luke's identity, even if Pete had no idea what help he had been.

But what stood out to Luke the most, as he read and reread the story, was the fact that there was no mention at all of Luke being the baby's father. In fact, it seemed that every attempt was made to keep that detail omitted. Luke finally stopped staring at the print, folded the paper up and stuffed it deep into the garbage. His face became tough with defiance. The baby was his and he would do everything and anything to keep her with him.

In the days that followed, articles about the kidnapping continued, but became shorter until they were pushed to other less visible pages and then eventually vanished, just like the baby. Luke began to breathe again.

Months passed, and his joy began to surface. Sophie was a chubby happy baby with huge blue eyes that made him marvel at her resemblance to his beloved Vee. Theta also seemed brighter. Her new role gave her purpose in life, and despite the occasional revelation of her past psychosis, she seemed to be back to her old self. They were a family. Every night when Luke held Sophie against his chest and slowly rocked her to sleep, he prayed their lives would continue to be blessed and full.

But his bliss was short lived.

He returned from a remarkably typical day at work with nothing on his mind but dinner and a shower. When he opened the door to the house, a strong sense of dread hung heavy in the air. The house was silent and dark, and Luke's detached mindset as he walked through the door immediately turned to panic. "Mama?" he called out.

He went from the living room to the kitchen, moving more quickly as each time he found the room empty. Luke went down the hall, and opened the tiny room he had turned into a nursery. Thankfully, there was Sophie, standing in her crib looking pensive. When the crack of the door filled the room with light she saw him and started to cry. He ran to her, and when he picked her up he could tell she had been there for a while. Her diaper was heavy and her face was red and swollen from crying. He quickly changed her. Then, he stood for a moment bouncing her, trying to comfort her fear.

His mind went from relief to anger to worry. Where could Theta be? Luke continued to search the house. He checked the garage, but found nothing. Then he went to the kitchen and stood searching the hills from the window above the sink. There she was, standing in the snow behind the house, her pants wet to the knees, rocking slowly and staring up at the hills. Luke opened the back door loudly, but she didn't turn.

"Mama!" Luke said, demanding her attention.

She looked over with exhaustion.

"What are you doing? You left Sophie alone. Why?"

"Sometimes I can hear it," she said, her voice cracking with fear.

Luke tried to pull his coat around Theta as she fidgeted against him in the cold. "Hear what?" he asked, annoyed.

"It's so loud. So strong, I can hardly think. I go black. My mind...it goes black with the noise."

Luke shook his head. "Mama, come in. It's freezing out here. The baby's cold." He took her by the arm. "Please come in."

She relented and let him lead her into the house. Once inside he made her change into dry pants and sit at the kitchen table while he changed and fed Sophie.

"Tell me what you mean by your mind going black," Luke asked Theta.

By this time, Theta had regained her composure and was feeling foolish and irresponsible. "I'm sorry Luke. I must have had a headache."

"You were standing outside in the freezing cold. Your pants were covered with mud and they were sopping wet. Where did you go?"

She furrowed her brow, upset at her own actions, and with a look of confusion. "I had to leave the house. It was dangerous for me to be in here. It's becoming strong. I can feel it all around."

A rush of woe fell over Luke. He had felt so confident and assured that life was going well that to hear her talk in her rambling and delusional tenor, disheartened him. "If it was dangerous to be in the house, why did you leave Sophie in here?"

She looked over at Luke with eyes that told him he already knew the answer.

He refused to give in to her insanity. "Don't you ever leave her again! I am sick of you using your craziness as an excuse. You have pills for your sickness, Mama. You have to take them…every day. No skipping. If anything happens to Sophie because of you, I swear I'll kill you myself."

In the three years that followed, Theta was distant but did what was expected. Only one other time did she give Luke reason to worry. For two weeks Theta went without bathing. When Luke confronted her about the smell, Theta refused to go into the shower because the veins of the fake marble tile looked like a face staring at her. She insisted the face had talked to her and told her to do things. Luke put a layer of duct tape over the "face" which was enough to satisfy her into bathing again. He checked her pill bottle every day, counting, to be sure she was taking them.

But it was months later, when the duct tape had peeled and she was kneeling down at the side of the tub giving her granddaughter her morning bath that the face spoke to her again. This time…she listened.

Theta Theotokis struggled to rid the world of the evil force she had conjured, but the beautiful face staring up from the water—eyes that looked at her with such incredible shock and dismay—also held an unwavering gaze of unconditional love. Theta's heart shattered as she saw the look of betrayal and mistrust in her granddaughter's dying eyes. The expression of "why?" was too gut wrenching for her to bear.

She had waited too long and now her bond was strong. With a clenched fist she smashed the tile wall where the "face" had prodded her on, saving the child from the last grasps of death. Theta wrapped her choking grandchild in a towel, hugging and kissing her fervently. Her love poured out, mixed with regret and the horror of what she tried to do and how she had failed. Theta sobbed, mumbling her apologies at both her inability to remove the awful curse and to the precious life she'd almost destroyed.

Chapter 35

Malad, Idaho, Early March, 2010

When morning came Stephanie was already gone. At first, I worried about the reasons why, but my attentions were quickly diverted when I overheard my grandfather talking with Aunt Elise in the kitchen.

Their tone went from whispers to low-pitched and angry barks. I peeked out the crack of my bedroom door and saw my grandfather seated at the table. Elise paced the linoleum floor. She was dressed in her work clothes, looking manly and tense.

"She's an adult. I doubt she's as innocent as you both think," I heard her snap. I knew she was talking about me by the way she motioned toward my room. Even though I knew she couldn't see me through the small slit, I leaned back for a moment.

Soon she left, and when I heard her car drive away, I waited in my room so it wouldn't be obvious that I was aware of their discussion. I tried to slip from my room to the bathroom, but my grandfather called me to him.

"I understand you went to Boise to see your father yesterday," he said. "You're old enough to make your own decisions now, but I don't like being lied to."

Both guilt and regret filled me and immediately tears rose in my eyes. "Oh, Grandfather, I'm so sorry," I said softly. It was the first time I called him that, but the name came easily and my remorse was genuine. "I knew that you'd worry, but I had to go."

He nodded. "You're right. I would have worried, but why didn't you just ask me to take you?"

I thought about that. What could I tell him without causing more problems with Elise and Uncle Lonny? "I didn't think you'd allow it."

Again he nodded. "Do you miss him?"

I felt my heart ache. "I always will."

He raised an eyebrow. "Aren't you happy here? That is all we've ever wanted."

I went to him and hugged his shoulders. "You've been wonderful. I love you both so much. But I had to find some things out for myself. I felt like there were parts of my life that were missing."

"Did you find what you were looking for?" he asked.

I lowered my head and gave a short laugh. "I don't know what I was looking for, but I found the truth."

"Are you happy?" he pressed.

I suddenly felt very unhappy. "Not really. It seems the more I learn about my life the more complicated and difficult it becomes."

He chuckled and then sighed. "That is life. You can either accept it or bury your head in the sand, but either way, eventually you must face it. It does no good pretending things will go away."

I smiled at him, and offered another hug.

"Sophie," he said. His voice was harsh. "You won't be going up to Stephanie's any longer."

I looked at him surprised. "Why not?"

My grandfather's face was pained. "Elise has told Lonny to leave. He's packing this morning and they'll be moving out."

They? I thought. "Stephanie?" I asked.

"She'll be going to live with her maternal grandparents. I'm sorry. I know she's been a good friend to you."

She was my only friend. I stood stunned at his words. "Why?"

He turned his chair to face me. "There are some bad things that we didn't know about your Uncle Lonny." He paused, picking his words carefully. "I hope he didn't do anything to you."

It was the same worry Stephanie had. I shook my head, but turned my attentions back to seeing Stephanie.

"Sophie, you can't...you shouldn't go up there."

"I have to. I have to talk to her."

"This isn't a good time."

"But she'll be gone. I'll never see her again."

My grandfather lowered his head, and didn't argue.

I skipped my normal routine and simply pulled on my jeans, an old sweater and boots. I grabbed my coat and left the house.

A chilly wind blew as though trying to keep me back, but nothing could have kept me from seeing her. I began to rethink what Stephanie said about the two of us living in the house in Arbon Valley. Maybe it could work, I thought. I wanted so badly to think that it might. I needed her. She was the one who kept me aloft and alive. I couldn't imagine being without her. Even though, just a few hours ago I was thinking of ways to talk her out of that very notion, knowing it was for her own good.

As I walked up the snow-covered lane to her house, I wondered what I'd find. Was I approaching a situation that could blow up in my face? But my concern for Stephanie pushed me on.

As I reached the house, I stopped and just studied it. Nothing was different except the car trunk was open, filled with boxes and clothing. I knocked on the door. The door cracked open. It was Uncle Lonny. He saw it was me and opened up, looking out to see if I was alone.

"Sophie," he said with an air of relief and pleasure. He shuffled me quickly inside. "I'm so glad you're here."

"You are?" I asked, skeptical.

He smiled and gave an exhausted laugh. "Oh yes," he said. "I'm so glad."

"Where is Stephanie?" I asked.

"I thought she was with you. When she heard how ridiculous your aunt is being, accusing me the way she did, Stephanie left. I can't blame her for being upset. To hear your stepmother calling me the names she did."

"She's making you move out." I looked around at all the packing in progress. Boxes were stuffed with books, clothes, and pictures; there was no order to any of it.

"Yes. But I'm glad."

"You are?"

He walked to me and tilted his head. His expression was apologetic and feeble. Uncle Lonny closed his eyes and tipped his head up. His face was covered in dark red stubble and the skin on his neck was puffy and paler than on his face. "I'm sorry it had to be like this, but I knew eventually my secret would get out."

I looked at him with question.

"I hope you don't hate me, but all this was for you."

"All what?"

His eyes started to tear and I felt the strange urge to comfort him.

"I have to leave because I love you. I love you so much, Sophie. And now that you're eighteen, we can be together."

I felt my head and heart revolt. I shook my head and tried to push him away, but he pulled me closer.

"Don't be scared. I know it's a lot to take in, but I know you appreciate all I did to help you, right?"

"Yes, but…" I squirmed.

"It's okay, Sophie. You said you loved me and now no one can stand in our way. I love you." He forcefully took my face and kissed me on the lips. He smelled of coffee and alcohol.

"Stop," I tried to yell. I struggled to move, but his grip was tight. I was stunned and sickened, and as I shoved against him with both hands I realized what he had just done. With one kiss, I knew his life was over. "What are you doing?" Then I heard the screen door in the kitchen slam shut. He quickly released me and, when I turned, there stood Aunt Elise. She was red faced with an angry, venomous smile.

Lonny stood straight with a surprising air of confidence. "What are you going to do Elise? Turn me in? You have nothing. I haven't broken probation because she's of legal age."

Elise's face went to stone. "Sophie, go home."

I nodded to her, terrified, and ran from the house.

The chill outside made me catch my breath, and I tripped as I tried to leap from the stairs. I knew what fate was about to befall my uncle. As I tore down the slick and muddy path, I felt as though I was hit in the back when I heard a gun go off. The shock struck me, and my legs gave out. I gave a half-cry, half-yell, not knowing if I should keep running, or if my stunned and paralyzed body would even allow me to move.

I turned around slowly, and saw Stephanie running from the small shed in the backyard into the house. Then I heard her high-pitched scream of horror. My body began to heave and I crouched down, shaking and sobbing at what I had done. I knew Lonny was dead, and I knew that it was because of me.

I had to hide. I couldn't face Stephanie. She knew the truth and now there was no denying it. Elise would tell her what she saw and Stephanie would know I had killed her father.

I ran to the back of the arena and into the old barn. From the loft, I sat looking out toward the lane. I watched my grandfather, his face pinched with despair, leave the house and hurry up the hill. I let silence fall around me as the reality of what happened settled in. It was then I let tears overtake me. I cried for Stephanie, I cried for Uncle Lonny and I cried for me. What Papa said was true and now I had undeniable proof. I was a pariah and a threat. The sooner I was able to run away, the better the chances were that no one else would have to suffer the same fate as Uncle Lonny.

A clamor of sirens filled the small valley. I watched and waited and soon two police cars and an ambulance turned into the drive. The sirens stopped, and I heard the pop of gravel under tires as they quickly made their futile journey up the hill.

I stayed at my perch in the loft, waiting until late in the afternoon. I was so cold, but I couldn't bring myself to come down. I saw Elise sitting in the back of a patrol car. She was deep in thought, and even from a distance I could tell she was satisfied with her actions. She wasn't sad about what she had done,, only sad that she had to do it. I felt my heart ache for her and it surprised me. I had never liked Aunt Elise, but for the first time I felt close to her—a connection that I didn't understand, but one that was palpable and real and I found myself praying to God to save her soul.

I kept watch, and soon my grandfather made his way back down the lane. His head was low, and his thinning hair was blown about. He was hunched with his hands buried deep in his pockets. When he came toward the back of the house, he felt me watching and stopped.

I had climbed back down the ladder and waited for him hesitantly at the barn door.

"Sophie, where've you been?" he asked, walking toward me.

I felt my demeanor melt and I ran to him, burying my head in his chest. "I'm so sorry," I cried.

He held me tight and rubbed my head. "Yes, it's an awful thing."

"I should have listened to you. I should have never gone up there. This would have never happened."

He held me out so he could look me in the eye. "Sophie, this isn't your fault."

I closed my eyes tightly.

"Sophie, listen to me. What happened wasn't your fault at all."

"But he's dead. She shot him because he was with me."

My grandfather nodded. "Yes. But you didn't do anything wrong."

I stayed silent.

"This is something much bigger than what happened today. There were things going on that we weren't aware of. I feel I put you in the path of danger. If anyone is to blame, it's me. It could have been much worse and I feel terrible I didn't do a better job of protecting you."

Protecting me? The irony made my head swim as the weight of what had happened settled in.

He walked me inside the house. Warmth wrapped around us and I looked at the clock, surprised that I had been sitting in the barn for over four hours. My stomach rumbled with hunger but I ignored it, feeling guilty that I still felt such human needs when Uncle Lonny was now cold and dead.

"What happens now?" I asked, as my grandfather stood at the sink washing his hands.

He took a seat at the table. "We pull ourselves together and go on with life."

I shook my head in hopeless confusion. "How?"

"It's difficult. Sometimes it feels impossible, but you do. You believe that things will get better. They always do. But it's up to you to believe it and go on with life."

I sighed, unconvinced and feeling helpless about being able to go on.

"Sophie, when your mother died and you were taken, I thought my life was over. I was so angry and bitter about what had happened, I turned away from my family, from my church, even God. I blamed myself and everyone around me. I hurt so badly, I didn't even want to live."

I nodded at him with understanding.

"I thought seriously about leaving it all. I would be free of the pain." His eyes became frail and distant. He bit his top lip as it quivered, then he looked at me with tears in his eyes. "When I think about what I would have missed if

I had given in to it." He shook his head, still looking at me. "I would have missed being with you. No matter how hard and terrible life may seem, there is always a reason to go on."

I wanted to hug him, but a question burned in my mind. "What if you're the cause of it all? Then what?"

"There is no such thing. It's called making choices, Sophie. Everyone has that. You didn't choose what happened to Lonny. He made that decision and so did Elise. You had no control over what happened up there."

What about the curse? I wanted to ask. How did that figure into making choices? I realized my decision to segregate myself was what I had to do to relieve my weary conscience. I would leave as soon as I could. I had the home and the money to support myself. I had just learned to drive my car and use a computer. The only thing holding me back had been school and Stephanie, and that was now moot. I must put all my efforts toward doing right by those who loved me. I must remove the risk by removing myself from their lives.

Chapter 36

Arbon Valley, 1996

My first memory of that day is of me sitting alone with the growing sense of terror slowly filling me. My hair was still wet and I was naked except for a towel. I remember pushing on my grandmother, trying to wake her up. Her wiry dark hair was tied back, but still sprawled around her face on the floor. Her face was still, but her eyes weren't all the way shut, so I thought I could rouse her.

When my father came through the door my feelings of relief quickly faded when I saw his despair. My eyes stung and my face was sore from crying for hours, but I cried again when I saw his tears. I was too young to understand the loss, so instead I wept from fear of the unknown and at the cold and robotic way he went about wrapping Theta's body in a large blanket and carrying it outside. He was quiet and walked with a look of emptiness as he went about the task. I pulled at his pants, needing his comfort, but he brushed me aside.

Eventually, I went to my room and crawled into bed. The knot in my stomach was from hunger and angst. I felt abandoned, even though my father was still busy in the house. I hugged my pillow and watched the shadows move on the walls just outside my door.

I cried myself to sleep, and I awoke to his nudging me from my nap. He told me to get out of bed and he helped me get dressed. Papa was still quiet, but when I asked at the back porch where we were going he bent down, and in a calm and consoling voice told me we were helping my grandmother get to Heaven.

We trudged up the hill. The snow was deep, with a solid crust. I kept falling through to my hips. Eventually, he picked me up and carried me the rest of the way. I was wearing my thick hooded coat, mittens, and a scarf wrapped around my neck. And even with my tall rubber boots, my legs were soaked and freezing.

"Be strong," Papa said, seeing me shiver.

At the age of four I watched as my father shoveled dirt on the body of the person who had fed me, dressed me and taken care of me since I was born. I watched as small glimpses of her holding me underwater flashed in my mind, yet I didn't realize the reasons why, or even what it was she was doing. All I remembered was the outpouring of love she expressed afterward and how good it felt to be held and cherished by her.

It was the reason why this memory was so strong, because ever since that day my father kept me at a distance, both physically and in his heart. I felt the strain and often caught him watching, deep in thought with scrutinizing eyes. I knew my existence was a chore for him.

As I grew older, he often took long trips into town — to shop, I thought. But he usually came back with just a few small packages.

Even with my solitary life, I knew what normal was from the television shows I sneaked to watch. I saw conversations, emotions, affection and conflict — all things that were missing from my lonely and sterile world. And I knew he missed those things too. Although we were together, being in each other's presence only added to the void.

It was this feeling that continually crept around in my head the longer I stayed with my grandparents.

Chapter 37

Malad, 2010

The morning after Uncle Lonny died, as I went to feed my chickens, I heard the sloshing rumble of wet and muddy gravel. I turned and saw a red car with an older couple coming from Stephanie's house toward the gate. I saw Stephanie lean forward in the backseat of the car. My eyes cried out sorrow and regret, but she turned away. She knew what I had caused, and I saw that she would never forgive me.

Stephanie leaned up to the old man and he stopped the car. She opened the door and slowly stepped out. I wondered what she was doing. We both stood motionless. She didn't blink, and watched as my pensive face melted away, revealing my weariness and shame.

Her face turned to rage and she started toward me, fists clenched at her sides, walking with quick, meaningful strides. I felt her anger and took a step backward, dropping the feed bucket with a loud clatter on the concrete floor. She shook her head, annoyed that I was backing away, and she called out, "Don't you dare run from this!"

At that I turned and ran with all my strength. The sense of flight took me back to my struggle under the water, and I felt the same awareness of the danger I was trying to avoid.

I heard her shoes pounding against gravel and cement, following my own. My breathing was loud, and I felt her gaining. I ran across the breezeway and toward the old barn. When I left the driveway, my boots sloshed into the damp pasture, slowing me down. "I'm sorry," I yelled to her, not turning back.

"No!" she yelled, tripping me and knocking me to the ground.

The combination of snow, muck and rocks made for a harsh landing. I curled up, hiding my face as she climbed over me, grabbing at my hands.

"Look at me!" she demanded angrily. She had pulled my hands away exposing my face, but I stayed curled up, with my eyes closed.

When all I heard was her breathing, I slowly peeked up at her. The morning sun framed her head like a halo.

"Stop thinking this is all about you. It isn't." Her voice was low and forceful.

I didn't answer, but looked at her straight on. She had mud splattered on her face and in her hair, and I felt cold, murky water seep into the back of my head.

She dropped my hands. "You're not cursed. You never have been. At first I thought it was quirky and kind of funny, but it's not anymore. This is real life, Sophie, and believing in this crap is ridiculous." She could see from my face that I didn't buy it. "I should have come forward a long time ago but I was too scared. This wouldn't have happened if I had said something years ago. *I* caused this, not you."

"But it was me. I'm the one he..." I couldn't say it. "I killed your father."

"No. You didn't kill him. Elise did. What he did was evil and he got what he deserved."

I shook my head.

340

"Yes, yes he did. He was going to molest you. Don't you get it? That's what he does." She lowered her face, letting the sun blind me. "That is what he did to me."

"No," I said, feeling my heart break for her. "You never told me that."

"I couldn't. I was afraid of him. I saw what he got away with and knew no one would believe me."

I tried to sit up so I could see her face. "What about Aunt Elise? Why didn't you tell her?"

Stephanie gave a quick huff. "He married Elise to get back to me. She was his probation officer. He spent time in prison for fraud and theft, and when he got out he met Elise and she pulled some strings, because he lied to her and made her think he loved her. That is how he got custody of me from my grandparents. He didn't want to be my father. He wanted to molest me. And when you came along, he lost interest in me and turned to you."

She put her head down, ashamed. "I tried to warn you, but part of me was so relieved that he was finally leaving me alone. I should have turned him in, but I always felt no one would believe it. I started saying I was gay and causing problems around town so he would become annoyed and send me back to my grandparents."

"Oh, Stephanie," I whispered, wanting to hold her.

She grabbed both my shoulders and put her forehead against mine. "I can't be happy knowing you think you caused this."

"But..." I started.

"Sophie, you have to think for yourself. Have you ever made a decision on your own?"

I looked at her, confused.

"Have you?"

"Yes."

She scoffed. "What?"

"Papa let me decide things. I always decided what was for dinner."

Stephanie threw her head back and laughed.

"Why are you laughing?" I asked, dismayed.

She rolled up and looked across the immense farm field. "What do you see out there?"

I looked over to where she was pointing. "The fields."

"What else?"

"The snow?" I asked, wondering where her questions were going.

"What color is it?" She softened and asked again. "What color is the snow?"

"White," I said, sharply.

Stephanie squinted and took a deep breath as she looked out at the field. "How do you know it's white? Who taught you that snow is white?"

"Why?" I asked, becoming annoyed at what seemed to be an idiotic question.

"Who taught you that snow is white? Did you read about it, or did you just know?"

"No. Papa told me."

She shrugged knowingly. "Yes. That is what I was taught, too. Snow is white. But look out there. What I see is silver, I see some pink and sometimes when the air is really cold, the snow is blue." The cold had pinched her cheeks red, and her lips were rosy and parted, letting her chilled breath escape in puffs of frozen mist.

I looked out at the field and studied the sparkling blanket of winter frost.

"Do you see it?"

I did. When the sun reflected off the mounds and dips of the pasture, I saw glints of color. "Yes," I answered, still skeptical of what point she was coming to.

She nodded. "So was your father wrong to teach you snow is white?"

I looked at her, confused. "No."

"Was I wrong for pointing out that sometimes it isn't?"

I felt a frantic pit of query form in my stomach. "What do you mean?"

She shook her head. "I don't have time to try and convince you any longer. Things aren't always what they seem, and just because you were taught or told something doesn't mean it's true. You are not the reason people died. Your friend was the victim of a cave-in. He walked in there, not you. Your mother died because something went wrong during childbirth, not because of you. And my father died because Elise shot him when she caught him trying to molest you."

"But, what about my grandmother?" The memories of that day were vivid in my mind.

Stephanie shrugged. She was drained and losing patience. "I don't know what killed her. But she was crazy, just as your father is crazy. Consider the source, Sophie. Just because your father said the snow is white, doesn't mean it is." She crawled off me and stood up.

I cried, confused and needy. I realized how much I'd miss her. "I don't want you to go." I stood up and felt the mud and water run down my back.

Stephanie hugged me. "I'll miss you too, but it's not forever. We'll hook back up someday."

"I don't know if I can go on without you," I said, sadly.

"You can and you will. Start trusting yourself. You can't control what goes on around you, or even what happens to you, but you can control what's up here," she said, tapping my forehead.

I listened to what she said but felt overwhelmed with sadness, knowing her leaving was inevitable.

She saw my doubt and hugged me. "All your life you've lived like you have some contagious disease. I told you I was going to save you, but the only person who can, is *you*. You'll never be happy and you'll never have a life until you rid yourself of Callidora. That's the only way you'll be free." She held me away from her. "I know nothing I say is going to convince you that you aren't cursed. It isn't something that anyone can do. Create your own destiny, Sophie. You have to find the truth yourself. But I want you to promise me something."

I looked at her with tear-stained eyes.

"Promise me you'll at least look."

I nodded and then she was gone.

The morning seemed warmer, even though a huge emptiness filled my heart as I watched the car drive away. I went inside, taking most of my clothes off in the washroom and quietly streaking my way across the house to the bathroom. I turned on the shower, and then stood looking into the medicine cabinet mirror at my mud-streaked and somber face. Strangely, I was happy for Stephanie.

As the car had made its way out of the gate and on to the main road, she had turned and looked at me from the rear window. I had stayed half-hidden behind the barn, but she smiled and waved. I gave her a distracted wave back, as I watched her leave. For a moment I didn't recognize her, and I squinted trying to see what it was that I found odd. As the car got smaller and the sky between us larger, I realized why she looked unfamiliar. In her face…I saw hope.

It was something I wanted to find in my own eyes, but it was still missing. The steam filled the room, and slowly I vanished from the mirror. I gave up trying to see my reflection and stripped off the rest of my clothes, carefully stepping into the shower.

I let the water hit me with its hot, soothing spray; it rinsed the dirt and grime from my hair and body. As I stood with heat and steam filling me, I felt my emotions come to the surface. I had spent too much time feeling sorrow and guilt. As I stood watching the grit flow off me and down the drain, I felt a rising in my soul that brought an incredible sense of relief. I inhaled, letting it fill every pore.

Chapter 38

The gate was locked but I knew where my grandfather hid the key. I pulled the car slowly onto the main road and said goodbye to the grandparents who were about to feel like I was taken from them twice.

I was going home. The drive was dark and lonely but I knew my place in this world was at the home in Arbon Valley. It was where I could go and be free. I was scared, but also at ease.

I had waited for my grandparents to go to bed, and then I took what I needed, including my art supplies and my new computer and cell phone, and quietly left the house. The stillness of the cold black night made my exit even more pronounced, but it wasn't until I was on the interstate and long gone that my heart fell with regret in not being able to say goodbye. They had been so good to me, so kind, even in the face of tragedy in their own lives. Their love for me rose above it, and I wanted nothing else in the world than to allow them every opportunity to find happiness.

As I drove, I thought about my grandfather's tender instruction and patience while teaching me to drive, even when I hurled him to and fro in the seat. I worried about his health and wondered if the close calls and quick jolting stops were too much for him. He simply smiled and corrected me. He never gave up, and soon we were driving up and down the road that led to the ranch. We never went any farther, but I knew where I was heading. I had watched as Carpo drove and remembered the simple path back to my home in the hills.

As the lights of Pocatello came into view, I felt my heart leap. I was proud that I had done this on my own. I took the turn toward Twin Falls, and watched as lights glimmered up from busy streets and businesses. It was almost midnight, but the town was still alive with activity. I felt a rush of adrenaline as I watched the bustle go by. Soon I was back on the dark and solitary strip of road, on my way to where most of my life had been lived.

When the headlights on my car splayed across the house, I marveled at how small it seemed. It was shut up tightly, and the snow-covered driveway was untouched by tires. I turned off the car, but I left the lights on as I went to the door and felt along the top of the jamb for the key. I put it in the knob and opened the door wide. The next test was the lights. A flip and they were on, illuminating the stale and untouched living room. I stepped inside. I was home.

After bringing my small bag of things from the car, I stood and surveyed the place. I went from room to room and let visions of past conversations, events, and simple memories fill my mind. It had been just over a year, but what had changed and what I'd learned felt like I'd lived two lifetimes; one taking it all in and the other to make sense of it.

Knowing the truth is why I was here. And after I reminisced and settled myself with the fact that I was really home, I went to my room and pulled open the accordion closet doors. Kneeling, I crawled in and pulled at the carpet in the corner. It came up easily, exposing the small piece of loose floorboard. I lifted it and there, underneath, was the gun—right where I had hidden it. I sat back on my heels and studied it. For its size, it had brought a ton of sorrow into my life and that of others. It was time for me to change that forever.

I stroked the cold metal of the barrel and knew what it was intended for. I imagined my father's hand wrapped around it, his finger on the trigger, as my own hand slipped into position. I felt the rancid taste of fate begin to heave at the back of my throat.

I went to the bathroom and splashed water on my face, trying to ease the churning in my stomach. I wiped the water from my eyes and stared at the rough metal box of the medicine cabinet. I touched it, thinking about that day Papa had removed all the mirrors. He was frenzied, and determined as he made his way in and out of each room, carrying them and placing them in a pile in the living room. They were all sizes and shapes. He had smashed the one in the bathroom because it was secured to the wall by the box.

I pushed on it and it clicked open. I swung the door wide and inside found several wrapped bars of Ivory soap, an old razor, and a neatly folded and detailed receipt for items taken by the police: aspirin, antihistamines, laxatives, antacids and Haldol (*oral*) for Theta Theotokis.

I had a vague recollection of seeing a prescription bottle in the box, but had never thought to read it. Grandmother had said that Theta had been ill. I ran to my laptop and was pleased to see that I had wireless internet in this rural setting. I quickly typed Haldol into my search box. What came up devastated me. I sat staring at the screen as a burning began to pulsate at the back of my eyes. The word was clear, and the reality of what it meant in my life rushed over me like a wave of sludge. Theta had suffered from schizophrenia. I saw her face, staring down at me through the water of the bathtub. Her eyes crazed and yet empty.

My stomach heaved and I ran back to the bathroom and leaned on the sink. I took deep breaths, clearing the nausea from my body and then began to cry.

Tears poured out as what was real in my life unfolded. What Stephanie had said about my grandmother was true. I wiped my eyes and tried to stand up straight. I had to be strong for what was ahead. My grandmother's illness made me sad and disturbed, but it brought enlightenment, and my world began to clear. I now knew my fate, but oddly my mind felt free.

My body however was weak. I needed strength and I needed food. I would go to the store. It was a big step for me, but I didn't care.

I started to close the medicine cabinet door and noticed some things sticking out of the corner behind the bars of soap. I moved them to the side and saw a yellowed piece of paper that had slid through the thin metal opening that was seated back into the wall. I pulled on it carefully and a small, square, hardened piece of paper slid out. On it was some official print and ink scribble. I squinted and read what it said. "John D. Baker M.D. Take one at first sign of symptoms. Theta Theotokis. Nitro stat 250mg." It was another prescription for my grandmother. The date on it was just a few days before I was born.

"Nitro stat," I said out loud. "Nitro..." Then my body tingled with what I realized. I already knew what that medication was for. My grandmother had heart problems. Just like my grandfather, who popped nitroglycerin pills when his chest throbbed out of control, she had a heart that didn't work right. But she didn't have her pills. The prescription was unfilled and stuffed into the medicine cabinet. Is that what killed her? As I stood staring at that old and discarded prescription and the police receipt for the

349

Haldol, I realized I now had rational excuses for her behavior and beliefs, and a cause for her death. If Stephanie had been there, she would say, "See? I told you so."

A qualm ran through my mind, but I pushed it aside. I pulled on my coat to go back out and find a store. As I opened the door, the cold air rushed in.

Instead of going back on the interstate, I followed the frontage road and went along the overpass into the small town of American Falls. Unlike Pocatello, the town was dark and sleepy. I drove slowly down the dimly lit streets, looking for signs of life. I saw a small gas station with a tiny convenience store that was still open. Two cars were parked on the side.

When I opened the door of the store, it looked empty. I looked around at rows of potato chips and candy bars, and wondered if the store was actually closed but they forgot to lock up. Down the aisle I saw a light from behind a slightly opened door. "Hello?" I asked, seeing movement.

The door swung open and a young man about my age with short dark hair and a long-sleeved plaid shirt stepped out. His eyes were big and he fumbled, trying to button his shirt. Then a girl with long blonde hair appeared, trying to look like she was bringing out a stack of soft drink cups from the room. Her hair was mussed and her lipstick smeared. When she saw me standing there, she gave a short relieved laugh.

"Oh, God, I thought you were my boss." Then he laughed, too. They fell together in a grateful and happy hug. She was pretty with a vivacious smile and perfect skin. She wasn't short but, next to him, seemed petite. "I'm sorry," she said with a friendly smile. "What can I help you with?"

"I need milk and some food. There was nothing else open in town."

The young man scoffed, "You can say that again." He was handsome with a confident swagger. "I'm surprised they keep this place open past ten."

The girl walked to the front of the store where two large freezers stood alongside a glass-encased refrigerator. "We have frozen dinners and there is cheese and milk. Is that what you needed?" she asked.

I nodded.

It was the first time I realized that neither had given me the normal wide-eyed glare I was used to. In fact, their attentions weren't on me at all, but on each other. The girl turned to the young man and flashed a smile. He leaned across the counter and tried to hold her hand but she pulled it away giving him a playful slap.

I reached in, grabbing a half gallon of milk and a prepared sandwich. I found a small box of cereal on the shelf, a few frozen dinners, and took everything to her at the counter.

She began to ring it up. "Where are you from?" she asked.

"I've been living in Malad. I used to live around here."

"Wow, cool bracelet. Where'd you get that?" she asked, pointing to my wrist.

It was the birthday gift from my father. The gems glistened in the dimly lit store, as I thought about what message my father had sent in giving it. I smiled at her. "It was a gift from someone in my past."

"Sounds mysterious," she exclaimed. "It's really pretty."

"Thank you," I said, feeling as if I was finally in my first normal conversation with a stranger.

I watched the couple flirt and tease in a wonderful and sweet dance that made my heart twinge for Damien. I longed for the smell and feel of his warm and welcoming chest, and wondered what would become of him. Would he fall in love with someone else? I imagined him in this playful ritual and my stomach fell. It was selfish to hope he wouldn't, but tortured me to know he would.

I unhooked the gold clasp and handed the sparkling strand to her. "Here, you can have it."

"*What?*" she asked shocked. "No, this is too expensive."

"I don't need it. I don't want it anymore."

Her eyes widened in pleasure. "Really? Thanks."

The young man stood up straight when I walked past. "Maybe we'll see you around," he said.

"Thank you," I replied with a smile. I left feeling afloat. I had journeyed out and it was not only a tolerable experience but an enjoyable one. They hadn't stared or gasped, or even known who I was. For the first time in my life I was anonymous, and it was liberating.

I looked out at the small town and dark countryside with new eyes. I made special mental notes and took in every sight and nuance I could. I wished it was daylight so I could stop and take a long, unhurried look at all those things in the Arbon Valley I had never enjoyed as a child.

When I got home, I took out my drawing pad and sketched the faces of the two young lovers in the store. Their joy in each other was powerful. I smiled as I sketched in between bites of the stale, but satisfying sandwich.

As I put the last shadowing lines on the portrait, I knew it was time for sleep. My body and mind were already drifting. I went to Papa's room and decided to sleep there. I had left as a child and returned as an adult. The girl with the pink lace bedspread was no more.

I remade the bed, turning the sheets inside out and trying to shake off most of the staleness from the past year. From my old bedroom, I brought my drawing pad and the gun. Sitting on Papa's worn but cushioned chair by his bed, I put the pistol on the night table. I pulled the bed covers back and crawled into bed. As my eyes closed, the walls of the little house seemed to pulsate with happiness that I was there, and I sighed...knowing I was finally home.

Chapter 39

Sunlight poured through the window and I awoke, wondering where I was. When the flood of the day before hit me, I stared at the ceiling, not knowing what was to come. I thought about the gun on the end table and decided to put it somewhere safer. As I pulled the drawer out, another receipt for items taken by the police was wedged towards the back. Among the items listed was yet another prescription for Haldol (*oral*). And the name on the receipt filled me with dread:

Miguel Sanchez.

Your father was crazy, like his mother was crazy.

I was filled with emotion, then realized I was not all that surprised; his long journeys into town…the small packages he returned with. The medicine had been the one thing that had kept Papa going, kept him working and supporting us all those years. I wept with relief.

I steadied myself and went into the kitchen. The floor was cold on my bare feet, and as I looked out the back window and toward the hills, I saw that it had snowed. A fresh, glistening blanket coated the valley. It danced in the morning sun and the crisp air seeped into the house, making me shiver. I wanted to take in the view, and soak in every part of the valley, burying it all deep into my soul. I tied my hair up and put on my hat, gloves and coat. At the back stairs I pulled on my boots then walked out into the little yard that had once been my playground.

In the garden patch, I stared at the rusted and frost-covered fence surrounding limp skeletons of old tomato plants. I recalled the smell of the shiny plump fruit, and it made me sigh. The chicken coop was empty, but I could still hear the clucks and pecks of the only pets I'd ever known. I held the clothesline pole and closed my eyes, as visions of Damien and Donny swinging carefree in the warm breeze filled my head. And I looked out toward the field that always held such anticipation and thrill for me, as I waited for Damien to appear on the ridge.

As tears started to well in my eyes, I pushed the thoughts aside. They were ghosts of my past, and they needed to be locked away. A chill ran up my back, making me turn and face what I'd always been told were ghosts on the hill. I squinted and strained to see if the haunting red flag still waved its warning to stay away.

Consider the source, Sophie. Stephanie's voice filled my mind. *Create your own destiny.*

The flag was there; still stark against its bright backdrop. I watched it and thought about my grandmother buried there. Both my father and grandmother had tried to kill me and failed. I wondered what they would think if they saw me there now.

As I started my walk back to the porch, I bent down to unzip my boots and heard a noise at my side. I saw a figure framed in the early morning sun, and my heart stopped. It was a man and he was coming toward me. Startled, I stood up and stumbled away from him. Then, as the shadow hit his face, Damien appeared. I gasped.

"What are you doing here?" I asked, stunned.

"I called your grandparents, but they said you had left in the night. I knew I'd find you here. I don't care what your father said, I am not going anywhere. I love you." He smiled and let out a joyous sigh. "I'll prove to you he's wrong." He took me by the shoulders. "I won't let his crazy superstitions do this to us. It's not real and I'll prove it to you."

Even with all I saw and felt in my heart, the long harbored and constantly reinforced fears of what might transpire made me hesitate. "But..." was all I could muster.

Damien leaned down and lifted my face to his. His eyes looked deeply into mine, and then he kissed me. My heart throbbed in my chest and I wanted nothing more than to hold him forever. I leaned up, giving in. He pulled me close and I felt the entire length of his body against mine. The warmth and strength of his chest and the smell of him fired in me an undulating passion that swept through my entire body, penetrating my soul. It was Damien. My love for him spilled out everywhere. I wanted more of him. I reached under his coat and felt his muscular back. His hands moved from my neck and enveloped me, pressing me even closer to him.

"Let's go inside," he said, breathlessly.

I nodded and we quickly moved up the stairs and into the kitchen. The door shut and he was kissing me again, moving me back until my body was braced against the wall. Together, we removed each others' coats, hats, gloves, boots – giggling as we fumbled with the heavy garments. Then he lifted me off the ground and cradled me in his arms. He started walking down the hallway. "What are you...?"

"Bedroom," is all he said.

My head spun as I nodded toward the door. He nudged it open with his foot and walked me to the bed. Gently he put me down, and then stood up straight and looked at me.

"Sophie," he said, softly. "I need to know that you can be happy and feel free. One day I'm going to marry you."

Damien pulled off his shirt. I felt my breath sucked from me as I took in his flawless and masculine form. He looked back with eyes that were both tender and determined. I swallowed hard, anticipating what he wanted and letting him know that I wanted him too.

We lay wrapped in blankets, feeling the incredible warmth and excitement of being together. My reservations and insecurities quickly melted when he kissed me again. He caressed my back as he nuzzled my neck. My body welcomed his touch, and the weight of his form gave me a sense of contentment and security I had never experienced.

Two shadows swept over the dimly lit walls of the room, moving, teasing and slowly joining into a single indulgent form.

The day was spent in bed. Holding, kissing, and being one. We rarely spoke; even as we reveled in the moments after, we lay staring out at nothing. We napped, ate cereal and reverted back to the days that he traced my face with his fingers. We were in awe, and I could tell he felt the same sense of overjoyed passion as I.

As the sun crept down behind the thick rows of aspen trees, we held each other in an exhausted and contented finale.

"I love you," said Damien, in a half asleep whisper. "I'll always love you."

"I'll always love you, too," I promised him.

That night my sleep was intense and dream-filled. Ghosts came, spilling out their stories to me one by one. As each appeared I went with them, watching from above as the decisions and actions leading up to their demise were revealed.

First it was my mother. I saw her clearly. Her spun gold hair and deep blue eyes were remarkable, and while I had never known her, I felt at ease with what she showed me. My birth was chaotic but her face, when I was wrapped up and placed in her arms, was angelic. Her love for me was evident as she nuzzled and kissed me, but then she was gone.

Next, I saw Donny so sunny and alive, his smile beaming and the bounce in his step just as I remembered. My heart lifted as I watched the breeze rustle his hair, but then just like a summer storm, his smile soon vanished... and so did he.

My body chilled as the next ghost appeared. It was Uncle Lonny. We stood apart and there was no warmth or attachment between us. It didn't take long for my feelings of anxiousness and fear to turn solidly apathetic, and when I looked over to face him, all I found was a small black scuff on the pristine marble floor where I stood.

The last spirit to enter my dream was my grandmother Theta. At first, I was afraid to look at her, but a light radiated from her chest and I suddenly felt at ease. Her body was young and vibrant and she embraced me with such love that I cried. I saw repentance in her eyes and knew she was content and forgiven. She gave me a red piece of cloth and held it in my hands, tightly closing hers around mine.

"Kill it or it will kill you," is all she said. She faded away, and I was left holding the red cloth. I looked down at it and began to weep. As though the cloth was melting in my hand, it became dark and thick like blood; and when I opened my hand, the word Callidora stared back at me. I felt a sharp stab through my chest and I gasped in horror.

Then I opened my eyes. My breathing was still shallow and I felt sweat on my brow. I realized where I was, and I turned quickly to see if Damien was still with me. He was. I gently touched his shoulder to convince myself he was real. He stirred and took a deep breath, but didn't wake. I carefully laid back and felt my body heave a sigh of relief. I stayed awake and just listened to his rhythmic breathing.

When the sun pushed tiny spires of light through the curtains, I quietly climbed out of bed. I returned with my drawing pad. Silently I took a seat in the old padded chair, and started sketching. I wanted a perpetual testament of what was real. As I worked, the glow of morning filled the room and the glistening shimmer of the day was everywhere. I relished the moment. I closed my eyes and in the hushed solace of the room, I heard two things-- Damien's uniform and contented breathing and the clock's methodical ticking.

I opened my eyes. The clock said ten fourteen. I looked over at Damien and watched his chest rise and fall. I stood up and felt both elated and bemused. In the new morning sun I stood and waited. My mind raced with plotting, memories, and what my destiny meant. *Kill it or it will kill you* rang out, shoving me out of my frantic thoughts.

I went to the side of the bed and bent down quietly. Damien's face was serene and sound. I found the gun and receipts, as I carefully leaned down and kissed Damien's forehead.

Chapter 40

As I stood at the top of the hill, I was overtaken by the beauty of the snow-covered fields and dusted trees. The brightness of the sun's shimmer made me squint. The valley was ablaze from a brilliant, cloudless torrent of sunlight that danced off the fresh new snow. During the night, it must have fallen in droves. A thick blanket covered everything. It reflected the light, making the day seem even more new.

The hike up the hill was both a physical and emotional drain. I needed to go and be with the ghosts on the hill and I needed to do it alone. I left the house after waiting for the sun to rise fully. I spent the last hour watching the clock and the rise and fall of Damien's chest.

I stepped onto the porch and took a deep, cleansing breath as I stared out and up at the hill. The old red flag fluttered its greeting and I sighed. In the brilliant light of the sun's crest just above the trees, I could see the familiar wave. I watched it just as I had as a little girl, imagining what was there and why it was so elusive. The hill wasn't far from our house, and seemed even closer than it had before. The ghosts of the valley didn't scare me any longer. It was time to put them and my fears to rest. I pulled my coat closed and walked out of the gate toward a place I had always dreaded.

The snow was deep but light; it kicked up in powdery bursts as I walked. The hill was steep, but the sun had risen fully in the sky and the breeze had stilled, making the air feel fresh and new.

As I hiked, I felt the desire to look back, but instead I pressed on, feeling that if I didn't keep my focus I would lose my resolve and turn back. The items were in my suitcase and I felt off-balance due to the weight of the gun and toaster. I was ready to be freed.

The farther I went, the clearer I could see the ragged, worn and faded red cloth dangling from a large wooden handle. When I reached the top, I turned and took in the panoramic view of the valley. I was troubled and a bit annoyed that I had never been able to stand and enjoy it before.

I marveled at the tiny house nestled perfectly at the base of the hill. I stood and listened…waited and watched. There was nothing but me and the vanishing monsters in my head. There were no ghosts or demons lurking in the trees, no spirits waiting to destroy me; there was nothing that could control me anymore.

I sat down on the back of my coat, taking in all that had surrounded me and yet had eluded me my entire life. The mysteries of what was out there were opened up, and as I pondered the time I'd spent hidden away from it all, I felt robbed.

I pulled the red handkerchief from the handle and held it tightly. I stuffed it in my pocket, yanked the handle and started digging a small grave next to the others.

The ground was hard, but not frozen, and I made progress from sheer adrenaline and will. The sweat and steam from my work was satisfying and when I finished, I smiled to myself, feeling pleased.

I knelt at the edge of the hole and took the red handkerchief, receipts, prescription, toaster and gun from my suitcase. Giving them one last look, I placed them in the hole and then stood up and pulled a folded piece of paper from my other pocket. I opened it and looked down at the distorted portrait of myself.

"It's up to me," I whispered and let it float down into the grave. With each scoop of dirt I placed on top, a part of me was restored. My doubt, fears and misguided worries were dug out and tossed aside with every spade full of earth. There were tiny bits of hesitation that lingered, but I knew the stronger I became the easier it would be to clean those out too.

When I had completely filled the hole I stood on top, gave the ground several solid stomps, inhaled until my lungs could hold no more, and then let it out slowly, feeling free.

I looked down at the house and knew who waited for me inside. Smiling, I started to hike back down the hill, but the glint from Winter's blanket that spread across the valley made me stop. As I stood taking in the view like a rebirth, I couldn't help but notice the snow.

I marveled at how deep it was, how endless it seemed...and how blue.

Questions for discussion

1. What different situations in the story question superstition versus religion?

2.How could the red bandana be seen as symbolic?

3.What were the different situations that had Sophie questioning whether or not she was cursed?

4. Why did the change in name from Luke to Miguel make such a difference in the story? Why did Papa get away with this disguise?

5. Why do you think Sophie gave her bracelet to the young woman in the store?

6. Did this book remind you of anything that has happened recently in the media?

7. Why do you think Sophie believed Papa?

8. What are your feelings about Papa? Do you feel sympathy for him or anger?

9. How does the title relate to the story?

10. Why do you think the writer planned the story with flashbacks instead of in a sequential pattern?

11. Identify and discuss the various themes in the story.

12. Each of the characters may play more than one role in the story. Identify what each one does. Vee, Sophie (Callidora), Luke (Miguel), Damien, Talia, Theta, Stephanie, Uncle Lonny.

CPSIA information can be obtained
at www.ICGtesting.com
Printed in the USA
FSOW02n0951170817
37472FS

9 781940 224886